Sally Brady's
Italian
Adventure

Also by Christina Lynch

The Italian Party

Sally Brady's Italian Adventure

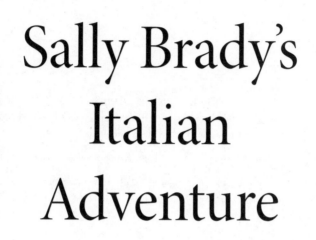

CHRISTINA LYNCH

ST. MARTIN'S PRESS
NEW YORK

First published in the United States by St. Martin's Press, an imprint of St. Martin's Publishing Group

www.stmartins.com

Design by Meryl Sussman Levavi

Image credits: Train photo: Library of Congress, Prints & Photographs Division, photograph by Harris & Ewing, pnp-hec-38800-38893; Bon Vivant image: iStock.com/Panptys; Ocean liner photo: Library of Congress, Prints & Photographs Division, pnp-ds-11500-11576

Library of Congress Cataloging-in-Publication Data

Names: Lynch, Christina, author.
Title: Sally Brady's Italian adventure / Christina Lynch.
Description: First Edition. | New York : St. Martin's Press, 2023.
Identifiers: LCCN 2022058081 | ISBN 9781250286154 (hardcover) | ISBN 9781250286161 (ebook)
Subjects: LCSH: Rome (Italy)—Fiction
Classification: LCC PS3612.Y5414 S35 2023 | DDC 813./6—dc23/eng/20221208
LC record available at https://lccn.loc.gov/2022058081

Our books may be purchased in bulk for promotional, educational, or business use. Please contact your local bookseller or the Macmillan Corporate and Premium Sales Department at 1-800-221-7945, extension 5442, or by email at MacmillanSpecialMarkets@macmillan.com.

First Edition: 2023

10 9 8 7 6 5 4 3 2 1

Yes, we wonder, what does it take to be a "decent person"? Maybe the most significant component is luck—the good luck to be born into a place and moment that inflicts minimal cruelty and thus does not require from us the courage to discern and resist its tides.

DEBORAH EISENBERG

Look back over the past, with its changing empires that rose and fell, and you can foresee the future, too.

MARCUS AURELIUS

I

Scavenger Hunt

Hollywood

1931

Sally

"Don't talk to strangers," Daddy said when he hoisted me onto the train that moonless night back in Iowa. "Don't trust anyone who doesn't look like you or talk like you. You got that?" I nodded. He kept going: "And don't act like a girl. You always make the wrong choice. Next time, whatever you're about to do, do the opposite."

My mother kissed my forehead and said only two words: "Be good."

Over the next few months, I found Daddy's advice a lot easier to follow. This afternoon, for example, I was standing at Franklin and Gower because Fountain and Vine was where I was going to stand. There isn't really an opposite to Fountain and Vine, but I thought anywhere but my first choice was probably safe. Me? Well, I tell everyone I'm sixteen and small for my age, but really, I'm eleven. I know my clothes look like I got 'em off a scarecrow who had a few rough winters. I try to keep 'em nice, I do. Yeah, someone stole my shoes. It's funny to be sweating in February—another upside-down thing about California. I probably should have moved to the other side of the street where there was shade.

My stomach was rumbling like a cement mixer, but I ignored it. How did I get there? I walked. Oh, you want to know how did I *get* there, like the whole shebang? Well, Daddy lost his job and the price of corn went into the basement and then Ma and Daddy didn't have any more money to buy food and then the well went dry and Ma got sick and there's five of us kids so they put me—the oldest—on a train and told me to find work and send money. That's what happened. No, I didn't cry. Neither did they—by that point, it was pretty clear crying wasn't going to change anything. What was the trip like? Well, I could tell you some stories that'd put hair on your derriere, as Daddy used to say, but the main thing to know was that there was other kids on the train, and all of us helped each other steer clear of the bulls—that's the railroad police and they carry clubs and they use 'em—all the way to Los Angeles. "There's plenty to eat in California." That's what everyone said.

That part turned out to be true, though of course there was a catch, like there always is. My jaw hit the floor when I saw those huge orchards. Seemed like a miracle after the dusty, dry farmland and dead trees I'd watched go by from the trains. Don't stick your legs out of the train door, by the way, or you'll get yanked off by them signal levers. But you couldn't get to the oranges and grapefruits and the fields of tomatoes, onions, and grapes. Men with guns and dogs chased us away. "Can barely feed our-selves," they said. "Keep moving. Go home." I offered to work and I meant it, but they laughed. I asked for work everywhere. I got nothing but no's. I had a standard answer for anyone who asked where my parents were: "Over there," I'd say confidently, thumb pointing over my right shoulder. Was I scared? Yes and no. I'd never been in a big city. Back home we don't have electricity, heat, or piped water in the house. I'd never seen so many dif-ferent flavors of people, not to mention all the tall buildings, streetlights that went on like magic, and so many cars. Apartments fascinated me. I walked along the streets at night looking up at the lighted windows, home upon home stacked on top of each other. I'd peep into the windows of Zu-kor's, with all those fluffy chiffon dresses, and slide quietly into the marble Perfume Hall at Bullock's just to sniff something good for a change. I loved the fancy columns, gold paint, and velvet seats of the movie palaces—I guess you could say every day was like the movie marquee that said TERROR AND DELIGHT. Terror and delight. Yeah, I was scared but also curious, lonely but never alone. There was no one telling me what to do, no rules except to find something to put into my belly.

That brings us to today. Was walking along Ivar, I think it was, and saw a flash of purple through the slats of a tall fence. Purple's my favorite color, you see. I shimmied up a tree to get a better look and saw a big green yard. The coast was clear, so I dropped over that fence. My toes sank into the cool, deep grass. It was paradise—and only a few feet from that griddle of a sidewalk. There was a cute little blue wood house, like a dollhouse made big. A tall tree gave shade and the leaves whiffled and whooshed lightly in the breeze. A lounge chair was covered with plump, flowered, fringed cushions with a book on 'em. *A Little Princess.* Never read that one. Next to the book was an apple. Red. Shiny. Bite already out of it. Who bites into an apple and walks away from it? I heard a screen door creak and then slam. A girl my own age stared at me with saucer eyes. She was so . . . clean. Even though she was a stranger, I decided to talk to her.

"Hi," I said. "Do you like Charlie Chaplin? I just love him. He makes me laugh and laugh. Can I finish your apple if you're not gonna?" I did my best Chaplin imitation and waddled toward the table with the apple on it.

The pigtailed girl opened her mouth and started screaming, half in fear, half in rage, "A hobo! A hobo's in the yard! A bum!"

I wanted to punch her right in the nose.

Footsteps clattered inside the house.

The apple or the flowers? It took two seconds to leap into the flower bed, yank a handful of flowers out of the ground, and vault back over the fence. I tell you, I didn't stop running for a mile. Listened for footsteps the whole time.

So that's how I came to be standing on this street corner, offering droopy purple flowers to passing cars, still thinking about the apple, how it would have crunched in my mouth, the way the tang of it would have made spit shoot up over my teeth. Daddy was right. Shoulda picked the apple.

I'm watching as the light turns red and green and red again, and the cars move and stop and move again like cows heading for the barn, and I approach a black car and just tap a little on the window. I hold up the flowers and smile. The lady inside looks away and hides behind her hat like I'm not there. I move to the next car. A man rolls the window down and growls at me to get lost. I stick my tongue out at him. Wrong choice. He opens the door and reaches for me, but the light changes and the cars move and I run back to the curb.

The flowers are pretty sad now. It's gonna get dark soon. I hate the night.

The light turns red again and the cars stop. I hold out the flowers and paste on my best smile and say, "Pretty flowers for your love on Valentine's! Get your Valentine some flowers!" and step off the curb.

"Hey!" I hear a voice. I turn and there's a cop coming down the sidewalk. Charlie Chaplin's scared of cops, and so am I. "Hey, kid," he says, "I wanna talk to you." I seen this happen to other kids and grown-ups too, hard fingers closing around a skinny arm. They disappear into paddy wagons and you never see 'em again.

I should run from this copper. That's what I was thinking. I was really tired, really hungry. But maybe that was the wrong choice.

The light changes and the cars begin to move. I feel like my feet are rooted into the ground. The brass buttons on the copper's dark-blue uniform sparkle in the sunlight. The copper grabs. I slip out of his meat hooks and run to a huge gleaming red Pierce-Arrow with a tan top and white sidewall tires that's just started moving. I jump onto the running boards, open the back door, and hurl myself inside.

Siena, Italy

1931

Lapo

Lapo put down the heavy black telephone receiver. They had the only phone in the area. It had cost a fortune to run the line from the nearest exchange just outside Siena through dense forests full of wild boars and giant porcupines and across mosquito-infested swamps to Belsederino, the half-ruined castle he'd bought on a whim. The phone line was physical proof of his fears about moving his American bride to this remote, abandoned property far from everywhere on twisted mountain roads. He'd hoped that slim black wire and its connection to the larger world would keep her happy in this wild place. The whole endeavor was also financial folly, a two-thousand-acre property that hadn't been farmed in a hundred years. A short time after the real estate deal closed, he had run through all the money his father had left him without making a dent in the work needed to make the place fertile and profitable.

"What's the matter?" asked Eleanor in English. The day he met her in Florence, she was little more than a girl, a lost tourist in a summer dress with lemons on it. Now she wore tall rubber boots and a pair of his pants held up with baling twine. Somehow, she still looked impossibly gorgeous, though he had to admit the scent of pig manure was at this moment overpowering her French perfume.

"*Niente*," he said. "Nothing." They did this a lot, carrying on one conversation in two languages. When he looked at her, his heart actually hurt, he loved her so much. "Just Giorgio," he said.

"Your book agent?" Her profile in the fading light was aquiline, her long neck accentuated by her bobbed hair. She still looked like that girl to him, though twelve years had passed since their wedding, and she was now mother to their three children. He had taken this beautiful exotic bird and caged her here in his castle using nothing but bonds of love, like a real-life Papageno. He felt terrible—she deserved a better life, the life of luxury and ease she was born to in Chicago, not the life of a farmer's wife in a foreign country, hanging frozen diapers by the fireplace in what was little more than an unheated pile of rocks miles from the nearest town.

"What did he say? Did he have news?"

He nodded but didn't elaborate. A couple of years ago, Lapo had published *It's a Dolce Vita,* a novel that was a thinly veiled diary of his and Eleanor's adventures restoring their run-down property. The comic story of a prosperous Florentine ex-playboy trying to convince the obstreperous Sienese peasants to embrace modern farming techniques, and inevitably getting his comeuppance by falling into pigpens, getting knocked over by sheep, and being stepped on by oxen, was a big hit. His favorite chapter was the scenting contest at a truffle festival, which went awry when a gruff gamekeeper's tame turkey beat the prize hound of the province's richest man, upsetting the local social order. *It's a Dolce Vita* was a mild success that at least gave them some cash to keep going on the endless renovations of the six falling-down farmhouses that, along with the thousand-year-old castle, made up the Belsederino estate. Though he'd been writing on the side since his school days, Lapo had never won a single literary prize, or really expected to. He wrote to transport people to a pleasant landscape where nothing too awful would happen. And to pay the bills, which multiplied faster than the rabbits who consistently ate anything they tried to grow. He hadn't told Eleanor the bank was threatening to foreclose. He couldn't bear to.

"What? Tell me." She sank down next to the sleeping Labrador on the sofa.

He felt if he said it out loud, it would be real. If he said nothing, it would fade away like a puff of smoke. And maybe it was just a puff of smoke. Maybe it was nothing. "Mussolini just said in a radio interview that *Dolce Vita* is his favorite book."

Eleanor's eyes widened. "Mussolini. As in Benito Mussolini?"

"Our Beloved Leader."

She jumped up. "Oh, my goodness! That's wonderful." She threw her arms around him, and the manure scent got stronger.

"Is it?" he said into her shoulder.

"Of course it is. It's amazing publicity. It'll be a number one bestseller. Congratulations!" She kissed his cheek.

"But."

"No buts. You always do this. Something good happens and you turn it into something to worry about instead of celebrate. You do that thing."

"What thing?" He knew exactly what she was talking about. A silly old superstition to ward off evil.

"This thing." She raised her index and little finger and made the sign of the horns.

He grabbed her fingers. "The horns always go down, otherwise it's un-lucky. *Caspita.*"

She laughed and said, "This calls for a celebration." She trotted out of the room, and he could hear her boots making the loose tiles clatter in the hallway. The floors shook and sighed in every wind. Maybe if the book did sell well, they could replace the beams, fix the broken windows instead of taping them. She returned with a bottle of wine, two glasses, and a cork-screw.

Lapo was staring out the window at the farmyard below them, where some chickens pecked at the dirt. Maybe they could fence the far pasture, maybe even try grapes in that field on the hill. Dig a new well instead of the one that produced salty, brackish water. "I suppose he's done some good."

"He's done tons of good. I mean, the malaria rates have dropped way down. That's a lot of lives saved. He's given this country a sense of pride again. Roosevelt loves him, apparently."

Lapo frowned. "But the violence . . ."

"He's not responsible for everything his supporters do. They love him."

"They *worship* him."

She moved a stack of past-due notices on the table out of the way and set down the glasses. "They're a little overly loyal."

"It's not healthy for the country. People should be able to disagree peacefully. We're not Neanderthals."

She worked the corkscrew until there was a satisfying pop. The wine gurgled as she filled two glasses with their own red. "Listen, tonight we're celebrating."

He managed to crack a small grin. "We might finally be able to afford all the things other people already have. Like indoor plumbing."

He loved her so much. He always worried she would awaken from her spell of love, realize she was married to a balding, middle-aged Italian who was a middling writer and a hopeless farmer, and walk away from this godforsaken place like any sane woman would have done years ago.

She raised a glass. "To you. And to wild luxuries like flush toilets."

He raised his glass. "To *Dolce Vita*." He sipped the wine. It wasn't terrible. With some French oak casks, they might even be able to age it properly and sell it abroad. "I wonder if he's really read it," he said.

"Does it matter?"

Behind his back, Lapo made the sign of the horns.

Hollywood

1931

Sally

I may as well have hurled myself onto another planet. I landed in the lap of Patsy Chen—yes, that Patsy Chen—who was on her way home from a frustrating day auditioning for a movie called *Dragon's Lair,* a murder mystery. Later I found out she'd wanted the lead, the brainy wife of the detective, but instead was cast in the role she always played: the evil seductress. Or better yet, the evil *attempted* seductress: she didn't have to read the script to know that Madame Wong would try to woo the handsome detective but fail and be exposed as a murderous viper.

The red quilted-leather interior of the Pierce-Arrow looked to my panicked eyes like the inside of a casket. I was still clutching my wilted flowers, speechless with terror at the sight of Patsy's black bobbed hair and sharp row of bangs, arched and plucked eyebrows, those oval eyes lined in black, and her crimson mouth, all set against that famous white-powdered face.

"Are you afraid of me?" she demanded.

I sure was.

"Why? Why are you afraid of me?"

I was too scared to even utter a squeak.

"If you tell me why, I will let you go. If you don't tell me why, I will . . . eat you!"

Patsy sounded more impatient than hungry, but I wasn't taking any chances. I swallowed twice, then found my words.

"You're Mrs. Fu Manchu!"

There was a long pause as palm trees zipped past the window when I thought for sure she would force poison down my throat or throw me to her dragon, but instead Patsy started laughing. She sat back in the red seat of the Pierce-Arrow and laughed and laughed. I didn't peg it for a happy laughter, more of an "I knew that cow was going to kick me" kind of laughter. "Where do you want to be dropped off? Where do you live?"

I smiled my best smile and said in my sweetest voice, "I love flowers. Do you like flowers? Which ones are your favorites? Mine are those horn-shaped ones. I don't know what they're called, but they're so pretty. Someday I'm going to live in a house covered with them."

"*Tecoma alata.* Flaming bells. That's what they're called. My house is covered in them."

"You don't talk like Mrs. Fu Manchu."

"No. In real life I don't. Are you a girl? You are, aren't you?"

"I'm sorry I thought you were a bad person."

"It's not your fault."

"I think you're actually very nice."

Patsy laughed again. "I wouldn't go that far. I'm just . . . like everybody else."

I nodded. Then I pushed my luck. "Do you like ice cream?"

Patsy's chauffeur offered to toss me out of the moving car, but to my surprise Patsy told him to drive us home. Home. We passed through iron gates and drove up a long circular drive to a golden castle covered with orange flowers overlooking the Pacific. "I've never seen the ocean before," I said. "It's so flat."

I followed Patsy through the giant wood-and-metal front door of the house, which was amazing and huge and had archways and red tile floors. I caught glimpses of suits of armor and heavy red-and-yellow-striped curtains and big green velvet sofas. When I ran my hand over the walls of the hallway, they were nubbly like dried mud. In the white tiled kitchen, Patsy's housekeeper, Aida, made me a plate of grilled cheese sandwiches that were deliciously buttery and gooey and crispy all at once. In between bites, I told them my story.

"I could work for you. Please?" I said, wiping my mouth. I desperately wanted to live in this house, stare out of the huge windows at the flat blue ocean, sleep under wooden beams, and walk on red tile. "I can clean, I can sew, I can take care of little ones. I can work in the garden. I'm really strong." All this was true.

"She could do the ironing," said Aida, handing me a dish of chocolate ice cream. "But I'm not taking a pay cut."

Patsy had a different idea. She grabbed me by my red hair and peered into my face. "Look at you. You're like an orphan out of Central Casting."

"Ain't an orphan," I said between mouthfuls. "Got a mama and a daddy." I continued to shovel huge spoonfuls of ice cream into my mouth in case they took it away before I was done.

"It's not what you *are* or *aren't*, it's how you *look*. Which is perfect. I'm going to adopt you," she said. "I'm going to be your mother. We'll call you . . . Sally."

"That's not my name."

"It is now."

Bologna, Italy

1931

Alessandro

Alessandro slipped out of the hotel room. It was absurd, the idea that a boy of eleven would be asleep by 8:00 P.M. He pulled on his leather helmet and goggles in the hope that people would mistake him for his hero Tazio Nuvolari, the race car driver. Nuvolari, or "Nivola" as everyone called him, had defied his doctors and won the Nations Grand Prix motorcycle race in a plaster body cast. Nivola jumped from burning cars at high speeds, raced cars while they fell apart, and, through sheer determination, won in cars that had no business winning. He broke all the rules, and yet people adored him. When Alessandro broke the rules, he just got yelled at. *"Come mai sei diventato cosi cattivo?"* his father would ask, more puzzled than angry. "Why have you become so bad?" Alessandro did know the difference between good and bad, *certo,* but fair and unfair had come to seem more important.

His family had traveled to Bologna so his father could accept an award. Alessandro and his sisters, Fiamma and Allegra, four years younger, were allowed to come along on the trip, but not to the ceremony. That stung, being left at the hotel with a babysitter. He hated being lumped in with his sisters. *You children.* Talk about *cattivo,* his sisters were horrible. Just this morning, when they were getting ready to leave Belsederino to get the train to Bologna, his sisters disappeared. His mother sent him to find them, interrupting a fantastic daydream in which he was piloting an Alfa Romeo P3 into the lead on the last lap, the crowd cheering him on. He stomped out and found his sisters in the shallow creek where they were expressly forbidden to play, sitting in the water in their dresses and their shoes, splashing.

"Go away," they shouted in tandem. "We don't want you here."

In the past few months, two things had happened. Alessandro had grown three inches, and everyone had become stupid and annoying. Like a sheepdog, he felt compelled by instinct to protect his sisters, but also like a sheepdog, he wanted to bite their tiny ankles, hard. They made him so angry. His parents, too, made him angry. Every request of his mother's—"Tidy your room, darling," "Would you get more wood for the fire?"—filled him with rage and resentment.

The hotel doorman frowned at him as he headed out the front door, and Alessandro realized he had remembered to put his jacket and short pants on but forgot he was wearing slippers. But then a black car pulled up. Alessandro took advantage of the distraction, pulled his goggles down, and darted into the cobblestoned street.

The theater was just a few blocks down from the hotel. That's where his father was getting the award. They'd passed it this afternoon when they walked around the city center. His mother had promised him they would see part of the auto race that was going right through Bologna today—Nivola himself would be there! But his sisters made them late and they missed the race. Alessandro was crushed, morose. His father tried to make up for it by buying them all candy at the central market as they toured the stalls. Alessandro knew he shouldn't sulk, he could see how it upset his parents—there was a part of him that wanted to throw himself into his mother's arms and say he was sorry, but he was a man now and men didn't do that. They drove fast and . . . it was unclear to him what else men did.

He made his way back to where the toy store was, but it was shuttered. He couldn't even look in the windows. He wandered down narrow streets in the darkness, hoping for something to happen, but nothing did.

He headed back in the direction of the hotel, feeling the cobblestones through his slippers. He turned down a street, sure he would find the hotel there, but he didn't. He turned back, unsure. At home he knew every inch of the property, but here . . .

To his relief, he came around a corner and the big yellow theater was in front of him. This was where his parents were. A famous conductor was going to be there, too. The Great Toscanini, his father called him.

"Who's Toscanini?" his sisters had asked.

"The greatest conductor in the history of Italy," Alessandro said as if it were obvious, even though he had only learned it the day before.

"You mean the guy who waves the stick?" asked Allegra.

He sighed with impatience. "He's the king of the orchestra," he said to them. "And Toscanini is the king of the kings. He's the most famous Italian alive. After Tazio Nuvolari, of course."

"What about Mussolini?" His sisters were obsessed. At school they had learned songs about Italy's leader that they sang day and night.

"More famous than Mussolini," said Alessandro.

The theater was all lit up with spotlights, tall columns along the front linked by soaring arches. The huge wooden door was open, and Alessandro wove his way through the people and caught a glimpse of a glittering chandelier before he was pushed along. He waited at the edge of a crowd on the sidewalk. He studied them, these *bolognesi*. When his neighbor Felice Pappone, who was two years older, heard Alessandro was going to Bologna, he rolled his eyes and said, *"Bolognesi di merda. Tutti grassi e pigri."* Yet Alessandro did not see anyone who looked either fat or lazy.

"What are you doing here, *ragazzino*?" asked a woman standing nearby.

"My father's getting an award from Il Duce," he told her. It was true. His parents had told him it was a great honor. Since it didn't involve race cars, it didn't seem terrifically interesting to Alessandro. The woman broke into a smile and said to the people around him, "His father is getting a prize from Mussolini himself." They were all very impressed by this, which was nice, and they handed him up to the front so he could see better. The crowd parted as a black car arrived. Alessandro watched as the door of the big car opened and a white-haired man got out. He was tall and slim, with a fluffy mustache and a red scarf over his tailcoat. Alessandro felt excitement sizzle through the crowd.

"That's him," a man standing near Alessandro whispered. "Toscanini."

Toscanini turned to help a young woman in a fur-trimmed coat out of the long black car. Alessandro wondered if he could risk bragging to his sisters that he had seen Toscanini and they hadn't. They would probably rat on him, tell his parents that he'd snuck out. He hated them so much. And yet when he was away from his family in Chicago last summer with his cousins, the atmosphere felt thin and oxygen deprived. He floated without meaning, a pale blue balloon loosed into a pale blue sky. Not like this morning when he waded, heavy with purpose, into the creek where his sisters were pulling crayfish from the shallows, screaming with fierce joy as the pincers pinched their horrible little fingers. They splashed and clawed at his feet and shouted *"Cattivo!"* and Allegra bit his knee and he grabbed them and dragged them, wet and shrieking with joyous rage, all the way back home. He wished they were here so they could see Toscanini, too.

Toscanini smiled at the gathered crowd, and Alessandro was happy he'd left the hotel, proud of his adventurous spirit.

"Traitor!" The word rang out over the sounds of cars and the dinging of a tram.

The crowd started catcalling, moving toward Toscanini as one and surrounding him. "Asshole." "Foreigner." "Capitalist." Alessandro was confused and afraid, but when he tried to push his way out of the circle, he found he was trapped.

"Who are you?" Toscanini asked the people. He sounded surprised.

"Real Italians, unlike you," a woman called. "Rat." "Parasite."

The crowd pushed forward around Toscanini and the young woman. Alessandro was shoved up against a newsstand. Pain shot through him as someone stepped hard on his foot. He got an elbow in his face. He looked down as he was jostled again and lost a slipper. His helmet came off and someone stepped on it, shattering the glass of the goggles. He reached for it, but someone trod on his hand. He came away clutching only a muddied program. ONE NIGHT ONLY, it read. THE IMMORTAL TOSCANINI CONDUCTS "ODE TO JOY."

"So you won't play the national anthem?" a man called out.

"The Fascist anthem," said Toscanini.

"You insult Italy," called a young man in rolled-up sleeves, "you insult me."

Alessandro could smell the menace, feel the hatred all around him, but he couldn't move.

"Wait in the car," the conductor said to the young woman behind him. "Lock the door." He tried to push through the crowd. Alessandro could see the vein in the old man's temple bulging. "I have work to do," Toscanini said to the people, angry now. "Get out of my way. Go home." He tried to shove the man in the black raincoat aside, but the man pushed him back. Someone lurched into Alessandro. A man in a black shirt and pants stepped forward and punched the conductor in the face. The old man's eyes widened in shock, and he put a hand to his cheek. There was a pause as everything froze for a moment. Then everyone began shouting *"Cattivo! Cattivo!"* and Alessandro screamed as the crowd surged forward and pushed Toscanini down.

Hollywood

1935

Sally

It would be a few years before I understood that Patsy's decision was both generous and self-serving. Adopting me was a smooth publicity move to put her in the public eye as a warmhearted maternal figure instead of an evil dragon lady, an attempt to open the studios' eyes to casting her in a wider range of roles. Patsy and her husband, George Brady, known to movie audiences as the loyal best friend who gets an arrow through the chest in dozens of westerns, tried to locate my parents, but their letters were returned as undeliverable. Undaunted, Patsy went ahead and announced to a gaggle of reporters that she and George had adopted me. I now lived for real in the huge Spanish-style mansion. I was photographed in a pink chiffon bedroom, in my private school uniform, and on my new pony, Chipper, always with an adoring Patsy by my side.

Every day I would wake up and look around in awe, run my hand over the dresses in my closet, rub the peach silk satin duvet against my cheek. I had my own pink-and-black-tiled bathroom that I did not have to share with anyone. I could fill the black tub with hot water and just sit in it, alone, and if the water got chilly, I only had to turn on the black ceramic tap.

"*Hola*, luckiest kid ever," called out Aida on a regular basis as she changed my sheets or brought in a breakfast tray. I had to agree with her. Like my mother, Aida had grown up in Mexico. Ma met my American father in Hermosillo, married him, and moved to Iowa, while Aida had come on her own to L.A. from Guanajuato at age sixteen. She'd spent the past thirty years in charge of Hollywood's literal and metaphorical dirty laundry.

Aida took me under her wing and gave me an interesting perspective on the new world I inhabited. She spared no one. She could be mean at times, especially when she compared Patsy's friends to exotic animals behind their backs, but she was also wickedly funny, which I loved. "Crazy" was her favorite description of most people who passed through our doors. And she cooked for me, special spicy dishes like my mother made with red-hot chiles, but also gooey cheeseburgers, crispy french fries, giant angel food cakes, and chocolate pudding so dense the spoon stood upright in it.

I spent four years in the velvety lap of luxury, then one day Patsy and I were poolside in our backyard when the phone rang. Patsy waved freshly lacquered nails at me, and I put down the movie magazine I was reading and picked up the heavy black receiver. Aida was on the line from the kitchen.

"*La bufala* came for a free lunch." Aida had also taught me the Spanish I didn't learn at home, and then some.

"Elsa's here," I said to Patsy, putting down the receiver. Elsa Maxwell was one of my favorite people in the world. While most Hollywood women were gloomy, starved, and painted, Elsa was large, hilarious, and real. She had a big square head like a box, a pug nose, and short curly hair, hence Aida's nickname for her. Elsa was a professional hostess, which meant very rich people hired her to throw very large and elaborate parties. She had single-handedly put Venice on the map in the 1920s with her brilliantly wild shindigs for the likes of Cole Porter and his pals. Elsa and Patsy had been best friends since their shared vaudeville days, and she often dropped by for a gossip.

Elsa appeared from behind a potted palm wearing a large, off-kilter straw hat and tortoiseshell sunglasses. Her linen dress was rumpled and slightly sweat stained. She set down two martinis on the side table and loomed over us, blocking out the sun.

"Sit down," she told Patsy.

Patsy looked up from the chaise longue where she was lying. "As you can see, darling, I am sitting down."

"Then sit up. This is important."

Patsy sat up and preemptively took hold of the martini.

"My sources tell me George filed for a divorce this morning," said Elsa.

"From me?"

"Who else?"

Patsy sighed and took a sip.

Turned out George was a good guy only in the movies. He'd apparently found himself a new starlet, as men generally did. I was hurt for Patsy, though she seemed unsurprised. "Well, I guess I should count myself lucky. Most Hollywood marriages have a shorter shelf life than a loaf of bread," she said. "This one was a can of sardines."

I liked George well enough, but I can't say I knew him. He was away on set most of the time, and behind a newspaper the rest of the time. Still, I was worried about what this meant for me as well as for Patsy. I was now fifteen, and I still had nightmares about ending up back on the streets.

"Don't worry," said Patsy. "He'll have to pay through the nose to get rid of us."

She underestimated him. When besotted with Patsy, George had danced to her tune. Now her spell had worn off. On set, George was known as a powerful man used to getting his own way. This was the George who stepped forward. That night, while eavesdropping in the doorway to the library while I was supposed to be in bed, I heard George threaten to have Patsy committed to a mental hospital if she sued him for alimony.

"Men are hyenas. They feed on our carcasses and crunch our bones with their teeth." I turned and saw Aida standing behind me. She shook her head and clucked her tongue as she disappeared back down the hallway, waving her feather duster back and forth at nothing.

Elsa was back poolside the next day to comfort a gloomy and frustrated Patsy. George was in the east wing and refusing to move out.

"I could plant nasty items in the gossip columns about him," Elsa offered.

"It will only backfire. You know George is always going to be seen as the handsome all-American golden boy who can do no wrong, and me— well, I'm Mrs. Fu Manchu."

"That's not fair," I said. They both turned to look at me as if they hadn't noticed I was there.

"It's the way things are, kid," said Patsy, patting my hand. "But we still have each other." Was it wrong that I wondered if that included the bathtub?

That night, I heard George threaten to get custody of me if Patsy tried to get the house.

"Don't forget that any judge would take my side," he said to Patsy when she barged in on him in the billiard room.

Again, not fair. But by this point in life, fair was about as real to me as Santa Claus.

Patsy's movie career was in a prolonged lull. *Variety* had recently dubbed her "box office poison," and not even dragon-lady parts were coming her way. Without George's support, money would be tight, especially the way Patsy lived, with champagne for breakfast and a couture wardrobe.

"I guess we're moving out," she said. We were enjoying our last days by the blue-tiled pool. I was trying to memorize every detail of the house: the angle of the roof beam against the tile, the color of the stucco where it faded from gold to pale red. The sun was setting in an orange streak over the ocean. Birds floated on the breeze and the air was scented with jasmine. It all seemed impossibly beautiful and fragile. Elsa had joined us, and we lay side by side on the lounge chairs, me in the middle.

I leaned toward Patsy and held up the page of real estate ads in *Variety*. I had circled two or three possibilities in red. "There's a two-bedroom apartment in Burbank. One bath."

"Ugh."

The last thing I wanted was to be a burden on Patsy after all she'd done for me. "I'll get a job," I said gently. "I can type fast enough to be a secretary. We've got to do some belt-tightening."

"It's much too embarrassing to be seen as downwardly mobile."

Elsa's eyes popped open. "What you need is a change of scenery. Yerp."

"Yerp?" I asked.

"What better place to hunt for a break from typecasting and a new husband than the Old World?"

✿

"I'll drop you off at a Swiss finishing school on the way," Patsy told me as Aida packed up boxes of our things. Aida was staying behind with George because he could actually pay her and we couldn't. We had all spent days crying about this, but like so many things, it was the way it was.

"Finishing school is a waste of money. I already know which fork to use."

Aida was insistent. "It's more than that. It's how to talk to dukes and princes, and lineages and lampshades and things. How to manage a staff."

I teased her: "You're manageable?"

She laughed and gave me a squeeze. "I'll miss you, kid. What's our motto?"

"*Comer los ricos.*"

Patsy rolled her eyes and waved a porcelain harlequin figurine at me. "Better to eat *with* the rich. At their expense. Finishing school will be your ticket. You'd be surprised what it's important to know in this world." I sighed. It was pointless to argue.

Elsa pulled strings with her pal Millicent Hearst, the newspaper magnate's wife, to land Patsy and me a stateroom on the SS *Giulio Cesare* to Naples. Elsa happened to be heading to Europe herself for "the season," when Europe's richest set migrated from chic place to chicer place, enjoying daily luncheons and nightly balls. She was perennially short on cash and hoped to replenish the coffers by throwing some top-class fetes.

"Don't I need a passport for that?" I asked Patsy.

"Hmm," she said, extending an index finger along her cheek. "I'll take care of it."

On the day we were leaving, I hugged Aida goodbye.

"Please come with us," I begged.

"I'm not a fish and so I am not crossing no ocean," she said. "But I got you something." She pressed a small manila envelope into my hand. "To remind you of home."

Siena

1935

Lapo

He and Eleanor were hosting a costume party to celebrate the completion of the wine cellar at Belsederino. All their friends and neighbors would be there, plus the obligatory aristocratic set, local Fascist Party officials who controlled the permits they needed to make and sell wine, and also *per forza* the industrialists whom one now felt compelled to include if one wanted to get things done. And there was still a lot to be done at Belsederino, so much to finish if he wished to leave his children a real legacy. Costume parties were all the rage now. Lapo found them silly, but Eleanor was insistent. "It will keep things light," she said. "Keep anyone from acting important." Eleanor's instinct was to deflate pomposity, even in herself. Because it was so far from his own nature, he admired the way she was able to laugh at serious things. Alessandro loved to join in her mockery, especially when it made his father uncomfortable. It worried Lapo. People got offended so easily these days.

Alessandro objected when he found the guest list on the kitchen table. "This guy's company makes bullets," he said, pointing to a name.

Alessandro was only fifteen. How could he even know that? He had been such a sweet little boy, but now Lapo felt a restless energy radiating off him all the time. He was still sweet and kind—he visited Fosca, their most elderly tenant farmer, every day, and did endless chores for her without being asked. He doted on his little sisters, who would try the patience of a saint. But any injustice, from someone kicking a dog to Italy's invasion of Abyssinia, enraged him. Privately, Eleanor and Lapo called him "The Angry Pacifist."

"I, for one, read the newspaper," said Alessandro in a tone that Lapo didn't particularly like. "And this one, he makes the screws that hold tread to tanks. How can you invite him here, Babbo?" Alessandro's use of the Tuscan word for "Daddy" didn't feel like an endearment.

"Alé," Lapo said, being careful with his words. "I understand your concerns. Of course I don't like it either, but this is the world we live in. Most of it is out of our control. Why don't you join us? You're almost a man. Men know how to talk to people, how to get along, how to accomplish things. There's an art to it that's important to learn. You should come to the party." Lapo admired his son, his belligerent sense of right and wrong, but he worried about him, too. Idealism led to heartbreak and poverty. The sooner Alessandro learned how the world really worked, the better.

Eleanor came in with a vase of flowers for the table, catching his last words. "What a wonderful idea. Of course Alessandro should come. The girls will be livid with jealousy, but they're just too young still. I'll make you a costume," she said. "Daddy's going to be Bacchus, god of wine, and I'm going to be a Pierrot."

"Okay," said Alessandro at last. "But I'll make my own costume."

✿

Eleanor had outdone herself. The wine cellar was beautiful, lit with candles that made the diamonds on the women's throats glitter. The brick vaulted ceiling echoed with happy party chatter. Lapo was deep in conversation with a local official who had blocked the drilling of a new well but after two glasses of wine was coming around to the idea. That was when Alessandro made his entrance.

Everything stopped. Lapo stared at his son and at the same instant took in the faces of his guests, their glasses suspended halfway to their mouths, their faces frozen.

Alessandro had polished his black riding boots to a high shine. He had dyed his khaki riding pants black, adding the jacket from his good black Sunday suit. He'd added medals, braid, to signify the highest rank in the land. In one hand, he held the globe from their library, ripped off its stand and spattered with blood. In the other hand, he held a riding crop painted gold, Il Duce's most distinctive accessory. But that was not the finishing touch. Atop his head Alessandro wore the papier-mâché mask that Eleanor had made for last summer's backyard production of *A Midsummer Night's Dream*. The decaying, lop-eared, idiotic grin of Bottom, the ass.

The Middle of
the Atlantic Ocean

1935

Sally

The ocean liner was sleek and comfortable, at least in the luxurious state-rooms Mrs. Hearst had gifted us. I had the maid's room next to Patsy's, with a tidy narrow bunk with a blue coverlet, and a round brass porthole. With its classic gleaming white hull, crisp green striping, and black-and-red smokestacks, the *Giulio Cesare* was a party on waves. There was a ball-room for the two hundred first-class passengers, as well as an outdoor bar and swimming pool. The waiters were all handsome and flirtatious and happy to gossip with Elsa. The ship also had a long-distance wireless tele-phone, which seemed like some kind of magic to me. Elsa was always on it, keeping up to date on the latest gossip on both sides of the ocean.

"Good news, doll," Elsa told Patsy as she plunked down onto a deck chair when we were a day from arriving in Naples. "I landed you a paying gig writing a weekly society column under a pen name with the Hearst syndicate."

"What's that?" I asked. Seagulls floated lazily overhead, and I waited for land to appear on the horizon. I was beginning to see why Aida had not come. Five days on the ocean was plenty for me.

"Wake up, kid. It's only a gigantic chain of newspapers that reaches millions of readers across America."

"What do I have to do?" asked Patsy.

"Describe all the swanky parties you attend while you're here in Europe."

"I hope I get invited to some."

"You will. You may be over the hill in Hollywood—"

"Thanks."

"—but you're still famous, beautiful, and wisecracking. Everyone loves you."

"You left out 'Oriental.'"

"That, too. But you're mostly going to be seen as an American movie star here."

"That'll be a pleasant change of pace. Who knew you had to leave your country to be seen as part of it?"

"People are just as hateful in Europe, but not about Americans," explained Elsa with characteristic pragmatism. "All you have to do for the column is describe who, where, when, and what they're wearing. Name and shame the princes canoodling with movie stars in castles. It'll be fun."

"People are going to care what I say? Since when?" Patsy pulled the lap blanket farther up over her as the sea breeze picked up. A woman passed us with two borzois on leashes, their noses lifted elegantly toward the wind.

"You'll be writing under a pen name. It's got to be a state secret who you are, or you'll be dropped like a stone and never invited to another party. That's the fun of it. All of America will spend Monday mornings guessing who's dishing the dish on the rich and powerful."

We all smiled at that.

"What's my nom de plume?" Patsy asked. She sounded brighter than she had since George asked for the divorce.

"The Bon Vivant."

Patsy clapped her hands. "I can see him now. He's a slightly world-weary, amused older man. . . ." Her eyes shone.

"French?" I asked, warming to the game.

"He had a French mother, I think, and an English father. German governess. Maybe a Hungarian riding instructor. Make that fencing instructor," Patsy said.

Elsa added, "He's seen it all but still finds life entertaining. Maurice Chevalier crossed with Cary Grant, with a pair of bird-watching binoculars, kid gloves, a martini shaker—"

"And a top hat," I said. I paused, then asked, "Where are we going to live?"

Patsy shrugged. "Nowhere."

✧

We landed in Naples, and I was shipped off to a Swiss finishing school. Patsy and Elsa hit the party scene and the Bon Vivant began captivating America with his Monday-morning columns in every Hearst paper, chronicling the comings and goings but mostly the naughtiness of princes and polo players. Patsy moved from hotel to hotel as the scene shifted every couple of weeks. Hearst doubled Patsy's salary and gave her a very generous expense account to make sure she could keep up with the bon ton. No one, but no one, suspected Patsy of being the Bon Vivant, which made the whole thing especially delicious.

The only problem was that because Patsy liked her cocktails, details of the parties were a tad hazy the next day. She landed in hot water when a British baron's daughter brought a libel suit against the newspaper because the Bon Vivant had her sitting on the lap of Prince Leopold at a villa in Monte Carlo, when she was in fact praying at Lourdes. Clever Patsy came up with a solution.

I was in a watercolor class when the finishing school's porter came to find me. We girls were only allowed to speak French at Brillantmont, and though I spoke some Spanish and could understand some German, I couldn't figure out a word of French. I was so homesick I wrote to Aida every day.

"Allons-y, allons-y," said the porter impatiently. He sounded like he was talking underwater. Finally, a snooty American girl said with an eye roll, "Your mother wants to see you." I stepped outside the white-and-green school building where a car and driver were waiting. I was whisked away through the Alps to magical Venice, caught a glimpse of a misty row of half-submerged buildings, was ferried to the Lido in a sleek mahogany water taxi, and finally escorted to a spacious suite in the majestic Grand Hotel des Bains.

"You're coming with me," Patsy announced from her perch on the massive hotel bed, barely visible in her fluffy bed jacket. A huge pink satin upholstered headboard arched over her, and a small white dog I'd never seen before nestled on the cream-colored silk satin comforter. The whole room smelled like lavender.

"Coming where?" I was still wearing my white painting smock over my pressed black school uniform and white blouse, my hair in two fiery braids. I may still have been holding a paintbrush tipped with Winsor Green.

Patsy stared back, studying me, and finally said, "The freckles have got to go. And electrolysis for that hairline." I raised a horrified hand to my cheek.

☼

We took the train down to Rome and checked into the charming old Hotel Hassler, then set out accumulating a wardrobe for me that any debutante would envy. My steamer trunks now bulged with chiffon and lamé gowns from Schiaparelli, and delicate evening sandals from Ferragamo. Patsy had Gian Paolo, Rome's finest hairdresser, dye my flaming-red hair platinum blonde and cut it short in the latest style. Now I had to iron waves into it every time I went out, which was annoying and time-consuming, though I had to admit the effect was dramatic.

"You're ready," said Patsy.

II

Monsters' Ball

Roman Revelry Afoot

The beau monde heads to idyllic Bomarzo this weekend to caper and frolic in the woods of the Orsini family's ancestral castle north of Rome. Rumored to be joining the revels is a veritable cioppino of who's who: shapely aviatrix Beryl Markham, the Duke of Anjou, Count Gottfried von Bismarck-Schoenhausen, Il Duce's jolly son-in-law Galeazzo Ciano, the Prince of Wales and his unsuitable and oh-so-secret American amour. Let's not leave out the ebullient Miss Lombard (and not coincidentally, the still very married Mr. Gable), Lord and Lady Lancaster, a matched set of Mitfords, along with a dozen young principi and principesse. Who will find amore in the sylvan setting? And who will don the ass's head of shame? The Bon Vivant will reveal all. . . .

Bomarzo

1936

Sally

A moonlit summer night in the overgrown garden of an estate outside of Rome. *What would it be like to live here,* I wondered, *with hundreds of acres all to yourself?* With plucked and repainted eyebrows framing my brown eyes, a jungle-red manicure and matching lipstick, foundation and white powder that turned my orange-gingham skin into smooth, snowy marble, and a white Grecian-style gown, I was making my debut into society tonight at the Monsters' Ball. The only hitch was that I, unlike everyone except the staff, was not there to have fun. I was there to eavesdrop.

The jagged outline of a castle loomed on a hill above us, backlit by the full moon peeking between gray clouds in the black sky.

"Don't be nervous. The rich are just like you and me, but more boring," whispered Elsa as we stood in front of a giant face sculpted out of rock. "That's why they need people like us around."

That stone face was twice as tall as I was, even in my high heels. I'd seen a lot of strange things back in Hollywood, but I'd never seen a garden ornament this bizarre. Of course Elsa chose only the most interesting places to throw her legendary parties.

"Make sure you meet our host. The man paying my bill. He's a good person to know," said Elsa. "Not the same as being a good person," she added with a laugh. "Just to be clear."

"What bad thing did he do?" I wanted to know what to be ready for.

"Good and bad are very slippery concepts, my dear."

This, I knew, was true.

✡

Though I was profoundly, intensely aware of how lucky I was, for the past five years I'd also felt like I was playing a game where the rules changed every day. I was surrounded by people who thought wearing the wrong hat was tragic and knowing the latest dance steps was genius. It was as if the rest of the world and all its woes didn't exist.

At sixteen, I was younger than all the other party guests at this massive fete outside Rome. Elsa, at the behest—yes, I just used the word "behest." Thanks to pricey private and charm schools, I was now a reformed ragamuffin, a veritable young lady, elbow-length white gloves and all. At the behest of the family who owned the massive garden and the ramshackle castle in the middle of it, Elsa had invited all of high society for a magical night under the stars. This, by the way, was all that rich people did—they lunched together, they went to the races, and they went to fabulous, over-the-top parties. But mostly they gossiped, and the Bon Vivant shared that gossip with the world. I was no shrinking violet, but let me tell you my palms were sweaty and my heart raced—there were a lot of famous and powerful people there. I spotted Myrna Loy, Countess Kitchener, Madame Chiang Kai-shek, and Prince Paul of Yugoslavia just in the first few minutes. It was like Rich People Bingo, and I had a winning card every direction I turned. I was filled with dread. The longer I talked to Elsa, the longer I could put off having to talk to any of the well-dressed strangers.

Patsy, always chic in her jet-black signature bob that gleamed in the torchlight, was getting a glass of champagne from an outdoor bar set up near the giant rock. In her forties but perpetually youthful, Patsy always looked gorgeous to me—lean and stylish in a silver lamé gown trimmed with feathers that floated on the breeze.

The ostrich plumes on Elsa's large bulldog head danced as she called to Patsy, "Watch yourself when you're stepping over the vines. They've really let the place fall into disrepair." A woman in a golden evening gown and a tiara came out of the bushes screeching with laughter, followed by a man in a top hat, white tie, monocle, and tailcoat.

"Are we in the lead?" the woman called to Elsa in an accent I pegged as Hungarian. Years of Patsy's parties back home with the likes of Peter Lorre, Greta Garbo, and Hedy Lamarr had made me something of an expert on accents. "I want to win this time. We found the dragon and the woman with the salad bowl on her head."

"Don't forget the elephant crushing the soldier," called Elsa as the man darted into the ogre's mouth and reemerged holding the next scavenger hunt clue and two fresh glasses of champagne. "The Count and Countess Kinsky," Elsa whispered. I watched in amazement as the countess managed to keep her glass from spilling while she and the count climbed over a tangle of ivy. They disappeared into the darkness again.

"You're a genius, Elsa," said Patsy as she downed her champagne and grabbed a cocktail from a waiter who appeared nearby with a fresh tray. I watched with concern as Patsy took a slug from the crystal tumbler. By age twelve, a year after Patsy and George had taken me in, and a year before Prohibition ended, I had learned how to make all the popular cocktails for my new parents and the unending procession of their friends winding through the mock Spanish hallways of the mansion. I was well aware that the sidecars Patsy and Elsa were drinking tonight were mostly cognac and deceptively delicious. Though Elsa frequently and accurately compared herself to a tugboat, Patsy was a tiny woman in very high heels who got drunk very fast.

"I don't see you taking notes," Elsa said to Patsy. "Don't you have a column to write?"

"Shh." Patsy put a bejeweled finger to her mouth. "Sally's taking notes for me, aren't you, darling? That way no one will suspect my secret identity."

I removed a miniature notebook and a silver pencil from my evening bag and waved them at Elsa, who grinned.

"Good girl. Someone told me today they think the Bon Vivant is either the Prince of Wales or Picasso. Ha!"

"Take lots of notes, darling," whispered Patsy. "Now Elsa and I must go mingle."

"Here's the guest list," whispered Elsa, slipping me a folded piece of paper as she and Patsy trotted off, giggling. Elsa called over her shoulder, "I'll tell you later who matters and who doesn't."

"Thank you, Miss Maxwell," I said with mock deference and a curtsy.

I was left alone to stare up at the monster's face.

Who matters and who doesn't. That was the problem, wasn't it?

Ducking my head to avoid the monster's teeth, I stepped into the beast.

Lapo

He heard Eleanor say in English to a blond girl in a white gown, "Well, if it's any help, I saw Marlene Dietrich over there." Lapo was busy studying a giant stone fish. The entire garden was such a strange dreamscape, twenty or more massive stone monsters overgrown with vines and creepers tucked into the dark forest amid half-hidden pathways.

"What is the world coming to?" Eleanor said, putting her arm around her husband.

"*Non lo so.* I can't imagine hiring an artist to sculpt that fish instead of buying a tractor." Lapo really wanted a tractor but was once again "overextended," as his banker put it.

Eleanor arched an eyebrow at him. "I'm not a historian, but I'm fairly certain there were no tractors in the sixteen hundreds when that was sculpted. And the artist's kids needed to eat, too. I'm so happy we decided to come to this party." She handed him a glass of champagne. Crickets chirped and the night air smelled like jasmine. "This is fun. I'm having fun. It's nice to get out of muddy boots once in a while."

And get away from the children, he thought. He smiled at her and nodded. "You're right. Though to me you're as beautiful in poo-covered wellies in the middle of a pigpen as you are here."

"I'm not entirely sure that's a compliment," she said with a laugh. She pulled him into a foxtrot in the moonlight as hidden musicians struck up a Cole Porter tune. He loved to watch her as they danced, and tonight she was especially beautiful. Her auburn hair was pulled back and up in some new style, and she was wearing a low-cut red gown that was soft under his hand on her back.

"'I get you under the skin,'" he sang softly in English. Then, when she laughed at this, "What? I get it wrong?"

"Nothing," she said. "I get you under the skin, too."

His beautiful American wife. This was her natural habitat, he thought—fancy parties, cocktails, interesting and accomplished people from all over the world.

"Why did you marry me?" he asked.

Eleanor flashed her smile and kissed his cheek. He could smell her perfume, citrus and roses. "You're being Italian again," she said, pulling his chin back to face her. "I can see it in your eyes."

He laughed. "I can't help it. I am Italian."

"Well, I'm not, and I'm going to have a good time tonight." She twirled and grinned at him.

"Lapo." He heard a voice at his elbow and turned to see his old friend Leone. They'd been schoolmates in Florence. The two men embraced as Eleanor and Leone's wife, Sara, greeted each other and went off to get them a fresh set of drinks.

"I haven't seen you in ages," said Lapo.

"You're so far south now."

"Siena isn't exactly Naples. I'm only two hours from you by car."

"True. But things are difficult right now. I wonder if I could talk to you for a minute." Leone's brow was furrowed with worry. Strange, Lapo thought—when they were boys together, Lapo was always the worrier, Leone the boisterous playwright, the artist playing pranks on the teacher, charming the girls.

"*Certo.*" The two of them stepped away from the crowd and walked toward a huge statue of a man holding something in front of him. As they got closer, Lapo was startled to realize that the stone giant was holding another man upside down by his ankles, tearing his legs off his torso. Lapo winced at the sight.

"You've heard about the new laws in Germany?" Leone lit a cigarette.

Lapo nodded. The Nuremberg Laws revoked citizenship for anyone with any Jewish parents or grandparents. They couldn't marry or have sexual relations with non-Jews or own businesses, among other prohibitions.

"It's obscene," said Lapo. "I'm sorry. Sara's family—?" Sara was from a prominent family in Berlin.

"Trying to get visas to leave. They've lost everything. I worry it could happen here."

Lapo shook his head. "La Sarfatti would never allow it." Socialite and art critic Margherita Sarfatti was Mussolini's longtime mistress and a key voice in shaping Fascist policy. Lapo knew her slightly. She had been born into a prominent Jewish family in Venice with a palace on the Grand Canal. Her late husband was also Jewish, as were many of her friends, who were among Italy's leading cultural figures. She consistently steered Mussolini away from antisemitism, arguing that aligning with Hitler would signal weakness to the Italian people.

"But if it does . . . can I count on you to help us? A man with your influence . . ."

Lapo blinked. "Of course," he said. "But Leone, it's not going to happen here. Stop worrying."

"But you would help us?"

"Yes. Please put your mind at rest. How are Sara and the boys?" At fourteen, Leone's twin boys were two years younger than Alessandro.

Leone exhaled. "All fine, thank you. We've just opened another glove shop on Via Tornabuoni. How are things going at Belsederino?"

"Bleeding me dry, as usual. This spring we renovated another one of the farmhouses. I couldn't leave the tenants without running water for another year. My banker wants to kill me. '*Signore,* a bank is not like a well. Sometimes you must put money *in* the account.'"

Leone laughed. "The kids?"

Lapo thought about Alessandro, his ardent, dangerous anti-Fascism and how it seemed to fuel his sisters' love of all things Fascist. "At a difficult age."

"And do you and Eleanor have running water in that castle yet?"

Lapo grinned. "Keeps me in shape to haul those buckets."

Leone hugged him. "I'm so grateful to you. I think I might even be able to enjoy this party now. We should probably dance while we still can, eh? *Andiamo.*" He headed back to the torchlight and the music.

Lapo looked up at the vicious giant's grimace and saw how the rain had worn away the expression on the face of the man who was being torn limb from limb.

Sally

It was two hours into the party, and I had nothing. I drifted through the crowd gathered around a bar set up next to a statue of a two-headed dog. What should the Bon Vivant say? *The night was warm and the darkness felt like an embrace.* No. That wasn't right. He was more irreverent than romantic. *Society's vultures gathered in steamy darkness to await the latest mistake they could seize on and pick over.* Too critical. *Everyone looked lovely in the warm darkness, even the portliest of society's matrons and patrons transformed into nymphs and fauns.* Yes, but I needed to name-drop, too. I had spent the last couple of weeks studying the photos and captions in every magazine at the newsstand outside the Hassler in Rome. I learned that the Savoias were Italy's royal family and part of what Patsy called the "European royal inbreeding program" and how to spot them: King Victor Emmanuel (bushy mustache), Queen Elena (tiny mustache), their globe-trotting son, Umberto (balding, underbite), and the dashing, athletic princesses Yolanda (big brows, tiny mouth), Mafalda (huge eyes, huge mouth), and Giovanna, now Tsaritsa of Bulgaria (tiny eyes, big schnoz). Then there was the next rung on the social hierarchy to memorize: the Italian noble families, among them the Borghese, Visconti, Brandolini, Colonna, Farnese, Franchetti, Corsini, not to mention the French, Spanish, Austrian, Hungarian, German, and British royalty and aristocracy. Peers, princes, counts, dukes, marquis, and marchesi. It would really help if they wore numbers on their backs like the Yankees. And I had to be able to recognize the creations of every major fashion designer at a glance.

"You're taking this very seriously," said Patsy. "I'm impressed."

"Movie stars and royalty, check, but what about polo players, prime ministers, and painters?" I asked. "Dali I would spot, but I could trip over Paul Klee and not recognize him."

"Don't worry about them. You'll learn who's who. But even an obscure princess is always worth mentioning. Back in Omaha, they love reading about royalty."

"They can't put food on their plates but they care what the Duke of Salaparuta had for dinner?" But then I thought of how I'd snuck into the movies when my stomach was as empty as my pockets.

"It's an escape," said Patsy. "A chance to live vicariously for a minute before you have to feed the kids breakfast and get them off to school. Every woman dreams of being a princess."

I wondered if that was true. Did my mother back in Iowa dream of tiaras and ball gowns? When I'd asked her about her childhood in Hermosillo, she wouldn't talk about it. Daddy worked as a pipe fitter here and at a button factory there to supplement the income from the unreliable cornfields on the windswept farm that was mortgaged to the hilt. Ma was often alone with us kids, working the fields by herself, me looking after the little ones. She never went to a single party that I could remember, though sometimes when Daddy was away, she'd tell us we were having a fiesta and make huge *tortillas de agua* and spicy salsa with tomatoes, apples, and tiny red chile peppers.

I also wondered if Ma, who had sewn all our clothes and washed them with water hauled by hand, would be happy to see me living in hotels, wearing fancy dresses, and eating off silver trays, or would she be horrified by the music, the dancing, the cigarettes, the backless gowns, the affairs, the cocktails, the cocaine and morphine—in short, the wild embrace of every sin imaginable, and a few more?

✿

I floated along a gravel pathway, the edge of my pleated Fortuny silk dress brushing against the snaking creepers. There were murmured conversations in the darkness all around me. I was trying to work up the courage to talk to someone. Back at the Hassler, Patsy had sent me on missions through the lobby to train me to strike up conversations.

"Why would anyone want to talk to me? I barely speak Italian. What am I supposed to chat about, the six months I spent at finishing school learning how to arrange flowers? I'm a nobody."

Patsy frowned. "Don't ever say that, or someone might believe it." She leaned in close to me so no one in the bustling lobby could hear us. "No one ever needs to know the truth about us. It belongs to you and me, and nobody else."

That part bothered me. My parents hadn't sent me away because they didn't love me. But still, Patsy made me understand there was something shameful there.

✿

An owl hooted nearby, startling me. I paused near a couple kissing on a bench under the gaze of a stone mermaid. I recognized Allegra Fiammetti, the youngest daughter of an aristocratic family, who modeled for Marie-Louise Bruyère in Paris, and Paul Brando, an American race car driver. Paul was married, and not to Allegra. I smiled to myself. *Yank speed demon hugs the turns with Venetian princess.* This was exactly the kind of juicy tidbit Patsy needed for this week's column. She'd be delighted. But then I thought of Paul's wife, who I'd read in the gossip pages was home in Chicago with their new baby. Wouldn't she be horrified to read on Monday that her husband was rubbing noses like Nanook of the North with another woman? Maybe this wasn't my problem, but it still made me queasy.

"Amore," said a voice at my elbow. I turned and saw a bright-eyed older woman. Her upswept hair was gray and her gown an elegant high-necked dark blue that I recognized as Chanel. A diamond pendant sparkled against the dress. "The entire park was created by a man with a broken heart." The woman spoke English with a British accent, as I'd noticed many aristocratic Italians did.

"Are you a historian?"

The woman smiled. "I'm an Orsini."

"Oh," I said. "So this is your party."

"My son's idea. For a hundred years, the garden has been allowed to become terribly overgrown, I'm afraid. It's going to take decades—and oodles of money, as you Americans say—to clear it out. Not how I would spend my inheritance, but he thinks it's romantic."

"I don't know the story of the garden."

"And you would like to?"

"Yes."

"An American with an interest in history—unusual." The woman lit a cigarette and offered me one from a silver case, but I'm not a smoker. Cigarettes make me sneeze. "Pier Francesco Orsini. Nicknamed 'Vicino.' Died in 1583. Rather interesting fellow. *Condottiero.* Do you know what that is?"

I shook my head.

"Leader of a sort of private army. Wealthy families had their own back then, you see. Might be a good idea now, but that's another story. Vicino was deeply in love with his wife, Giulia, from the very powerful Farnese family. Marriages in that time were usually a matter of wealth and power, not love."

"Nothing's changed in that department, far as I can see," I said.

The woman laughed. "Well, theirs was truly a love match. He had to go away all the time, fighting various battles for years and years on end, but she stayed true to him and bore him five sons and two daughters. Despite being related to popes, they were Epicureans. Does that ring a bell?"

"Something to do with food?" I realized as I said this that I was hungry. I'd been so focused on gossip hunting I forgot to grab canapés from all those passing waiters.

"Pleasure, which of course includes food. Epicurus believed that life is best spent avoiding pain and pursuing pleasure."

"Isn't that just common sense?"

"An American with a sense of history who is not a puritan? Now I am really amazed." I heard a distant band strike up "Night and Day." "I think Vicino saw all that blood and war and violence and realized the sheer pointlessness of it. The whole time he was away, all he wanted was to be back here with Giulia in this beautiful place. At one point, he was captured and held prisoner, not knowing if he would ever see his family or home again."

I inhaled the scent of jasmine and pushed away feelings I didn't want to feel right now.

"Finally, finally, a treaty was signed, and he was released and able to come home for good. And then Giulia died."

"Oh." I felt a catch in my throat and tears brimming. Was it dumb to feel sad for someone who died hundreds of years ago?

"Vicino was devastated. He built the garden of monsters—'the sacred wood,' as he called it—as part of his process of grieving. No one quite understands what it all means. Have you seen the crooked house?" She took me by the hand and led me through the torchlight to a small two-story building. Her grip was cool and firm. The place looked like a normal, sweet little house, except it was leaning sharply to the left.

"Earthquake?" I asked.

"He built it that way. It's perfectly safe. Come inside." I followed her into the little house, where everything was solid, but tilted. "My husband died last year," said the woman. She leaned against the topsy-turvy fireplace. "I think this is the perfect expression of grief."

I felt faint. "Excuse me, *Principessa*," I said. "Thank you. It was nice to meet you."

"I didn't catch your name."

My name. I had memorized so many of them to get ready for tonight. What was my own? Who was I?

Manners demanded I answer her. I extended a trembling hand. The floor tilted down and the ceiling tilted up and my head was swimming.

Finally, it came to me. "Sally Brady." As the words left my mouth, a burning sensation rushed up my throat and I found myself on my hands and knees on the wall, retching.

Lapo

Lapo passed a fountain where a young woman was leaning over and splashing water on her face. He approached with concern but was waved off by Principessa Orsini.

"She'll be fine," said the *principessa. "Tutto bene."*

Lapo nodded and kept walking. As a father, he found the current vogue for cocktails troubling. Like all Italians, he had been drinking wine since he was a child, watered down, of course, but it had trained him to know how much alcohol he could handle without getting drunk. Though of course some people struggled with their drinking, as a culture, Italians were not heavy drinkers. Then the Americans brought sidecars, Tom Collinses, gin rickeys, and Hanky Pankys across the Atlantic. The shift to hard liquor had definitely changed parties, along with the desire to forget the cares of the day. The young people today danced faster, laughed louder, and got into a lot more trouble.

"I think I'm getting old," he told Eleanor when he found her chatting with Count Galeazzo Ciano. Ciano was suave and handsome in his black tie, and Lapo was slightly jealous of how Eleanor was laughing at his jokes. "I thought you were in Shanghai," Lapo said to Ciano, shaking his hand. The son of an admiral, Ciano had grown up in part on a large estate in Tuscany. The admiral and Lapo's father, who had made a fortune with an international hat business, were friends, and Lapo and Ciano had known each other socially since they were in their twenties.

"You're behind on the news, old man," said Ciano. "I'm just back from Ethiopia."

Lapo frowned. He found Mussolini's desire to reenact the far-flung land grabs of ancient Rome disgusting. The fact that the Italian Army was invading Ethiopia and building an empire in East Africa while many Italians were illiterate and malnourished was obscene. He felt Eleanor grab his arm before he could speak.

"Darling, you must congratulate Gally," she said with a strained smile. "He's just won a medal of valor. He's a war hero."

For slaughtering innocent people, Lapo thought. *People just trying to defend their own land.* He shuddered at the thought of some foreign army invading and taking over Belsederino.

Eleanor forced Lapo's glass up in a toast.

Ciano smiled and leaned in to whisper, "Tomorrow you will read in the papers that I've been named foreign minister."

"It helps to marry the boss's daughter," said Lapo, and Eleanor gave him a discreet kick.

Ciano laughed. His marriage to Mussolini's daughter Edda was widely known as strategic, not romantic. He was a famous and unapologetic lothario, despite having three children at home. "I am even mentioned in the American gossip columns," he said with pride. "Alongside Clark Gable and the Prince of Wales. We are the playboys of the Western world, according to the Bon Vivant. He sees more than the OVRA," Ciano added, referring to Italy's secret police, who used a vast civilian network to keep tabs on pretty much all Italians.

"I'm going to go powder my nose," said Eleanor. "Don't you two get into any trouble while I'm gone." She disappeared behind a sphinx, shooting Lapo a warning glance over her shoulder. Ciano was slick and obnoxiously ambitious, but Eleanor had always reminded Lapo that this made him a good person to know. Ciano had helped them get loans and grants to finish renovating the six ancient farmhouses on the estate so they could house families. He had pulled strings to get them money for a school for the tenant farmers' children. And his appointment as foreign minister was a huge deal, especially with Hitler's rumblings. But Ciano was also part of the regime that had created its own grassroots militia of black-shirted thugs who harassed and beat up opponents of the Fascist Party, as Lapo's own son had witnessed firsthand in Bologna. He still shuddered to think of that.

"Congratulations," said Lapo through gritted teeth. "*Auguri*. Please don't let us get pulled into this mess in Spain, no matter how much Franco begs."

Ciano nodded. "I'll do my best to keep Italy out of any European wars, even if it means keeping Il Duce busy in Africa."

Lapo went to slide away, but Ciano stopped him with a hand on his sleeve.

"I have a proposition for you," he said, putting a conspiratorial arm around Lapo's shoulder. Ciano lit a cigar and exhaled a cloud of smoke. "Il Duce is looking for a new ghostwriter."

Lapo felt slightly sick, but forced interest. "*Davvero?*"

"He's been watching how Stalin has crafted his public image. Thinks a book about his life would be a good move, and maybe we'll make it into a film." Ciano began walking, pulling Lapo along.

"La Sarfatti's biography is the definitive one, no?" Mussolini's mistress's 1925 telling of Il Duce's life story had run to seventeen editions in eighteen languages. Fluent in English and well-connected all over the world, Margherita was not only Mussolini's confidante, lover, and ghostwriter, but also his chief propagandist, using her friendship with Millicent Hearst to place pro-Mussolini articles in American newspapers, and singing the dictator's praises to American audiences, including FDR.

Ciano lifted an eyebrow. Lapo sensed his distaste for Sarfatti, and marveled at how Ciano maneuvered his way into power, knocking others out along the way like billiard balls. "Il Duce is looking for something more fresh, more . . . compelling. Something to elevate the way people see him."

"Oh. Well. I can recommend some writers."

"He wants you."

They had stopped in front of a statue of a snarling dragon.

Lapo's mouth was dry. He steadied himself before speaking. "I . . . I'm honored, of course. But you know I've retired from writing. The farm takes all my time these days."

Ciano's eyes held his. "Your son will be doing his mandated military service soon, no?"

"He's barely sixteen."

"It's amazing how fast they grow up. When he does get called up, it would be best if he stayed away from the front lines. I saw terrible things in Addis Ababa."

Lapo kept his mouth shut. Ciano put a hand on his shoulder. "Think it over. I told him you're just the man for the job."

Sally

Much as I wished it to be, my evening wasn't over. After I apologized to Principessa Orsini and dabbed some water on my face, I circulated through the grounds of the park, desperately looking for people doing or saying things worth gossiping about. I needed to find someone newly engaged, cheating, freshly pregnant, landing a new movie role, wearing something especially daring or gorgeous, or saying something outrageous. First, I trailed a duchess through a labyrinth, then eavesdropped on a conversation between drunken young aristocrats, watching the alcohol loosen inhibitions. But it was all fuzzy, indistinct, at a distance. I couldn't quite make out what anyone was saying—the Italians spoke too fast for me to follow, and the British clipped their words. The French turned their backs on me, not even pretending politeness, and the Germans broke no rules of decorum except in the volume of their disdain for everyone else. I found myself always outside the circle, with no one to talk to, and nothing to write in the little notebook with the silver pencil.

I wished I were one of the men with trays of drinks. People said and did outrageous things in front of the hired help, as I knew well from Aida's stories. "The day George tries to fire me," Aida had told me, "I'm calling that gossip lady Hedda Hopper." Now I *was* Hedda Hopper. Or at least her competition.

I wandered back to the giant open-mouthed ogre where I began my evening, hoping to find Patsy and Elsa. My feet ached in the pinching pumps, and I was exhausted, not to mention mortified that I'd vomited in front of a princess. I longed to go back to the hotel and my comfy bed there.

As I approached the ogre, I heard voices but didn't see anyone. *American voices,* I thought. I found a photographer crouching outside holding a big camera with a massive set of flashbulbs on top. The kind of stoic professional who dogged celebrities on the Via Veneto, he was barely more than a boy my own age, in an oversized shiny tuxedo. He gave me a wink and put a finger to his lips, nodding at the ogre. I realized the voices were coming from within the stone sculpture. The carved room inside must be an echo chamber, with whatever anyone said wafting out, warped but perfectly audible, through the nostrils and eyes of the ogre. Now the inscription over the ogre's mouth made sense: EVERY THOUGHT FLIES FREE. I took out my notebook and copied down the conversation as fast as I could.

"Look, I love you."

"You know we can never be together."

"We'd be happy."

"Not for long. Listen, darling, I can get away from time to time. Why does anyone have to know about us? It's none of their business. Why the need to throw it in their faces?"

"I'm sick of hiding in the shadows. Love is love is love. I want you to come live with me."

"I'll come."

"For how long. Forever?"

"I can get away for August."

"Not enough. It will break my heart."

"Oh, stop. What do you really want?"

"I want to stop hiding. I want the world to see me as I am. To see us."

This was perfect. A love affair, clearly illicit, the kind that sold newspapers. I waited to see who the lovers were. The photographer had his camera up, ready.

I gasped as the two figures emerged from inside the mouth of the ogre. Flashbulbs popped and the two women threw up their white gloved hands, temporarily blinded by the glare.

Elsa and Patsy.

Sally

Patsy said nothing in the car on the way back to Rome. I pretended to sleep while the sun rose and the chauffeur navigated the empty winding roads.

When we arrived at the top of the Spanish Steps, a workman in gray overalls was scraping the name off the front door of the hotel. "Il Duce thinks 'Hassler' is not Italian enough," he muttered. "So as of today, it's the Villa Medici."

I helped the drunken Patsy to bed, set three glasses of water and an aspirin on her nightstand, and then retreated to my own room. I sank into the cool, smooth white linen sheets and ran my finger over the raised blue border around the duvet as if I would never see it again. I arranged three delightfully fluffy pillows behind my back, trying to memorize the sensation.

I flipped open my notebook and placed a steno pad on my knees.

Just before noon, the connecting door to Patsy's room flew open. "I've got to get on the horn and dictate my column to New York," Patsy said as she bounded in, all manic energy in her chiffon peignoir.

I lifted my eye mask. "You're bright as a daisy this morning." I was wiped out. "Relax. I wrote it for you." I handed Patsy the steno pad and rolled over into the sweet softness of my pillow.

There were a few moments of blissful quiet, then Patsy exploded. "I can't send this!"

I sat up, annoyed. "Why not?"

"It's . . . old news. It's all about some Italian guy who died in the fifteen hundreds. Who cares about him?"

"He was scarred by his experience in the war and built the garden and dedicated it to his dead wife's memory. The Bon Vivant's crusty old heart was melted by this beautiful tale of lost love."

Patsy plopped down on the bed. "Listen, kid, I'm very grateful to you for trying. That was sweet of you. But America needs gossip, not history."

"Does it?" I was irked.

"Didn't you see anyone getting a little tipsy?"

"Yes, I did." I pressed my lips together and stared, but Patsy ignored the hint.

"And anyone playing a little footsie, but with their lips?"

"Yup."

"Well, why didn't you write about that? This is . . . boring."

I exploded. "You don't remember, do you?"

"Remember what?" Patsy looked worried.

I sighed. "You and Elsa were having one of your private conversations inside the monster. Except it was an echo chamber. And there was a photographer outside. He heard everything and took a picture of the two of you coming out of there. What's going to happen to us now?"

Patsy was quiet for a moment. Then she said, "We'd better announce my engagement."

Now my eyes were wide open. "Engagement?"

"Let's see that guest list." Patsy grabbed Elsa's guest list off my nightstand. "How about Sonny Whitney? He's between marriages. Polo players make excellent third husbands."

"He was there with his mother."

"Were they ever apart? Was he drinking?"

I shook my head. Patsy ran her red fingernail down the typed list of names. "Georg!" she said brightly. "Baron von Hohenheim. He bought me a bracelet during a rough crossing one time on the *Aquitania*. His wife ran off with a Brazilian sugarcane tycoon last year. He's perfect."

I caught a glimpse of the travel clock on the nightstand. "It's almost six P.M. in New York. If you don't like what I wrote then we'd better get cracking."

Patsy sat on the edge of the bed and dictated a new column to me, one full of innuendo about flirting, nuzzling, and drunken hijinks I knew had never taken place.

"You know, the party was actually pretty boring," I said.

"Nobody wants to read that. They want to read about people having fun, being naughty. Breaking the rules."

"What's Baron von Hohenheim going to say when he reads he's engaged to you?"

"He'll send flowers, I'm sure. He's very well-bred."

"And . . . Elsa?"

"What about her?"

I paused, then said quietly, "That Italian photographer. It could ruin her. And you."

Patsy tapped out a cigarette and lit it. I sneezed as she said, "America will never hear a thing about it. Disgusting lies."

By this point, I had seen all kinds of love. No one needed to tell me to keep what I saw to myself; it was just something I absorbed, that you could gossip about love affairs between men and women, but what happened between men and men or women and women in the shadowy corners of the pool house or in the moonlit garden was private. I felt an aching sadness for Patsy, and for Elsa. For every bold and unashamed Tallulah Bankhead asserting her right to love whoever she wanted, I knew there were many others forced to hide their true selves.

I watched as Patsy ripped the pages from my steno pad and went back to her room. I heard her telephone the hotel operator and request a line to New York. After a few minutes, the operator rang back and the call was put through.

"Take this down," shouted Patsy into the phone. "Dateline: Rome. Headline: Secrets of the Eternal City. The Bon Vivant got an eyeful of I-talians at play at hostess extraordinaire Elsa Maxwell's Monsters' Ball. Talk about a Roman orgy! 'I came, I saw, I conquered,' announced one well-known American playboy as he left a certain young princess swooning on the terrazzo. This swanky soiree made the shindigs at Hearst Castle look like church socials. Is the Prince of Wales going to abdicate the throne for his American divorcée? If I were a betting man, and I am, I'd put my money on him telling Windsor Castle to send their crown where the sun never sets. . . ."

As Patsy dictated a series of lurid and very colorful lies as seen through the eyes of a fictional older man, I picked up the newspaper that had been slid under our door while we slept. I frowned at the headline and began reading. I looked up when Patsy came back into the room.

"The Italians have taken Ethiopia," I told Patsy.

"Taken it where?"

"They've invaded and seized control of it. Haile Selassie fled, and the King of Italy has declared himself emperor of East Africa." I held up the newspaper.

Patsy opened the curtains and sunlight streamed in.

I tapped the front page with my index finger to get her attention. "And Spain—it's officially in a civil war now."

"Darling, you're very grim today."

I wasn't letting go of my worry this time. "I think this is very important."

"Not to us it isn't."

"Look." I shoved the paper into Patsy's hands. Patsy looked down at it and a moment later shrieked with laughter.

"What?"

"Do you see the byline on this story from the front in Spain? Virginia Cowles. I know her."

"You do?"

"She was a society columnist, just like her mother. Father was a Park Avenue psychiatrist. Little bit shady, there were some lawsuits. Virginia was a debutante. Elsa introduced us at Newport. Tiny little thing. Very chic."

As Patsy spoke, I caught a glimpse of myself in the mirror. Staring back at me was a strange blond woman-child with plucked eyebrows and a high white forehead. She looked like a Kewpie doll, vapid and empty eyed. *Ma wouldn't recognize me right now,* I thought. *She would walk right past me on the street.* "I wonder how well that pays," I said to Patsy. "Maybe I should be a war correspondent."

"I bet you'd meet all kinds of interesting men."

"I'm serious. I don't think I'm cut out for high society."

Patsy took my hand and squeezed it. I could feel her rings. I wanted to go home, but what did that mean? I had no home.

"You are beautiful, smart, and twice the human being of any of these fucks." When Patsy swore like a sailor, it meant she was serious. "Someday you'll realize I'm right. Now we'd better order breakfast," she called to me over her shoulder as she disappeared through the connecting door. "This afternoon we're off to Deauville for the Grand Prix, and a whole month of parties. The Bon Vivant is going to have a very full dance card. Giddyup!"

III

Imperial Masquerade

The Bon Vivant

SCHUSS AND SHINE

The winter season kicks off in style at St. Moritz this weekend, where everyone who's anyone is gathering like a herd of water buffalo to ski and be skeen. The Bon Vivant will don his binoculars and bring you the blow by blow of the water-hole courtship at Badrutt's. . . . Life of the party Lupe Vélez celebrated her divorce from Johnny "Tarzan" Weissmuller in Klosters this week—will she land back in the arms of horse opera-tor Gary Cooper or swordsman-about-town Errol Flynn? . . . Rumor has it the temps in snowy Switzerland have nothing on the chill generated in Windsor Castle by rumors that a certain American duchess refers to the new Queen as "Cookie." . . .

St. Moritz

1938

Sally

Before I opened the heavy red envelope, I made a mental note of what I was wearing: slim black ski pants, a red-and-white sweater that fit tight to my waist, and a knit hat with leather-edged dark glasses perched on top. Elsa had recently thrown a "Come as You Were" party where guests were ordered to attend in whatever they were wearing when they opened the invitation. My fellow guests had appeared in street clothes, tennis whites, riding attire, and one Alsatian baron came wrapped in a hotel bath towel. I showed up in a hair salon smock and a headful of curlers. I wasn't going to make that mistake again.

"Oooh," I said when I ripped open the envelope and read the heavy engraved card inside. "Charlie Foix-Renard's throwing a masked ball in Venice," I called to Patsy, who was unlacing her ski boots by the front door of our room in Badrutt's Palace Hotel in St. Moritz. The Swiss Alps towered outside the picture window just like on the postcards. The whole thing didn't look quite real—I felt the backdrop had been painted by a Hollywood scene painter and would roll up any second, revealing the padded walls and rigging of a soundstage.

"Now? Venice is freezing in the winter. What's he thinking? No one will come. I need a hot bath before dinner." Patsy limped toward the bathroom and I heard the water running. "I'm all bruised," she called.

I joined her as the little marble room filled with steam. Perched on the edge of the tub, I checked my manicure. "That'll teach you to ride a toboggan disguised as the Earl of Dudley."

"I think it's awful they banned women from the Cresta Run. It's unfair." Patsy added Epsom salts to the water and then a few drops of oil, which filled the room with a piney scent.

"I agree with you. Women should be allowed to decide for themselves whether to ride a small piece of wood headfirst at fifty miles per hour down an icy ravine, though I have no idea why anyone would want to."

"To put color in my cheeks."

"Try rouge next time. Listen, Charlie's party is in July. An Imperial Masquerade. We're supposed to come dressed as famous rulers from history."

"Any excuse for Charlie to dress up as Caligula." Patsy lowered herself into the tub with a happy sigh.

"The Marquis de Sade would be more appropriate. Don't leave me alone with him next time, all right?" Charlie was an aging French tycoon with roving hands. "Six months to get a costume ready. People are going to go all out. Who should we go as?"

"They'll expect me to be Empress Wu, who killed her family and slept her way to the top, but I'd rather be Alexander the Great. I could ride in on a winged horse."

"That was Pegasus. Alexander rode Bucephalus."

"Make sure you get a guest list in advance."

"Relax. I've got a Ph.D. in High Society," I assured her. "I know exactly who had soup at the starting line snowbar this morning and who greeted the day with whisky. I know who enjoyed twelve minutes alone with whom on the cog railway, who nuzzled whom on the motor sleigh, who lunched at the Corviglia hut with whose estranged spouse, and who bet on whose thoroughbred at the snow races. I know who's at the bar at the Kulm right now, and who's sitting where in the hotel dining room tonight."

"You're a regular Mata Hari, kid. Pass me that sponge."

I now penned all the Bon Vivant columns. To preserve secrecy, only one editor in New York knew Patsy's identity, and no one knew mine. That gave us a double layer of protection, and made the beau monde wild to uncover the BV's real name. The idle rich were both outraged and delighted by "his" encyclopedic knowledge of their love lives, and the public's fascination with them. I'd made household names of obscure dukes and duchesses, starlets, writers, and musicians. The BV wrote about how Hedy Lamarr wore all her jewelry to a dinner party so she could flee her abusive husband in style, and how Decca Mitford had followed her handsome beau, Esmond Romilly, to the Spanish Civil War. I'd scooped *Vogue* when Wallis Simpson wore an evening gown decorated with a crustacean.

And speaking of Wallis, I did love a scandal. Over the past two years, I had mastered the art of writing juicy gossip in the voice of an aging flaneur without getting us hit with any more libel suits. I had spies among all the hotel staff, including the waiters, who wore ice skates as they carried trays laden with cocktails to skating patrons, and the maids, who brought extra towels while getting an eyeful of who was sharing a bed. They were delighted to tell me what they learned while moving invisibly among the rich and famous, and I added what I learned while being a good listener at dinner parties and polo matches. I made sure to be fresh-faced and pleasant without being distractingly pretty so I could listen without being seen or remembered. I still missed my family and thought of them every day, but to be honest my life pre-Patsy was feeling further and further away, a sepia-toned, fading photograph. My nickname for my steamer trunk was "Home."

Meanwhile, Patsy had starred in four Italian and two German films, several of which featured more nudity than I thought was wise. She had also briefly dated a kleptomaniac Belgian count who employed a full-time valet to return the loot he lifted, along with flowery letters of apology and testimonials from doctors that he suffered from a genuine and incurable medical condition. The Bon Vivant column was a huge success, which was fortunate. In sharp contrast to the heirs and heiresses in our social circle, Patsy and I had to survive on what we earned. We kept expenses down by not owning an apartment or a car and staying in the cheapest rooms at the nicest hotels. We accepted all invitations, and went weeks at a time as houseguests, dinner guests, and yacht guests, without paying a cent for anything. It was a precarious game—we could attend parties but not afford to throw them, and could stay for weeks at someone's château or villa but not return the favor. As long as we kept moving and stayed charming, no one would care, but if there was a whiff of poverty around us, we'd be cast out of the magic circle. And of course, no one could know we were actually spies, reporting to the unwashed masses about our friends.

I had come to the conclusion that a good marriage for either of us would solve a lot of problems, but that was easier said than done. It didn't take twenty-twenty vision to see that titled men without money were delighted to marry Americans, just as long as they were wealthy heiresses. Untitled men with money gravitated to the young European or British princesses, whose titles and charm would smooth their arriviste edges. And titled men with money could have any woman they wanted, and did. "Count van der Noot stole my heart, but then his valet returned it," Patsy said when summing up her last romance. Her long-term financial plan was to find a suitable next husband, but in the meantime, she was having as much fun as possible— with women and men—while shopping for him. My long-term plan was to find a wee castle to call my own. I wanted a roof over my head that no one could take away from me, ever. Since it was unlikely I was going to make enough money to buy real estate, I needed to land a manse the old-fashioned way: by marrying a man who owned one. I supposed some people would see that as shallow, but I fully intended to love this hypothetical home-owning man. The crucial part was that I needed to chronicle scandals and not cause one if I was going to win the heart of Prince Charming.

I slipped into a white fur-edged gown and smoothed my hair, resetting the waves with my fingers. Changing for dinner was one of the rituals I had come to enjoy. I could be a hard-charging tomboy during the day—ice-skating, sledding, skiing—and an elegant lady by candlelight in the evening. I was no longer startled by the blond, alabaster-faced woman looking back at me from the mirror. If I had become a little cold, if my laugh rang a little false, it wasn't good or bad, it was just what had to be done, like stealing the flowers that day in Los Angeles.

"Come on, Mother," I called. "The Duke and Wallis are supposed to make an appearance."

"You must call her the Duchess," said Patsy, emerging perfumed from the bath.

"Only to her face. She reminds me of a whippet. Little beady eyes."

"Beady eyes that stole the heart of a king and made him give up his crown. You should do so well for yourself."

"What about love?" This was a game she and I played.

Patsy kissed my cheek. "You and I weren't born so lucky. For us, love is fun, sex is power, and marriage is business. Don't ever mix them up or you'll be in real trouble. Rules for happiness."

We made our way down to dinner in the hotel dining room. An elaborately carved wooden ceiling sat atop high white walls with arched doorways. The parquet floor was famously waxed to a high shine and just as slippery

as the ice rink outdoors—more than one grand lady had landed on her duff
there. Iron sconces held tall white candles, and a massive fire roared in the
fireplace. All the men were in white tie and tails, their jackets cut away in
the latest style. They were all identical, poor dears, while each woman had
to be unique—the greatest horror was if someone wore the same dress as
you, and looked better in it. I spotted Mrs. Harrison Williams, who always
made the "best dressed" lists, confident in a Vionnet gown with a gold-
lamé-wrapped bodice and a gold embroidered tulle skirt with a daring
slit up the front that only a divorcée could pull off. Poor little Brenda Duff
Frazier, who had confessed to me that she often got a stiff neck because
if she moved her head it mussed her hair, looked miserable but nonetheless stunning in a Balenciaga long-sleeved gown with scalloped paillettes.
Josephine Baker, Parisian nightclub sensation turned industrialist's wife,
was sporting an elegant, simple Mainbocher, a sharp contrast from the
banana skirts that had titillated audiences. We circulated through the dining room, greeting with the lightest of air-kisses all the friends we'd seen
only hours before. The phrases were always the same: "You look *divine,*
darling." "Have you heard about dear [someone else]'s *tragic* faux pas? I
was *dying* for her." "I had a letter from [royalty] and he said to send you
his *very* best." It was all about status: if you showed deference, you were
accepted, but you also needed to prove your worth via wit and (the highest
form of currency) gossip. But one could never gossip openly—it had to be
shared lightly, like a condiment, as if one didn't really care.

Patsy nodded at a man in his sixties who was recently widowed. "Baron
von Stettmeyer. He would make a good first husband for you. Heart condition."

I didn't want a first husband. I wanted a keeper whose stately home I
would move into, redecorate in a modern way, host parties in, and live in
happily ever after. The man was fuzzy in my imagination, but the house
was not: I wanted grand lawns, a cozy library, a dining room that would
seat twenty, and a bathroom all to myself. With a huge tub. In exchange
for lifetime residency, I would be an excellent wife in every way. I was sure
this would work out just fine.

Thus I ignored Patsy and made mental notes for the BV column. Count
Velsky was sitting awfully close to his cousin, the Countess Velamirovich.
Rudy Gutierrez was crowing about his triumph in snow polo today and

making the Marquis of Milford Haven, who had fallen off his horse, buy the drinks. I spotted a new young gentleman I hadn't seen before at the Duke of Devonshire's table and stopped to compliment the ancient, deaf Duke on his curling.

"Your sweeping, Your Grace, was a thing of beauty," I said, hoping he would introduce me to his guest. Comings and goings were always fodder for society columns: *Mr. Smythe Flum-Flum has joined his cousin Lord Hoo Hah for a weekend in Biarritz. . . .* Though Patsy was the original Bon Vivant, I had elevated the BV to worldwide fame by perfecting "his" arch, sophisticated, teasing tone. I was already making mental notes about what the BV would say this time. *The newest lanky laddie to join the alpine hijinks here in this charming cuckoo clock of a Swiss village has large gray eyes and slicked-back dark-blond hair, a British Fred Astaire. His laughing eyes have buckets more life in them than those of the standard-issue aristocrat, who tends to have the personality of a glass of tap water.*

"My cousin Roddy," the Duke said at last. "Viscount Lumley. This little minx is the delightful Miss—" The Duke never remembered anyone's name. He didn't have to.

Lumley. I mentally flipped through *Debrett's Peerage.* Wasn't there a little manor in Surrey that was set aside for the younger son of this clan?

"Call me Sally," I said to Roddy, extending a gloved hand. "My mother is Patsy Chen, in case you're wondering which hole is mine in this advent calendar."

He stared at me, confused, as they always did. "The film star? But you're not—"

I sighed. "I'm adopted."

"Oh. How interesting. And are you also in the movies, Miss Chen?"

"Miss Brady. Chen is my mother's stage name. I've run fast enough to escape the klieg lights so far." I had the sense he was assessing me. The firstborn sons had to keep the bloodline pure, but younger sons like him were sent out to hunt for a meatpacking heiress from Chicago or a cod maven from Boston to replenish the family coffers. I had to exude wealth I didn't have.

"You can take me for a spin if you like," I said to the viscount. "Put me through my paces, check my teeth." This would give me a chance to discover a tidbit for the column and determine his real estate holdings.

He laughed and took my arm and we eased into a waltz.

"The variety of people here is . . ." he said.

"Reminiscent of a day at Coney Island?"

"Back in England, one knows everyone at every house party."

"How cozy."

"I find it tedious."

"So you're okay mingling with the masses, Lord Roderick? A little 'them' with your 'us'?"

He laughed again. I liked his laugh. It was a kind of restrained howl. "You're making me sound like a real sap," he complained.

"Who, me? You're the one doing the talking."

"Miss Brady, you're cruel. I may be a viscount, but I'm not a snob, I swear to you."

"Well, if you were, this place would probably delight you. A good number of the guests and half the staff at this hotel are defrocked Russian royalty of one stripe or another. Even the servants are titled."

He narrowed his eyes in glee. "You're correct that we British hardly consider anyone important except our own."

It was my turn to laugh. "You do travel in close-knit packs, like fleas. My favorite is when the Brits just shout in English at anyone they suspect of speaking a foreign language."

"That's how I got here from the train station. Everyone finds us rude but fascinating. But not you?"

"No one cares what I think," I said with a sly smile. "I'm a mere child."

"You seem awfully grown-up to me."

The song ended. I said, "Evenings in St. Moritz appear high-spirited, but generally follow timetables and mating rituals as fixed as migrating waterfowl's. It's time for me to rejoin my mother. Enjoy your evening, my lord." I bobbed a quick curtsy (thank you, finishing school), and he bowed.

"Handsome," said Patsy, after I had crossed the room as casually as possible. I began picking daintily at my shrimp cocktail. I would have loved to wolf it down. I was starving, but my time on the streets had taught me to manage hunger. Only dowager duchesses were forgiven a thickened waistline. There was a part of me that couldn't wait to get married so I could finally eat a full meal.

"He wouldn't win a blue ribbon at the Iowa State Fair," I said, but the truth was I did find Roddy attractive. And perhaps the attraction was mutual. In fact, several times during the rest of the evening, I found him staring at me from across the cavernous, antler-chandeliered dining room. What had started as a shallow bit of house hunting was taking a different turn.

"Titled and rich," said Patsy. "Officer in the British Army. I hear his parents will give him Marsden Manor as a wedding present. Charming place. Lovely park. Eighteenth-century house. Library." She raised an eyebrow. "Modern plumbing." Patsy cared nothing for real estate. Security for her was something completely different: freedom. She wanted to be able to run away. I wanted to be able to stay.

"Good views?" I asked.

"Excellent. And he's a younger son, which means less scrutiny on a fiancée."

"Doesn't that bother you, that women are checked out like prospective brood mares, bloodlines and hip width and dowry?"

"Marriage is—"

"Business, I know."

"You're eighteen and not getting any younger. Now is the perfect time for your first marriage."

"I'd never pass the background check."

Patsy dropped her social smile. "Don't be afraid to lie. Do you think Wallis announced on her first date that she was born out of wedlock and grew up poor? Hell, no. Don't forget the rules for happiness. Sex is power. The only power we have. Use it. Once they fall in love with you, they don't care where you fucking came from."

✿

The next morning, I was in my ski garb having an espresso at the hotel bar when I heard a voice behind me.

"Miss Brady, word has it you're quite the sportswoman."

I turned and saw Lord Roddy wearing slightly comical puffy wool plus fours over brown-and-orange argyle socks. His ski jacket tapered elegantly to his waist, and he wore a shirt and tie underneath it.

"Dressed to kill?" I asked.

"Touché. Princess Alexandria was supposed to join me for a chamois hunt but she has opted for a day of ice-skating instead. I've decided to lay down my arms and hit the slopes. Care to join me?"

"Where are you headed?"

"Diavolezza, I think. I've heard the views are marvelous."

"Off piste? Did you hire a guide?"

He waved his hand. "I'm all the guide you need."

Lapo

He joined Eleanor at the outdoor tables alongside the ice rink at the Kulm. Tuxedoed waiters in ice skates carried silver trays of drinks one-handed. Women were swathed in furs and men in loden. Everyone looked jolly, and most people were drinking, despite the early hour.

"You would never know that Europe is on the brink of war," said Lapo. He looked down at the morning paper. "German bombers killed a hundred people in Barcelona. Hitler's meeting with the Japanese ambassador. Mussolini wants Corsica and Djibouti. But what's on the front page? 'Crown Prince Paul of Greece weds Frederica of Hanover.'"

"What time are we meeting the owner?" asked Eleanor.

Lapo and Eleanor had come to St. Moritz to buy an apartment. Leone had given them the money. As non-Jews, they were less likely to be searched at the border, across which Italians were forbidden to bring more than fifty lire. Lapo was alarmed to see Switzerland preparing for war. Posters on the walls of every village and train station ordered, not urged, Swiss citizens to stockpile at least two months' worth of food. Rumor was that Switzerland would likely pull out of the League of Nations and return to the official neutrality it held during the Great War, when it had housed tens of thousands of wounded prisoners of war from both sides of the conflict, an agreement convenient to all concerned. The rich of any nation could stash money and loved ones there out of harm's way.

Skaters glided past them, and Lapo sipped his amaretto. He felt vaguely offended to see all these people having fun when things were deteriorating so fast. But on the other hand, what could any of them do to stop this inevitable slide toward war?

"Let's skate," said Eleanor. "It will cheer you up."

A few minutes later, he found himself gliding over the ice. Eleanor was right—it was good to move, and he felt his mood lightening. There was nothing he could do about any of the terrible things that were happening in the world, except this one thing he was doing. He was helping his friend. He shifted his weight and let his feet draw a huge circle on the ice.

Eleanor skated over to him. "Guess who I ran into?" she asked, looping her arm around his. They skated along in unison. "Charlie Foix-Renard. He's invited us to a party in Venice. An 'Imperial Masquerade.'"

Lapo frowned.

"Don't make that face. You know I love to dress up."

The idea of traveling to Venice with lots of luggage, putting on some heavy and no doubt hot and uncomfortable costume, and going to a crowded party sounded awful to him. "Imperial Masquerade" was an apt description of the world right now. Alessandro's ill-fated disguise would be, unfortunately, perfect. But Eleanor had a glow in her cheeks that wasn't entirely from the skating and the cognac. Their life on the farm was so isolated. He realized that having a party to look forward to would cheer her up.

"*Va bene,*" he said. "Let's accept. That sounds fun. Can I be Mark Antony to your Cleopatra?"

"Yippee!" she said, releasing his arm and doing a spin.

"My elusive writer," came a voice from behind him. Lapo turned too fast and his feet went out from under him, and *boom,* he was on his ass on the ice. He looked up to find Count Ciano laughing and extending a black-leather-gloved hand to him. His camel overcoat was trimmed in mink. "You can't escape me now. Let's have a drink."

"I can't. I'm—" He realized he couldn't reveal his real purpose in coming here. Buying property outside of Italy was frowned upon as a sign of disloyalty, that is, unless it was in a country that Italy was invading. And the suitcase of cash he was carrying could land him in jail. "Eleanor and I are going skiing."

"Don't break a leg. Later, then. I'll meet you in the bar at five."

✺

Eleanor and Lapo found the apartment smaller and darker than described, and way overpriced. They bought it anyway as there was nothing else for sale in the area. Lapo couldn't picture Leone and his wife there; their Florence apartment was so gracious and beautifully furnished. This one had low ceilings, worn floors, and leaking windows. Still, real estate was always a good investment. No doubt they would make it absolutely lovely in time. He made an appointment at a lawyer's office the next day to sign the papers. He would bring Leone some good news for once. He and Eleanor stopped in a chocolate shop to buy treats for Alessandro and the girls.

"I'm just so busy with the estate," he told Ciano as they sat in the Renaissance Bar at Badrutt's. Ciano had chosen a spot in front of the fireplace that Lapo found uncomfortably public, two wing chairs in the middle of the room. Still, it smelled of cozy cedar and pine, and the heat the carved-stone fireplace gave off was welcome in the drafty space. Lapo was happy he didn't have to huddle side by side with the foreign minister on a barstool. The gentle glow from the sconces on either side of the fireplace illuminated only a few couples having a predinner drink. He'd rather not be seen with Ciano, if he could help it. The count was being groomed as Mussolini's successor, it was rumored, but at the same time, people said he was getting too big for his britches, and Mussolini wasn't thrilled with how rampantly Ciano cheated on his wife Edda, Mussolini's daughter.

A waiter brought them a selection of cigars, and the logs popped and crackled.

"We've put in several new wells and piped water to the houses and fields. The irrigation is allowing us a longer growing season," Lapo said.

"Did the tractor help?"

"Immensely. I loved the old oxen, but I have to say the tractor gets the job done a lot faster."

"So you have time to write?"

Lapo shook his head. "I'm busier than ever. And Eleanor is starting a school for the farmers' children."

Ciano blew a large puff of blue smoke. "That's wonderful. We'll have to arrange a visit. Yes. The whole thing is marvelous. You're a genius."

"I am?"

"We've been looking for a place to be our model for agricultural reform.

An ancient estate reclaimed and brought into the twentieth century by a gorgeous young couple? I love it. Il Duce will want to visit."

Lapo choked on the cigar and wiped his eyes. "The Cubans are always so strong," he said.

"We'll arrange it with the local officials. Brilliant idea. Splash it all over the papers."

Mussolini at Belsederino? Lapo tried not to be aghast. "I don't know. I wouldn't want to let you down. I mean, the place is still rustic. It's not a showplace."

"That's fine—it's a work in progress. Like Italy. Pointing toward the future. But someday, we're going to want that biography."

"You must have better writers on your list," Lapo said.

"We want *you*. Your country needs you."

Lapo paused. Alessandro was now seventeen. He'd have to do his compulsory military service when he turned eighteen, but Lapo imagined with Ciano's help he could arrange for his son to have something cushy and safe. Right now, the boy was asking to go study in Prague to escape the overbearing Fascist curriculum being forced down his throat at home, but Eleanor was afraid to let him go so far away. "You don't think if there is a war it will last long, do you?" he asked Ciano.

Ciano chuckled. "It can't. Italy is utterly unprepared for war. After Africa and Spain, we simply can't afford it. I said that to Il Duce just the other day. We can't possibly let ourselves get dragged into this insanity."

"What did he say?"

Ciano rolled his eyes. "He's jealous of Hitler." He signaled the waiter for another cocktail. "All the more reason to keep his focus on domestic successes. Like your farm."

Sally

Roddy grinned, and I felt things unfurling inside me that were going to be hard to refurl, dammit. I told myself this was purely research for the Bon Vivant column. But then there was Marsden Manor. If I played my cards right, I could end up welcoming my guests to my stately home. *Our* stately home. And why not? I was as good as any English broad, wasn't I? Why couldn't I pull a Wallis? But if I was really going to hunt big game like Roddy, I needed to stay in control.

Roddy held my gloved hand as he helped me up into the red wooden sleigh and handed me our skis. I settled into the furs, and he sat close to me. My breath was an icy cloud, and the bells on the big bay horse's harness jingled as we climbed up through the gray stone town. I stuck to polite questions about his winter activities. He told me it was only his third visit to St. Moritz, because he generally preferred the skiing in Klosters.

"But my cousin told me the girls are much prettier here," he said.

"And have you found that to be true?"

"So far, yes. Present company included."

I blushed against my will. This man was part of an inbred, incestuous, snobbish caste that fancied themselves better than all other humans, just because of who their parents and grandparents were. This assumption of innate British superiority had propelled them to colonize huge chunks of the planet under the banner of bringing "civilization" to the so-called savages, while in fact exploiting and oppressing those they ruled. My own country had thrown off the British yoke. So why was I so damn delighted Lord Roddy was paying attention to me? Was it just the hope of having a permanent address? Or did I really like this guy? Was Wallis this confused when she pursued her prince?

We transferred from the sleigh to a series of rope lifts and then hiked up even farther, nearly to the mountain's summit. I was warm from the exertion and the sun, and the wind felt icy on my cheeks. The snow was soft and powdery under my skis. The sky was a stunning clear blue, and the blinding white peaks below and all around us seemed unearthly, like we had climbed up to Valhalla.

"It's so beautiful" was my brilliantly original comment. Though my brain was devoid of wit, my heart soared in places like this, and I felt some kind of ancient connection to nature, a sense of the sublime that broke through the volcanic crust of irony and good manners that had smothered me.

"I thought we could run down the glacier to the Morteratsch railway station. I hear it's better than six miles," said Roddy.

I'd never done the run without a guide. "Yes, it's wonderful," I said. "But we've got to look out for crevasses."

"Can see all the way to Libya today."

I glanced back to the familiar, easy slopes where everyone else was descending, black ants in the sugar bowl of the huge white mountain.

"You're not thinking better of this, I hope?" Roddy asked.

"Of course not," I said, and pushed off. There had been lots of snow this winter, and I was happy to see the rocks were well covered. I glided down through the powder, steering my wooden skis into even, beautiful curves. Roddy shot out ahead of me, dropping fast toward the village far below us.

I paused to catch my breath and savor the moment. Life was so strange. I was skiing down a mountain in Switzerland. I thought about my parents and my brothers and sisters—Victor, Michael, Mary, and baby Margaret, who was only one when I left. What were they doing at this moment? I felt a twinge of guilt. Why was I living this bizarre fairy tale while they were— where? Trying to feed livestock amid fifteen-foot snowdrifts? Building the State Street Subway in Chicago? It was so unfair. I had done nothing to deserve this luck. Yet no one else I met seemed to question *their* luck, which was magnitudes greater than mine. It never seemed to occur to them that they could have been born into a life other than this one. Or that they should be kind to those who had less.

"Come on!" called Roddy. "Let 'er rip." He shot down to the left side of a couloir.

I followed him, keeping my eyes on the expanse of white snow in front of me, ready to stop on a dime if I spotted the shadow of a crevasse. The gaps in the glacier's ice sheet could swallow a skier and drop you fifty feet to your death without warning. The stories of skiers hung upside down, trapped for hours or days, were hair-raising.

Despite the wariness, I loved the way I felt on the snow. At first it had been difficult to keep the long wooden skis from crossing over each other, but after several lessons, I'd learned to shift my weight from foot to foot, and ski edge to ski edge, to turn. I leaned forward now, feeling myself speed up and schuss through the snow, making the powder sigh and spray around me.

I caught up to Roddy, whose lean form was silhouetted against the snow. "Your cheeks are pink," I said, gliding to a stop.

"Take a gander." He put an arm around me and pointed into the distance. "What's that?"

I loved these peaks and was happy he was interested in knowing their names. "Schlarigna. And those are Vadret and Languard."

I felt his hand shift to my left breast, and then the right. "And these?" he said, leaning into my neck.

Yes, I was a virgin. In fact, I had never even been kissed. I know, I know, all I ever wrote about was people kissing each other at parties, and who was sleeping with whom. But that meant I was busy spying, not participating in the fun. I had kept myself apart and unknown for good reason. But those reasons were blurring with the feel of Roddy's hands on my body. . . . I found myself dissolving and expanding in a way that made me think of molten glass in the hands of a Venetian craftsman. "I—" I sounded like I was choking on a sandwich. Roddy reached down and released our boots from the ski bindings.

"I can't stop thinking of you." He kissed me, his lips on mine soft at first, then harder. With clinical detachment, I had spied on so many couples as they necked. The Bon Vivant even ranked people's kissing like an Olympic diving judge on a scale from French (high) to British (low) using descriptors like "messy, sloppy, dry, anemic, gymnastic, electric," always implying that his own technique was world-class. Roddy's arms closed around me, and we fell onto the snow.

This was unexpected, and I found myself pushed down into the cold hardness of the snow-baked crust in a way that was suddenly less romantic and more like high school wrestling.

"Wait." This was all happening very fast. My body was still unfurling, but my brain was full of Patsy's voice reminding me of the rules, and the Bon Vivant's sly lists of what men wanted. What did I want? A husband? A house? Or just to feel his skin on mine?

Roddy was on top of me now, pressing me deeper into the snow, fumbling at my ski pants, pushing my sweater up. I could feel his breath, and his weight was heavy, his hips grinding into me, and—

Oomph. I pushed back at him and said, "Hold your horses!" That was pure Iowa talking. I didn't know what to say next, so I stuttered, "I—I'm a good girl." He laughed and slid his hand below my waistband and into my culottes and said, "Yes, you are, and you deserve to have a lot of fun." He moved his hand gently and I couldn't stop myself from exhaling sharply. He took his hand away.

"You want me to stop?" he asked.

I honestly didn't know what to say. I felt angry and embarrassed. He saw that, and laughed again.

"Stop laughing."

He rolled next to me on the snow. "I'm not laughing at you," he said. "I want you to enjoy this. I really do. I am a gentleman, after all. And an officer in the British Army sworn to uphold the honor of the Crown."

"You're not acting like it."

"You're right. I'm terribly sorry. I don't know what got into me. I'll cease and desist, of course. Though I may be off to war soon. Laying my life down and all." He lay there without moving and stared at the sky. I waited, but he didn't resume his attention, and I realized that bothered me, too.

What was the right thing to do? I suddenly felt like the teenager I was. It all seemed so blurry. My body had very definite opinions, however.

I took his hand and put it on my stomach. After a few minutes it felt warm and he wasn't moving it, so I wriggled a bit underneath it. Still the hand just lay there, a lifeless instrument. I took his hand again and slid it down into my pants. Yes, I did, and I refuse to be judged for that. You try rolling around with a lord at a Swiss resort and walking away calmly just when things are getting interesting. I moved my hips and finally he un-curled his fingers, and once again I was hot glass. . . .

He rolled onto his side and kissed me gently. "I really like you," he whispered. "In fact, I think it was love at first sight."

I know, I know, but come on. I was eighteen.

"Really?" I sighed.

"Uh-huh."

I still felt the need to test him. "Aren't you going to ask me who 'my people' are?"

Roddy looked into my eyes with surprising sincerity. "All I care about is who *you* are. And you're marvelous. I really think I'm in love with you, Sally Brady."

Love. Love! It was so unexpected, so spontaneously marvelous. So . . . wonderful.

"I know what I want," he said, his voice husky. "What do you want?"

"To be a chatelaine," I said.

"What?"

"You. I want you." I closed my eyes and he rolled onto me again and kissed me. This time, reader, I didn't stop him.

✡

I didn't quite know what to say afterward, so I chatted gaily about the surrounding mountains as we put our skis back on and resumed our trek down the slope.

"I saw a big goat over there once," I said, pointing to a rock outcropping.

"Race you down," he said, and took off in a swirl of powder.

I was relieved and unsettled, but told myself it was all fine, Roddy and I were together now, and he did love me, he'd said so, and love made it all okay. I would marry him and be a perfect wife and live in a beautiful house and be happy. I made graceful turns and thought about how yesterday I was just a girl, and today I was a woman in love, making love, and he was a man of wealth and position, and we were in love, and everything would be all right, love, modern plumbing, and table settings and bone china and engraved stationery and . . .

"Help!" I heard a faint call from somewhere off to my right. *"Aiuto!"* I slowed and skied to a knoll and scanned the slope below. I caught sight of a figure below me. "Help!" called the person again, waving his arms and ski poles.

I could still see Roddy to my left. "Roddy!" I cupped my gloves and shouted, hoping he could hear me over the wind in his ears.

I stood there shouting until he stopped and looked back at me. I waved my arms and pointed to the right and sidestepped over to where I could drop into the chute that led toward the person needing help. I skied down to him and saw he was in his thirties. He was in expedition-ready ski gear, all boiled wool and oiled canvas, with glacier goggles. He had a rope tied to his waist and I saw that he had dropped it into a crevasse. I gasped and stepped back. I hadn't even seen the crevasse until I was right on top of it. Clearly, neither had he. I was sure it had been invisible until the snow gave way under his companion's feet.

"Il mio amico," the man was saying in Italian. He seemed exhausted and terrified. "My friend fell in. He's alive, thank God, but I can't get enough traction to get him out. I've tried and tried." He was panting and deeply upset, almost crying.

"It's okay," I said. *"Sono qui."* I said my friend was coming, too. We would help.

I went as close to the edge of the crevasse as I dared. As the ice sheet of the glacier expanded and contracted and shifted in the day's warmth and cold, it created these terrifying, deadly fissures. This one was only about three feet wide, with a blue light reflecting out of it. I could hear groaning from inside. "He is trapped upside down," said the Italian.

Roddy appeared and we quickly pulled off our skis and created a human chain. The poor devil's skis were caught on the sides of the ice wall, which had saved his life but also trapped him facing downward, headfirst. Once we had him secured by our own weight, his friend called to him to remove his skis. I couldn't see from my vantage point at the end of the chain, but I pictured the poor man, hanging upside down in that terrible hole, having to reach up and remove his skis. I gasped as his full weight hit the rope. For a second, I thought all three of us would be pulled down with him, four people at the bottom of a crevasse. My feet sunk deep into the snow and stopped the slide. The three of us hauled on the rope until the man appeared. He was purple faced and moaning. We laid him in the soft snow.

"I think my leg is broken," he said in Italian. *"Rotto."* His face went from purple to ashen as I watched the blood drain out of it. He was trembling and his teeth were chattering uncontrollably.

"He's in shock. We have to get him out of here. I'll go for help, get a sled," said the unhurt Italian who had waved me down. "Can you two stay with him until I return?"

"*Aspettate.* Wait," I said. I translated what the Italian had said for Roddy, then I added, "I watched how to do this at ski school. We need to move him now or—" I glanced at the man. "We should take my skis and lash them together. We'll lay him on them and then we'll use the ropes to tow him. One of you will go in front to watch for more crevasses, and one behind to stabilize him." The instructor at Cervinia had made us practice it ourselves until we could haul each other around. I explained the plan to the Italians, adding to Roddy, "We need to move quickly." I could see the man was losing consciousness.

The three of us rapidly built the makeshift sled from my skis and got the injured man onto it. Roddy went in front and the Italian behind.

"What about you?" Roddy asked me. "Without your skis, how are you going to get down?"

He did care about me. My heart took wing in the most annoyingly clichéd way. Of course, I was worried about how to get down the mountain alone without skis, but I did my best to sound bright and confident, the kind of plucky girl any man would love. "I'll start walking," I said. "At least it's all downhill from here."

Siena

1938

Alessandro

He spent weeknights with a friend whose family lived in the center of Siena. He missed home, but it would have been impractical to travel all the way from Belsederino to the city every day for university.

An unusually tall, gangly boy just about to turn eighteen, with black curly hair and big feet, he was seen as something of an oddity by his classmates. It wasn't because he hated Fascism in a place where everyone vocally embraced it. He did hate Fascism, but he had made a promise to his parents to keep that to himself. His classmates made him feel like an outsider because his mother was American. He was not quite Italian in their eyes, and they called him *lo straniero*, "the foreigner," or *l'americano*, despite the fact he was born in Italy. Yet when he visited his mother's family in Chicago, his American cousins also treated him like a foreigner. "Dago," they called him to his face, or "wop." When he finished *liceo*, his mother talked about him going to the United States to college, but Alessandro wanted to go to Prague. He had never visited the city, but he felt the lure of its history, its magic, its place as a cultural crossroads. In his imagination, it was a city that welcomed all and ostracized none.

"I want to see Prague Castle. I want to look at the sky from where Tycho Brahe saw it. I want to see the Kunstkammer, the emperor's cabinet of curiosities. I don't want to study just the kings and the battles. I want to study the way everyday people lived."

In the end, Alessandro had given in to parental pressure and enrolled at the University of Siena, itself one of the oldest schools in the world, dating back to 1240. Here, it was the Middle Ages under scholarly focus. Alessandro found his professors and classmates to be obsessed with the golden age of the Sienese Republic, which didn't officially end until the city was conquered by Florence in 1555, but had been dealt its mortal wound by the Black Death of 1348. Of course, he valued the fact that Siena was a sensible, thriving constitutional republic with a medical school and a bank at a time when the rest of the world was still figuring out how to hold a fork. That wasn't what his professors focused on, though. They talked only about the glorious wars, the strong leaders, the private armies, the brave knights, the chivalry. When he asked about civic life, they frowned. "We're under pressure," one professor whispered to him. "They control the curriculum. The reading lists. I have to feed my family. If I lose this job . . ."

It became clear to him that Mussolini's embrace of imperialism and the need to support that with nationalism meant that all Italian scholars were pressured to produce works lauding or proving Italians' innate strengths, their inherited greatness, their genetic exceptionalism. One of his professors had to scrap a study of Dante in favor of Filippo Tommaso Marinetti, a Futurist and ardent Fascist author of "War, the World's Only Hygiene."

After his party joke fell worse than flat, his parents warned him it wasn't safe to be openly anti-Fascist, though they assured him they agreed with him. "We just have to keep that to ourselves," they cautioned. "Even in front of your sisters." He liked that he and his parents were in a secret circle that the twins were shut out of. Little monsters. They absorbed all the Fascist drivel that was pumped into them in school, and had an unnerving habit of raising their manicured right hands at random moments and shouting the Fascist motto, "Believe, obey, fight!"

☼

Alessandro walked down Via Camollia toward Piazza del Campo in the hunched pose he'd adopted since his growth spurt at thirteen. He turned the corner onto Via Banchi di Sotto and was surprised to find several Blackshirts at the front gate of the university, checking everyone's papers.

"What's going on?" he asked someone in the crowd of students.

"No Jews allowed," a boy in a striped shirt said. "New laws just passed."

"What do you mean 'no Jews'?"

"You're fine, *americano*," said an older boy he recognized with a faint mustache and a black tie. "They haven't banned all foreigners, just Jews."

"Not all Jews are foreigners," Alessandro said. "You sat in the same history class as I did. Jews have lived in Siena since the twelve hundreds. Our classmates, our friends are Jews."

"Well, now they can't go to our school."

Alessandro was speechless.

"Go home," the guard said to the boy behind him. Alessandro knew him slightly. Daniele.

Rage blossomed inside Alessandro.

"If he can't come in, then I'm not coming in either," shouted a young woman Alessandro recognized from the library. Alice. "*Sì, sì,*" shouted others. Before he knew what was happening, Alessandro had joined a throng of angry students who streamed down to Piazza del Campo. It felt so unbelievably *good* to set free his feelings at last, to stand shoulder to shoulder with people who believed what he believed. He'd thought he was alone all this time, that he had to hide his truth, but he wasn't and he didn't. In the piazza, they all milled about chanting, "*Italia per tutti!*" and "*Basta con il razzismo!*" He felt alive, empowered, joyous, finally standing up and fighting for what was right. They marched and chanted, circling the piazza. People hung in the windows watching them, curious.

Without warning, squads of Blackshirts poured into the piazza. He froze, midchant. He watched as two of them grabbed the boy next to him and hit him over the head with truncheons. He watched Cinzia, a girl in his world civilization class who read to the blind, drop to the ground under a rain of blows. He tried to pull them off her and was smacked in the face himself. He stood up to face a pistol. The Blackshirt met his eyes and Alessandro saw in them that he meant nothing to this person. Nothing. Alessandro put his hands up. There was nothing to do but run. He was nearly trampled as the student protestors bolted out of the one unguarded entrance to the square.

He didn't bother going back to his friend's apartment. He boarded a bus and, keeping his eyes down, went straight back to Belsederino, walking the last three miles on foot.

He arrived home at the castle trembling, in shock, sobbing, his white shirt spattered with blood.

✡

"We're leaving Italy tomorrow!" his mother announced that night at dinner in the great hall. Eleanor had lit every candle in the elaborate candelabras, as if to exorcise the hate that was infecting her adopted country. His country. Or was it his country? If they could decide that people who had lived here for seven hundred years were foreigners, where did that leave him? Half-Italian? Not Italian? Did he even want to be Italian? Could you choose?

"We're all going!" his mother concluded.

His father agreed. His sisters listened wide-eyed, too shocked for the first time in their lives to protest.

It was decided.

✧

He was reading in his favorite spot atop the tower of the castle the next day. His mother hated it when he went up there because the whole structure was somewhat unstable. But he trusted the old building to take care of him. He sat in a corner on the roof, surrounded by crenellations and capers and tiny oak trees.

He was halfway through a book of poems by Elizabeth Weston, a sixteenth-century English poet, the only prominent female writer of her age. She was stranded in Prague at the court of Rudolf II after her stepfather, Edward Kelley the alchemist, fell out of favor and died there. A stranger in a strange land, penniless, she wrote to save her life. Her poems were full of the formal classical and religious language of her era, but her own emotions came through clearly:

> *I lead my reluctant muses through all extremities*
> *and can find no path forward or back.*
> *Hence the time has come for grief without end,*
> *and I have left behind the outer boundary of my hopes.*
> *I am tormented, and seek solace for my wretched fate.*

It comforted Alessandro to hear her calling to him across the centuries. Another "foreigner" trapped in the only home she really knew.

His mother had left early that morning to drive to the American consulate in Florence to ask for visas for her husband and children. His sisters were packing, whining about having to miss their society debut at the

Imperial Masquerade in Venice. They chilled him, his sisters. They were such perfect little Fascists, reveling in Italy's strength and swooning over the picture of Mussolini that hung in their room. "Italy is the greatest country in the world," they loved to chant. "And Il Duce is the greatest leader in history."

Babbo was meeting with some people in the estate office to do the paperwork necessary to keep the place running while they were gone. Alessandro was supposed to be packing, too, but when he went to choose what books to take, he wanted them all. How long would they be gone? Years? Would they ever come back? Who would he be in America?

Alessandro heard a car and assumed it was his mother returning, but when he looked out from between the crenellations, he saw Felice Pappone getting out of a black Alfa Romeo.

Pappone was the son of Belsederino's game warden, and two years older than Alessandro. They had grown up only a kilometer apart, but it may as well have been a thousand. Alessandro liked to rescue baby birds; Pappone liked to crush them. Alessandro liked to climb trees and play his violin, while Pappone liked to hang around the village and cheat at cards. Pappone hated that Alessandro's father was *"il padrone,"* while his own father was forced to patrol Lapo's forests and raise his game birds—in short, to take orders from him.

Alessandro was not surprised when Pappone joined the Fascist militia, Mussolini's personal police force. Pouring castor oil down people's throats and keeping *schedature*—index cards that noted key details on every single person in the area, especially their loyalties or disloyalties—were right up his alley.

He wondered what Pappone was doing here today. The local Fascists were deferential to his father, but it was worrisome anytime a Blackshirt made a house call.

"Your *babbo* is useless," Pappone had said to Alessandro when he was fourteen. "He doesn't know how to do anything. He inherited money. That's it. He's a pathetic parasite."

"He can write a villanelle," Alessandro replied.

St. Moritz

1938

Sally

I watched Roddy and the Italian disappear down the slope with the injured man on the makeshift sled. I began walking, but without my skis, I found myself post-holing into the deep snow. Every step was arduous, and that village was far, far below me. No one else was around. I was terrified of falling into an unseen crevasse. Clouds rolled across the sky, blocking the sun, and the light became flat. It was hard to see very far in front of me, and my depth perception was off, so I kept lurching and stumbling. I thought I was making progress, but then I came to a cliff face. "Dammit!" I shouted. Yes, even good girls like me swear under the right circumstances. I had to crawl my way back uphill and try another path down. Meanwhile, the light was fading fast.

"Stay calm," I told myself. "Don't think. Keep walking."

As long as I kept moving, I wasn't cold, because walking in the deep snow was such hard work. But when I stopped, the cold cut through my jacket and sweater. I couldn't feel my toes.

After an hour of steady downhill progress, I let myself stop to breathe. The village in the valley below did not look any closer. I tried to take a step and plunged into a drift, sinking in up to my waist. I fought back panic as I realized I could freeze to death out here in my stylish ski outfit, the prettiest corpse on the mountain. I clawed my way forward with my gloved hands, fighting back tears.

The voices inside my head started to shriek. Why was I here, in this place, with all these rich, famous, titled people? All they cared about was playing. This man, this stupid lord, had had his way with me, taken my virginity, and left me. I thought I was going to get a house out of it? Who was I kidding? I wasn't one of "them" and he had abandoned me here to die. I cursed my own bovine stupidity. I should have gone to college or gotten a job instead of feeling obligated to leave with Patsy. Or was it worse than that? Was I just unwilling to let go of an easy, parasitic life? And then the real guilt burst forth like a tiger. I should have gone back to Iowa to search for my lost family. Still, that feisty little red-haired kid inside me made me keep walking.

At last, as the sun was sinking below the mountain, I heard voices that weren't coming from inside my own head. "Sally!"

"I'm here!" I shouted hoarsely. I waved my arms as figures on snowshoes came into view.

It was Roddy, dear, darling Roddy, along with half the Corviglia Ski Club and all the St. Moritz Tobogganing Club. There may have even been a St. Bernard or two, or maybe that was just a hallucination. The Bon Vivant, whose voice had been strangely silent during my ordeal, took note of the flushed faces of Noël Coward, Jacques Cartier, Conte Rossi, Harry Hays Morgan, and Philippe de Rothschild. These notables carried lanterns, and someone thrust a flask toward me. Another wrapped me in a deliciously soft fur.

"I'm fine," I said, feeling the need to be jaunty and sporty again. I handed the flask back after taking a long draw on it. "Just cold and tired. Though that cognac hit the spot."

I was bundled onto a toboggan. The group sang and shouted as they made their way down, led, of course, by Coward. That man has a tune for every occasion. Jokes flew around me, though to my disappointment, I missed most of them due to fatigue as the sled bumped along. When we got down to the village, the entire crew of us piled into the tiny train for St. Moritz.

"We had them hold the train and warm up a special car just for you," said Roddy. My fingers and toes and cheeks prickled as he lifted and carried me into the warm train car and plopped me down onto the wooden bench. Love was back in full flower in my body, and all was forgiven.

"Damn Swiss," said Morgan, sinking onto the bench between me and

Roddy. "Haven't they ever heard of upholstery?" All the flasks came out as the train began to chug its way back down the valley. Morgan smelled like anchovies and whisky and pipe tobacco.

"How's the man with the broken leg?" I called over to where Roddy was playing a hand of cards with Noël and Philippe. Did I blush involuntarily as his eyes met mine? Dammit, I did.

"Getting plastered, in both senses of the word. He's going to be fine." Then he was back to his cards.

Once in St. Moritz, I was carried on the shoulders of the rowdy crew through the streets and straight into the bar of Badrutt's. They sang "She's a Jolly Good Fellow" the whole way.

"Goodness," I said as they set me down onto a barstool.

"Oh, my Lord," said Patsy, rushing over. "I was out of my mind. Tell her, Coco."

Coco Chanel, swathed in furs, nodded in agreement. "I haven't seen your mother that upset since Luise Rainer won the Oscar," she rasped in French.

I noted that Patsy had still managed to dress for dinner, and appeared to have enjoyed a few cocktails to boot. Still, her maternal concern was charming.

"Drinks all round," called Roddy. "A toast to Sally Brady. Heroine of the Alps."

I happily accepted a glass of hot mulled wine. "Thank you. But I didn't actually save anyone."

"*Non è vero.*" The crowd parted and I saw the injured Italian, whose leg was in a long white cast propped up on a barstool. "Without your keen eyes and quick thinking, I'd still be in that hole in the ice. The drinks are on me. And I think I'm in love with you." I blushed again, everyone cheered, and I looked over at Roddy to see his reaction. He was looking away. I could see he was talking to another girl—who was it? I craned my neck while trying not to fall off the barstool. Dammit! The Honorable Miss Edith Featherstone. A third cousin of the King's. Double damn. Love began to gasp for air inside me as if I were holding a pillow over its face. I made myself turn away and forced a smile at the crowd gathered around me.

My health was toasted over and over, everything and everyone got blurry, and tales of the rescue were embroidered until they bore little resemblance to the truth. The fire blazed in the huge fireplace. Roddy was nowhere to be seen. Love heaved its last breaths and quietly expired. I was surrounded by happy people trading stories and singing songs of their exploits, yet I felt hollow and brittle and unhappy. But I couldn't show that. Never. It wasn't done, my dear. I gave everyone my brightest smile. "I feel like a Viking princess," I said.

"Marry me and you will be," said the son of the king of Norway.

"You're already married, Olav," said Patsy, shoving him aside and handing me another glühwein.

The alcohol kept my energy up, but eventually the exhaustion of the day took hold. "I'm going to bed," I announced.

"Have dinner sent to Miss Brady's room," said Patsy to the maître d'.

"On me," said the Italian.

"And flowers," said Chanel. "On him."

"Thank you and good night, *bonne nuit, buona notte, gute Nacht,*" I said, and Patsy and I waddled to the elevator.

✿

Once free from the public gaze, I fell onto the eiderdown of my bed and slept until morning. I awoke to find my room filled with flowers, chocolates, champagne, and one large cuckoo clock. Patsy was drinking the champagne, of course, sitting on the foot of my bed in her peignoir.

I flipped through the cards on the night table, trying to appear nonchalant. "How sweet of everyone," I said.

"If you're looking for Lord Roddy's calling card, it's not there," said Patsy. "He left this morning for Chamonix with that boring sheep Edith."

I wanted to roll back into the pillow and cry, but instead I said, "Bye-bye, Marsden Manor," pretending all I cared about was a lost house.

"You were competent, darling. Kiss of death. Be helpless. Look at poor Beryl. She's good at everything and men run from her like a house on fire."

"So I should have let that poor Italian die on the mountain instead of taking charge of the situation?"

"Small price to pay for landing a lord, I'd say."

I burst out laughing at this and to her credit, so did Patsy. She put her arms around me and kissed the top of my head. "Rules for happiness," she said.

"Isn't one of them coffee?"

Patsy poured me a cup, which was a first. In fact, I'm not sure I had ever seen her pour anything. She'd summon Aida or a hotel waiter from halfway across a polo field to get a pour.

"You got quite a lot of attention," she said, downing her champagne. "Is the Bon Vivant going to write about yesterday's dramatic rescue and the heroism of a certain young lady?"

I shook my head and sipped the blessed liquid. "That would be a very bad idea. It will all be forgotten by tomorrow. You're still the star around here."

Patsy raised her glass. "To my precious girl. You're all I have in the world."

Have. Sometimes I felt that's what I was to Patsy, a possession. But then I thought of all the things she had done to try to give me—a random kid who had jumped into her car—a good life. Things Patsy, working her fingers raw in her family's Chinatown laundry as a child, enduring taunts and slurs and worse, had only dreamed of. But almost freezing to death yesterday had made me stop and think. Was Patsy's definition of a good life also mine? I loved all these nice things—who wouldn't?—but was the nonstop party-going really living, or was I just skating on the beautiful surface of life?

I didn't blame Patsy. Patsy would never in a million years be accepted as her true self in the country that passed the Chinese Exclusion Act, saw homosexuality as a crime, and banned mixed marriages even in the movies. So she had become an actress, playing vixens on-screen and off-. She had taught me to also play a role, never revealing too much of myself to anyone, always keeping a socially acceptable mask in place. I didn't really want to live that way, but what choice did I have? Imagine if I'd said to Roddy, "We were so poor I didn't have shoes until I was ten years old." Would he find that charming or repugnant? What if I told him that Aida had plucked lice from my hair, and that I had eaten garbage to survive? And that I would do it again if I had to?

I remembered how tired Ma was at the end of the day, the hard work she put in just to survive. She had married what she thought was a hard-working American who would take care of her in the land of plenty to the north, and she still ended up broke and starving. "Be good," she'd said to me. At times I felt I had lost my moral compass, and yet at other moments I wondered whether a moral compass was a fixed thing at all. After all, other people didn't seem to worry the way I did.

I eyed Patsy's fresh glass of champagne. "You're starting early today," I said.

"I'm warming up for lunch with the Windsors. And you, my dearest one, have an invitation from the Baron von Stettmeyer." She gave me a long look. "For winter golf. The ball is orange. It's all the rage."

Baron von Stettmeyer had a forty-room schloss outside of Salzburg.

I met her gaze. "Tell the baron I will join him," I said.

Siena

1938

Lapo

He needed to tell Leone he was leaving the country, but he was struggling to find the words. It felt shameful. Maybe he should say nothing. Better not to worry Leone. He just needed to give him the documents for the apartment in St. Moritz. "I think you should leave Italy now," he said. "Don't wait until things get worse. The apartment in Switzerland is safe." He offered him a whisky. They were settled in leather chairs in Lapo's office at Belsederino, surrounded by ledgers, architectural plans, and drawings for irrigation, fields, a new barn. Children's artwork covered the walls, and the Labrador slept under his desk. Alessandro and the girls were packing while Eleanor was in Florence to get their visas. He bit his tongue when he thought of leaving. How could he just walk away? he wondered. But he saw again the blood on Alessandro's shirt and knew they had to go. Italy had become unlivable. "Promise me you will go," he said to Leone. "These new laws—"

"Let's not speak of them." Leone's hand shook with anger as he clutched his glass. "My family has lived here for twelve generations, but suddenly we're not 'Italian.'"

"Mussolini is just appeasing Hitler to get support for his colonial adventures."

"Please don't try to justify it."

Lapo's face reddened. "I'm so sorry. That's not what I meant. I—"

"I want to transfer everything, not just the apartment in Switzerland, but everything I own—the apartment in Florence, the estate in Fiesole, the business—all of it to your name."

Lapo gasped. But of course this made horrifying sense. The new laws, laws he himself had said would never pass, made it illegal for Jews to own property, send their children to school, serve in the military, employ non-Jews, or work. Anything not transferred would be seized by the state.

"You're the only person I trust to give it back to us when this is all over. If it's ever all over." Leone put a hand on Lapo's sleeve. "Please."

He sighed. "I didn't want to say, but we might go ourselves. My wife, she thinks we should go to America."

Leone was surprised. "Oh. Of course. I understand." He looked crestfallen. He sat for a moment, then put his glass down and stood up. "I should go," he said.

"You'll go to Switzerland?"

Leone shook his head. "I refuse to leave Italy. This is our home. I'll find someone to sell the houses to, on paper. Someone who will restore them to us when sanity returns. If you're leaving, you should do the same. The bastards will seize it all."

✡

Lapo sat there for an hour after Leone left, immobilized by the thought of losing everything he and Eleanor had worked for.

He heard a car outside. At least Eleanor was back. Eleanor, who made everything all right. Wherever they went, whatever horrors they would face, at least they would be together.

He heard a banging on the door and, mystified, opened it.

There stood Felice Pappone in his black uniform, as proud as a toad.

Lapo smiled. "*Ciao,* Felice," he said to the boy he had known since birth. "How are your father and mother? I have some jars of peach jam Eleanor made for them. . . ." He turned away to grab a basket she'd made up. Signora Pappone loved the peaches from the castle garden.

"You will address me by my proper title," said Felice Pappone.

He ignored the tone. The boy was always a bit officious, even as a wee pup. Lapo turned back, offering the basket. In return, Pappone handed him an envelope.

"There's no need," said Lapo. "They're a gift. You're family."

Felice Pappone stood taller, his face locked in a sneer. He nodded at the envelope. "That is a draft summons," he said. "Your son will report immediately for his military service or be considered a deserter and shot."

IV

Fascist Party

The Bon Vivant

ROMANS UNLEASHED

Spring has sprung in the Eternal City, where the fashion shows brought out the young things and the old guard to see what we'll all be wearing next fall.... Miss Schiaparelli's comedy-themed collection of harlequin evening coats and dresses festooned with tinkling bells was a light touch after last fall's trench-brown-and-camouflage beach pajamas.... Princess Maria Francesca gave a delightful luncheon for two hundred of her closest amici.... Curvier than an Amalfi roadway, Miss Mimi Petacci is making her cinematic debut in Le vie del cuore, *which sounds like a description of her sister's friendship with a certain stylish and powerful head of state. One thinks the film will be a winner in Venice next fall or heads will roll....* One little marchesina *found a furry creature in her bed at a house party at Ninfa last weekend.... We all thought it might be a lost satyr from Lord Desart's deliciously naughty celebration of Saturnalia last winter, or maybe roving son-in-law Ciano up to his old tricks, but, alas, it was only a tiny hedgehog. Who knows—she may enter it in the dog show next week!*

Rome

1941

Sally

"I'm not going to let you get skunked out of singing your opera," I said to my pal Lila as we stood in line for exit visas outside the foreign ministry in Rome two days after some faraway place called Pearl Harbor was bombed. Of course, I thought it was tragic and shocking—I'm just telling you we had no idea where that was. Despite the fact it was midmorning and we were visiting a government office, we had donned the latest, most chic fashions. I sported a fox fur jacket and a darling little pointed harlequin hat I adored more than life itself. Lila wore a fabulous pink boiled-wool jacket with big white hand-shaped buttons and a black fur hat with a matching muff. Lines in Italy were a rarity—usually this was a culture of scrums, not queues—but men with guns were keeping us in order. In two hours of shifting back and forth on our sky-high heels, alas, we had only progressed from the lowest of the hundreds of marble steps to just under an imposing bas-relief of a screaming eagle holding twigs in its talons above the front door. Everyone in line around us was talking about how Mussolini was about to declare war on the United States. We were there because Il Duce had just issued an order expelling all American citizens from Italy. That stung, let me tell you. No one likes to be asked to leave the party. But before we could get on a plane or train, we had to have a little piece of paper called an "exit visa" in hand.

Despite the Fascist edicts, I will admit I was sorry I had to leave, and miserable at the thought of the U.S. and Italy going to war. Over an island no one had ever heard of on the other side of the world? It made no sense to me. Unlike certain British aristocrats and a notable American pilot, I was no fan of Fascism, but I loved living in Rome. I had made a home for myself there. As the Bon Vivant, I supported myself in the style Patsy had accustomed me to even after she moved to Texas with her new husband, a ninety-five-year-old oil baron who called her his "concubine." Lately I was saving on rent by being the long-term houseguest of Lila Poncelet, the latest wife of an American tool and die maker known as "Percy the Screw King." Lila was exactly half the age of her famously frugal husband and living alone in a spacious Rome apartment overlooking Piazza Navona while studying opera at an elite music school. I made a perfect roommate for her, with my connections and knowledge of the Eternal City. It was as close to domestic bliss as I had ever experienced.

And what of my love life? I'd seen Lord Roddy again at a garden party at ethereally beautiful Ninfa later in that spring of 1938. He was now aide-de-camp to a general, and he'd been charming, of course, and tried to steal a kiss despite the presence of his new wife Angus—I mean Edith. I'd seen them again at the Imperial Masquerade in Venice, where I'd chosen to dress as the female pharaoh Hatshepsut in an Egyptian headdress, sheer gown, and strategically placed necklace. He'd lunged for me in a gondola on the Grand Canal. He took it surprisingly well when I pushed him overboard.

"Love, sex, and marriage are three separate things," Patsy reminded me that night in the Gritti Palace. "You're just lucky you didn't get knocked up in St. Moritz."

"Would he have married me?" I wondered.

We both knew the answer was no.

I chose to remain free of entanglements after that. If there was home-ownership in my future, it would be up to me to make it happen, I decided. I would start to save money to buy a little house somewhere. A cottage, with climbing jasmine and a white picket fence. I tried to be frugal—I had a jar under my mattress and everything, but I kept raiding it when I needed cash for taxis and hairstyling. Oh well, I thought. I had time. My work as the Bon Vivant was all-consuming, between maintaining social contacts via a vigorous lunching schedule, writing the actual columns, cultivating my network of informers among the beau monde's hired help, and keeping up appearances with visits to dressmakers and beauty salons. I was too busy for romance or putting down roots. My steamer trunk was still "Home."

Even after Italy joined Germany in its war with France and England in June 1940, after which British lords and Gallic marquis were banned from Italian soil, I carried on secretly chronicling the antics of Rome's glamorous young elite. Despite curfews, blackouts, and rationing, members of Italian high society continued to gather and frolic, just as American high society had rumbaed, sambaed, and fox-trotted through the Depression. German, Austrian, Hungarian, and Bulgarian aristocrats still traveled down to Rome on private trains for "the season." All through 1940 and '41, I filed columns about the silken-haired countesses and handsome *principi* and their salons and what they wore to this ball or that luncheon or the newest, chicest beach resort, as if people all over Europe were not fighting and dying. I wasn't the only one—the society pages of every newspaper were full of luncheons, fetes, and debuts. I told myself that American readers needed some frothy silliness to balance the bad news coming out of Europe. Maybe it would help if people recognized that the desire to flirt and fall in love was universal.

I made sure to be useful to my hostess, Lila, who'd said right up until that very morning she "had it on good account" from hubby Percy that the U.S. would never enter the war. Lila was eager to finish her studies with a famous Italian opera maestro. Was she sleeping with him? Does a nightingale sing at night? I was just happy to keep her company and be useful. I never left toothpaste in the sink, never drank the last bottle of wine, and was remarkably forgiving when she threw impromptu parties, which she did frequently, being a friendly type and having a generous monthly allowance from Percy. I whipped up great midnight *spaghettate* for roomfuls of Lila's hungry pals, and I was always willing to stay up late and listen to her talk about how she wished her globe-trotting better half would pay more attention to her. Lila and I became fast friends. We were quickly labeled *le ragazze,* the girls everyone wanted to have at their parties, which made my job as the BV easy.

The ole Bon Vivant became even more bold and saucy, tongue firmly in his cheek but also unmistakably affectionate to the world "he" chronicled. I had to keep it light, even as the world turned dark. Yes, in the '30s, as the BV, I had written admiringly of Mussolini's movie star machismo and brash personal style. "That tasseled fez!" I pecked into the keys of my portable Smith Corona. "Too too too fabulous! And spurs! Who doesn't love a good pair of spurs?" I would remind you that back then, Il Duce had quite the fan club stateside, too. But as his regime became more authoritarian, and anti-American rhetoric intensified, I had steered clear of mentioning politics or heads of state, and privately I began to worry, tossing and turning in my emerald silk satin pajamas. If Lila left Italy, I'd have to find another place to stay, or head back to the U.S. Where would I go? Texas was out. Patsy had fallen in love with an aviatrix who'd stopped to refuel on the ranch. She'd followed her to China, where the daring pilot hoped to be part of the Flying Tigers, the Americans helping China fight off the invasion by imperialist Japan. My family back in Iowa had never resurfaced, swallowed up by the chaos of the Great Depression. Rome had been my home for the past five years, and I couldn't imagine leaving it.

I kept Lila pumped up about her upcoming performance of the heart-wrenching aria "Vissi d'arte" from *Tosca* in the spring recital celebrating her graduation from music school. "Percy will be so impressed," I told her. Mussolini's announcement that foreigners were banned from appearing in performances of any kind put the kibosh on those plans. Still, I convinced Lila to stay a few more weeks, just until the show jumping in Piazza di Siena was over. We always admired the handsome cavalry officers on their gallant mounts. Or did we mount the officers and admire the horses? I'll never tell. . . .

Then a pair of Mussolini's black-shirted militiamen appeared at the door of our apartment and told us we had to get an exit visa and get out.

"This is scary. I want to go home right now," Lila said, breaking into tears. "Why do we even need the visa? Let's just go to the airport and beg them to let us on any plane out of here." Lila had been unable to get in touch with Percy for days.

"Don't panic. It's going to be okay." The words came without even thinking. This was my role, after all, from birth. "It's just a piece of paper," I said. "A formality. Probably a chance for them to collect one last tax from us."

I encouraged Lila to dress to the nines to signal our status, and we bravely marched to the imposing palazzo of the Office of Foreign Affairs, where we now waited in a long line of Norwegians, Danes, Hungarians, Poles, and one very confused Irishman in a yellow rain slicker who seemed to think he was going to meet the Pope. Hours passed, and the line inched forward. I used some of Lila's last stash of cash—they wouldn't let us take money out of the country anyway—to buy us lemonades from a vendor with a cart.

"How much money is left?" Lila asked nervously.

"Don't worry," I said. "Soon we'll be on a plane home."

What kind of work could I do back in America? I wondered as the line inched forward. There were already plenty of society writers stateside, people with better connections than I had on that side of the Atlantic. I wondered if I should float the concept of working for Lila in some capacity. The idea was embarrassing, though. "I wish you could at least get to sing your song first," I told her. Lila had practiced the hell out of that tune, to the point where I heard it in my dreams.

"I don't care about that anymore. I just want to get out of here."

I turned and looked out at the vast sea of people in line along the steps. The sky was clear blue over the stunning cityscape of domes, spires, monuments, and red tile roofs. Mussolini had mostly prohibited flying planes over the city to preserve "the essential character and beauty of Italy," as he put it. I could see the twin black chariots atop the bright white wedding cake of Il Vittoriano, and the huge obelisk in front of St. Peter's. Rome was so chaotically gorgeous. "You could sing it now," I said.

"I can't."

"Come on. Last chance before we leave Rome. Talk about a captive audience. Great acoustics. Majestic setting." I pointed. "There's the Pantheon. Even the gods are listening. Nothing in America is going to be like this."

Lila shook her head.

At that moment, I heard a low buzzing sound, and a blue biplane flew into sight, low over the rooftops. The color made it hard to see against the azure sky. I stared up as it came into focus, shielding my eyes from the sun's glare. The pilot in the open cockpit waved jauntily at us and began tossing papers into the air. They fluttered down over the city as the plane circled and then disappeared.

People scrambled to pick up the papers as they landed. I grabbed one out of the air before it hit the ground. It was a picture of Mussolini with a pig nose scrawled over it. Over "Italy for the Italians" had been written "Italy for Me, None for You!"

"It's just some political cartoon," I said, showing Lila. Despite my encyclopedic knowledge of Italian high society, now it was better to feign ignorance of the complexities of Italian politics. Under the eyes of the gun-toting Blackshirts at the top of the steps, people around us dropped the papers as if they were burning their hands. No one wanted "opposition sympathizer" on their *schedatura*.

"I think you should put it down," said Lila, nudging me as a guard held us in his sights. I grinned, theatrically crumpled up the paper, and dropped it.

Inch by inch, the line moved forward, and the people in front of us emerged from the ministry each with a stamped and signed exit visa, even the Irishman. Finally, I was motioned inside the building with a wave of a pistol.

"See you at the airport," I told Lila, giving her a jaunty salute for courage.

I crossed the marble-floored hall, my heels tapping. The façade of bravura I'd adopted started to slip away. I made myself notice what I was seeing, hearing, smelling right now. I saw ornately curved metal grills on the windows, frosted glass barriers between cubicles, uniformed civil guard officers with hats with the insignia of the flaming torch. I found that if I could set aside the terror that went with being in the bowels of a Fascist bureaucracy, it was all deliciously stylish. I took a deep breath and headed for the window the guard motioned me toward.

"I love your epaulettes," I said to the functionary, smiling broadly to show how friendly and cooperative I was as I handed over my American passport. He didn't look at me, which was a shame, as I'd done my blond locks in a special way involving a roll and a twist I'd seen on Lana Turner at Deauville. He examined my documents.

Finally, the functionary looked up and said, "No exit visa for you."

Knock me down with a feather. "What? Excuse me? *Mi scusi?*"

"No visa," he said, and pulled the shade down. My stomach dropped. What did that mean? The guard with the gun motioned me back outside, where I found Lila sitting on the marble steps wadding up the hem of her dress and crying like the Little Match Girl.

"I didn't get an exit visa either," she said. "He wouldn't say why. I'm scared. What are we going to do?"

Her distress blotted out my own. "We'll figure it out," I said lightly, offering her a hand up. "Let's go find the ink-stained wretches." This was what we called the foreign journalists who hung out at Caffè Greco. I liked to drop into the ancient watering hole and listen to them palaver about the decline and fall of everything. They'd all been kicked out of countries be-fore, and I felt sure they'd know what to do.

The two of us clattered past the Spanish Steps on our platform heels, Lila clutching her fur muff in glum despair, poor lamb chop. A group of schoolchildren stood in front of a giant statue of Mussolini while a teacher described how the dictator had invented electricity, the automobile, and pizza. As the Italians say, *esagerato.*

I pulled open the wood-and-glass door of Caffè Greco and we passed walls chockablock with artwork of all types and tastes all the way to the back room. It was quiet, with few customers, but I spotted Allen from the *Herald Tribune* at a marble table and waved. As Lila sank down on a leather banquette, I ordered us a couple of glasses of fizzy prosecco to lighten the mood, and put it on Allen's tab, of course.

I settled in next to Allen and Lila on the banquette where, according to legend, Casanova had worked his magic on many a Roman lassie. Allen, who was in the running for a Pulitzer that year for foreign reporting, was in his midforties and had a balding head that gave him a reassuring, fatherly air. I'd always admired how he charmed and calmed his sources into giving him the inside scoop on Mussolini's regime.

"You two are high-profile hostages," he said when we told him we'd been denied exit visas. "I don't know what'll happen to you when Mussolini declares war on the U.S., but he must think you're worth something."

"Lila, maybe, but me?" I said. "I'm not a VIP." No one here knew I was the Bon Vivant. Just as it had always been, only one editor in the New York office of the Hearst Syndicate, Max Orson, was the keeper of my secret. I hadn't been able to reach him for a week, and I thought it unwise to try to put a call through to New York now.

"Do you really think there's going to be a war?" Lila asked Allen, her hand trembling a little as she held her glass.

He nodded. "We'll all be enemy aliens. Members of the press will likely be traded in a diplomatic exchange for Italian journalists in the U.S. Any other Americans still in the country will be put into camps."

"Camps?" Lila's eyes were wide. "Like with tents and shared latrines?"

"But they won't hurt us, right?" I said.

Allen shrugged. "No guarantees of anything in this world."

Truer words.

"My husband will figure something out," Lila said to Allen. "Can you get word to him? I've sent telegrams but I don't think they got through."

"I'll try, but everything we write is censored before it goes to New York. For now, I would consider that you're on your own."

✡

The next day, Mussolini appeared on his balcony in front of a crowd of thousands packed into Piazza Venezia. Lila was at home in the apartment, packing in hopes that help would arrive, but I ventured out to witness history. I was crunched between a teenager standing on the seat of his bicycle and a large mastiff held by a stern elderly man in a gray fedora. The mastiff's breath reeked of sardines and it was gently drooling. Of course, I had dressed up for the occasion, in a bright yellow bolero over a full-skirted black crepe de chine Chanel day dress.

I could see that in person, Mussolini was short, with a large torso and a manic energy that made him seem larger. He wasn't handsome, but he did have a certain testosterone-heavy charisma that would have caught the attention of a casting director. He wore a black uniform with red and gold stripes down the side of the trousers and shouted into a microphone that echoed from speakers around the piazza. I could see droplets flying through the air over the crowd. "Bit of a spitter, isn't he?" I joked to the elderly man holding the mastiff's leash, hoping to make him smile. The man turned and stared at me, then motioned to a nearby policeman. Even I knew that the OVRA had spies everywhere looking for traitors. I just hadn't taken it seriously before. Now I realized I was hemmed in on all sides, unable to move. The policeman was shoving people aside, coming closer.

"The time has come to declare war on our biggest enemy. . . ." Mussolini boomed from the balcony.

"I only meant—" I started to say to the hostile patriots around me. A long trail of saliva drooped from the mastiff's mouth toward my favorite pair of open-toed sling-backs. It landed on my left big toe as I said, "the dog!" at the exact same moment Mussolini shouted, "The United States of America!"

Siena

1941

Lapo

He stared at the pattern the leak made on the wall. The white plaster was tinged a slight rusty color, and around it, the ancient beige floral wallpaper was peeling away in long petals, surrendering to moisture and gravity. He peered up at the ceiling, trying to see where the water was getting in, whether it was a crack in a tile or loose caulking around a beam, but it was unclear. If Eleanor were here, she would see the damage as beautiful, like the wrinkles in an older person's face, signs of a life well lived. To her, this constant decay was part of the charm of living in a thousand-year-old castle in Tuscany. As an Italian, he could see the beauty, but he also knew that mold, rot, and mildew were brewing underneath.

He had pulled strings with Ciano so that after basic training, Alessandro was sent not to the Russian front, where death seemed all but certain, but to German-occupied Prague as a guard at the Italian embassy there. In return, Lapo could no longer escape writing Mussolini's biography. Or autobiography, because besides fighting a world war, Mussolini was also supposed to be the author of this new work. At least there was that—Lapo would be anonymous.

"Make it exciting," Ciano had said on a call from Palazzo Venezia in Rome. "Adventures."

"Adventures?"

Lapo waited for him to elaborate, but instead Ciano said, "Hang on, let me put MinCulPop on." This meant a functionary from the Minister of Popular Culture, in this case a particularly humorless woman named Marta, who he discovered took her job of protecting Mussolini's public image very, very seriously.

"You understand the honor?" Marta said.

"Yes, of course, very honored. But are you saying you want me to make things up?"

Her voice was clipped and impatient. "The world needs to know about Il Duce's bravery and brilliance. We'll give you a few days to come up with an outline. Do not fail us. We'll be in touch." She hung up.

That was three days ago, and Lapo had spent all of the intervening moments in agony, veering between what the famously mercurial Mussolini might want the book to be, or what valid reason Lapo could give *not* to write it that wouldn't leave him ruined, or dead, and Alessandro stranded in Prague without protection.

Today he had come up with fragments of an outline, but he was struggling with the physical-bravery part of the story, so he wandered down the cool tiled hallway into the kitchen, packed coffee into the moka, screwed it back together, and, while waiting for it to boil, made a quick catalogue of his own worst fears: being trapped underwater, having an insect climb up inside his penis, having his face vomited on. The moka began its *pop-pop-pop* as he stared out the window, watching the tips of the cypress trees wave in the breeze.

Yes, Mussolini was a *stronzo totale,* a cartoonishly vicious and amoral tyrant, but Lapo, as ghostwriter, could choose to see that as an opportunity to let his imagination roam freely. He could make up childhood obstacles for Il Duce to recount for his readers: poverty, certainly, and some bullying, lots of hard work. There should be breathtaking examples of physical bravery, too. None of it would be true, of course, since Lapo had it on good account from Ciano that Mussolini's bravery went no further than boxing with men he paid to lose.

Sitting on his desk were comic books that his children had brought back illegally from those childhood summers in Chicago. MinCulPop had banned American comic books, with the rather strange exception of Mickey Mouse. Fiamma and Allegra loved the crime-fighting detectives Slam Bradley and Speed Saunders, Superman and Batman. They—and apparently millions of other people—went wild for these simplistic and

violent stories. The Fascists hadn't banned them because they were American, they had banned them because they were popular. He could use that
model. He plotted the chapters in his mind: Mussolini would not only
break free of the underwater rock ledge that was trapping him beneath the
azure waters of . . . *Sardinia!* but would save a beautiful naked woman and
help her to the surface. Mussolini would survive thirty—*fifty!*—days in a
jungle alone, eating the insects that tried to assault his every orifice. When
someone punched him, Mussolini would . . . Here Lapo's imagination and
the comic books failed him. In truth, he wished to hold Mussolini underwater until he drowned, let insects eat his penis from the inside out, and
have overfed Rottweilers vomit on his face. The coffee shot up into the
top part of the moka, and Lapo poured it into a chipped, flowered teacup
and padded back down the hallway to the room in the tower of the castle
where he wrote, or, more accurately, the room where he thought about
writing.

The smell of the coffee as he raised it to his lips was like passing a hand
over a fogged mirror. He sighed and crossed out the only word on the
paper. If Eleanor were here, he knew what she would say about the offer
from Mussolini's people. Would he admit to her that they had threatened
him? *Do not fail us.* It was subtle, but he knew how these things went,
how writers were silenced, punished. Salvemini was forced into exile. Mat-
teotti was not so lucky. He wished he could hear Eleanor's voice. Mussolini
had blocked telephone calls to and from Italy, and OVRA seized the mail.
Probably if Lapo wrote the book, he would be allowed to write to her.
Another reason to swallow his pride, his ethics, and his morals, and write
the damn thing.

12 December 1941
Belsederino

My love,
Alessandro is safe in Prague and I am safe here. The sink is stopped up
again, and mice have gotten into the pasta. I can hear you laughing. "You
wanted to live in the country!" you're saying. There are definitely still moments when I question that decision. But then I throw open the shutters
and look out over this landscape. Even in the midst of a world war, the sea
serpent undulations of the hills are calming and peaceful, sparrows nest
under the eaves, capers grow out of the stone walls. These hills, even these

ancient buildings, have lived through so many wars before. It comforts me a little that this place has seen so much conflict. Even though the people are long dead, it's still here. Our home.

Lapo filled the pages with ink even though there was no way for him to get them to Eleanor. It was dangerous to leave them lying around where loyal Fascists might do a random unannounced house search and find them, so he could only burn them or hide them. Last night, he'd glued one inside the binding of a book about nettles. But it kept him sane to imagine Eleanor sitting at the window of her childhood bedroom in the brick mansion outside Chicago, reading his words, their girls not far away, perhaps even getting ready for a party. *It makes me so happy to think of you safe there, even though it means we are apart. Plus, I get to practice my written English, which is sadly rusting. I remembered "sinuous" today.*

Lapo tried to live bilingually in his head, translating everything he said and thought, a way of holding on to Eleanor, but this morning he could not remember the word for "spoke," as in a wheel. He and his estate manager, Roghi, were fixing one of the horse carts now that all the fuel had been seized for the war effort. When they finished, he traipsed back to the castle to look up *raggio* in the battered old English/Italian dictionary.

He looked over at the Labrador sleeping on the sofa, his fur yellow against the worn red upholstery. "Should I write the damn book?" he asked the dog, who lifted his head briefly, his third eyelids slowly retracting to reveal deep brown eyes with gold flecks. *"Allora?"* Lapo pressed him. But the dog just sighed, curled up more tightly, and went back to sleep.

Eleanor and the girls had not left in 1938, as they had all hoped to, because of Alessandro's draft notice. After June of 1940, when Italy was officially at war with France and England, he had begged her to leave, but she stayed until June of '41, when it was clear things were going to get uglier and uglier. Even then, she wanted to send just the girls to Chicago, but Lapo argued they would suffer without her, especially if war between Italy and the U.S. did break out. The twins' habit of greeting everyone with the Fascist salute wasn't going to make life easy in America. The only solution was for Eleanor to go, and for him to stay here.

When I said goodbye to you and the girls, I was sure that Mussolini's bluff would soon be called and Italy would be out of it all within days. I assumed we had learned the lessons of the "Great" War. What an idiot I seem now. We Italians—who are supposed to be the keepers of history!—have forgotten it all. Mussolini is a clown, an actor pretending to be a caesar. When he thrusts out his jaw and struts, when he stands on balconies and shouts about decadent democracies, when he arrests his enemies, people think he's strong and a real leader. It's so laughable as to be absurd to me, but I can't say that out loud. Even more than when you left, the Fascists are everywhere, ready to pour castor oil down the throat of anyone who disagrees with them, or worse, deliver a bullet to a traitor.

At least Eleanor and the girls had a place to go—so many trying to flee Europe did not. Leone's cousins had ended up on a boat to Shanghai. Other refugees floated around the globe, rejected everywhere. But was the U.S. actually safe for Eleanor?

I worry now that Italy and the U.S. are officially at war, your neighbors will judge you because of your connection to me and this country. I pray Alessandro never has to fight American troops. I can only hope that a history of goodwill between our two countries will keep all of us safe. All the Italians who resettled in the U.S., all their children and grandchildren. And all those Grand Tour visits? Is there an educated American who doesn't have etchings from Venice and Rome? This can't last long, can it?

Lapo paused. From outside the open window of his writing room, a swallow darted in and circled the room, then zoomed out again. As much as he missed her, he was glad Eleanor was away from this madness. He wished Leone and his family had gone with them. Mussolini was leaving Italian Jews alone for now, but he was imprisoning foreign Jews in camps all around the country. Lapo put his hand on the dog's head and looked into his eyes, begging him for an answer. *How long will the nightmare last?*

He poured himself a grappa and got back to work.

Rome

1941

Sally

"I'm not going to plop down on a tufted hassock, file my nails, and wait to be arrested as an enemy alien," I said to Lila over a Negroni at the bar in the Hassler. I refused to call it the Villa Medici, even after its extensive renovations in 1939. It had been the Hassler since the 1890s, and the Hassler it would remain, no matter what the sign said. Mussolini's ban on foreign words and names was funny until it was annoying. Now to use the word "cocktail" instead of *"arlecchino"* was a crime. And why was a cocktail a "harlequin"? No one had a good explanation.

"Un'altro cocktail," I said to the bartender with as much aplomb as I could muster. To Lila I added, "We can sit at home sulking and crying, listening for the knock on the door, or we can go out drinking and dancing and eat everything delicious in sight." I was as much trying to convince myself as Lila. We were screwed.

A clock chimed from a tower nearby, and a hotel manager dutifully turned on a large radio in the bar. This meant it was 11:00 P.M., the hour when all of Italy was expected to listen to the Italian State Radio broadcast. The martial strains of "Giovinezza" played, and then Il Duce's magnetic voice came booming through the room, talking about American degeneracy and how the Roman Empire was back in all its glory. "The truth is that men are tired of liberty," he boomed. "Tired of peace. War alone brings up to their highest tension all human energies and imposes the stamp of nobility upon the peoples who have the courage to make it."

"I can't take it," said Lila, and headed home, leaving me to scan the bar for friendly faces to pass the time with. I spotted Alba Farnese, the daughter of a marchese. We'd met at a weeklong house party at Ninfa outside of Rome. It was the most marvelous garden I had ever seen—waterfalls and ruins and tons and tons of flowers. I had spotted a wan, thin girl always hovering on the edges of conversations. I had befriended her, and as we walked under willows and along beds of lilies every morning, she told me with very un-Italian candor that she was her parents' only child, the end of their family name. It was as if she had absorbed the weight of that disappointment into the cells of her body, making her hair limp and her skin pale. It was a strange curse of a lot of aristocratic families I'd met, that they struggled to produce a male heir to carry on the name. Since I found the idea of primogeniture and inheritance in general repugnant, I wasn't especially sad about the names on family crypts fading from history, branches pruned from the human family tree. *People could solve this problem really easily,* I thought, *by valuing daughters as much as sons.* Or valuing all humans, not just the ones who looked like them, not just the ones who claimed, like show horses, to be "better bred." On our walks, Alba confessed she felt unwanted by her husband, cast out by her parents. She complained that even her babies refused her breast. I could see she was as loved as a mosquito—even her voice had that grating whine. One night I "saved" her by removing a tiny hedgehog from her bed. I suspected her philandering husband had left it there as a sort of taunt to poor Alba. He was from an equally prominent aristocratic family, and his wedding to her barely put a dent in his schedule of female conquests.

This was the first time I had seen her since Ninfa. "Alba, you look lovely," I lied. She was even more thin and pale than I'd remembered, and it was obvious she'd had more cocktails than a proper young Italian lady should. Her dress, however, was stunning: a black-and-white-striped number in silk satin. We greeted each other with the requisite kiss-kiss, and I led her to a banquette in the corner. We slid onto the red leather, and a waiter instantly appeared with champagne, which was interesting, given the anti-French rules. Alba downed her glass and poured herself another.

"I just came from the opera," she said. "There was no one interesting there. War is so boring." She downed another hefty glass of champagne in one gulp.

"How is Silvio?" It was only polite to ask after her husband.

"He's with his mistress," she said, louder than was really needed.

I raised my glass. "Then we must toast his health and wish him a bout of diarrhea."

She began to laugh.

"Sudden, and unexpected," I went on. "A lot of it. At a very bad moment. Like a fire hose."

She was now guffawing. "Sally, you really are the best," she said.

"Can I refer you to a good divorce lawyer?"

She shook her head. "My parents love him. He's from such an *old* family," she said angrily. "They blame me for our problems."

"That's really unfair. But it's not their decision to make. Leave him anyway," I told her. "Times are changing. A woman doesn't need someone to take care of her."

Alba looked at me in silence, then said, "I do."

She got up and left.

I stared into my drink, surrounded by dark wood, leather upholstery, gilt columns, and frescoes of old Rome. The bartender said amiably, as he topped up my glass, "How about one more for my favorite degenerate?"

"Il Duce does say it's better to live one day as a lion than a hundred as a sheep," I said. "Fill 'er up!"

☼

Everyone I ran into in Rome knew what was about to happen to me, and they seemed mostly apologetic. "It won't be so bad," restaurant owners said as they let me eat for free. "You're a member of café society, and just a girl. You're friends with everyone who matters." I wasn't so sure about that. My dance card was suspiciously empty all of a sudden. Over the past few nights, I had consumed comforting buckets of fettuccine, waistline be damned, all by myself at Alfredo on Via della Scrofa. Alfredo, who had been sustained by generations of American tourists, piled pasta on my plate himself. *"Mangia, mangia, piccola,"* he crooned through his white mustache while wielding his signature gold fork and spoon.

Then one day, Alba's father, the marchese Aldo della Gherardesca, invited me to lunch at his vast Roman apartment.

"I don't know if I should accept," I said. I worried he'd try to enlist my help in keeping Alba in line.

"Go," said Lila. "Definitely go to lunch. Get him to help us."

The apartment in the Parione district, a short walk from the Pantheon, was decorated in what the BV had dubbed "Euro old money" style. Portraits from different eras of bilious-looking people were crammed onto the walls many rows high like an oil-and-canvas checkerboard. "That's seven centuries of my family," said the marchese with an arch smile, as if he were introducing me to live people. "They watch over me day and night."

"What happens when you run out of room for portraits?" I asked.

He laughed. "We build another room. Sometimes I feel I may buckle under the weight of all that family history. I mean, I'm not complaining, of course, I know my privileges are immense, but the pressure to not be the last of one's line or the one who loses the family fortune . . . it has crushed many."

Velvet and leather sofas were dotted by pillows embroidered with wire-haired dachshunds and Scotties, as well as live, sleeping versions. Needlepoint footstools tripped you at every turn, and a million picture frames cluttered every surface. Jade-green marble floors and an indoor fountain lent an air of casual decadence. In the formal dining room, a uniformed waiter offered me gleaming silverware from a tray before each course. The wine was from the marchese's own estate outside Siena—Cielocade, with a label of a huge oak tree.

"It's not safe for you in Italy," he said. He was slim and very vigorous for his age, dressed in a beautifully tailored black blazer and monogrammed striped shirt, hair slicked back.

I nodded but felt it would ruin the mood to show fear. "Not much I can do about it without an exit visa," I said, spearing my penne arrabbiata.

"I could hide you in the wine cellar," he said with a twinkle in his eye.

Though he had always seemed like a nice man, I wasn't sure whether to take the offer seriously. It sounded like the plot of a Peter Lorre movie.

"There's also my estate outside Siena. You're always welcome, you know. Tuscany's a hotbed of anti-Fascism, and Siena's got a long history of welcoming strangers—you could hide there, wait out this madness."

"I wouldn't want to cause you any difficulties."

He waved off my concern with a thick white linen napkin. "Mussolini needs to keep people like me on his side. If we start helping the Carla Rossellinis of the world, he's sunk."

I'd heard the name, but didn't know her. "She's the publisher of that underground magazine?" Someone had shown me a copy of *Are You Kidding Me?*, a small magazine printed in violation of Mussolini's censorship laws. It mocked Mussolini the way Chaplin's *The Great Dictator* did, and Groucho Marx's *Duck Soup*, by turning him into a Punch and Judy carnival act.

"Commedia dell'arte," he said. "Very dangerous stuff."

"Dangerous? Why do they even care?" The pasta tasted so good I wanted to lick the plate.

"You underestimate the power of comedy," he said. "It may be the only thing that gets Italians to wake up and fight back against Fascism. Carla is not her real name, of course. She's feminized the name of one of Italy's leading anti-Fascists, Carlo Rosselli, founder of Giustizia e Libertà, who was assassinated in '37. No one knows who she is, but there are some guesses. One of Il Duce's former lovers, or the daughter of an industrialist, or a university professor."

"Maybe she's just a regular person who got fed up and decided to do something about it," I offered in defense of the common man, or woman.

"Whoever she is, she's Mussolini's worst nightmare." He dabbed at his mouth with the white napkin and made an almost invisible nod to the waiter. The pasta bowls were whisked away. "You know he banned women from flying—he thinks they should stay home and be baby factories. We all know how he feels about having his authority questioned, much less made fun of. If she is indeed one of his ex-lovers, she could dish some serious dirt on him. His thugs are desperate to catch her, but she's stealthy. No one knows where she keeps the plane that's the color of the sky."

"I've seen that plane," I said. I thought of Beryl, poor lost Amelia, and Patsy's aviatrix. These women who defied gravity and more.

The waiter arrived with a salmon filet, slices of perfectly cooked steak, and a green salad. That was followed by small scoops of vanilla ice cream doused in espresso.

"Real coffee," I said, letting the dark liquid linger on my tongue. Coffee had not been available in months, even for the well-connected, and I was amazed to taste it again.

"I can't stand that faux stuff," said the marchese. This was a tacit admission of two surprising points: he did not support the regime, and he violated its trade embargoes by buying on the black market. Apparently he wasn't worried about his *schedatura*.

In the foyer, I thanked him for lunch, and he took both of my hands in his. "Even though we've only known each other a short time, I feel I know you well," he said. Despite my friendship with his daughter, I was afraid this was a seduction in process—vulnerable young woman and powerful older man—but all he said was, "Please come to me if you need anything." He let go of my hands, the butler showed me out, I rode to the ground floor in the tiny private elevator, and I was released like a trout back into the chaotic streets of Rome.

�֎

I was dressing for dinner when the police arrived. Lila was at the largely abandoned American embassy, trying to get someone to intervene in our case. I heard the buzzer, thought it was my taxi, and slipped into a smart little low-cut maroon velvet number with wide straps and a pair of sheer black hose, which I have always found to be reliably slimming. I briefly considered the sensible stacked heel pumps, but opted for my sky-high black Ferragamos—did I mention my growth spurt ended at five foot two? I longed desperately to be known as "that statuesque blonde with the legs." I grabbed my emerald-green velvet cape, put on a pair of diamond earrings Lila had lent me, and opened the door. Two policemen in gray overcoats and fedoras stood there.

"Oh," I said, with my usual eloquence. I wondered if it would be bad manners to telephone the marchese and ask for help so soon after lunch. "I think I should change," I said to the men.

"Why? You look perfect," they said as they ushered me out the door, one on each side, assuring me this was just a formality and I would be allowed to return to the apartment later. One of them said he had a cousin in New York. "Yankees, Giants, or Dodgers?" he asked me.

"You know, I did apply for an exit visa," I said politely. "I tried to leave like your government asked. Do you know why I wasn't allowed to go then?"

They shrugged and gave the Italian equivalent of "dunno": *"Boh."*

Just that afternoon, I had tracked down Allen and privately confessed I was the Bon Vivant, swearing him to secrecy. "Do you think as a member of the press I can avoid being interned?" He told me that, most likely, journalists would be briefly detained, but that I would qualify for a diplomatic exchange if I could prove I worked for Hearst. "Diplomatic exchange." Just the phrase sounded as quaintly formal as gently slapping one's rival across the face with a chamois glove, having a duel where of course you both fire high, and then going out for a champagne breakfast together. Good manners all the way, just my style. On the other hand, once I told the Italians, the news would be everywhere. I would never be invited to a party again, and plenty of members of high society would be delighted to see me shot at dawn.

I forced myself to notice the fine herringbone weave of the policemen's coats, the luster on the ribbon of their hatbands. *These men seem like very nice people,* I told myself. *It will all get straightened out.*

The two detectives took me on foot to police headquarters, the three of us merrily trading stories about New York hot dogs and our favorite Broadway musicals (*Anything Goes,* of course). Once we were inside the large white building with the ubiquitous gigantic screaming eagle on the front, they tipped their fedoras and left me standing in a hallway under a portrait of Il Duce. It was as if the soundtrack of my life changed from Cole Porter to Beethoven's Fifth. Black uniforms strolled briskly back and forth. Everyone looked angry and mean and busy. My outfit no longer felt chic or charming, but offensive. I had a faint metallic taste in my mouth.

Finally, the unmarked door outside which I was standing opened, and a goon grabbed my arm and pulled me in. He wore the uniform of the carabinieri, the branch of the Italian Armed Forces responsible for law enforcement. Redesigned under Mussolini with operatic flair, the carabinieri uniform included ballooning black jodhpurs, a red jacket with two rows of brass buttons, and a white sash, as well as a giant plumed hat.

"Violence is not necessary," I said with icy froideur. "I want to come in. I've been waiting outside for an hour to straighten all this out. I'm a member of the press." I had decided to portray myself as a regular journalist. "I write for the Hearst Syndicate. You know, the group that published all those flattering stories about Il Duce? Well, up until last week. You can't expect them not to be a little catty now."

"*Zitta,*" said the goon, commanding me to silence. The police official in a rather nicely tailored gray suit looked up from his desk. He was wearing a Fascist Party pin in his lapel, but I thought I glimpsed a flicker of humanity in his eyes. Or maybe he just looked tired. I spotted a small beige stain on his white shirt collar I was dying to blot for him.

"You're not on our list of journalists friendly to the regime."

"I'm very friendly to the regime," I said. "I'd even say I have a crush on the regime. I know we can straighten this out."

"Thank you, Sottotenente Favagrossa," the official said to the carabiniere.

I stifled an unexpected laugh. The name "Favagrossa" meant "large bean" but was also rather naughty slang for one's manhood. "Sorry," I said. "Sorry."

"Your Italian is good," said the official through narrowed eyes.

Favagrossa glared at me.

The official said, *"Documenti?"* and held out his hand. A portrait of Mussolini hung in this room, too. It felt like the dictator's eyes were following me as I reached into my evening bag for my passport. Favagrossa snatched the beaded handbag away from me and dumped it out on the desk. He ignored a very nice lipstick and the little envelope Aida had given me as a parting gift and grabbed the American passport and handed it to the official.

The official opened a huge dark-green-and-gilt calfskin ledger and began to slowly enter the details of my existence in black fountain pen. The leather and the ink gave off a mix of reassuring school smells.

"Your handwriting is beautiful," I fawned.

He ignored me and carefully, letter by letter, inscribed my name. Address. Place of birth. Date of birth. Passport number. Date of issue. Place of issue. Tourist visa. Date of issue. Place of issue. Necessary seals issued where and when, with serial numbers. Double-checked and rechecked.

My heels were starting to bother me and I shifted from foot to foot. "Are we off to the airport now?"

"I have studied your *schedatura*. You are an enemy of the regime, *signorina*," the official said, putting down his pen and looking me in the eye. "As such you will be sent to a prison camp until the war ends or you die."

Not the best news I'd ever had. "I tried to leave! You wouldn't give me a visa!"

He shrugged.

"Please! I tried to play by your rules. You can't change them now."

"I'm afraid we can."

"I'm a member of the press. You're supposed to put me under house arrest in my apartment until I get sent back in a diplomatic exchange with Italian journalists."

"*Signorina*, you entered Italy on a ninety-day tourist visa five years ago, yet you claim you are a journalist. You have no bylines. This is all very suspicious. You're a prisoner of war and possibly a spy."

"Spy?" I laughed, and decided I would have to put down all my cards.

"Yes, in the sense that I spy on rich, stupid people who kiss each other at parties. That's where my spying begins and ends. I'm a gossip columnist. I'm the Bon Vivant." I threw open my hands and waited for a response.

He laughed in hostile disbelief. "The Bon Vivant is a man," he said. "Everyone knows that."

"What's a Bon Vivant?" asked Favagrossa.

"A boulevardier," I said. He frowned. "A flaneur," I tried. No luck. "A party girl," I said at last. His eyes lit up. "The Bon Vivant is not a man," I went on. "I've made you think that, but he is . . . me . . . I. I am he. *Sono io, il Bon Vivant.*" I bowed theatrically.

"Do you have proof of this?" asked the official. "I think the answer is no. You'll be imprisoned until the war ends."

"But—"

"This war will be short," added Favagrossa. "Mussolini says so, and Mussolini—"

"Is always right. I know, I know," I said. "I really am the Bon Vivant. There must be something we can do to work this out."

"Take her away," said the official. Favagrossa took my arm. I put my hands together, beseeching the official, using my best, politest Italian. "*Vi prego . . .*"

Think, I told myself. *Think. These are men.* How could I use their egos against them? "Wait. I have information," I said. Favagrossa stopped. The two men looked at me. *Good first step. Now what?* I tilted my head at Favagrossa and made eye contact with the official. "It's very delicate. For you alone, sir."

With a nod of his chin, the official sent Favagrossa out of the room.

"Not the freshest egg in the Easter cake," I said.

"His father is the Undersecretary for War Production," he said with a slight eye roll. "What do you have for me? If you really are the Bon Vivant, it will be juicy."

I took a breath, trying to stay focused and think how I could steer him the way I needed to. "I have information on a German official stationed in Italy. I was witness to an indiscretion at a party. If I tell you, you could use it if you need to."

The official straightened his collar. "I don't really care for the Germans myself. They are heavy drinkers. And they are fond of pranks."

"Famously. Terrible pranksters. Very unpleasant. And this is a good story. Homosexual behavior. Very frowned upon by the führer." It would be unsporting to name any actual gay men, but there were a couple of really nasty womanizing German officers I would love to tar with that brush.

The official thought for a moment, then shook his head. "I want to know the names of Italians who are against Il Duce."

I kept my face a blank. Of course, I could name several right off the bat, including the marchese who had offered to hide me only today. "I don't know any," I said.

"I think you're lying. You're exactly the kind of girl people would speak freely in front of. A sweet little American. Tell me. I'll give you house arrest instead of prison."

"Don't you want to know what the German did? The color of the women's underwear he was wearing as he—"

"Give me a name."

"All of the Italians I've met wholeheartedly support Il Duce." By the way, kids, you don't have to cross your fingers when you fib if you're saving lives.

He took off his hat and rubbed his face with his hand, then lit a cigarette. It was considered patriotic to smoke the Italian state brand, despite its famously awful-tasting tobacco. I sneezed several times.

"Then it can't be helped. You're an American spy, and you must go to prison for the rest of the war." He moved to push the buzzer that would summon Favagrossa.

"Wait. Listen. To tell the truth, I'm not even really an American," I said.

He looked exasperated. "What? What are you talking about?"

"I'm Mexican. Maybe."

"Mexican, maybe?" He was taken aback. "You have an American passport."

"It was obtained using false documents so that I could attend finishing school in Switzerland."

"Finishing school?"

"It seemed crucial at the time, I promise you. It's a long story, but I was adopted by Patsy Chen the movie star when I was eleven. You know Miss Chen's work?"

"Mrs. Fu Manchu?"

"Well, yes, and other, more nuanced roles. You see, Patsy didn't actually legally adopt me. She was afraid they'd block it, because of the anti-

Chinese laws." The words poured out of me in my most rapid and correct Italian. The hilarious part was that it was the truth. The very complicated truth. "My American father was working at a mine in Mexico when he met and married my mother. I was born there, but we moved back to Iowa when I was a baby. Patsy wrote to the hospital in Hermosillo where I think I was born but we couldn't get a copy of my birth certificate." I took a breath. "So to get the passport so I could go to finishing school, Patsy had the props master at the movie studio make a fake birth certificate for me. That's what we used when we applied for my passport."

The official stared at me in disgust and horror. "A fake birth certificate?"

"Yes. You see, my real parents put me on a train to find work when I was eleven and I've never been able to locate them again."

The official frowned and pointed to his ledger. "This is why we Fascists keep records of everyone's movements! And why we have many, many stamps and seals on official documents! Didn't the stupid Americans realize your birth certificate was fake? And what happened to the real birth certificate in Mexico? And where are your real parents?"

I turned my palms up. "I don't know."

"Barbaric. This is why we are at war with the Americans. No understanding of the importance of recordkeeping. So this information, it's . . . *wrong*?" He gestured to the black ink entry.

"I'm afraid so."

"You're Mexican?"

"My mother was Mexican. She became American, I think, maybe, but she was Mexican when I was born. And I was born in Mexico. Maybe I'm Mexican on paper, and that seems to be what you care about most—?"

He shook his head in horror, threw up his hands. "There's no way to correct this ledger for Americans. And I don't have a ledger for Mexicans," he said. "I would have to start a new ledger. These ledgers are expensive. They are handmade in Bergamo from the finest Italian calfskin."

The official stared at me, his mouth a tight line. Outside in the hallway, I heard a muffled scream. I leaned one hip against the desk and picked up a tiny rubber soccer ball the size of a plum from his blotter, examined it, and put it down again. "Mexico has not declared a side in this war, so if I'm Mexican, then technically I'm neutral, like a beige divan." I flicked the ball toward him. It rolled across the desktop.

"But you're not Mexican. Look at you. You're obviously American."

"Are we going off looks? Because if we are, there are plenty of redheads in Italy. Legacy of the Celtic invasion of Italy in the B.C. era, right? So you're actually a little Irish, like me."

"I am one hundred percent Italian."

"If my Celtic forebears made whoopie with Italians while they were here invading and then retreated back to Ireland, then it's possible I'm part Italian, too."

"You're not Italian. At least according to this passport."

He captured the ball in his hand before it went off the edge. He continued to stare at the ledger and smoke.

"Part of my father's family also came from Germany."

He squinted. "Are you Jewish? Because that's a whole different ledger."

I shrugged. "Could be. We never talked about religion back in Iowa, but the bar mitzvahs I went to in Hollywood were nice. I might have been baptized in Mexico, though I'm not certain, and I've taken Communion just to be friendly now and then, though maybe I wasn't supposed to, was I? Patsy's family is kind of Buddhist. My adopted Chinese grandmother tried to teach me to meditate, but you have to sit very still. What do you think about Confucianism? I find it very interesting."

"You're making me ill. Everyone should know who they are and what they believe."

"I know exactly who I am and what I believe. I'm me. We're not livestock, so lineage doesn't matter. All humans are created equal. People should always treat each other kindly, especially if they're strangers. That's it. That's who I am and what I believe."

"Completely impractical."

"Only if your goal is to divide instead of unite. And by the way, I'm sure you're aware," I added, "that his eminence Benito Mussolini was named for Benito Juárez, a Mexican? Doesn't that sort of make me, as a Mexican Irish German American, an honorary Fascist? By *blood*?"

He narrowed his eyes and smoke wafted from his nostrils.

I tried a softer tack. "Don't you think documents are just useless?"

"Excuse me? Do you see what my job is?"

"But a piece of paper is not a person. It can't capture a person's story or define them. What does it matter if my name is Sally or Ethel or Anastasia?"

"Your name is who you are." He flicked the ball back across the desk. I caught it.

"It isn't. It's just what others call me. We define each other and our-selves by everything except what really matters, don't we?" I closed my lips, leaned down, and blew the ball back straight toward him.

The official narrowed his eyes and took a long drag on his cigarette, then pushed a button on his desk.

Siena

1941

Lapo

He was at his desk, trying his best to write about Mussolini's childhood. It was a few days before Christmas, and outside his window, he could hear his farm manager, Roghi, working with the young horse, shouting at him, the clatter of chaotic hoofbeats. He knew Roghi was pushing the colt too hard. Roghi believed in taking a firm hand with animals, and usually Lapo did, too, but in this case he knew that letting the young horse stop, calm down, and come back into a relaxed state would be much more effective in the long term than pushing him to obey, obey, obey as he got more and more frantic.

He made himself put a sentence onto the paper: *I'm nine years old, very strong, much stronger than my classmates. I don't know why, so I ask my father. He says, "Because you are destined for greatness, my son."*

A wave of nausea and despair crashed over Lapo. He threw the pen down as if it were scalding and rushed to the window.

"Roghi!" he shouted so the slightly deaf old man would hear him down in the round pen below the castle. "I'll be right there! Take a five-minute break." Roghi looked up and nodded, stepping back and lowering his whip until the young horse, sprinting back and forth in the round corral, slowed to a stop. The horse was sweating on his neck and flanks and his nostrils puffed rhythmically.

As Lapo trotted down the stone steps inside the cool depths of the tower, his boots echoing on the well-worn stairs, he thought about the day he met Eleanor. He relived this scene frequently as a way to calm himself. It was 1919. The war was over and the Spanish flu epidemic had subsided and life seemed full of possibility again. Of one thing everyone was certain: there would be no more wars like that one. No country would be so insane as to provoke another Pyrrhic conflict. It was a sunny day in Florence, and she was so cute, a curvy American girl in a tiered and draped summer dress and a vaguely nautical hat, too summery for February. American girls of her age and social class were rarely unchaperoned, and she confessed she had escaped her rather tiresome aunt. She asked for directions in broken Italian in Piazza Santa Croce. He was instantly smitten. He asked her to coffee, which turned into lunch, which turned into a stroll around the Duomo, then an *aperitivo,* then dinner, then a gelato from a special place a long walk away on the other side of the Arno.

Over huge cups of pistachio and *cioccolato* gelato topped with wafers, Lapo explained that he was from the less-than-picturesque industrial outskirts of Florence. As a young man, his father worked in a hat shop just off Piazza della Signoria. His father did not go to university or come from wealth, but he was an intelligent, charismatic, and ambitious man. He managed to buy the shop, then the factory that supplied it, and then ride a wave of thirst for Italian straw hats for men and women that swept the world and made him rich. Lapo, to his father's chagrin, did not wear hats—he found them hot and uncomfortable. When he graduated from *liceo,* his father gave him a beautiful boater, but when a gust of wind blew down the Arno and carried it away, Lapo did not run after it. Nevertheless, he went to work in the family business. "A year ago, my father had a stroke that incapacitated him. I inherited a hat empire that includes three factories and twenty stores around the world, including New York, London, and Rio de Janeiro," he said almost apologetically.

"Wow," said Eleanor. "A hat magnate. Nice. So what's your average day like? What did you do today?"

"Today is Saturday," he said. "No work. I like my weekends free."

"So you can lunch with unchaperoned American young ladies?"

"Usually I'm with clients who want to buy things." He told Eleanor that that morning he had gone to see a remote property with an American businessman who had gotten rich in the war supplying steel to the Defense Department.

"I can't stop thinking about the place," he told Eleanor as she bit into a wafer. "I can't stand the idea of it being turned into a country home for some rich family who'll come for two weeks a year."

"Is it because they're Americans?" She was sitting back with her arms crossed.

He shook his head. "It's because he bragged to me about making the war last longer so he could make more money."

She grimaced, and stared into the distance, then turned back to him. His stomach leaped when her eyes met his. "What does the name 'Belsederino' mean?" she asked.

He grinned. "'Sweet little . . . derriere.'"

"Seriously? You're making that up."

"I'm not! *Bello* means 'pretty,' of course, and *ino* is 'little.' *Sede* is 'seat,' like 'chair' but also 'headquarters.' And also . . . the part of us we sit on. So when you put it all together, the slang means . . . like I said." He shrugged.

She laughed. "What would you do with your sweet little rump?" she asked, stealing a spoonful of his *cioccolato*. Lapo had never met an American girl who was so daring, and yet so proper at the same time.

He surprised himself by unspooling a dream of resuscitating the ideal medieval estate: wine, olives, wheat, game. Ancient breeds of horses and cows. "And . . ." he added, "I've always wanted to write. You know, novels and plays and poems." He imagined a sort of ongoing salon, the many rooms of the castle filled with houseguests who loved the outdoors, writing, making art and music, and eating the food and drinking the wine made there.

"That's wonderful," she said. "You must do that."

"It'll never happen," he said with a sigh.

"Why not?"

He signaled to the waiter to bring the check. "What, I'm going to sell the family business and become a farmer and a writer?"

"Is that what you want?"

He stared at her. "Yes, but . . ."

"We only get one life," she said.

"How do you plan to spend yours?"

She smiled and looked away at the fountain in the middle of the square. "We women are supposed to aspire to nothing more than marriage and motherhood. But I'd like to do more. I want to spend every day doing things that make the world better, not worse. I think that's the lesson of the war. That we need to work hard at peace so war doesn't happen again."

He laughed and then saw that she was offended. "I'm not laughing at you. I'm marveling at your ambition. How does one make peace, do you think, outside of the League of Nations?"

"I don't know. It's a little paralyzing, frankly. The truth is, I have no idea what I'm going to do. I suppose it will depend on who I marry."

He took her hand, semiserious. "We could build it together," he said, wanting to dive into her eyes. "A place that is beautiful and nurturing for everyone who comes there. It could be a farm, a school, a meeting place. Very, very old and very, very new."

She didn't say anything, just smiled and looked at a tour group of English widows in black dresses and veiled hats following a tall man with a bowler hat and a black umbrella who was warning them not to talk to the Italians, who were "all thieves." Lapo paid the check and said, "Now I want to show you the view from the top of that bell tower."

"Are you hypnotizing him?" Roghi asked.

Lapo laughed drily. He realized he had been staring at the horse, lost in his memories. "I'm giving him a moment to calm down and think," he said. "You need to give a young horse time to relax or he won't learn."

The horse began to lick his lips and chew on his tongue.

"See?" said Lapo. "Now you can ask him again."

Roghi grumbled as Lapo took the lead rope and asked the horse to move in a small circle around him, one hind leg stepping over the other.

"Perfect," said Roghi. "You speak horse. I don't."

Lapo was about to ask the horse for a trot when he heard a car. Gasoline was rationed for the war effort and passing cars were a rarity these days. He and Roghi both turned to see who was arriving. The plume of dust settled to reveal a black Fiat 2800. The car had a long nose and four doors in an aerodynamic torpedo shape. The door swung open and there was a long pause as a familiar figure, a portly man in a tight black uniform, struggled out from behind the steering wheel, stood up, and brushed himself off. He gave them the Fascist salute. Lapo hadn't seen him since he'd dropped off Alessandro's draft summons.

"*Ciao*, Pappone," said Lapo.

Lapo's casual tone seemed as always to irritate the young officer. "*Buongiorno, signori*," he said with great officiousness. "I have come on government business."

"Any news from my son?" asked Lapo, who refused to kowtow to this carp of a man. "The mail doesn't seem to be working very well these days." He knew he shouldn't have said it—Pappone took any criticism of Italy personally—but he couldn't help himself. He knew Alessandro was guarding the embassy in Prague, but Lapo had heard nothing from him in weeks. It wasn't like his son not to write—he remembered when Eleanor would take Alessandro back to the States for summer vacations. He would send his father a postcard every day just for the joy of knowing the piece of paper would land in his hands a few days later. Alessandro loved paper.

"I'm not supposed to reveal classified information, but I may as well tell you he's in Prague," said Pappone.

Lapo bit his tongue. "Yes, I know that. Is there fighting there? The radio doesn't tell us anything." Italians were only allowed to listen to the state radio station, and all it ever reported was good news.

"We're winning the war," said Pappone dismissively. "Today I have come to collect Boranni Michele." He inverted the first name and last name as per Fascist protocols. "He must do his military service."

Michele was Roghi's grandson, and Lapo grabbed Roghi's arm and closed his fingers around it hard to silence him. "Michele is away in Siena," Lapo said. "At the market. We'll send him to you when he gets back."

"I would sooner shove a woodpecker up my ass!" exploded Roghi. "I will not send my grandson off with this dipshit—"

Felice Pappone, who was fifty years younger than Roghi, fifty pounds heavier, and four inches taller, punched the older man as hard as he could in the face.

"Stop!" said Lapo. "*Basta!*" But Pappone pushed Roghi to the ground and straddled him, then continued punching his face. "*Basta,* for the love of God."

With every inch of his body, he wanted to grab a rock and smash Pappone's head in. But he knew that Pappone was fully capable of unholstering his revolver and putting a bullet through his and Roghi's heads.

"I'm going to meet Il Duce!" Lapo shouted. "Mussolini himself!"

Pappone stopped. Roghi's face was a bloody mess. Pappone stood up. The horse snorted. "What are you saying?"

"It's true," said Lapo. "I'm doing some writing for him. I'm going to Rome next week to meet with him."

Pappone's eyes were wide. "Il Duce," he said. "What an honor! Will you tell him about me?"

"Of course," lied Lapo. "But I'll need Michele to be my personal assistant. Someone must type up my notes."

"Of course," said Pappone. "I understand. I will procure you a typewriter. The most modern available."

"Italian, of course."

"It goes without saying. An Olivetti. Top of the line."

"*Va bene.*"

Roghi groaned. Pappone looked down at him. "Excuse me, *signore*," he said to him. "But you must show some respect for the uniform."

"*Testa di cazzo,*" said Roghi as Pappone's car sped off in a cyclone of dust. Lapo helped him to his feet. "You're working for Mussolini now?"

Lapo sighed. "I guess I am. And so is your grandson."

Rome

1941

Sally

Favagrossa gave me a choice: we could take the tram to Le Mantellate, the women's wing of the Regina Coeli prison, and he would pay, or we could take a taxi that I would have to pay for. Apparently this was standard practice in Italian arrests going back to Julius Caesar.

"Traditions are important," he said.

I gave Favagrossa the once-over. Men like the official were difficult, but this kind, not so much. Spoiled sons of powerful daddies. "Let's splurge on a taxi, sweetheart," I said, waving the last of my lire.

Favagrossa nodded. "You are my sworn enemy," he said. "But I like your style."

✡

The taxi stopped in front of a huge and inelegant pale-yellow building with bars on the windows. Favagrossa, who it turned out was a student of the history of incarceration and torture, told me that Regina Coeli dated back to 1654 and had been built as a convent but had housed prisoners since the late 1800s. "Now it's full of foreigners and enemies of the regime. This prison is famously terrible," he boasted, warming to his topic with a huge smile. "Wait until you see. Just being there is a form of torture, and then sometimes there's real torture, too," he added without malice. "You will know that you are powerless before the Italian state."

"That's how all my relationships begin," I quipped, "but usually I get my way in the end." Favagrossa really brought out the worst in me.

"Arrivederci, Sally Brady," said Favagrossa as he left me in the prison's intake area.

I took a deep breath and made myself look around. It reminded me of the locker room of my elementary school back in Iowa, complete with physically impossible genitalia scratched into the tan paint of the battered lockers. The stern female warden was wearing an unflattering boxy blue dress and low heels. I wanted to tell her that her shoes did not show her ankles to their best advantage, but her type was never in the mood for a makeover. The matron's expression never changed as she ordered me to undress. She didn't even blush. She was not impressed by the emerald cape, the wine-red crushed-velvet gown, black heels, or beaded evening purse I handed over to her. Still, I made an effort to be a model prisoner, giving her a polite smile.

The matron dumped out the contents of my much-abused purse and made me take off Lila's diamond earrings.

"What's in the envelope?" she asked me, opening the little packet Aida had given me when I left.

"Magic beans," I said.

She wrote down a list of my items and put them in an envelope and put the envelope in a cubbyhole with a number on it attached by a clothespin.

"Will it be safe there?" I asked. Lila would never miss the diamond earrings, but the little manila envelope was sacred. I always kept it with me.

The matron inspected my dress and the emerald velvet cape inch by inch as I shivered in my black lace bra, silk culottes, and stockings. I was awfully glad I wasn't wearing the old ones with the holes in them. I wondered if she was looking for tiny weapons hidden in the seams, or just admiring the craftsmanship. The matron gave my garter belt a good snap. Then she stared at my face and checked it against my passport.

"Sally Brady," said the matron.

Ha!

Once I'd been checked in, the matron motioned for me to dress again. She handed me a loaf of bread, an empty metal pitcher, a crumpled tin cup, and a sticky wooden fork and spoon, then a stained straw mattress that wouldn't pass muster as a goat bed, and a thin, tattered wool blanket. I had to juggle all these items as the matron preceded me down winding flights of concrete stairs lit by flickering light bulbs and through narrow passages where water seeped through the stones.

Notice, notice, notice, I told myself. Pay attention to the details. What would the Bon Vivant say about this? *Readers, my latest adventure had me far from the madding crowd indeed, deep beneath the Tiber River, in the footsteps of naughty popes and gorgeous scheming Borgias.* The truth was that it was cold, dank, and smelled of urine and despair. I could hear rodents scuttling in the dark corners. From inside the cells came moans, sobbing, and even some laughter, though I was pretty sure the inmates weren't passing the time playing charades. The matron pulled open a heavy wooden door and shoved me inside a cell, then slammed the door behind me.

My eyes adjusted until I could see by the dim, caged light bulb that there were two middle-aged women sitting in the cell already. I had expected the Italian version of Lizzie Borden and Bonnie minus Clyde, but these two looked in dress and manners like the sensible, well-behaved ladies sitting on every park bench in Italy, watching their grandchildren and gossiping with the neighbors. They smiled politely and pointed to two empty iron bedsteads that matched theirs. I chose the one on the left and set down the straw mattress and the moth-eaten blanket. There was a shelf above the bed for the cup, pitcher, and utensils. I kept the bread under my arm, unwilling to sacrifice it to the rats. There wasn't much room in the cell beyond the bedsteads, especially given the ominous-smelling metal bucket occupying one corner. Home sweet home.

After an awkward silence, I offered a quiet *"buongiorno"* to my cellmates. They nodded, staring at me as if this were a stage show and I the star attraction.

I was grateful not to be alone. The women looked frightened, unsure of me. I took a deep breath, then smiled broadly and held out my hand. Mussolini had outlawed handshakes in favor of the Fascist salute, but I just couldn't bring myself to respect that rule, even in prison. "Sally Brady," I said enthusiastically, as if we were all meeting at a society soiree. *"Piacere conoscervi.* And in case you're wondering about my outfit, I'm not a prostitute," I added with a laugh. "Not that ladies of the night are undeserving of respect. Quite the opposite. I'm sure we can all agree they should earn medals, not to mention health care and pensions."

The ladies frowned. I went on, "I'm a journalist. American. That's why I'm in here. Enemy alien."

"Aaah," they said in unison, with long exhales.

"My son built a radio," said the one in a brown tweed skirt and black loafers.

The other woman, who was wearing a blue tweed skirt and brown loafers, said, "And my crime is that I said while buying some fruit that I thought Mussolini had gained some weight."

"You're in jail for that?"

They nodded. One of them put a finger to her lips and pointedly looked around. "They could be listening."

I jumped up and examined the cell more closely, looking for peepholes or hidden microphones. The women were mute with terror.

I spoke to the light fixture hanging overhead like I'd seen Barbara Stanwyck do in some movie. "Hello, I just want to say that I love the aesthetic of the Mussolini regime. Big fan. Everyone looks good in black. I don't care about politics, but I love Italy. And if you're listening, we could use some better light bulbs in here. A lady looks only as good as the lighting allows. *Grazie!*" I sat down again.

"I admire that you are not frightened," said the woman in the blue tweed skirt. "But please do not antagonize them."

"Okay, but if we're frightened, then they've won, haven't they? Just tell yourself that you're here and you're alive and nothing *that* bad is happening."

"Yet."

"No 'yets.' Stay in the present. Are you in pain right now? Does anything hurt terribly?"

They shook their heads.

I threw back my head and laughed loud, startling them. "Do it," I whispered. "Laugh. I do it at parties when I feel nervous. It makes you relax, even when you don't think you can."

They gave little chuckles.

"I'm . . . puttin' on my top hat," I began singing. As the women watched in shock, I stood up and danced around like Ginger Rogers, leaping from bed to bed, twirling as if I were having the best day of my life. "Tyin' up my white tie, brushin' off my tails . . . !"

I threw myself down on the mattress, panting. "Your turn," I said. "Come on."

"*E' pazza*," whispered one of the women to the other.

"Trust me," I said. "This kind of crazy is what it takes to get through something when you're really scared."

The women looked at each other, then one of them sang quietly, *"Ba-ba-baciami piccina."*

"Do it!" I cheered, laughing. The lyrics translated as "Ki-ki-kiss me, baby." "Sing it loud and proud!"

"O bi-bi-bimba birichina," the woman sang on. "Na-na-naughty little girl."

"Better, right?" I asked them. "Less frightened?"

The cell door swung open again and a skinny brunette was thrust in.

"Lila!" I said, hugging her. But now I was scared. If Lila was in here, who was coming to get me out?

Prague

1941

Alessandro

"Documents, please." Alessandro stood at a roadblock made of wooden sawhorses at the Pařížská entrance to Old Town Square. No civilian vehicles were allowed in the square, and concrete barriers funneled all foot traffic to his checkpoint. Prague was the intensely beautiful and historic city he had imagined it to be, and this was its magical center. On the one hand, he was delighted to be immersed in history. The gray paving stones under his boots had been trod by alchemists, emperors, heretics, and revolutionaries. The famous Astronomical Clock was just around the corner. The ornate pastel façades were only the latest buildings to preside over ten centuries of war and peace and shopping here. A light snow was falling, and the city was breathtakingly gorgeous, yet Alessandro was miserable. He wasn't here studying history, he was here making it, a minor supporting player in a Fascist extravaganza of epic proportions.

He checked the identity card of a middle-aged woman in a blue raincoat. She was scowling in her knitted scarf and collar while juggling several heavy shopping bags, her rubber boots half-submerged in frozen slush.

"Well?" she said in Czech-accented German, her hand outstretched for the card, her purse hanging open. She unleashed a torrent of Czech at him.

"Just a moment, madam," he said in Italian-accented German. He stared at the documents. As an embassy guard, he'd been trained to spot fake papers, but he didn't speak or read Czech. "Just look for a red seal," the officer who trained him had said, referring to the wax stamp that was obligatory on residents' ID's. "Blue seals are bad, red seals are good." This woman had a red seal.

"You may proceed," he said. She stomped off and an old man with a skinny white neck stepped forward. The man was carrying a piglet under his arm, a sleek brown thing that Alessandro had no doubt was about to be dinner for a German officer. The pig stared at him reproachfully as he checked the man's documents. Red seal. "You may proceed," he said. He had not had any blue seals, ever.

He had seen distressingly little of Prague, even after the Germans strong-armed the Italians into staffing some of the city's checkpoints. Both armies were feeling pinched by their eastern push into Soviet territory, and there was no love lost between the so-called Axis allies, each of whom suspected the other of shirking their duties. To avoid trouble, at night the Italian soldiers were locked into their barracks, a repurposed old pensione on the outskirts of the city. The hallways were loud with the pent-up energy of young men. Alessandro tried to drown out the noise by disappearing into books. He had discovered an odd assortment of reading material in the lost-and-found closet on the ground floor of the hotel, near the back entrance. The books were in every imaginable language. He read Hemingway in English and Proust in French, and he tried to decipher Thoreau in Arabic, but failed.

Under Mussolini, of course, displays of brute strength were considered masculine, and studying was frowned upon as "girlish." "Why do you carry those things around? Nobody reads books!" the other soldiers taunted him, but he didn't care. Books took him everywhere he wanted to go. He also loved music of all different eras, and missed his parents' extensive record collection, which contained everything from Gregorian chants to Duke Ellington to Japanese court music. And Toscanini, of course. Ever since Bologna, Alessandro had loved his music and admired the way the old man continued to stand up and speak out against Fascism.

Alessandro's shift at the checkpoint was supposed to end at seventeen hundred, when Carlo took over. Carlo was from Livorno. They'd met in basic training. Carlo was chronically late because there was a Czech girl he liked. Alessandro's hands were cold, and he stomped his feet to keep warm. He checked his watch. A quarter after already, and no sign of Carlo. He couldn't abandon the checkpoint, though. He had to stay until Carlo arrived. Documents, the Fascist obsession with documents. Though it didn't start with them—the stationers' guild in Siena was one of the most powerful in the Middle Ages, because of course written records were essential to a smoothly functioning government. They made the elaborate ledgers with parchment pages, leather covers, and gilt lettering that were required for every kind of record keeping for merchants, guilds, estates, city offices, armies. By the fifteenth century, when factories in Colle di Val d'Elsa, near Siena, were supplying paper to the entire Tuscan region, paper was power.

Alessandro checked the ID of a girl of about ten, and then of a tired woman in her forties in a pink jacket. Red seal. Red seal. God, Carlo was irritating. Like all Livornesi, always late. He looked down at a blue seal. He shook himself back to the present.

He looked into the eyes of the person who had just handed him her ID, a young woman about his own age in a yellow knitted hat who was carrying a shopping bag under her arm. In it, Alessandro could see a plaster statue of a red-hatted gnome. The girl blinked. He looked at the ID again. Maybe it was just the fading light. Was the wax of the seal red or was it blue?

"Okay?" she asked.

Her eyes were full of fear. He was frozen with grief for her, for what would have to follow. She would be detained, interrogated, probably arrested. Sent to a camp. And for what? Because she was maybe Jewish? Maybe a teacher who had told her students that a free press mattered? Maybe a poet who had dared to mock Hitler's stupid little mustache? Maybe just someone who knew someone like that?

He closed the cover of her ID card and handed it back to her. "Proceed," he said.

✡

Carlo arrived at half past and took over. No apology, of course. Damn Livornesi. Alessandro went back to the hotel, ate his canned rations, and dove into his tattered paperback copy of *Agosto, moglie mia non ti conosco* by Achille Campanile. It was a comic novel about a group of steamship passengers who mistakenly don chastity belts instead of life preservers when abandoning ship during a storm and then have to endure misadventures in a beach resort while trying to rid themselves of the contraptions. It was absurd and ridiculous, but so was his life right now, under the command of General Geloso, or "General Jealous," as Alessandro thought of him. It made him feel closer to home to read about Italy.

At ten to eleven, he was still reading when his fellow soldier Capraldo knocked on his door and slipped in.

"What is it?" No doubt he needed to borrow a razor, or a shirt.

Capraldo looked around, terrified. He was crying silent tears.

Alessandro sat up. "What?"

Capraldo took the book from his hands. He grabbed a pen off the side table and opened the book to a random page. *They shot Carlo. He let someone through the checkpoint. She set off a bomb at army HQ. I'm so scared.*

Capraldo tore out the page and ate it. Alessandro watched him chew and swallow. Then he slipped out of the room, and Alessandro was alone.

Rome

REGINA COELI PRISON
1941

Sally

Lila was sobbing and bruised. She was not dressed any more practically than I, in wide-legged champagne silk satin palazzo pants and a black silk shirt with broad lapels. She curled into a ball and whimpered. I covered her with the emerald velvet cape.

"Look at us," I said, sitting next to her on the bunk and stroking her back. "A couple of jailbirds. Swingin' door Susies."

"I'm scared," said Lila through tears. "I'm really scared. Aren't you?"

"Sure, but that doesn't help. We've been singing and dancing to lift our spirits. You should sing."

"No," said Lila.

"It helps. Sing a little."

"Stop it," shouted Lila, swatting my hand away and sitting up, her cheeks streaked with tears. "This is serious!"

A stricken silence fell over the cell.

"You're scared," I said at last. "But try not to worry. We have bread to eat. We have water. We're going to get out of here. They're not going to send Mrs. Percy the Screw King and her best pal to the guillotine." It sounded pretty hollow even to my ears, but Lila nodded and wiped her nose with a corner of the cape. "Look at this place." I tapped on the oozing walls. "This is going to be a helluva story to tell old Perce."

Lila gave a half-hearted smile. "He's going to be impressed I made it through this," she said.

"It used to be a convent," said one of the women.

"They should not put this one on the nun recruitment posters," I said.

"They threw me against the wall," Lila said. "My arm hurts where those bastards grabbed it, and my ribs are sore."

I examined her arm. "Nothing broken, though?"

Lila shook her head.

"Wait until Percy hears about this. He'll say, 'No more steel widgets for the Italians who laid a hand on my wife!'"

Lila smiled. "He thinks I'm a hothouse flower."

"You're tough as mule hide! Why, they practically beat you half to death and here you are, still standing. Though there are other forms of violence." I gave her a wink. "Low-quality cashmere. Unlined trousers. Perry Como."

Lila laughed. "I think he's dreamy."

"They've got to release us any minute. Someone is going to telephone someone, and a discreetly gigantic amount of money is going to change hands in the form of some deal for screws for submarines or airplanes. Then you'll go home and laugh about this."

"*We'll* go home," said Lila. "Thanks, Sally. You always know what to say."

Lila told me about her visit to the American embassy. She described how the last of the officials were busy emptying filing cabinets and having a big bonfire in the courtyard. The place was clogged with aging rich Americans who'd been living in Italy for decades in their villas and were now complaining mightily and demanding the U.S. "do something."

This did not surprise me. "Clearly they forgot Italy is not the forty-ninth American state," I said. "And Roosevelt is not their butler."

✖

When we woke up the next morning, and the morning after that, it was much harder to keep laughing and making light of things. Lila ate her wormy bread. I stopped singing for the other prisoners. We both had serious regrets about our wardrobe choices.

"They're going to leave us to rot in here forever," said Lila.

"I don't think that happens to people like you."

"Oh no, it does," said one of the women. "People die in this jail all the time. Even famous and well-connected people."

"How very egalitarian of them," I said.

"So now you are understanding how it works in Italy?" whispered the woman in the brown tweed skirt. "This is what they do, they wear you down so that when you leave here, all you want to do is go home and make no more waves."

✡

The matron appeared at the door the next day. She flashed us the smile of a Tyrannosaurus rex and announced to all of us, "You can get your sentence reduced. If you want to."

"We haven't actually been tried yet," I pointed out. "So we don't know what our sentences are. Can we talk to the Red Cross, please?"

"This is a great honor. A patriotic service to the nation."

"The American ambassador, maybe?"

The matron frowned. "I am telling you this is a great honor!"

"Sorry. We're listening."

The matron's expression melted into something almost human. "Mussolini needs to keep his strength up."

One of the women in tweed said, "A nice broth?"

The other added, "Or a hearty pasta, maybe with chickpeas?"

"Is he ill?" I asked.

The matron sighed and shook her head. "Quite the opposite. He's full of vitality."

A dim light bulb went off. "Sex," I said.

"Oh my God," said Lila.

"Il Duce requires companionship. Female companionship. Loyal Fascist visitors. Every afternoon at three."

The two Italian prisoners started to titter a little.

"Does Signorina Petacci know about this? Because I have seen the claws on that tigress." Claretta Petacci was Mussolini's not-so-secret mistress, more than thirty years his junior. The ladies giggled knowingly.

The matron let out an angry shriek: "This is not a laughing matter! This is our leader we're talking about."

"I don't think he wants me," said one of the ladies. "I'm as old as his wife."

"Me, too," said the other.

The matron said, "Il Duce does not wish to compel any woman to perform this wonderful, honorable duty, and he welcomes a diverse assortment of ages and body types. One is only required to be healthy. He is very generous to women who perform this essential national service."

No one spoke.

"Very well," said the matron. "Your loss."

"Wait," I said.

"Sally!" said Lila.

"Hang on. I just have a question, *signora*."

"*Signorina*, please."

"*Scusi*. No offense intended. Have you done it? Have you volunteered? You have, haven't you? I can tell." I couldn't resist.

The matron frowned and blushed a little and said, "I have been honored in this way."

Everyone's eyebrows went up.

"It was the happiest night of my life," said the matron with a sigh.

"Night? You stayed over?" I asked.

The matron shifted a little. "It was not a long encounter, but it was like being touched by God." She slammed the door.

"Jeepers creepers," I said.

"This is bad," said Lila. "We have to get the hell out of here."

For once, I could find nothing comforting to say.

✿

On day four, we watched as our cellmates were released, their families having successfully paid the requisite fines. "*Buona fortuna*," they said as they left.

✿

On the morning of day five, Lila said, "Would you do it?"

"Do what?"

"Make whoopie with Mussolini?"

I thought of Patsy, who had made excellent arguments for the separation of sex, love, and business. But Mussolini? "Nope."

"Never? Not even to save your life, or the life of someone you love?"

"Let's not think about it. We're getting out of here."

At the end of the day, the door clanked open and the matron pointed at me. "You. You're getting released. They've decided you don't matter." Lila began to whimper. I thought of my time on the trains, and on the streets of Los Angeles. I'd learned not to get attached.

The matron stood there waiting, door open, but I didn't move. *Dammit*, I thought. "What about her?" I pointed at Lila.

The matron shrugged. "She matters."

"Then I'm not leaving." Don't go thinking I'm a saint or something—it's just that I knew Lila wasn't made of Percy's steel. That kid couldn't find an elevator button on her own.

"Sally, go," Lila said. "Go. Don't be stupid. Go."

"Nope," I said. "I may not matter, but I'm not leaving you alone in this salt mine." I sent the perplexed and suspicious matron away.

"I love you, but you're crazy," said Lila, hugging me with her scrawny arms. "You did not have to do that."

"If I hadn't convinced you to stay in Italy a little longer, you'd be at the 21 Club in New York eating a steak and Caesar salad."

Ten minutes later, the matron was back. She looked at Lila. "You."

Lila squealed with glee and moved toward the door. I followed her, but the matron put a hand up. "Only her," she said to me.

"I thought I didn't matter?"

Lila's eyes went wide, and she glanced at me. Then she gave an apologetic half smile and averted her eyes. I stood rooted to the spot, feeling my stomach fall through to the floor. Lila followed the matron out. The cell door shut with a clang.

I made myself put my hands on the stone walls of the cell. A familiar dullness settled over me. A deep numbness. I went to the door of the cell and put my face to the small barred box in the center of it. I could smell piss, and mold. I could hear distant yelling. I ran my tongue over my teeth, finding a stray bread crumb. *I'm here.*

I opened my mouth and sang.

"Vissi d'arte, vissi d'amore, non feci mai male ad anima viva . . ." "I lived for art, I lived for love, I never hurt a living soul."

It was the aria Lila had been scheduled to sing at the recital.

My voice, rising in volume, echoed off the stone walls of the prison.

Perché, perché, Signore,
Perché me ne rimuneri così?

God, why do you repay me so?

Siena

1941

Lapo

When Lapo spontaneously told Pappone that Roghi's grandson Michele was his assistant, thus saving the boy from military duty, he had only a hazy sense of Michele's schooling. Michele's parents had abandoned the boy as a child to be raised by his grandparents. Under Mussolini's regime, a national Fascist curriculum had been created and students were put on career paths very early in their schooling. Michele, from a farm family, was educated mostly in farm techniques and manual labor. This, combined with a lack of interest in the printed word, did not make him the ideal candidate to be an amanuensis.

Today they were going to meet Il Duce himself. Lapo had summoned Michele to the castle at dawn. Since the boy was up every day to do farmwork, this was not unusual, but today Lapo studied the eighteen-year-old carefully. Curly sandy hair. High cheekbones. He was strong but lean. His brown eyes were calm and kind. Still, he was a teenage boy, so there were things Lapo worried about.

"Michele, it's important that you remain silent in the presence of Il Duce." He practically choked on the title.

"*Sì, signore.*"

Somehow, this did not feel like enough. He heard some of the farmers gathering for a chat outside his window. "Let's go for a walk," he said. Probably none of the farmers living at Belsederino would report him to the Blackshirts, but Felice Pappone's father could be among them, and every Italian knew that what you said, even out of doors, was being heard and possibly noted on your *schedatura* at police HQ. People made careers out of ratting on one another, and sometimes accused neighbors of making antiregime statements just to get even over a broken engagement or a noisy dog. Italy had become a nation of nasty little tattletales.

He led Michele out behind the castle into the woods. The oak trees arched welcoming arms over their heads. The branches were full of warblers and doves, redstarts, goldfinches, and nuthatches. He felt a sense of relief in nature, far from other humans.

From the pocket of his canvas jacket, Lapo produced an American poetry anthology he'd found in the castle library. Although foreign words were officially banned, foreign works of literature were not yet being burned in massive bonfires, as many Italian works were. Lapo had been horrified to turn a corner in Siena and find a group of Blackshirts outside the library burning works by Jewish, Marxist, and anti-Fascist authors. The flames reached high above his head, and the militia members stood around it, arms crossed, modern-day Savonarolas, smug in their certainty that they were keeping their fellow citizens safe from polluting thoughts.

"I'm going to read you something," he said to Michele as they sat under the oak tree.

> *I met a traveller from an antique land,*
> *Who said—"Two vast and trunkless legs of stone*
> *Stand in the desert. . . . Near them, on the sand,*
> *Half sunk a shattered visage lies, whose frown,*
> *And wrinkled lip, and sneer of cold command,*
> *Tell that its sculptor well those passions read*
> *Which yet survive, stamped on these lifeless things,*
> *The hand that mocked them, and the heart that fed;*
> *And on the pedestal, these words appear:*
> *My name is Ozymandias, King of Kings;*
> *Look on my Works, ye Mighty, and despair!*
> *Nothing beside remains. Round the decay*
> *Of that colossal Wreck, boundless and bare*
> *The lone and level sands stretch far away."*

Lapo finished reading Shelley's poem and looked at Michele, hoping for a sign of comprehension. "'Sneer of cold command'?" he said. "Sound familiar?"

"Ozymandias is the name of your bull," said Michele.

"Yes," said Lapo, unwilling to spell out exactly what he needed Michele to understand, in case the boy was not as trustworthy as he seemed, or not smart enough to keep his mouth shut. "What's important is that the man thinks he will rule forever, but he doesn't."

"Yeah. Too bad."

Lapo sighed in frustration. He realized Michele was raised on a farm and was used to butchering pigs, lambs, rabbits, and cattle. Maybe it wasn't the right poem to prod him into an understanding of human ego and cruelty. "I just want you to understand that our lives are in danger."

"But we're good people," he said.

"That depends where you're standing. To some people, we're good, but to others we might seem bad, for exactly the same reasons."

Michele frowned. This clearly did not square with his worldview or sense of self. They walked silently back to the castle. Michele went off to help his grandfather with some fencing the young horse had knocked down. Lapo went back to his writing room and stared out the window until Pappone showed up to drive them to Siena in his black Alfa.

Siena's train station, a newly built Futurist masterpiece, was below the ancient city walls, a long walk downhill from the famous fan-shaped piazza at the city's heart. Lapo had not been to the city in many months, and as they circled it to reach the train station, he wondered what life was like now in the piazza above him. Did couples still walk hand in hand in the evening? Were there any tourists left to gawk at the brick heights of the Torre del Mangia? He had no idea. The daily newspapers reported only the stories the Ministry of Popular Culture told them to write. Without real sources of news, he was essentially living the life of a peasant in the nineteenth century, when peasants rarely left their villages and knew nothing of the world outside. Radio filled with nationalist propaganda was not even worth listening to, so he rarely did. Newspapers kept people's attention away from government policy failures by splashing the front pages with distracting stories about grisly murderers, pedophiles, and foreign terrorists. He had to acknowledge that back in the era of reading six daily newspapers, spending hours on long, unmonitored phone calls, and reading and writing sheaves of uncensored letters every day, he had joked to Eleanor about how wonderful it would be to be cut off from the world, without ever thinking he would be.

They boarded the train to Rome. Michele said, "I've never been on a train before." He wiped dust off the window and peered out. The train lurched once and pulled out of the station slowly. Michele's eyes widened. "*Caspita*," he said, impressed. They were alone in the compartment, and the train was not one of the newer models. Loud clanking noises accompanied their progress down the tracks.

"Today your job is just to take notes." Lapo opened his briefcase and handed Michele a stenographer's notebook, one of a dozen that Pappone had given him in a blatant attempt to get Lapo to mention him to his beloved Duce. The typewriter, some ribbons, pens, and a ream of paper were all safely back at the castle out of reach of the Labrador's inquisitive jaws.

"What do you want me to write down?"

"Anything Mussolini says. Try to get the exact wording."

Michele looked doubtful. "I can't really write that fast."

Lapo sighed. "Try to get the big ideas down. Things I'll need to remember later when I go to write the book."

"Right," said Michele, then added proudly, "I've never read a book. I watched a big bonfire of them the other day, though. Those things really burn."

Looking out the window, Lapo was relieved to see the Italian countryside was still the Italian countryside, a glorious patchwork of fields, orchards, and forests punctuated with farmhouses, and towns perched on hilltops. It was comforting that the view hadn't changed since Lorenzetti painted his murals for the town hall in Siena in the 1300s. The train lurched to a halt. Lapo slid the window down and put his head out. He could see there were soldiers on the tracks. The conductor came down the gravel alongside the tracks and shouted up at the passengers. "Delay for repairs," he called over and over.

Michele just stared out the window for the hour they were stopped. Lapo admired his ability to calmly do nothing in silence; he himself yearned for distraction in moments like this—a newspaper, a book, the radio, someone to talk to. He filled the time by writing questions on the steno pad for his meeting with Mussolini. He made a list down the page vertically:

Family?
Childhood?
Education?
Teenage Years?
Young Man?
Rise to Power?
Present?
Personal life?

Now all he had to do was fill in the gaps.

A female militia member came down the train aisle, knocking on the compartments. When she got to theirs, she glared at Lapo.

"Contribution to the war effort?"

Lapo gave her a blank stare. "My son is in the army," he said. "Not to mention the local militia has requisitioned wine, hams, oil, and crops, as well as our motor vehicles."

She didn't miss a beat. "Well, you haven't given anything today." The woman fingered her pistol. "You should both be in uniform, serving your country. I'm fining you."

Lapo sighed and forked over some lire for him and for Michele. These kinds of bribes were becoming increasingly common. Mussolini had gone from bringing law and order in the early years of his reign to destroying it. Now every bully, male or female, was part of his militia and taking full advantage to terrorize anyone not in uniform. On sidewalks in cities, they pushed people into gutters and attacked those out after dark, even sometimes in broad daylight. If they came upon anyone who was "not Italian looking," according to their undefined set of criteria, they beat them to death, and there was no recourse. The judges were all party loyalists, and actual justice was considered laughably archaic. No one even expected it anymore.

Finally, the train was moving again. The trip to Rome took five hours. Lapo remembered Mussolini's promises, the new trains that actually ran on time. For a while, they did, but no longer. Il Duce's dream of empire had bankrupted the country. Now everything was under repairs, or just broken, no funds to repair it. Italy itself felt broken to him. It was strange to live in an era when things were going backward. He wondered if this was what it was like as the Roman Empire collapsed. The Roman roads were a marvel of engineering that allowed the empire to expand all the way to England and Egypt. What did people think as those roads fell into disrepair and bandits made passage difficult and deadly? The empire took hundreds of years to expand and thrive but collapsed within a hundred years—one lifetime. What was that like to watch? One of the reasons that the cause of the collapse was so debated by historians was the lack of first-hand accounts—and accounting. Without written records, it was all spec-ulation. That was the genius of censorship—there was no truthful record of anything to contradict the state's version of what was.

But they'd lived *here*, those people who had watched progress go back-ward. Were born here, died here. Walked these same hills, tended their flocks, worried about their children. Lapo wanted to reach through time and ask them what they saw each day as it happened. Though, really, he didn't have to ask. It was like this. It was the slow replacement of wise and far-thinking leaders with selfish and corrupt ones, the increasing difficulty of finding the products you needed, the worry about food, the rise of ig-norance and conspiracies, and the pervasive sense that things were not going to get better, the desire to hold tight to what you had even as it was torn away from you. Throw in some disease to speed things up. A natural cataclysm or two that felt like divine revenge. He was reminded of when Alessandro was about five, and was sitting calmly in the garden playing with a small teddy bear in the grass. One of their dogs, a rambunctious greyhound mix, galloped up behind the boy, went over the top of him, grabbed the teddy, and kept going. The boy's expression—shock, fear, rage, amazement—was exactly what Lapo felt all day, every day.

The train station in Rome was filled with troops boarding special trains to far-flung destinations. A Blackshirt met them there and whisked them away in a huge black car with flags flying. Lapo saw almost nothing along the way, in part because of his own terror. He stared at his hands, willing them not to tremble.

Rome

1941

Sally

"Isn't there *anyone* who will pay for your release?" the matron asked. "Family member? Friend? Neighbor? Lover?" She was almost kind in her frustration. "Anyone who'll just pay for an upgrade to a better cell?"

"You can do that?"

"Of course you can do that," she said with a snort.

I shrugged. It was fairly disheartening that I had spent years cavorting with the rich and famous—attended their weddings and funerals, slept in their homes—and yet I couldn't think of anyone I could call on. The marchese, yes, but I didn't want them to think he was pro-American. Finally, someone occurred to me.

I gave her the name of the Italian I helped save on the mountain in St. Moritz. I didn't have a phone or precise address for him. I had no idea what his family status or profession was, but he was skiing with well-connected people that day. It was worth a chance.

Her eyes narrowed. "You know this man personally?"

"Yes. Well. Sort of. We met once."

She snorted. "We'll see," she said, and slammed the cell door with extra vigor.

Lapo

They were sitting in one of the reception rooms in the Villa Torlonia. They had waited thirty-five minutes for Mussolini to appear, which gave Lapo time to tamp down his anxiety, practice what he was going to say, and study the oval space. Every inch of it was decorated—intarsia floors, trompe l'oeil columns, alcoves for life-sized sculptures of Greek gods and goddesses, frescoes of putti circling above the sculptures' heads, and a painted paneled ceiling with a huge glass chandelier.

"I like the naked ladies," said Michele, pointing to the floor design.

"Those are maenads, followers of Dionysus. They achieved ecstasy through frenzied drinking and dancing."

"I'm kind of getting hard," said Michele.

Then the door was flung open, and Mussolini strode in, followed by a lanky lion cub. Lapo was both charmed and terrified by the sight of the wild animal. The lion sniffed them, perched on a chair, and began licking its fur. The dictator was instantly imposing—always in motion, the heels of tall black riding boots clacking on the floor, his tight black uniform and sidearm like something the bad guy would wear in a cowboy movie. His eyes darted around the room. Lapo and Michele sprang to their feet, but Mussolini motioned them back down with a smile.

"I don't have much time," he said, adding to Lapo, without rancor, "That's an ugly tie," and then, just as amiably, "Do either of you box?"

"A little," said Michele.

"Good," said Mussolini. "Very good sport. Very good for the mind and body. I box for an hour every morning. Keeps me on my toes." He illustrated with a few jabs. "What about bridge?"

"I play," said Lapo. He didn't really, had only been roped into a game or two with American visitors to the castle, but it seemed important to find common ground. He hoped they weren't going to play now.

"I love bridge," said Mussolini. "Keeps the mind sharp."

"I'll put that in the book," said Lapo, and they were off and running. Mussolini spoke at a machine-gun pace that felt twice as fast as most Italians.

"People want to know my story," said Mussolini, launching into a monologue. "And they deserve to know, they should know, they'll be honored to know. It should be studied in schools, as a model for the modern Italian. It's an Italian story, a story of Italy, a story of what she can be, what she should be, what she should aspire to be. A story of a man who loves his country, and whose country loves him. A man who will fight for his country! A man who tames lions! A grand Italian adventure!"

The lion snored and Lapo nodded politely—wondering if he was being enthusiastic enough—and when Mussolini paused for breath, he asked why he had chosen him for this honor.

"You wrote that book about dragons," Mussolini said.

"Dragons?"

"Yes, you know, where the hero is a boy who realizes the whole world is evil and he's the only good person and he has to slay the dragon to put things right again."

"*Dragon Slayer of Vico?*"

"Yes," said Mussolini impatiently. "It's my favorite book."

"Oh. Count Ciano said—"

"Ciano! Don't speak of him. Preening peacock."

Lapo realized with no small amount of shock that Mussolini was thinking he was the author of the badly written story for nine-year-olds about a fairly misogynistic little boy whose nastiness leads him to kill a friendly dragon. He thought about correcting the misunderstanding, but then he remembered all the people counting on him. His desire to survive through the end of this meeting. "Ah," he said. "Dragons. Of course. Yes."

He nudged Michele, who wrote down "dragon saliva."

Mussolini smiled with all his teeth and said, "I thought you'd be perfect. Just write like you did in that one, but about me."

"I can do that," said Lapo.

The lion cub growled, grunted, and began to gnaw on the arm of the priceless antique chair it was perched on.

Mussolini stood up and paced back and forth, monologuing again. "Italy is like a child who needs a strong father. A father who's loving but stern, a father like only I can be. A father who will bring out the best in his people, who will inspire them to serve and love their country. Not like the traitors who seek to undermine me and who hate our country and who only want to sell us out to foreign dominion! They don't want Italy to thrive! They want it to die and be served for dinner to their foreign masters. They want to own our land, put us in debt to them, force us to do their bidding, take our resources, pollute our land, and force us to exist only as a playground for their bored elites. We are so much better than that!"

Lapo was reminded of his father, of the speeches he would make at the dinner table. As a child, Lapo had thought his father was strong and wise, but as he grew up, he saw him as petty, insecure, controlling. Eventually, he saw him as needy, with an emotional black hole at his center, and felt compassion for him.

"Yes, sir."

"Good man. I'm sorry I don't have much more time for you today."

"I totally understand, your eminence, but I do need to know about your life. I read the Sarfatti book, but—"

"No, no! Drivel. The woman's a traitor. I've given orders to find every copy and burn them. Don't use anything from that. I'll have my assistant give you what you need. Stand up," he said to Michele.

Michele did. Mussolini put his fists up. Michele, cautiously, did the same. The lion watched, its eyes glittering. Mussolini danced a little, then threw a quick punch. Michele sidestepped it. The lion swatted at their legs as they danced past him. Lapo was chanting internally, *Don't hit him, don't hit him.*

Mussolini threw another punch, and again Michele sidestepped it. Then Michele's fist rocketed out and smacked Mussolini in the jaw.

The world stopped.

Lapo's breath was frozen. Michele stood still, eyes wide. Even the lion gaped in shock. Mussolini didn't move, just stood there with his mouth open. Finally, he wiggled his jaw and put a hand to it. "Nicely done," he said. "I'd like you to stay here and be my sparring partner. You'll give him to me, of course?" said Mussolini to Lapo.

"I—"

"Go right through that door," said Mussolini to Michele, who glanced at Lapo and then walked out of the room.

"He's only eighteen," said Lapo. "Needed on the farm. A really good boy."

"And you will write a really good story," said Mussolini, his eyes as black as his boots. The lion jumped off the chair, yawned, stretched, and casually shredded a Turkish carpet with his claws.

"*Andiamo,* Ras!" ordered Mussolini.

And with that, Il Duce and his lion were gone.

Lapo was crushed. How could he tell Roghi that he'd lost his grandson? That the boy was now the sparring partner to the dictator? Probably he would have been safer going to the front lines. Lapo sat there trying to figure out what to do under the supercilious eyes of the Greek gods until a young woman in a pink cardigan and a tweed skirt and round glasses came to get him. She was carrying an armload of clippings. They seemed to be mostly photo ops from Fascist newspapers—Il Duce in a plane, Il Duce on a horse, Il Duce on a tank. He squinted closely at the tank, which looked suspiciously like it was made of cardboard.

"Hmm. I don't know if you can help at all," he said to the woman. "But Michele, Il Duce's new boxer, he's a very good boy. Maybe not so smart. But good at heart. Very needed on the farm, as soon as Il Duce can spare him. If you could keep an eye on him . . ."

"I can't," she said. "Also, I know you're not the right author. Ciano told me. But the other one opposes the regime and I didn't want Il Duce to have to kill his favorite writer. He's actually a very sensitive man."

An antique clock ticked nearby. "Ah. Okay. I understand. Before I go," Lapo said, "are there any red flags I should know about, things Il Duce really does not want to see in this book? I mean, I don't want to do anything to . . ." "Get killed" seemed too strong. "Upset him," he said.

She turned a bland smile on him. "Nothing that I'm aware of," she said. "Though he does hate the color green." Her eyes strayed down to his tie.

"Okay. Good to know." Lapo realized as the light flashed off her glasses that this woman had access to military communications. "I wonder, can you tell me anything about where my son is? He's in Prague, a guard at the Italian embassy. I haven't had a letter lately. It would give me the peace of mind I need to write."

"The Germans control Prague, so I have no news for you. Is there anything else I can do for you today? Would you like to call your wife in Chicago? I can get you a line."

Lapo froze. He was both suspicious and elated. Everyone knew the phones were tapped, even for minor calls within Italy. Still, even just to hear Eleanor's voice . . . "It would be okay?" he asked timidly. "I mean . . ." Was this some kind of loyalty test?

She smiled again. "It's fine. You can use this room." She opened a small door, and Lapo ducked down to enter a room about one meter by one meter. There was a black phone on a table, and a plain chair. Nothing on the walls.

"Your car will be here in five minutes," she said, and shut the door.

Lapo lunged for the phone. Fortunately, he had memorized Eleanor's phone number in Chicago. Would she be home?

It rang ten times, then the line went dead. "Eleanor," he said into the ether. "Eleanor. I'm okay. I hope you're okay. Are you okay? I love you, I think about you all the time, I write to you—"

Lapo realized he could hear breathing on the line.

"Hello? Is that you, Eleanor? Who's there? Who's there?"

The breathing continued.

"I love you," Lapo said, and hung up, heartbroken. He had his hand on the door when the phone on the table rang. He stared at it, then picked it up and said a cautious hello.

"Honey! Where are you? I was sleeping." Her voice melted him. Then he was suddenly paralyzed by what Eleanor might say next.

"It's a long story," he said, "but I'm in the Villa Torlonia, in Rome. Just for today. They let me make a call. I . . . I can't talk, but I love you."

"Alessandro? How is he?"

Lapo's heart sank. "He's fine," he said. "Just fine. We're all fine. And you?"

"I'm fine." He could hear the caution in her voice. She was putting it together. Torlonia. One phone call. The OVRA listening in. "The girls are fine. They miss you. I miss you. We miss our home. We pray this is all over soon. Are you sure you're okay?" She was keeping it light, and he could hear the stress of that.

Or maybe it wasn't Eleanor at all, but an actress imitating her voice.

They did that, he'd heard, the OVRA, to try to get people to say things they shouldn't. He pushed the thought away.

"Listen, my love, I don't know when I can call again. Just try to feel me with you. I'm there, in my heart. Right next to you. To all of you."

"Me, too." And then she was gone, the call dropped, or ended.

Sally

Without any warning, the matron had come for me that morning, delivered me upstairs, and returned my handbag. The envelope from Aida was safe. Even the diamond earrings were there. Gone was the brusque manner, the rudeness.

"I am all apologies," she said, as if I were checking out of the Ritz. "I hope you enjoyed your stay here, Signorina Brady."

I was so surprised that it took me a moment to respond. "I take it you reached my friend?"

She nodded. "He is indeed a well-connected gentleman. You should have told us of your connection at the beginning. Much trouble could have been avoided."

I assumed an imperious air. "I like to be taken on my own merits," I said. "Not on my connections."

"Connections are everything, *signorina*," she said. "You are a foreigner so perhaps it is different where you come from. But someone who knows a man like that—life is a little easier, as of course his circle is quite wide."

Now I was deeply intrigued. I didn't want to admit I had no idea what valuable product—steel? wheat? guns?—the skier made, or what royal family he was part of, but I really wanted to know.

"You reached him at home?" I asked.

She gave a little smile. "At work, of course. It's a Tuesday."

I thought some more. "He was very busy today?"

She nodded.

"I suppose I will see him on the ski slopes," I said.

"I'm amazed he can get away," she said. "War is such a busy time for men like him."

Armaments, I thought. *Grenades, or machine guns*. "Yes," I said. "We're counting on him, aren't we? I know I am. Personally."

Now it was her turn to look surprised, and also a bit disgusted. She took a step back. "I suppose as long as there are brothels, we will need him, and as long as there are men, there will be brothels. Good day, *signorina*. Please give the doctor my best on your next visit. I hope he can cure your syphilis."

And with that, she backed out of the room into her office and shut her door. I barely had time to laugh before the other door was flung open.

"L'Americana!" Sergente Favagrossa threw wide his arms in greeting as if I were the best friend he hadn't seen in years. "Didn't I tell you this place would break you?" he said triumphantly. "Was I right? Huh? I was right. You look terrible."

I feared he was right.

I was exhausted, but I refused to give this idiotic piece of meat any satisfaction. "Give me a chance to get my hair done and I'll freshen up just fine."

"C'mon, admit it, we broke you. Damp, rats, dark, weird noises, terrible stench, and random screams in the night. It's the whole package. You Americans have nothing like this."

"You'd be surprised," I said.

"I don't believe it," he said, adding, in English, "Italy—best prisons ever!"

✿

Favagrossa took me back to Lila's apartment. I turned the key and pushed open the door, not sure what I would find.

Lila was gone, but all her clothes and belongings were still there. Strange.

"Nice place," said Favagrossa. The apartment was indeed quite lovely in a decaying old-Rome way, with high ceilings and faint tracings of faded frescoes on the ceilings, dancing nymphs and goat boys with flutes. The plumbing and electricity were also a tad historic—if you flipped the light switch too vigorously, you might get a quick shock. "My father frowns on requisitioning apartments, but this is tempting." He stepped to the tall windows to admire the view of the Roman Forum. "Hey, look, you can see where Julius Caesar was murdered!" He grabbed his own collar. "The senators

seized him by the toga and stabbed him to death, right there on the steps."
He acted out the death scene for me, falling to the floor and barely avoiding his own sword.

"Did Lila leave the country?" I asked. During my days in the cell without her, I'd tried to sort out my feelings about Lila, but had decided it was too much. Judge not, lest ye, and all that.

"*Boh*," said Favagrossa, getting up with a shrug.

He flipped through old copies of *Vogue, Punch,* and *The Tatler* in the living room while I bathed and changed my clothes. "Pack one bag," he called. "That's it. Not one thing more."

"Plus a handbag," I said.

I reluctantly chose a plain navy-blue wool dress, not much livelier than my old school uniform. I felt anonymous, informal, and unspecial, but also warm and ready for anything. Unwilling to totally surrender to practicality, I pulled on a faux fox fur jacket and high-heeled ankle boots.

"Really?" said Favagrossa when I emerged from the bedroom.

"I can't be short. I just can't," I said. "Where are we going? The airport?"

"A surprise." He grinned.

I was suspicious of that grin. He was clearly a sadist, but also insecure and longing to impress me. He balked, however, when he saw that my "suitcase" was "Home," my Louis Vuitton steamer trunk that Patsy had bought for me. "You said one bag. This is technically a bag," I pointed out. "I'm not leaving behind all my clothes. A woman without her clothes is . . . a plucked chicken. My Schiaparelli evening suit? That's protected under the Geneva Convention."

"You don't have respect for me."

"I have total respect for you, sir."

He nodded. "Better. You're paying for the taxi." He put a red armband on me that screamed POW in big white letters.

"Pow, like Superman," I said, miming a punch. "Pow, pow."

"Do not mention Superman," he whispered. "Even though he is very amazing."

The taxi took us to the train station, which was full of soldiers in uniform who were chanting at the top of their lungs and angrily waving scarves at each other. I was mystified until I grasped that each troop had its own chant and was aiming to drown out everyone else's while flicking their scarves in unison. Favagrossa grabbed a luggage cart and shoved the trunk onto it, then pushed it to a spot under a huge clock. "Wait here," he said. "I will buy us two second-class tickets to Siena. Or you can pay for first class, but it has to be for me, too." He waited expectantly.

"*Boh,*" I said and turned out my pockets. "I'm broke."

Favagrossa looked disappointed. "I hate second class," he said. "The bathrooms smell and the seats are uncomfortable. Honestly, Sally Brady, you and I deserve better, despite the fact that you're a prisoner of war."

"I couldn't agree more."

Once we had our tickets, we made our way to our assigned train car, Favagrossa pushing the cart while complaining about how heavy it was, how noisy the station was, how people threw trash on the tracks, how no one had respect for anything. People stared at my red armband and moved aside as I walked past. One old man put his face in mine and spat. I was shocked and disgusted—even as a "hobo" kid, I had rarely been the focus of such intense hatred, but I remembered Patsy talking about how she handled this kind of thing when she was a girl. I calmly raised my sleeve and wiped my cheek and kept walking. We had to walk past all the first-class cars to get to the second-class ones.

I tuned out the hostile crowd and Favagrossa's sense of wounded entitlement and self-pity and looked up at the faces of the people in the compartments we passed, wondering if I would see any of my high-society pals. I spotted one of the minor princesses three cars down. I'd been to luncheons at her house many times and was a bridesmaid at her daughter's wedding. During a tea dance, I'd even saved her parrot Maurice from Lady Cheshire's very determined terrier, at the risk of my fingertips. She saw me, clearly recognized me, and averted her eyes.

We jammed ourselves into a second-class car heading for Siena. It was ancient, hazy with cigarette smoke, and the heat wasn't on. I sneezed several times, and shivered a little, even in the fox fur. All the seats were taken, so we had to stand the whole way, just outside the bathroom under a poster that proclaimed MUSSOLINI MAKES THE TRAINS RUN ON TIME!

"I hate second class," repeated Favagrossa every time the bathroom door opened.

"I bet growing up as the son of a general, you didn't have to travel second class a lot."

"You'd be surprised. My father enjoys torture. Regretting those boots?" he needled me. He, like everyone else in all of Italy all the time, was smoking. I sneezed.

"Not for one second," I lied as we swayed with the motion of the train and I tried to breathe through my handkerchief. "What's in Siena?"

"You'll see," he said.

The train had two speeds: slow and stopped. When we creaked to a halt for the umpteenth time with no explanation, Favagrossa and I both let out angry sighs. I took my lipstick out of my purse. I put a finger to my lips, and as Favagrossa watched, I changed the poster to read MOUSELLINI MAKES THE TRAINS RUN LIKE SHIT. I added big Mickey ears on Il Duce's head.

His eyes got wide, and then he put his hands over his mouth to stifle a laugh.

He snorted. "You have gone too far. You are funny, Sally Brady. Very bad girl and bad prisoner, but very funny. I'm going to pretend that didn't happen. Never do that again. The OVRA, they will report us both. *Dio mio.* What your *schedatura* must look like." He kept laughing as he made me wipe off the poster.

Five hours later, we arrived at the station in Siena. Favagrossa looked at the trunk and then up the hill at the city above them. "Two kilometers uphill," he said. "I hate Siena and I hate the Sienese. Assholes. I hate them more than I hate the Pisani and the Livornesi, which is a lot." I had always been fascinated by Italians' open scorn for other Italians, and their rampant, absurd stereotyping. I wondered if it was an intrinsic part of human nature to hate everyone who wasn't like you, which begat a need to find difference at any cost. Favagrossa thought Milanesi were liars, Lucchesi were cheats, and Livornesi were bad drivers. On the other hand, those from Carrara, where he was from, were flawless. "Like our marble." All Italians not from Carrara thought the Carraresi were backstabbing anarchists.

He began to shoulder the trunk. The Fascist militiaman yelled over at him.

"Carabiniere!" he called out. "That is beneath the dignity of your uniform." Favagrossa flinched and dropped the trunk. "Make the prisoner carry her own luggage, *porca miseria.*"

Favagrossa put his hands on his hips. "See? Assholes. And from a militia member! I am in the *real* armed forces." He fumed some more, then said, "I'm not going to be your pack mule any longer. Follow me, prisoner." He marched off, leaving me and the trunk to follow.

I began to slowly push the trunk up the damn hill. The city walls looked farther and farther away and that trunk got heavier and heavier until it felt like the world itself was inside of it. I thought of Ma, how she spent most of every day in the fields, carefully laboring just at the edge of her strength, knowing she would get up the next day and have to exert the same effort again, and again, and again, never asking for pity or getting it because everyone we knew was in the same boat. Since leaving Iowa, I had been spared that kind of hard physical life. I was soft. I walked more and more slowly, then stopped to sit on the trunk. I noticed Siena smelled different from Rome. Pine. Bread. Earth.

"Come on," shouted Favagrossa. "I don't have all day!"

"I'm coming," I whined, pushing the trunk once again, heaving and sweating and stumbling on the cobblestones. A car went by, and the young women inside jeered at me, *"Straniera di merda!"* "Shitty foreigner." Thanks, ladies.

I inched my way up to a massive brick wall that soared at least fifty feet over my head in a medieval show of defense. I'd made it. I stood panting in front of an arched opening in the wall decorated with white marble.

"This is Porta Camollia," said Favagrossa. "The Sienese are terrible people but the history is interesting."

"You mean someone was executed here?" I'd caught on to the events in history that captivated Favagrossa.

"Ha, ha. Yes, of course. Many violent deaths. The city museum is not far from here. All the medieval torture equipment that was on display is now back in use over there in the Medici Fortress, militia HQ." He pointed down the hill. "You should see the thumbscrews in action."

I stared up at a beautiful sun symbol over the gate, and a huge heraldic crest.

A militiaman stopped us. I studied his uniform, which, as the Bon Vivant, I had spoken of so glowingly. Black shirt, black tie. The edges of the black jacket were embroidered with gold flames and the famous Fascist twig bundles that signified unity, whereas Favagrossa's Royal Army lapels had stars. There was some problem with Favagrossa's papers, and the Blackshirt made him wait while he confirmed some information with a colleague who looked like he was taking a nap. I suspected the "problem" was that the first man was actually illiterate. Finally, the Blackshirt waved us through.

"*Testa di cazzo*," muttered Favagrossa.

"You don't like the Blackshirts."

"They are loyal to Il Duce and not to the generals," said Favagrossa. "This bothers me. Our armed forces should be united under one command, not working against each other."

"So maybe Il Duce and not the generals should have supreme command over all of you?"

"Il Duce is a brilliant leader," said Favagrossa with a sniff, "but he did not go through the academy in Modena. He is not a trained military expert like others."

"Like your father."

"Exactly." He leaned in close. "There have been some mistakes recently. A lost opportunity in Dalmatia. Excessive bravado in Macedonia. I will not say more."

Finally, he stopped in front of a six-story brick building with flags flying out front. I looked up at the sign.

"Hotel Excelsior?"

"*Sì.*"

"I'm staying here?"

"Happy surprise, right? Welcome to house arrest," said Favagrossa. "Courtesy of Il Duce. But you can thank me." He leaned toward me, and I realized he expected a kiss.

"When the Americans come and bomb the shit out of Italy, I'll put in a good word for you." I was hot and tired and it just kind of slipped out. I flinched as Favagrossa grabbed my arm and made a fist.

Close your eyes. Don't resist. Don't fight back. I was a kid again, back in the rail yard, facing down a group of kids just as hungry as I was, but twice my size, and all boys.

The blow didn't come, and I opened my eyes and he was still staring at me, his arm once again at his side. He sneered as he said, "No one's coming to save you, sweetheart. America is nothing but a weak band of mongrels at each other's throats."

V

Supper Club

The Bon Vivant

Welcome to the Bon Vivant's nightly broadcast on Radio Siena. Nighttime is the right time for dancing and air raids here at the lovely and charmingly boarded-up Hotel Excelsior. All the best people are interned this season, not counting the Yanks in the press corps who've been holed up here on Il Duce's tab since Hirohito rained lead confetti on Pearl Harbor. Lucky 13 is yours truly, who got stuck in Rome when they closed the exits. My task is to teach everyone to dance the rumba, the boomps-a-daisy, the mambo, and to play bridge. . . . The rumor on the sixth floor is that we'll have clean towels next week, and whispers about room 603 having chocolate were proven correct to a favored few. In his cups last night, Allen revealed his middle name is Leslie. The height of the social whirl this week will be the backgammon tournament in room 608. . . . Someone tell the RAF to keep it to a dull roar while we continue with our nightly talent show. . . . And now, a special request from Betsy, "Chattanooga Choo Choo . . ."

Siena

1942

Sally

House arrest was strange, but a hell of a lot better than prison. We were a baker's dozen of Americans locked in a luxury hotel in wartime, far from the front. Could have been the plot of a movie, except it was stunningly boring, like being on a cruise where we never got to port, or summer camp in the Catskills during a monsoon. Were we suffering? Not by most definitions. We could not order off the hotel menu, but were served three quite decent meals a day that might include *pici cacio e pepe*, roast chicken, some hearty bean soups, and always a quarter loaf of saltless Tuscan bread. We couldn't buy hard liquor (gasp!), but we could purchase wine or settle for a small glass of the house red. The one hard-and-fast rule was that we were not supposed to leave the hotel.

I had a single room, 602, that would have been five stars if the windows weren't blacked out and covered with plywood, diminishing its charms considerably. Still, it was home for now, so I laid out my comb-and-brush set and emptied my steamer trunk into the closet. One whole floor of the Excelsior was for the American internees: me; my old pal Allen; his wife, Terri; four other journalists and the wives of three of them; Anthony, a Black jazz singer from L.A. who was on tour when war was declared; Ron, an Italian American from a wine-making family who was being forced to take sides; and Betsy Skinkhaven, a humorless elderly woman from Chattanooga, Tennessee, with gray skin and hair who owned a hotel in San Gimignano and swore she was going to keep filing lawsuits against Mussolini until she got her rightful property back. I had dubbed us the Thirteen. There was no sign of Lila.

"Did she make it out of the country?" I asked Allen.

"I don't know. They haven't allowed us any contact with the outside world."

I'd been to some awkward parties in my life, but this guest list made for especially tough conversations. We had nothing in common other than our nationality and weren't quite sure what to do with ourselves. For a couple of days, we all stayed in our rooms and read the newspapers we already had, now a week old. Once I had memorized everything including the classified ads (WANTED: SHOE TREES WOMEN'S SIZE 5), I started creeping into the hallways to see if anyone had any new information on when we were going to get out of there. No one did. Then we opened our doors and got to know one another. Terri, brisk and practical in plaid dresses, mentioned at least once in every conversational exchange, no matter how brief, that she'd been a copywriter for an ad agency before she got married and quit to follow her husband around the world. I sensed she regretted that decision. She discovered a pack of cards and a Monopoly game in a lost-and-found box in a hallway closet, and organized tournaments. Anthony got a few of us to sing in a nightly talent show competition we dubbed "Radio Siena," even though of course we were forbidden any access to an actual radio. I emceed the talent shows to try to keep everyone's spirits up, but it was a slog: musically about all we had in common was "Happy Birthday." I taught myself to juggle. I watched a coy flirtation develop between Betsy and a stooped elderly waiter who brought her tea every afternoon.

"You must have an Italian boyfriend," Terri said to me one day as we played gin rummy in the lounge. "Your Italian is so good."

Though she was not to the manor born, Terri struck me as a type of woman I'd seen quite a bit in high society: very intelligent, with not enough to do. I guessed the wives of foreign correspondents found themselves in that same trap. Boredom drove them to pry into the lives of others. There were always heavy doses of unasked-for interference and opinions.

"I have an ear for languages," I said.

"Oh, c'mon. Some things you only learn in . . . private."

"I had some fun in Rome," I said cautiously.

"But no real romance? That's a shame. Half the fun of being young is falling in love."

Ah. I saw where this was going. Matchmaking, usually in ill-advised directions, was a major activity for this kind of woman. I decided to play along.

"I just don't feel pretty. I don't think men are attracted to me."

"You're very pretty!"

"I could use some hair color."

"Why don't you let it grow out to your natural shade? It's red, isn't it? I can see it coming through. Blond doesn't suit you. Doesn't go with the freckles. The men will be all over you."

Irritated, I played four hearts. "Do you ever worry that we go to so much trouble to look attractive, but men just see us as something to use and discard?"

Terri looked over her cards at me. "Oh, honey. Well, certainly, that's how some men think about women. Okay, a lot of them. But some want to fall in love and marry their best friend. Allen did."

I was reasonably sure that back in Rome, Allen had been having an affair with his Italian secretary, but I was not unkind enough to point this out.

"What if he's the only one?" I asked.

Terri put down four diamonds. "We'll be back home soon, and you'll only have American men to choose from." She leaned in close and whispered, "And they're not very romantic."

That told me more about Allen than I wanted to know.

"You should fall in love with a handsome Italian," said Terri. "I'm going to help you make that happen."

"I hope he makes house calls."

✡

Lying in bed that night, listening to the sounds of troops marching under my blacked-out window, chanting their war songs, I thought about what Terri had said. Maybe love wasn't such a terrible idea. I was only in Italy for as long as internment lasted, then I'd be plunked down in America with no family, no contacts, and no job. After the disaster with Roddy, I'd avoided romance. I should have some fun now. What else was this damn war good for? That's what Patsy would say, anyway.

But who to have this hypothetical wild romance with? The hotel staff, with the exception of Betsy's elderly waiter, wanted nothing to do with the Thirteen, knowing full well that their *schedature* would fill up with red marks if they consorted with the enemy. Having an affair with one of the other twelve would be convenient, but seemed a bit incestuous. If it went wrong, I couldn't walk away. As the Bon Vivant, I had learned a lot about how people take sides in a breakup.

I needed to get out of the hotel.

Lapo

"Each one of them is Christ on the cross," said a despondent Roghi. Lapo and Roghi were walking the vineyard at Belsederino, going up and down the rows examining the soil and the leafless trunks of the vines. In the weeks since the visit to Rome, Lapo had apologized over and over. Roghi had taken the news about Michele becoming the dictator's sparring partner with great stoicism, but Lapo knew he had let the old man down.

Each vine had a central trunk and two outstretched arms that visually echoed the crucifixion, and they were the estate's saviors. Wine was their big cash crop, along with olive oil. If the grapes were unhappy, it would be a very bad year for everyone. Though they could easily grow enough food and raise enough animals to feed themselves, the government was requisitioning more and more of what they produced. Germany had not chosen Italy as an ally for sentimental reasons—Hitler was demanding that Italy's fertile fields feed its army and hungry Germans across its expanding empire. Making and selling wine this year would give Lapo a financial cushion to face the uncertain days, months, and years ahead. Plus, he had government agricultural loans to repay—he was acutely conscious that Mussolini's regime could call in those loans at any point.

It was February, and as if being at war was not bad enough, they were also in a freezing drought. Olives tolerated cold nights but not a prolonged freeze. Their grapes were more resilient, but the plants would need some water to get through this month. They'd have to coddle the grapes if they wanted wine, and the olives if they wanted olive oil, not to mention plant the wheat soon for bread and pasta, and in a month or so start a rotating set of vegetables in the farm gardens. They also needed to tend the fig, pear, and apple trees in the orchard. These were the staples that had fed people on this land since before recorded history, and he hoped they would feed them next summer.

"I don't know," said Roghi, looking at the cloudless sky. Lapo knew this was code for "we're all going to starve to death."

"It will rain," he said, although he shared the older man's fears. Roghi and his wife, Luisa, were bent and hardened by the decades they'd spent as sharecrop farmers. They were the first family Lapo had invited to come live at Belsederino. They contained so much wisdom in their graying heads. He knew he should take notes when Roghi talked about how the color of the soil should look at the time of planting, and when Luisa looked at the sky and knew it was the right moment to find a certain mushroom, stalk of wild asparagus, or wild herb that would cure a headache. He worried that if he didn't get that knowledge down in some form, it would die with them, but despite a rather stolid exterior, Michele seemed to have absorbed an amazing amount. Lapo reminded himself that oral traditions were vibrant, too. At least as long as the chain of transmission existed.

Michele was missed on the farm. He was young and strong, and now he and all the others in their twenties and thirties were gone, leaving only the older generations to do the hard physical labor of growing food to keep them alive. The past two months without him had been difficult on all of them, and Lapo had not gotten much writing done.

"We're going to be all right," Lapo said. "Look how far we've come already. You and I rebuilt Belsederino. It was dead, and we brought it back to life."

"It was merely sleeping," Roghi said. He was in charge of the vines and the olives, but he really helped Lapo with almost anything he needed, including the horses, which had now become their only means of transportation besides bicycles. He and Luisa had made Amoroso into the charming place it was, with its cool stone and brick, uneven terra-cotta floors, wooden shutters, space for animals below and people above, climbing jasmine, a bench under the linden tree, and a table on the patio that was always ready to welcome guests.

Roghi and Lapo went over the list of what needed to be delivered, repaired, planted, fixed, or rebuilt that day. Mulino was the millhouse on the river below the castle, where apparently the footing of the bridge was crumbling and needed to be shored up. Volpaia was the sunniest house, sitting exposed to the elements out in the stone-walled pastures. That's where Lapo's favorite tenant, Fosca, lived and kept her sheep and cattle. Fosca was in her nineties but stronger than Michele. Lapo checked on her as often as he could, and she always greeted him with a pail of milk and a cheery hello. She was their cheese maker, producing large wheels of *pecorino* that sat in rows on wooden shelves in her aging room. Though most people ate it aged, Lapo loved the cheese when it was only a few days old, melting in his mouth with the sharp tang of fresh milk and grass. On winter nights when they were too tired to cook, he and Eleanor used to melt it in a frying pan and scoop it up with bread while reading poetry aloud to each other and playing records on the Victrola.

"Volpaia needs a fencing check."

"Got it," said Lapo.

"The chimney's smoking again at Castagneto." Castagneto was the house buried deep in the chestnut forest, where in ancient times the *carbonaio* supplied charcoal for the estate and to sell in Siena. That's where the Pappone family lived—Felice's mother, Prima, and his father, Giovanni, who worked as Lapo's game warden, keeping poachers away from the woods and monitoring the health of the fields and forests and all their inhabitants. Felice grew up there, though he was now quartered at the fortress in Siena. Lapo still held out hope that there was some good in Felice Pappone, that somehow one day he would wake up and say, "I've been a horrible person, but now I will do better." He realized the futility of this hope, but held on to it nonetheless.

"Smoking chimney, got it," Lapo said. It was going to be a long day.

"Without Michele, it's going to be hard to get it all done," said Roghi. "We're going to need some diesel to run the tractor."

"Is it essential? We didn't even own one until a few years ago."

Roghi rolled his eyes. "We had young men around then. If we want wine, it is. When it finally rains, you don't want the weeds stealing all the water from the grapes. Guess we shouldn't have sold the oxen after all."

This was a justified dig at Lapo's expense. He'd wanted the tractor, and Roghi had fought it, pointing out that farmers had worked without tractors for tens of thousands of years, and it would make them soft to use one now. "In one generation, the knowledge of how to farm with animals will disappear," Roghi had said. "And then if the damn machines stop working, we're going to be screwed."

He was right, of course. They were now utterly dependent on the tractor, which was utterly dependent on diesel, which was impossible to get.

Roghi said, "We can try it with the horses, if they're strong enough. I have my doubts. This clay soil is like stone. They don't call it *Maremma amara* for nothing." Bitter Maremma.

"All right," Lapo said. "I'll see if I can get us some fuel."

He'd have to pull strings, which always meant different strings would be pulled in return, unknown strings. Ciano's plan to bring Il Duce to Belsederino had fortunately not come to fruition due to war pressures, but a swarm of officials and reporters had come for photo ops that led to multipage spreads in *Il Popolo d'Italia*, the official newspaper of Fascism, proclaiming Belsederino to be a triumph of modern Italian know-how. Preparing for the visit and farming had allowed him to postpone writing the biography, but his excuses were running out.

That night, Lapo looked at his bank statement, open on the desk. Pathetic. He had eighteen people on the estate who were counting on him to keep them safe from the war. Writing a glowing biography of Il Duce was not such a terrible sacrifice. People had lost their families, their homes, all their savings. What would he lose? The ability to look at himself in the mirror? He could take down the mirrors.

Pappone's car was followed not by the diesel tank truck Lapo was expecting, but by a delivery truck painted black. The paint was flaking and Lapo could see a *panificio* logo underneath. He waited, perplexed, as Pappone parked about a hundred yards away in the empty field, heaved himself out, removed a riding crop from his left boot, and used it like an airport mechanic to wave the truck into alignment with his car. He then opened the metal doors at the back of the truck and began gesturing to whatever was inside. Lapo was confused, then shocked as people began to jump out. Tall, short, male, female, young, old, of every shape and size, they had one thing in common that stood out to Lapo: they were city people. Pappone strode over to Lapo.

"*Buongiorno,*" said Lapo cautiously. "I was expecting diesel for the tractor—?"

"I have something better for you," said Pappone, with a grand gesture of his riding crop. "Farmworkers."

Lapo frowned. "Uh . . . with all due respect, these do not look like farmworkers."

"They're enemies of the state," said Pappone quickly. "You'll be in charge of them."

"Enemies of the state?!"

"I'm a violinist," offered one older man in a thin winter coat.

"I teach linguistics at the university," called a stout woman smoothing her plaid skirt. Two little girls who looked to be about eight and ten ran off behind her.

"Stagehand," called a young person with a crew cut.

"Shut up," said Pappone. "You spoke negatively about Fascism and now you are all farmworkers."

Lapo struggled to understand. "Dear Pappone, am I to understand that you want me to employ these people? I don't have any way to pay them."

"You don't have to. They're prisoners. They will work in exchange for food."

"I don't have enough food to feed them."

"They are here to grow their own food."

"What?"

Pappone snapped, "They complained about our new Italian society, so they have lost their rights. They must do useful work and take care of themselves and then we will reconsider their status in a year or two."

"Why am I in charge of them? I'm not a prison guard."

Pappone's face reddened. "You are the beneficiary of all that is good about the new Italy. You have lots of land that can be used to feed its occupants."

"These people are not strong-backed farmhands, they're educated city people. Maybe they do criticize the regime now and then. Why is that something worth getting jailed for? Criticism helps us improve."

"Dissenters have no place in Italy."

"Look. I'm not going to argue politics with you. All I need is diesel to run my tractor and then I can feed half of the city. But with this crew and no tractor, we may not even survive until summer. Please take them away."

"It is your duty to give them a chance to feed themselves."

"Is it my duty to let them starve if they can't?"

Pappone turned to the group assembled by the truck. "Unload the tents, you lazy assholes. And the shovels! I brought you lots of shovels," he said to Lapo as if he had brought filet of salmon. "They were supposed to go to the Russian front to dig trenches, but I thought they would be more useful here."

Lapo sucked in his breath. "These people are going to live *here*?"

"That way they can work harder. Round the clock. They have tents, and they will dig pit toilets. I've brought a month's bread rations to tide them over until the vegetable crops start coming in."

"A month? Even if we start today, we won't have food in a month. This is crazy. It's suicidal."

"Are you questioning the wisdom of Il Duce?"

"I'm questioning the wisdom of burdening me with thirty more people to look after when I'm supposed to be writing a book for him."

"Fine," said Pappone. "I will shoot them instead. That's what political prisoners deserve, anyway. I was trying to be kind. And save on ammunition." He turned to the group and yelled, "Okay, line up. One behind the other." He whispered, "I will try to save bullets by shooting two at once."

Lapo, frozen, whispered, "What are you talking about? Are you insane? These are human beings. Some of them are children."

"Exactly. So save their lives. Take them off my hands."

✡

"You're finally doing a great thing with that writing of yours," said Pappone through the car window as he circled before pulling out onto the rutted road. "Not telling those stupid little stories of unimportant people. People need to know Il Duce's story. That's what's important."

Lapo had no response for this. He stood immobilized by panic, watching thirty people with soft hands and nice shoes and pathetically inadequate winter clothing wander about, struggling to lift heavy canvas tents, confused but much less frightened than they should have been.

"Oh, I almost forgot," said Pappone, retrieving a letter from his inside pocket and handing it to Lapo.

Lapo glanced down and saw it was from his son. He restrained himself from ripping it open. No doubt Pappone had already read it. Pappone gave Lapo the straight-armed Fascist salute and pulled away. The truck followed him, rattling over the bumps and stirring up a tornado of dust.

"I'll be with you in a minute!" Lapo called to the new inhabitants of Belsederino, who were standing about in awkward groups amid piles of luggage. One woman was holding a cage of parakeets, another a caramel-colored domestic rabbit. "Welcome!" To himself he muttered, "Madonna, mother of God, help me."

He turned and Roghi's wife, Luisa, was standing there, feeding the chickens, throwing out handfuls of grain to the eager birds, who pecked and squabbled with one another.

"You did the right thing," she said. "But Gesu Cristo, what the hell are we going to do?"

✿

Roghi and Luisa agreed to help the new arrivals set up their camp in the orchard a short way from the castle. The rows of apple trees would give them a sense of order and individual space, Lapo hoped. He said he would be back soon with whatever food he could find and a plan. He disappeared into the castle, trying to appear calm and confident. His heart was pounding.

First things first. He opened the envelope and removed the letter. Doves cooed outside the doorway as he read Alessandro's neat handwriting. When he finished reading, he sat down on the wooden bench in the hallway and tried to process his feelings. Alessandro said he was fine, Prague was beautiful, and the unit assigned to the embassy was also assisting the German Army "in keeping order." He did not say exactly what that meant. To anyone else, the letter was full of dedication to the Fascist mission, but Lapo could read between the lines. Alessandro described life in Prague as "beautiful as our old horse Clivia." Clivia was indeed beautiful, but also impossible, unpredictable, and dangerous, and they had ultimately sold her. He said he was mostly inspecting documents at checkpoints around the city, which made him feel as proud as "Prince Inga of Pingaree." Eleanor had read to the children from the L. Frank Baum books as a child. Lapo knew he meant the book where Inga saves his people when they're enslaved by evil raiders from another land. That book scared Alessandro so much as a little boy that he hid under the covers during those chapters. He ended by saying there was a rumor they were being reassigned to Greece soon, "because our Italian Army is as strong as Hercules." The censors would think he meant the Greek god, but they'd had a spaniel named Hercules who was so terrified of everything he never left Eleanor's lap. Alessandro was afraid, unhappy, in danger.

Even if Lapo could summon comforting words, there was no return address to write to him. *O God,* he thought, *please help me. I know I have not been a good Catholic, but I haven't been a terrible one, either. Please help my son.*

But he couldn't wait for God on this one; he needed to work every possible angle to keep Alessandro from being transferred to the front lines. He looked over to where Roghi was directing the prisoners to set up their tents. He had a couple of hours before anyone would expect a meal. He jogged upstairs to his study and sat down to write.

Sally

"We should find you an Italian artist. Or maybe a soldier, but not one of those ardent Fascists. Or a chef." Terri and I were teaching Allen to play bridge, which he said made his brain hurt. Anthony made up the foursome.

"Hmm," I said, staring at my cards. I was finding Terri increasingly tiresome. Frankly, I was finding all of them—and myself—tiresome. It wasn't really their fault—I had cabin fever. We all did.

"What if I just had an imaginary affair? Isn't the crush the purest expression of love because it's not acted on? It runs free in whatever direction it wants, then dies a peaceful death, and no one cries or throws themselves out a window."

Allen, who loved flaunting his knowledge of Italian history, said, "Pia de' Tolomei. Sienese woman whose husband accused her of adultery and threw her out a window. Thirteen hundreds, I think. Mussolini made domestic violence legal again, you know. Keep that in mind when you're dating Italians."

Anthony put down a trick. "Stick with the crush. A good crush can change your life. Look at Dante and Beatrice. He only saw her once, on the street, but he spent his whole life in love with her, and she inspired his greatest work."

"Come on, you guys, a crush is not going to cut the mustard," said Terri. "Sally is young and beautiful. She needs to fall in love."

I was mad now. "You guys must be really bored if you're spending your time thinking about my romantic possibilities."

"Everything else is grim," said Allen. "With the windows all boarded up, you're our sunshine."

Tears sprung involuntarily to my eyes, and I fake coughed and turned away. "Sunshine" was what Ma used to call me. *La luz del sol.* My father didn't like it when she spoke Spanish to us, but I loved it. I barely thought about my childhood these days. Where were Ma and the others now? Baby Margaret would be twelve this year, older than I was when I left home. Victor was nineteen, about to turn twenty. It hit me that he was probably in the U.S. Army or Navy by now. Or the Air Force—would he fly the plane that dropped the bomb we all dreaded on our heads?

☼

I stood in the lobby and studied the situation. The Thirteen tended to gather there all day playing games, drinking coffee, and chatting. Today the *New York Times* correspondent was playing gin rummy with the United Press correspondent. I knew that when we commandeered the piano to sing campfire songs, it deeply annoyed the hotel staff and the nonprisoner guests, most of whom were military higher-ups. Like good Americans everywhere, we tended to ignore the stares and blithely carry on at maximum volume. The tuxedoed hotel manager, a staunch Fascist who saluted and fawned over every Italian or German official who came through the revolving doors, loathed the noisy Americans.

I stepped over to the piano and sat down. *What is the most annoying song in the world?* I asked myself. "Home, home on the range . . ." I belted it loud enough to drown out an air raid siren. The manager frowned and glared at me. When I finished three rounds of the song, and three of "Clementine," I stood up and marched toward the revolving door.

"I'm going out," I announced to the guard. "*Vado fuori.*"

"No, *signorina,*" he said, blocking me. "*Non é possibile.*"

"Please? There is zero reason to fear that any of us Americans under house arrest will try to escape Siena."

"Still, is called house arrest," he said.

The manager came over, looking peeved.

"What is going on, *signorina*?" he demanded. "What do you want now?"

"Can't we think of house arrest as more of a concept than a rule? If you let us go out during the day, the hotel will be so quiet and peaceful without us."

The manager considered this as I hummed a few more bars of "Clementine." He said to the guard, "They're all going to be sent back home within a few months anyway, right, as soon as the diplomatic exchange can be negotiated?"

"Yes," the guard said cautiously.

"What if we just did a mandatory check-in once a day? Make it twice. Morning and evening. They can leave the hotel during the day—"

"Dawn to dinnertime," I said.

"Eight A.M. to eight P.M.," said the manager to the guard.

The guard went to talk to his superiors.

"Congratulations," he said when he returned. "You can go out."

"Hey, everybody—" I started to say.

"No." He stopped me. "Just you. No one else. You can bring back whatever they need."

La luz del sol?

"If you violate the rules," he continued, "we will shoot one of them. One person will die each time you are late returning."

I assembled the Thirteen in the ballroom, where we held our talent shows. "Good news and bad news," I began.

Naturally, they were miffed. I was seen as disloyal, and some people said I shouldn't go out at all, if no one else could.

Terri intervened on my behalf. "She can get us cigarettes," she said.

"And hair dye."

"Strawberry jam."

"Ribbons."

"Razor blades."

"Pinking shears."

"Stockings."

"Chocolate!"

"An American newspaper."

"Better toilet paper."

"Typewriter ribbon."

"Drawing paper."

The list of things they wanted went on and on, most of which I would never be able to find during wartime, but I promised to try.

I donned my navy-blue dress and ankle boots. I made sure my POW armband was visible—that was one of the rules, that I could never take it off when

I was outside the hotel. I had a special pass from the guard that I also carried with me. I chose the adorable pointy harlequin hat by Schiaparelli—not practical in the least, but so chic.

As the others watched, I walked past the guard and stepped outside the plywood-boarded front door for the first time in two months, ready to breathe and feel the sun. Of course, I forgot it was February, and I found myself immediately soaked in a freezing rain, since my adorable hat covered about three square inches of my head. Still, I stood there until I began to shiver, taking in the slate-gray sky, the wet pavement, the grinding roar of passing trucks on cobblestones. I crossed the street to the *tabaccaio,* bought all the cigarettes our ration cards would allow for everyone else, a copy of the fashion magazine *Gioia* for me, and went back inside. Freedom!

Prague

1942

Alessandro

It looked like the snow was falling only in the broad cones under the streetlamps, not in the darkness beyond, but of course it was piling up on everything—the parked cars, the tanks, the concrete barricades, and Alessandro's own head. He was standing in Wenceslas Square, holding a gun, making sure no one expressed any political opinions. At his back was the massive equestrian statue of the saint, the patron of Bohemia. He knew this square, or rather this very long rectangle, had been the traditional site of political gatherings and protests for centuries. The Germans knew that if there was any place in Prague the Czechs would choose to protest the Nazi knee on their necks, again, this was it.

Trains were leaving Prague every day, taking the city's Jews to a fortress called Terezin.

He had to get out of this war.

A Panzer rumbled past in the nightly show of force. It blared the German national anthem from speakers on the front. Six German soldiers sat on top, pointing their guns at anyone left on the street. They passed a bottle around, then one of them threw it through a shop window with a loud smash. Alessandro remembered something a professor had said about how as societies collapse, they spend more and more on war, police, and prisons. That professor had then disappeared. Alessandro had sat in the lecture hall that first semester, a skinny kid with wild hair, envisioning a future for himself as a professor or an artist, or a writer like his father. He would travel the world and live at Belsederino. Raise a family there. He was pretty sure he had imagined actual butterflies. That it would be an existence of peace and love was a given. By the end of that year, that imagined halcyon future was obliterated. Less than four years later, he *was* the police, and the war, and the prison. He couldn't remember the last time he had seen a butterfly.

Bundled figures hurried along the sidewalks. It was nearly eight, when curfew began. The snow had quieted the city.

Because the suicide bomber got through the checkpoint, the Germans came and took Carlo away. The Italians assumed they shot him. No one talked about it. Alessandro felt a poisonous mix of fear and guilt. He didn't eat. He didn't speak to anyone. He did his guard duty, he marched from the embassy or his assigned checkpoint to the barracks in the pensione and back. He didn't even read, he just lay in his narrow bed staring at the ceiling. And then, on the second night, just before eleven, a trumpet suddenly blared through the hotel. He jumped out of bed and mustered in the hallway for one of the periodic inspections they were subject to. As his commanding officer stormed through the rooms, overturning furniture and berating the men, Alessandro recognized what the trumpeter was playing. It was *The Radetzky March*. He knew the piece well. Strauss composed it to celebrate the squelching of northern Italy's attempt to remove itself from Austrian dominion in the 1800s. It was a stupid thing to play to inspire Italians to greatness. The Fascists acted as if these wonderful ideas of empire and domination were only logical and natural and that of course they would succeed, ignoring the fact that humans always find a way to throw off authority. He knew that Italy would eventually, like a horse whose rider beat it while starving it, throw off Mussolini, and the Czechs would throw off Hitler. But how many innocent people, regular people, would die in the process? Why did the world have to be yanked around by a handful of power-hungry assholes, again and again and again?

As he stood in the freezing hallway in army-issued underwear in a rigid salute, it hit him how stupid it was to blame himself for Carlo's death. Neither he nor Carlo should have been shot for letting the woman through, because no one should have provoked her to give up her life to protest the occupation of her city, because no one should be occupying the city, because the entire war was wrong. He was filled with a rage he could barely suppress.

His commanding officer berated a few people for tarnished buttons, spattered boots, and unauthorized pornography. Then they all went back to bed. At dawn they were back to their duties at the embassy, outside the barracks, or at checkpoints. The Nazis were now keeping the Italians far from Prague's Jewish population—which made Alessandro suspicious. He decided to start keeping his eyes open for a way out. He was angry at the snow, the never-ending cold, the slush, the way people walked or didn't walk, talked or didn't talk, the beige food, the gray sky, his fellow soldiers, his own feet. His rage fueled him—it kept guilt and depression at bay, gave him forward momentum—but it also consumed him. He lost more weight and had terrible nightmares. In the moments after he awakened every day, fear threatened to overwhelm him. He would snarl at the nearest person for anything at all—"What are you looking at, asshole?"—and suddenly he was functioning again. In a way.

Then he ran out of anger. He snapped at a fellow soldier who'd just given him a candy bar. "What the fuck is this?" And then he started to laugh. Couldn't stop, just laughed and laughed. Couldn't summon rage anymore. But he couldn't allow other emotions to rush into the void, so he retreated into a safe robotic dullness. He had the sensation he was at the bottom of a swimming pool, hearing everyone talk through six feet of shimmering water.

Unfortunately, things got worse. Within days of the bombing of their HQ, the Germans had instituted huge crackdowns on the Czechs, and they were making the handful of Italians in the city do some of the dirty work. Alessandro found himself harassing innocent people for doing nothing except walking down the street, going to school, or riding the tram. He was supposed to arrest anyone who had a gnome in their yard because it was now a symbol of opposition to the Nazis. He retreated further inside himself as he waved his gun in their faces, and he saw them retreat inside themselves. He feigned aggression; they were not feigning fear and hatred.

He marched back and forth in front of the statue of Wenceslas on his horse, humming, peering out into the snow, willing himself to find some way out of this war. He sent a silent prayer to the alchemists, the heretics, the revolutionaries of the past. Prague felt like it had subterranean magic to him, as if all this concrete and stone under his feet had been poured over a secret cache of magic that was one day going to start leaching out. It would emit a strange sulfuric odor at first that would come out of manholes, then maybe a hissing sound people would hear in certain cellars, then boom—a cloud of white rabbits would appear over Prague Castle. Magic would be back with a vengeance, enveloping the city in illogical, irrational joy.

"Beautiful night," said a voice nearby in Czech-accented Italian. He turned and saw a man in his sixties or seventies, tall and thin, a white goatee under a black hat. "It's cold. I brought you some soup."

Alessandro hesitated. Was this a trap?

"It's not poisoned," the man said with a laugh. "I'll show you." He took a spoonful himself. "Garlic soup," he said. "Czech cure for a hangover, but it's also good on a cold night."

The other Italian guard called out, "I had it the other night. Delicious. Bring more next time." He waved Alessandro toward the man. "I'll cover for you."

Alessandro frowned, but walked over and took the bowl and tasted it. It was delicious. "Why are you being nice to us?" he asked. The soup warmed his insides. The garlic was pungent and diffused through him like an embrace.

"You're Italians. You're far from home. You probably hate the cold. Where are you from?"

"Tuscany."

"Ah. The most beautiful place in the world."

"Prague is beautiful, too."

"Yes. Listen. I want to tell you about this spot."

Alessandro stiffened. Was this a setup?

The man whispered, "You know that this is where the Czechs gathered to protest the Nazi 'protectorate' two years ago?"

Alessandro nodded, thinking of his own failed protest in Siena. He'd heard thousands of people had appeared in November of '39, carrying signs, singing, and chanting. The Germans opened fire on the crowd. They had later shot nine students who organized the protest, and sent thousands of others to camps.

"I wasn't here then."

"It was a terrible day."

"You were there?"

"Do you know something of the history of the Czechs?"

"I do. I am—was—a history major. I wish I could go up to the castle to see where Kafka lived, and the Arcimboldo self-portrait in the National Gallery."

The man laughed. "Another Italian far from home. I was a history major, too. That was a long time ago. Eventually I changed to business."

Alessandro finished the soup and handed the bowl back to him. "Thank you."

"Do you know the Czech word *pamětnik*?"

"I'm ashamed to say I don't know much Czech at all."

"It means 'witness,' but more than that. It's the word you use when you are talking about someone who is a firsthand witness to history."

"Like you, being there for the protest?"

The man looked right at him. "And you. The anger is not so visible right now, but make no mistake, the Czech people will reclaim their country."

He walked away, the snow swirling around him as the darkness consumed him. The streetlights clicked off one by one down the square, and the lights of the city with them. Alessandro was standing in total darkness. It was silent until he heard the crunch of boots on snow.

"Bit of a screw loose, right?" said his fellow soldier. "Going on about old shit no one cares about. I mean, this is Germany now. Get over it. But the soup is good."

Alessandro nodded, feeling the gentle burn of snowflakes on his cheeks.

Siena

1942

Sally

The next day, I dolled myself up as warmly as I could and headed out. It was cold, but at least the rain had stopped. The city was a labyrinth constructed on several steep hilltops, I discovered, a warren of twisting, narrow streets that led me up and down in circles or dumped me at dead ends at the city walls. I got lost, then found I was not far from the hotel after all. I finally made it to the heart of the maze, Piazza del Campo, where Terri had told me the famous Palio horse race was held twice each summer. Thinking of romance and hoping to at least bring a good story back to the Thirteen, I ogled the young soldiers piling up sandbags. It was the first day of Lent, and I was conscious of the fact that everyone I passed had ash on their forehead, while I had no ash but my red POW armband. I was stopped by a militia patrol in the piazza, but the man just read my pass and waved me on. It was all much more low-key than I expected, after months of being cooped up.

I made my way back to the hotel well before my curfew and found everyone waiting for me. I handed out their smokes, lipstick for Betsy, curlers for Terri, and a few other shopping requests. They all waited eagerly for a story from the outside world. I told them what I had seen, the places I visited, but I could see it wasn't grabbing them. They wanted an adventure. If they were going to live vicariously through me, I owed them some thrills. I vowed to try harder the next day.

I kept going back out every day, in all weather. I was careful to adhere to the rules so I didn't lose my privileges (or get anyone shot). I always wore my red armband, even when it clashed with my outfit. But because of the armband and the fear that talking to me would end up on their *schedatura* as "fraternizes with the enemy," no locals wanted to actually interact with me. I bought things, I walked around. Some people muttered insults at me as I passed, but mostly they averted their eyes and left me alone. I was persona non grata, invisible. I could see that my reports at the talent show the Thirteen held most nights were disappointing. As a nightclub performer, I was bombing. The whole talent show started to feel depressing, and we began skipping nights. The Thirteen turned inward once again, and people seemed listless, like zoo animals. Every day was the same. I needed to be way more entertaining to keep their spirits up.

Since my pass didn't seem to have geographic limits on it, I began to venture outside the walls of the city, past the men with machine guns who smoked bottomless packs of cigarettes. They barely glanced at my documents, and I tried not to sneeze in their faces. I was surprised by how little they cared about me. The hills that surrounded Siena were sensuous curves, mostly deep reddish brown in this winter season. I borrowed one of the hotel's bikes so I could go farther and still make it back in time. Because Siena was uphill from everything around it, this meant at the end of the day, I was pushing the bike. But it was worth the effort—I felt free in the cold wind, vistas stretching before me. For the Thirteen, I described the farmers in their clean winter fields, stark orchards and bare vineyards just starting to sprout tendrils and leaves. The new travelogues raised a flicker of interest. "Any flirting?" asked Terri. Unfortunately, I told her, the farmers were all women—apparently all the men had been called up to military service.

The hotel kept our ration coupons for food, but I liked to linger outside bread shops because of the wonderful smell. One cold and windy day, I was inhaling the scent of fresh-baked bread in Via di Città when I felt a hand on my bottom. I turned around, instinctively lifting my arm to slap the offender, and found myself accosted by a sour-faced young Blackshirt officer. He grabbed my arm and held it, his face close to mine. "Prisoner," he growled. "It's illegal to wear trousers. Take them off."

I looked down at my sensible and warm tweed pants. "Here?"

"Yes. Right now. Do it." His pig face grinned at me.

There were people passing by, averting their eyes, doing nothing. I didn't seem to have a choice. I pictured walking back to the hotel, all the way across the city, in my silk culottes. Would a band of jeering Fascists follow me, or worse? Just as I was putting my hands on my belt, I felt a whoosh of air, and a woman holding an old-fashioned broom made from twigs thrust herself between me and the Blackshirt.

"Felice Pappone, *you're* wearing trousers," she said. She herself was wearing gray flannel pants and a white apron. I recognized her from the bakery.

The Blackshirt shouted at her in inflated fury, "I am a man!"

She narrowed her eyes. "All the men are at the front. If we women have to do their work and ours, we should at least be able to wear what we want."

He spat at her, "Il Duce does not believe women should wear pants, and Il Duce is always right."

"First he outlaws pants, then divorce and contraception. It's too much."

"Italy's population needs to grow." He was not backing away, and neither was she. I admired her. I never saw people stand up to Fascists.

"Oh, really?" She waved her broom. "And who's going to feed all these children you want us to have? I didn't even get my flour allotment this week."

I could see she was getting the man's goat. His face turned red. "I'm writing you up, *signora*," he said, putting a finger in her chest. "This is going on your *schedatura*."

"Excellent. Please make sure you write that I am not happy you men have decided a husband beating his wife is no longer a crime."

"Definitely not in your case," he said, which made her eyes blaze even more. I was trying to inch away into the shadows.

"And now we women can only work in family businesses? You think you can decide that you own our bodies?" Her face was right in his. "You think we don't notice that we're starving to death and you're sending our sons to die in far-off places?"

"It's the fault of the American capitalists," he said, gesturing at me.

"She's a girl," she said fiercely. "A guest here. You try to make people fear the wrong monsters, but we know who is to blame for all of this."

He turned on me. "Go back and change!" he shouted.

✡

I recounted the story to the Thirteen that night in the ballroom.

"You got lucky," said Betsy.

"I'll say," said Terri. "That lady was brave." Everyone seemed to have a story of Italian neighbors and friends standing up to the oppressive Fascist laws in small ways, whether it was running a black-market business, evading taxes, or mocking the Blackshirts. Not all these stories ended happily—as it was for the women I had met in prison, punishment was often severe.

We were sitting in semidarkness on the floor of the ballroom, drinking the house red. Lit only by a few candles, the room was ornate, with high ceilings, made for the kind of formal gathering I used to write about. Now it felt intimate and real, a participant itself in the stories we were sharing.

"I guess we're lucky we can go back to America," I said. "But it's funny that I don't feel that way."

"Me either," said Betsy.

"Except for Fascism, I love Italian culture," said Allen, a sentiment echoed by Anthony, Betsy, and the others, half sprawled on pillows on the Turkish carpets. "And I'm not just talking about the food. They have a healthy perspective here on life that Americans don't."

Our conversations about Italy always went this way—they inevitably led us back to an analysis of America, our homeland. I talked about my family's poverty, and the way I was treated as a child on the streets of Los Angeles. I talked about the ridiculous waste of wealth I saw as part of my job—money spent on lobster bisque and ballroom decorations when so many people were living on the streets. Allen talked about corruption in politics, and nepotism. Betsy talked about being an unmarried woman, how people looked down on her, and how she couldn't get a loan without a male cosigner. Terri talked about her first marriage and how it was impossible to get a divorce unless one person claimed battery or adultery. I talked about Patsy's experience of growing up in Chinatown and Hollywood. And Anthony finally felt safe enough to speak up about racism and Jim Crow laws. "I've never voted in an election in my life," he said. "And not for lack of trying." He spelled out a reality that the rest of us couldn't even imagine— schools without books, neighborhoods that were off-limits, getting turned away at hotels and restaurants, being treated worse than a stray dog. "I don't live in the same America you do," he said. "It's a different country."

"It's true," said Betsy quietly. "People say 'that's just the way things are,' as if that's any excuse. I hate it, but I don't know how to change it."

"It's disgusting," said Terri. "Here we are, telling the Europeans we're going to make the world safe for democracy when we don't even have it at home."

Ron, the Italian American winemaker, who had stayed silent for several days, hovering on the edge of our circle, exploded. "You people are terrible!" he shouted, leaping to his feet. "I've never heard such a bunch of whiners in my whole life," he thundered. "America is the greatest country in the world!"

Everyone was stunned into silence. The ballroom suddenly felt cavernous, our circle on the floor small and vulnerable.

"In many ways it is," I said at last. "But it's okay to admit it's not perfect. That's what makes our country strong, that we can say that. Italians can't."

Ron's face turned a deeper shade of red, even in the half-light from the candles, and he huffed through his nose. "Our boys are dying to keep you ingrates safe!" he shouted, and stormed out of the ballroom. I hardly saw him after that.

✿

One blustery, unseasonably chilly day in early April, I decided to forgo the bike ride I had planned and stay inside the city. I was admiring some paintings in the Palazzo Pubblico, memorizing each detail so I could describe them later. One was a painting of a city that kind of looked like Siena, if you squinted. Horses, falcons, hills, castles, fields, farmers, knights. Workers, dancers, threshers, weavers, hunters. Everyone looked happy and busy. An angel labeled SECURITY hovered over the open gate to the city as people came in and out.

The other huge mural also depicting the city was in poor repair due to water damage, but the horned devil in it was eye-catching.

"You must read it right to left," said a voice at my elbow. I turned and there stood a very, very old woman with bright blue eyes leaning on a cane. She was stylishly dressed in a Chanel knit suit, her white hair elegantly swept up and her jewelry simple but obviously expensive. "The painter did that to throw you off, so you'd feel doubly unsettled looking at it."

I was so shocked that after months of silence someone was actually talking to me that I stumbled over my words.

"How interesting," I said in Italian. "Thank you."

"The tyrant is cross-eyed, but you see that, can't you? Justice, of course, is bound and gagged at his feet." She paused, then pointed a gnarled finger toward another corner of the mural. "Disease. And there we have armies clashing on the darkling plain," she added in English. "Governments were being overthrown regularly when it was commissioned in the thirteen hundreds. The idea was to remind the politicians of what their higher calling was. To have a huge illustration right here, where decisions are made, of what the effects of good and bad government are."

"Oh," I said. It all made sense now.

"Of course, Florence has much more beautiful masterpieces, but I do love this one. There's nothing like it anywhere else in the world. Do you know Florence?"

"Only a little," I said. "I've been to some wonderful parties in Fiesole."

"Ah, the Berensons and the other Chiantishire foreigners in their lovely villas. You'd think I'd be angry they've colonized some of the prettiest places to live, but really I'm grateful. Very few Italians can afford to live that way and I'd hate to see those palaces turned into Futurist apartment blocks. Florence is where I'm from. The Florentines and the Sienese are like cats and dogs, you know."

I saw the guard across the room staring at us and frowning.

"I should go," I said.

"I could use some help with the lift," said the woman. I smiled politely at the guard as I helped her into the elevator. She held on to me and I was forced to get in with her. The woman said nothing as we jolted downward. "Let's go have an ice cream," she said brightly as the elevator doors opened on the ground floor and she trotted off into the freezing air.

I shivered at the thought. "I don't have any money, I'm afraid," I said. "I really need to get back to my hotel."

"I have money."

I pointed to the red armband, in case her vision was impaired or she didn't understand. "I'm under house arrest. I'm an American."

"How delightful. One of my sons married an American," she said. "Let's go just here, in the piazza. They have a sundae I love, with wafers. It's the bee's knees."

I laughed out loud at the antiquated American slang and let the old woman take my arm again. I had time before I needed to be back, and it was exciting to speak to someone other than the Thirteen. We walked slowly against the cold wind across the piazza and up to a café just to the left of the fountain. There were a few empty outdoor tables set up, umbrellas waving in the breeze. An old man with a stooped back in a long apron greeted us solicitously, not seeming to care about my armband. The woman asked after his schnauzer, who apparently had a limp.

"Better," the waiter said. "The tea you said to make is helping."

"You should have some of it, too." The old woman ordered ice cream for both of us, and the waiter disappeared. She turned to me and whispered, "The only men left to work are too old or too broken to be at the front."

By reflex, I glanced around at the other tables. Did she not understand that people ratted each other out to the OVRA constantly in exchange for protecting themselves and their families? This network of spying neighbors meant the secret police were effectively listening in on every conversation happening all over Italy. The kind of comment the old woman just made would land her a nice *schedatura* in a file at police headquarters if anyone was listening. I wondered why she would talk to a prisoner of war at all. *Maybe she wants to practice her English,* I thought, or maybe she was just lonely. Or crazy. Fortunately, it was so unseasonably cold and windy that no one seemed to be listening.

I looked out over the piazza, which, despite the war, was full of people going about their daily business. Men in suits with briefcases and fedoras, women in stylish dresses, gorgeous handbags, and fetching hats with small veils or jaunty feathers, children in school uniforms. A few soldiers goose-stepped past. Everyone but us seemed to have somewhere to be, and someone to be with.

"How do you know so much about dogs?" I asked her.

"Just an animal lover," said the woman. "When you get to be ninety-three, you know things."

"Ninety-three? Really?"

"Yes. I was born in 1848."

"That's . . . so long ago."

"Yes and no. That was another era of upheaval and war in Italy. My parents were part of the fight to throw off Austrian rule and unite Italy. Now I wonder if that was such a good idea. What is your name?"

"Sally Brady."

"Is that your real name?"

I was startled. "Um . . ." I said.

The woman leaned in and whispered, "You must practice. Learn to say, 'Of course it is!'"

I was mystified, and more than a little alarmed. How could this woman know my secret? "Of course it is," I said cautiously.

"Much better. You can call me Clio. I don't like informality, but I will tolerate it from you because you're an American."

This woman was definitely odd, but then again, she was small and frail and ninety-three years old, so not much of a threat.

"I should probably be getting back to the hotel."

"We haven't even gotten our ice cream yet. Don't be rude to an old lady."

I smiled, but felt slightly trapped.

"I'm tired of wars," Clio said. "I'm tired of men and their fighting."

The waiter arrived with two gigantic ice creams, the biggest I had ever seen, even counting Schwab's in Hollywood. Multiple scoops, whipped cream, cherries, huge chocolate wafers.

"Gee" was all I could say.

✿

As the Thirteen gathered in the ballroom that night, I was revved up that I had a story to tell. The others felt my excitement, and the talent show had the whole baker's dozen present. Anthony sang "Sophisticated Lady" to kick us off, but before we got to my report, the air raid siren went off. We were forced to file down into the hotel basement with the staff, where we were forbidden to speak. My story would have to wait. This wasn't a false alarm— the walls shuddered and dust fell on us as we heard explosion after explosion. It lasted for hours. The Italians down there turned angry eyes on us. And who could blame them? This was the Allies bombing them into submission, while their jobs were to cook us food and give us clean linens once a week. It wasn't fair.

Of course, the local papers, controlled by the MinCulPop, included only false reports of the air raid ("the weak and pathetic Allied bombers were shot down by our brave Italian Air Force and no damage was done"), but we heard whispered rumors that Siena's train station had been hit. I was nervous about going out into the city the next day, but made my way to the piazza unmolested. The city felt subdued, and I kept my eyes down the whole way. I was buying a comb for Betsy at a small shop when I heard Clio's voice say my name.

"*Buongiorno*," I said cautiously.

"Let's go have another ice cream."

I was nervous about sitting so prominently out in the open, but Clio insisted we take "our table." We ordered and sat in silence for a few minutes as people passed us.

"I have a granddaughter your age. You remind me of her," she said at last when the ice creams arrived.

I smiled politely and busied myself with my *gelato al limone*.

"Do you know about the racial laws?" she asked me.

"A little," I said cautiously. "Jewish people can't have Italian servants."

Clio nodded. "They can't send their children to regular schools, or own businesses. It's atrocious. But not as bad as in Austria, of course, where the Germans have taken over."

"I heard it's bad there." I was being drawn into a conversation I didn't want to have.

Clio looked around again. "My son was living in Vienna. The Italian government has closed the border to Jews fleeing Austria."

"Are you Jewish?" I asked quietly.

"I'm not. But his father was. And his wife is. So my grandchildren are three-quarters Jewish, by the ridiculous Italian laws. They don't even practice. But we're all genealogists now, I suppose."

I nodded. The ice cream wasn't tasting so good anymore. It was just cold in my mouth.

"But there are ways, of course. My granddaughter made it across the border." She leaned in even closer. "She's hiding here in Siena."

I blinked. "Oh." I wondered why she was trusting me with this.

Clio laughed, guessing my thoughts. "You have a very honest face. And you're an American."

I blushed. "Thank you, I guess."

"She'd really like to get out sometimes and walk around. But she can't, of course, because she has no visa to be here. If she is stopped . . ."

"They'll arrest her."

"They'll likely deport her back to Austria. And from there . . . you know what's happening?"

I nodded. Allen and the other journalists at the hotel had talked about what the Nazis were doing. People put on trains and never heard from again.

"You can move freely around the city? You have this privilege?" she asked.

I nodded. "I can't take off the armband. And I have to be back by eight."

We sat in silence. I knew what was coming.

"Would you . . . I know it's a lot to ask. It's risky." Clio didn't look at me.

"Give her my armband and pass so she can walk around? I think they'd shoot both of us."

"Not you. They wouldn't hurt you. That would be a diplomatic incident."

My laugh was as mirthless as hers. I knew I would be shot if I helped her.

We finished our ice creams in silence. I felt trapped. A girl my own age. Guilty of nothing. Hiding in some windowless room.

"I'm sorry," said Clio. "I shouldn't have asked. Thank you for listening to an old woman. I will find another way to help Anna."

�

The whole way back to the hotel and as I changed for dinner, I debated whether I should tell any of the others about my meeting with Clio and about her request. The fewer people who knew, the better. In the end, out of caution, I said nothing. I gave the Thirteen a charming rundown of a soccer match between twelve-year-olds that ended in a melee, a blow-by-blow of a conversation between two women about the laundry strung between their buildings ("Your socks? My socks!"), and a description of the smell of Selleria Maffei, the saddle shop in the corner of the piazza ("bliss").

"So, if the Nazis are as bad as they say, why isn't anyone in those countries doing anything about it?" I asked Allen as we made our way back to our rooms.

He turned and stared at me. "They missed their moment," he said.

Prague

1942

Alessandro

He was in Charles Square, looking up at the trees, feeling the freezing rain on his face. These trees had seen so much history that didn't make it into books: regular people coming and going for a thousand years. It was a palimpsest of a place, overlapping eras, buildings, ghosts, but the trees were still here. Witnesses.

Alessandro was there to betray a friend. He had been approached by his commanding officer to entrap another soldier. The other soldier was someone no one liked, and yet there was nothing you could point to about him that was unlikable. He didn't snore, he didn't whine, he didn't shirk, he did share. In other words, he was a normal human being like the rest of them, but every group needs a scapegoat, and this poor little shit had somehow drawn the short straw. Alessandro, relieved *he* was not the scapegoat, felt compassion for him, and had befriended him on the sly, when no one else was looking. When on guard duty together, they talked about movies. The soldier liked comedies, the stupider the better, which were not Alessandro's favorite, but the soldier's exaggerated acting out of scenes involving men in drag and idiotic families on vacation were funny and helped pass the time. He was from Bergamo, a small city outside Milan.

"I hear you're not feeling well," said Alessandro's commanding officer one day when he returned from patrolling the outside perimeter of the Jewish ghetto. They were in the lobby of the pensione, standing on a cheap green carpet under an ugly chandelier.

"No, sir," said Alessandro. "I'm fine." Good Italians never showed weakness of any kind.

"So I guess you don't want the ten days' leave I was going to offer you? You could go home to Italy."

Alessandro's eyes snapped open. "I would very much appreciate that, sir. For my family's sake."

The officer frowned. "Not the American side, I hope?"

"No, sir. My mother left Italy. My father is still there. He's Italian."

The officer grunted. "I hear he's very loyal to Il Duce."

Alessandro didn't like hearing this, but agreed, as it seemed the smart thing to do. "Of course, sir."

"So you don't harbor any loyalty to America?"

"None, sir. I am completely Italian."

The revolving door let in a gust of frigid wind.

"Well, if your mother's a foreigner, you'll never be really Italian, like me, but you can serve the *patria* and Italy will reward you for it."

"Whatever I can do, sir." He could hardly believe the shit that was coming out of his mouth. This is what they did to you.

"I'm tired of Toad." This was the unit's nickname for the scapegoat.

"He unites us in our dislike of him, sir. That's a service he provides. He's good for morale."

The officer raised an eyebrow. "That may be, but he's been disrespectful. To me."

It was Alessandro's turn to be surprised. "When, sir?"

"When? When I'm talking to him. He . . . sniffles."

"He has allergies, sir."

"Yes. *Allergies.* But it's more than that. He annoys me."

"Yes, sir."

"But I can't reassign him to the front for that."

"No, sir."

"I want you to find a better reason for me to get rid of him."

"I don't understand, sir."

"Oh, for God's sake, see if he'll offer to sell you something on the black market. See if he visits Czech prostitutes. Maybe he colludes with the enemy. Plant one of those stupid gnomes in his room. Be creative about it." The officer swatted at a potted plant with the gold riding crop that was issued to all of his rank.

"What's going to happen to him?"

"He'll be fine. He'll get to go work on the German weapons-testing program."

"Oh. As an engineer?" Alessandro knew Toad had a degree in engineering.

"Sort of. It's an indoor job. Better pay. Regular leaves. No chance of being shot." He swatted again at the palm, this time succeeding in severing a frond.

"That sounds good, sir."

"Yes. I mean, since you're pressing me that way, it does involve having the weapons tested on you." *Swat.*

"Like, they shoot you?"

The officer turned, his crop raised, and Alessandro flinched involuntarily. "I just said he won't get shot! Pay attention. No, these are other forms of weapons, like gases and diseases." He gave a little shudder and a chuckle and shoved the crop back into his boot. "Makes one long for the old days of trench warfare. That's when men were men. In the Somme. Reminds me, did you get the new shovels we were issued?"

"Mine didn't have a blade so it was more of just a stick."

"Blades are for sissies. Not men like us. So you'd like that leave?"

"Ten days' leave? I can get the train to Siena?"

The officer smiled. "The ticket's on the army. Let's make it two weeks' leave. Gives you more travel time. Not that you'll need it, because the trains are always on schedule."

"Thank you, sir."

☼

So here he was in Charles Square, waiting for poor Toad to show up. Alessandro had casually let slip that he had a crazy hankering for American chewing gum. In truth, Alessandro disliked gum, always thinking it made his American cousins look like dairy cows.

Toad, grateful for the kindness Alessandro had shown him, was eager. "I'm sure I can find some."

"It's illegal, though," said Alessandro. "Because it's American."

Toad rolled his eyes. "Come on. It's gum."

To celebrate some no doubt trumped-up victory on a distant front, the

Italian soldiers had an hour after their duty was over before they had to appear at the barracks. Toad and Alessandro had agreed to meet here, in Charles Square. Just two guys meeting for a beer after work.

The rain stopped, and Alessandro sat on a bench near a bronze statue of an old woman. She stared at him in complete and utter disapproval. The name on the black marble plaque said KAROLINA SVĚTLÁ in a particularly beautiful antiquated typeface Alessandro admired.

"She was a writer," said a voice at his shoulder. It was Toad.

"Can you read Czech?"

Toad laughed. "My girlfriend told me. Světlá's a symbol of Czech national pride. That's why the Nazis are talking about melting the statue to make weapons."

"They are?" Alessandro was amazed that Toad was so casual about what he knew. He must really trust Alessandro.

"The Czechs have a plan to steal it and hide it." Toad removed two beers from his pocket and a packet of Wrigley's Spearmint, which he handed over with a flourish. "What are you giving up for Lent?" he asked.

My soul. They sipped their beers.

"She used to write under this very tree," said Toad. "It's a—"

"Witness," said Alessandro. "I was just thinking about that, what these trees have seen."

"I was going to say golden rain tree, but yes."

They sat next to each other with their backs against the rough bark. The beer was slightly bitter.

"Cheers," said Toad. "To friendship."

Alessandro was convulsed with guilt. "They want to transfer you out," he blurted.

"I know. I'm expecting it any day."

"Really?"

"Yes. This is my third unit in three months. No one wants me. I'm too kind."

Alessandro was struck by the truth of this. That was it. The thing about him no one could put their finger on. "Yes," he said with a laugh. "You are. You're too kind."

"It drives everyone in the military crazy. We're not supposed to be kind. We're supposed to be tough. But this is the only way I can be."

"I'm worried for you."

Toad put his hand over Alessandro's. "I'll be fine. Or I won't. But I won't—can't—change. Kindness isn't weakness."

Alessandro didn't move his hand away. He realized how long it had been since someone had touched him in kindness. Since he left home.

"I can't bear this anymore," said Alessandro between swigs of beer. "I'm not cut out for this."

"I know. But you'll be okay."

"Don't say that. You don't know that."

"I do know that. You'll be okay. I don't mean that I'm promising you'll survive this, but you'll be okay."

"What do you mean, like, in heaven after I die? I'm not a believer."

"Me neither. I mean, nothing formal. But I know that I have a moral compass inside me, and I have to follow it."

Alessandro realized he had tightened his fingers around Toad's, as if he were drowning and only Toad could save him.

"'What does it mean to be an Italian?'" Toad said, mimicking their commanding officer. "They keep harping on that. To me it means being compassionate, a little hedonistic. Enjoying the pleasures of life and not taking it too seriously. Connecting with others."

"That's not what Mussolini thinks being Italian is."

"Yeah. But it's not just him. My job before this was monitoring the foreign press. I read about this insanity everywhere. Countries expanding their borders, monopolizing resources, feeding this giant need for growth, for *things. Eccoci. In guerra.*" "And here we are. At war."

"So Fascism is everywhere?"

"It's not always called that. But there's exploitation and empire-building everywhere. And always at the root, hatred and intolerance. And money."

"What about America? My mother and little sisters are there."

"America. You heard they're interning anyone with an Italian, Japanese, or German last name? Doesn't matter how long your family's been there."

Alessandro sat up and stared into Toad's eyes. "What?"

Toad looked deeply pained. "In Canada, too. It's all so wrong."

He saw that Toad's eyes were large and brown, like his dog Ettore's. They seemed to contain all the wisdom of the world, but also all its pain and sadness. He wanted Toad to comfort him, to save him, to wash away his fear, his sins. He leaned in and pressed his lips against Toad's. He felt a sense of connection that brought him enormous comfort, a sense of safety, a sense that everything would be all right. He closed his eyes and put his face against Toad's neck. Toad didn't hit him or even move away.

"Someday I'll find a society that values kindness," said Toad. "Hasn't the definition of a good person pretty much always been the same? Don't be an asshole." Toad stroked Alessandro's cheek with his free hand.

Alessandro was filled with love, which in turn filled him with terror. He looked up and caught the disgusted gaze of Karolina Světlá. "What if it's impossible to be kind without hurting someone else?"

Out of the corner of his eye, he saw Toad smile. "Better to die kind than survive cruel," Toad said.

A piercing whistle blew. The military police moved in, shouting and shoving black hoods over their heads.

Siena

1942

Sally

I hovered on the edge of the piazza. The place never ceased to fascinate me, the beating heart of Siena. With multiple entrances and exits and its strange, tilted floor, it was a stage on which the dramas of the day played out. Children ran, dogs frolicked, but also men argued and women held each other tightly by the arm as they gossiped. I was only an observer of all this. On the third day, I spotted Clio. She was moving slowly in her camel-colored overcoat, carrying shopping bags with bread sticking out. I slid in behind her on the street and waited until I was sure no one could hear us. "Once. I'll do it once," I said. "Just for a few minutes."

We agreed to meet again in the piazza the next day. I went back to the hotel and wondered if I was making a terrible mistake. But the thought of someone having to stay in hiding for years on end was so awful.

The next day, it was crisp and breezy, and Clio was right on time, in a tailored pale-pink linen duster and a bright blue chiffon scarf with polka dots. We sat at our usual table, but just had coffees instead of ice cream.

"I don't think we should be seen together after this," I said.

"Or the opposite. I'm ninety-three and no one cares much what I do. I'm invisible, and no one wants to be caught looking at you. But you're right, we must still be careful. I want to set a pattern of being out with you so that people get used to seeing me with a girl with a POW armband," she said quietly. "A girl who is ashamed and keeps her face down. Who wears hats. That way, no one will get a good look at your face. They'll assume you're working for me. A slave. They exist, you know. Thousands and thousands of political prisoners. Usually they're men in gray, digging ditches or building walls. People pretend not to see them, just keep walking or driving as if they're not there." We walked slowly up Via della Galluzza to the birthplace of St. Catherine, where we admired the delicate arched loggias inside the courtyard.

"Catherine had her first religious vision when she was just a little girl," said Clio. "Her family was in the wool trade, and they wanted her to marry. Instead, she said she wanted to dedicate herself to Christ, so she cut off her hair to make herself undesirable. That didn't convince anyone, so she went into a sort of lengthy trance."

"St. Catherine stood on this actual spot?"

"Yes. Right here in this house. Eventually her parents gave up and let her do as she pleased, and she dedicated herself to the poor. She became shockingly powerful for a woman of her time, for anyone of her time, really. She traveled, and was involved in politics, wars. She launched a crusade, and wrote influential letters to generals and princes. She even convinced the Pope to move the papacy back to Rome from Avignon. She was strange and marvelous."

We wandered into the shrine, which was an explosion of white and gold and brightly colored frescoes on the ceiling. I preferred the cool simplicity of the loggia.

"Think of a little girl in a hostile world, bending it to her will that way. She just took control."

I put my hand on Clio's arm. "I'm ready," I said.

We made our way through the maze of the city and down an alley so narrow it felt like people living across from each other could reach out and touch hands. All the shutters on the second floors were closed, but I wondered if anyone was peeking at us from the darkness inside. Clio looked back and forth until the street was empty, then unlocked a small brown wooden door in a brick wall, and we went in.

It was a small apartment with low ceilings. I guessed it was probably built in the Middle Ages, like most of central Siena. We entered a tiny living room with a huge fireplace. Clio tapped twice on the floor and opened the door to what seemed to be a regular closet. I heard a shuffling, then the back wall of the closet door shifted. Out came a young woman about my age. We stared at each other. Anna was pale, slim, with auburn hair and freckles. We were not identical twins by any stretch, but the resemblance was close enough that strangers might not notice.

I gave her my coat and hat and armband. "One hour," I whispered. As Anna and her grandmother were about to leave, I said, "Wait," and gave her my shoes. Women always notice other women's shoes.

I spent the hour looking around the apartment and trying to calm my nerves. What if they never came back? What if they were late, and I was late, and one of the Thirteen was shot as a result? I needed a distraction. There was only one book in the apartment, and it was in German. I almost laughed out loud when I saw the title: *Eine kleine Prinzessin. A Little Princess.* I thought back to that day in Los Angeles when I stole the flowers and launched myself into Patsy's car. Life is strange.

Though one side of my father's family was German, I didn't know them and I didn't speak the language. What does it mean to be descended from people who lived somewhere if you know nothing of their culture? If I had grown up in Germany hearing Hitler speak instead of Roosevelt, would I have been marching for him? Is our sense of right and wrong reliant on the stories we're told?

After about an hour of struggling to decipher the words, and just when I was getting worried about the time, I heard footsteps. I climbed into the hiding space behind the closet. I had assumed it would be a small space, but it was a ladder. I climbed down the ladder, not sure what was at the bottom. I had no light. I felt a cool breeze move; it smelled like dirt. I could hear water moving slowly. I reached out and touched walls close on either side of me. I was in some kind of tunnel. I immediately felt the panic of claustrophobia. Fortunately, I heard two knocks and clambered back up the ladder and emerged from the closet to find Clio and Anna. Anna's cheeks were rosy and she was smiling.

"*Danke. Grazie,*" she whispered, squeezing my arm. "Tomorrow?" she asked. I sighed, certain I was making the right decision, and also the wrong one.

✡

The next day, Clio and I met in the piazza again and hiked up Via della Sapienza to visit San Domenico, a huge Gothic church with a soaring wooden ceiling. "The basilica was damaged during the occupation," said Clio.

"In 1917?"

She laughed. "No. That war was fought up by the border with Austria. I'm talking about the occupation by the Florentines in the fifteen hundreds. An aggression that's never been forgiven. My Florentine accent makes me persona non grata here even today—I got a frown this morning buying oranges. '*Ma Lei é da Firenze*,'" Clio said, mimicking a snobbish shopkeeper. We wandered the airy spaces of the church.

"Leaders came and went and armies marched back and forth, but how much did life really change for most people?" I wondered aloud, my voice echoing off the walls. "I'm thinking about the women."

Clio nodded. "We cook, we clean, we give birth to children, we raise them, we grow food in the garden, we make clothes, we tend the animals. It's always the same, across most cultures. We women rarely have power over our own choices."

Clio pointed to a smaller room off the main part of the church. "There's a chapel there with Catherine's mummified head on display. Anything you want to ask her before we visit the museum?"

"You don't have to entertain me first," I said.

"I want you to know something of our history," said Clio. "It's important."

✿

Each time Clio took Anna to Piazza del Campo for an ice cream or a slice of cake, they brought a treat back for me. Clio didn't want us to speak in the apartment in case neighbors were listening, so I couldn't really interact much with Anna, but through gestures I understood that she (like me) loved the simple fruit tarts and torta della nonna, while Clio preferred the rococo creations like Zuccotto. None of us could stand Siena's most famous dessert, *panforte*, which Clio said was like trying to chew a deflated soccer ball.

I asked Clio about the hiding place. "Is that some kind of tunnel?"

"It's part of the Bottini," she explained. "Siena is a city with no river or lake for water, so in the Middle Ages, they began to tunnel under the city and channel the water table into a system of slowly fed irrigation tubes that piped to fountains and wells. The Bottini are extensive and ancient, spreading under the whole city, though it's not one system. They're kind of an engineering miracle. In 1914, the city built an aqueduct to bring water from a spring on Monte Amiata, so the Bottini are only used for a few of the fountains these days. There are miles and miles of them."

"So that's where she hides?"

She nodded. "It's risky, because they do patrol them now and then. Plus there are collapses, dead ends. You wouldn't want to be stuck down there."

I nodded, thinking of the panic I'd felt in the darkness.

Each time Clio and I spoke, she didn't ask, but I offered. "Tomorrow?"

I said nothing about Anna or Clio to the Thirteen. I didn't want to put me or them in danger. I continued to give my nightly reports at the talent show, and to buy them the little things they needed with the money they were able to get through the Red Cross. Some people got letters (heavily censored) and packages (opened), but I got nothing. No one knew where I was. I wondered if readers missed the Bon Vivant. Or did Hearst hire a new Bon Vivant to take my place?

May came, and I continued to meet Clio to explore some aspect of the city and then let Anna use my armband and pass almost every day it wasn't pouring rain. I thought of it as "the switcheroo."

After one of our rambles, I asked Clio about her childhood as we sat in the piazza. She told me about life growing up in Florence, but said the house she really loved was a country place they used to go to up in the mountains outside of Siena. It had belonged to her mother's family, which had deep roots in Tuscany, part of the old nobility.

"It was at one time an *eremo,* a hermitage," she said.

"I thought hermits were like trolls, just characters in fairy tales?"

She laughed. "These were highly religious individuals who chose to live alone, far from civilization, as a spiritual practice. The church built dwellings for such people to retreat to for extended periods. But this one was deconsecrated long ago. It's half-ruined and hidden in the woods not far from a castle, just like, as you point out, a fairy tale."

"Are you a princess?" I asked.

"Only when I'm getting my hair done. I'll take you to the *eremo* some-day," she said. "You'll love it."

I waited for Clio to say more, but she didn't. She just sat there, looking out over the piazza, her eyes clouded with memory. Finally, she said, "Enough about me. You should tell me your story."

I sipped my tea. "I don't really like to look backward. You trip and run into things when you do that."

"I didn't like to look back either, you know, for a long time. No one in Italy did. My parents didn't. There's so much history here that it's easier to ignore it. We all just looked ahead into the future. And now look."

"At what?"

Clio opened her arms to take in the whole piazza. "War. Again. We wanted Italy to be strong and wealthy, to have a sense of itself as a nation. And it got us this. I watched it happen. And did nothing."

"You had a family to raise."

"My life has not mattered. And by doing nothing to stop Fascism, I'm to blame for it."

"Your life does matter. It matters to me. I want to know more. Please tell me more about the *eremo,* about your life. I'll write it down." I produced one of the notebooks I used to take notes for the Thirteen.

"The *eremo* is a magical place. My life, on the other hand, is utterly unexceptional."

"The history books are all about men. We never get to hear the stories of the women. Tell me. I'll decide what to write down."

"*Va bene, va bene,* I'll talk, but why write any of it down?"

"You can give it to your family. I would kill to know my family's story, what their lives were like, what they thought about things. I don't even really know where I'm from. I mean, I know my mother is from Mexico and my father's family came from Ireland and Germany at some point, but I don't know what my grandparents' names were, or anything about them." I felt suddenly very blue about all of it.

"That's so sad," said Clio. "All those traditions and stories, family lore, passed down from generation to generation, and then—poof—nothing. I'm so sorry."

I thought about the old marchese in Rome. "Do you know Aldo della Gherardesca? He once told me he was being slowly crushed under the weight of his family's history. That's the other end of things, right?"

"I do know him, yes," said Clio. "Quite well, in fact." There was a layer to her answer that I wondered about.

The sun hung on the edge of the piazza, rays slipping out from under the edge of a black cloud. It gave the bricks an eerie glow.

"I don't even know if my brothers and sisters are alive. I have nothing."

Clio took my hand and squeezed it gently. "You can't see it yet, but you have everything."

VI

Trade Partners
and Dance

The Bon Vivant

The stoic Thirteen greeted the New Year in style, or as close to it as we could muster, in the hallway on the sixth floor, the ballroom being previously reserved for a very serious generalissimo and his Fascist party. . . . Terri sported a new Rita Hayworth do for the evening, and was threatened with arrest for wearing palazzo pants and talking too loudly. We danced to the tune of Radio Rome, and bit our tongues when our radio host for the evening turned out to be Fifth Columnist Ezra Pound. . . . Rumors of our release have been greatly exaggerated, but hope springs eternal, like boils. . . . This week's croquet tournament has been postponed in favor of an egg-laying contest among our new flock. Will the chickens outproduce the canaries? Put your money where your beak is and join the fun!

Siena

1943

Lapo

It was a year since Pappone had brought the political prisoners to Belsederino. Lapo remembered addressing them that first night, feeling honesty was the best approach. He laid out the fact that it was winter and there was not enough food. He told them he would understand if they walked away, but that likely the militia would shoot them. He explained that without fuel for the tractor, they were hampered in their ability to farm, but they did have seeds, basic tools, and land. "We can survive if we all pull together," he said.

"Who made you the king of Italy?" snapped a young man in his twenties who was in law school when he was arrested. Lapo wondered why the man was dubbed an enemy of the regime, but didn't ask.

"Belsederino is not a monarchy," Lapo said. "And there are enough of you that you can certainly rise up and kill me. But Roghi is the person with the knowledge of how to grow food that can save us. So I wouldn't kill him."

"And if you kill the *padrone,* I will definitely not help you," said Roghi. "He may be a landowner, and that is inherently unfair, but he's a clever and useful man. I would suggest you put up with him."

Lapo had to laugh at Roghi's summation.

And so, they had all gotten to work. They'd divided into groups: one to unearth the old farm machinery that was half-buried in the olive grove. Though it had only been a few years, the trees had grabbed the pieces of metal and enveloped them, and the workers (Lapo couldn't bear to think of them as prisoners) had to use axes to chop them out. Then they tried to piece them together and use them. This was a harder task, but there was an older man in the group who had done some welding, and one woman who had learned woodworking from her grandfather.

Another group set up housing arrangements, with some families moving into empty rooms in Luisa and Roghi's house, and some into the castle. They debated sending some people up to Fosca or the other far-flung farms, but decided for the appearance of penal servitude it was best to keep the group together. They brought two cows down for fresh milk, and some sheep and pigs to breed in hopes of meat.

There was a list of chores, including cooking, laundry, teaching the children, animal care, weeding, and more. There was always more work than there were people to do it, and everyone was busy all the time. Jobs rotated, though you could choose what you were best at. Any shirkers were quickly reprimanded by the others.

Weeks, then months passed. On sunny days, the group was almost cheerful, but when it rained and the temperature dropped, misery spread like a bad cold. Lapo had to physically stop Tommaso, an engineer in his seventies, from burning books and furniture to try to keep warm. Lapo couldn't stand the sound of the children crying because they were hungry and gave up his own meals as often as he could, though Roghi told him to keep his strength up or they would all suffer. They worried about the crops all the time.

Last spring felt like a miracle: fresh green shoots in the garden and fields. Kale, arugula, chard. Lapo marshaled the whole crew to reinforce the fencing to make sure wild pigs and other creatures did not get in. They raided every ancient junk pile on the farm for wire, and posts, and cut trees for more. Guard duty was established to keep watch for hungry birds.

Now it was winter again, and he worried about their food supply. They had carefully preserved and stored enough to get them through, but the army could take it at any point. Still, right now, things were all right. He was piling up the olive trimmings in preparation for a bonfire this evening. It was a waste of firewood, but it would boost morale. He thought they could sing songs, and maybe have some contests of strength and wit. That would let people showcase what they had learned, and laugh a little. The last rays of the winter sun were warm on his head. He stopped what he was doing and stood tall and stretched. He could hear the sound of people and work all around him. He realized he felt something he hadn't felt in a long while: contentment.

Luisa appeared at his back. "A fox got six of the chickens," she said.

His contentment vanished. Six chickens meant six fewer eggs, six people who wouldn't get protein tonight. He'd always loved foxes before. Before. When foxes were symbols of quaint English traditions, of cleverness. Now they were bloodthirsty demons threatening the lives of people he felt responsible for. He felt a murderous rage, the male response to a threat. But then his intellect kicked in and reminded him that the fox was just doing the same thing he was doing, feeding his own. And now the fox had learned to eat chickens, which would eventually lead to him getting trapped and killed, ending his foxy family line. Fewer foxes meant more rodents eating their crops, invading their supplies and homes. All the living things at Belsederino were connected, whether they liked it or not. He had committed the sin, not the fox, in not making the chicken coop secure enough. He sighed, his anger gone, replaced with disappointment. He, the so-called steward of this place, was not doing a good enough job of protecting all its inhabitants from each other.

"How's the book coming?" Luisa asked.

Sally

It was a blustery spring day. Despite the frigid temperatures, we were headed to the piazza and our usual table that we'd been occupying for more than a year. Routines mattered. They made us invisible. The waiter came to collect our empty ice cream dishes. Clio ordered us two coffees.

"Give me your notebook for a second," said Clio. I handed it over, and she drew on one page, then handed it back to me.

"A map. So you can find the *eremo*," she said.

"I thought you were going to take me."

"Just in case I'm busy and you want to go."

I looked at the map. She had drawn an odd-shaped mountain, a river with a dogleg bend in it, and a crossroads with four cypresses on one side and three on the other.

"No place-names? No road names, even?" I asked.

"That would make it too easy to find."

✕

When I returned to the hotel, I found the Thirteen in a state of excitement. "They've set the date," said Terri, opening the door of her room when she heard my key in the adjacent door. "We're going home next Thursday!"

I rushed to dress for dinner. I slid into the wine-red velvet sheath. The menu was rabbit stew, which Clio had said was her favorite when she was little. I had written down a story from Clio's childhood when she pretended to be a rabbit, practicing stillness in the face of danger. "Why would anyone care about this?" Clio had said. But I loved her stories. As I pinned up my now-red-again hair, I wondered if I would live to be ninety-three and tell my own stories. Where would I be in the year 2013? It sounded so far away, but if I was lucky, it would be a date I would live to see. Or unlucky, I thought, if things just kept getting worse.

"Guess you're going to miss out on that love affair," said Terri, as we headed down in the elevator.

"Maybe Italy itself was the love affair," I said.

✿

"I'm leaving in a few days," I told Clio. It was painful to say it. I worried about her and about Anna. We were back in the black-and-white-striped Duomo, staring at the marble inlay floor, which was chaotically filled with churning figures from mythology and biblical history.

"The whole theme of the floor is the slow attainment of wisdom," Clio said. "But the path isn't easy." She led me over a few steps and pointed down at a gruesome scene of children being torn from their mothers by soldiers.

I turned away, my heart in my throat.

"Slaughter of the Innocents," said Clio.

✿

"My mother taught me that Mexican culture venerates the *abuela*, the grandmother," I told Clio the next day. The sun was out, and we were admiring the Fonte Gaia in the piazza. "But I never had one. Would you be my honorary *abuela*, even though we'll be far apart?"

Clio laughed, pleased. "Of course. And your *nonna*, too. But I will be so sad to see you leave. Let's go to the Fontebranda today. I'll add my tears to it." We'd been putting off the medieval fountain because it was a long way down from the piazza, which meant a long way back up again afterward.

"Are you sure you're up for it?" I asked.

Clio nodded, and we made our way down Via di Fontebranda to the large crenellated baths. We passed a noisy bar with a blaring radio. I headed toward a bench to give Clio a rest.

"Can anyone hear us, you think?" I whispered to her when we were settled.

We scanned the street.

"Listen," I said. "I want to give your granddaughter my spot on the train to Lisbon."

Clio's eyes widened. "No," she whispered. "It's too much. No."

"I've thought it through. Before they realize she's not me, she'll at least be in Portugal, and maybe even on the boat to New York. The other Americans won't say anything. I don't know what she'll do there, but I can give her some names of people who might help. It's risky. If the officials catch on, I guess they might send her back to Austria. That would be worse than being here."

Clio said, "And you'd stay here? If she has your papers, you won't have any."

A man with a large mustache came down the narrow cobbled street. He lit a cigarette and leaned up against a building, watching us. Clio took my arm and I "helped" her down the street. The man didn't follow us.

We stared into the fountain.

"The wool makers washed the textiles here in the Middle Ages," Clio said. "Catherine's family." She whispered, "You're a miracle."

A man passed us on a bicycle, bumping over the cobblestones.

"You'd have to go into hiding," said Clio. "I'd hide you."

I nodded, thinking of the narrow, dark tunnel. Part of me hoped Anna would say no, that she didn't want to take the risk of being caught.

The next day, Clio and I met in the piazza as usual and made our way to a quiet spot just inside Porta dei Pispini. We sat close on a bench so we could talk. Black military cars zoomed back and forth through the gate, their tires rattling on the paving stones.

"She said yes," said Clio. "She wants to go. But, Sally, are you sure you still want this? It's so dangerous."

"I want to do this."

We sat in silence and stared at the soldiers marching by, eyes straight ahead.

"Why?" Clio asked at last.

"Because I always make the wrong decision."

Lapo

The boy watched the dragon savage the body of the teacher who had given him a bad grade and then drop it in a bloody mess on the ground. The head rolled right to the boy's foot. Her eyes were open, her mouth in a grimace as if she were telling the class to sit still. He saw the dragon shake out his enormous leathery wings, unfurl them like huge sails, then fly away to his lair. The boy turned and headed down the rocky trail into the town, holding aloft before him the head of his enemy like a lantern in the darkness.

Lapo finished the chapter and sat back, his fingers aching from pounding the keys. He had gotten caught up in the storytelling in a way he hadn't in years. There was a thing that happened, when the walls around him faded away and he was *in* the place he was writing about.

He felt a little dirty admitting it to himself, that he had enjoyed writing today. But that's because none of what he wrote was in any way tethered to reality. He was writing a fairy tale about a boy who tamed a dragon and commanded it to eat his enemies, fulfilling a divine prophecy that he would rule the land. While piling words on top of one another, he allowed himself to forget that he was writing a foundational myth that would create a cult of personality intended to allow an abusive dictator to maintain power over the Italian people. He glossed over the truth: that young Mussolini was expelled from several schools for violence, including stabbing a little girl when he was only ten.

No one would believe this shit anyway, Lapo told himself. *Dragons? Magic chalices?*

Then he remembered how Fascist propaganda had warped minds across Europe. Conspiracy theories abounded. People believed things that were absurdly far-fetched, like that Jews were Satan worshippers who drank the blood of children. And that the Roma people engaged in witch-craft. The herbalist sold remedies for the curses, and everyone made the sign of the *corne* to ward off evil. It was laughable until it wasn't, until the conspiracy theorists began to take up arms, commit violence, run for office, and win. Until bureaucrats turned the classification, incarceration, and eradication of entire groups into a policy and an industry.

But would Italians actually believe that dragons existed and that Mus-solini had the power to tame them? Or would they, as Lapo hoped, laugh? Maybe they would find the whole thing so offensive that they would rise up and overthrow the dictator. Lapo poured himself a glass of wine and pondered this as he put a pot of water on to boil for his bowl of pasta. Flour was getting harder to come by, and he was excited when Luisa told him she'd led a group in making pasta by hand this morning. She shared a small bag of *pici* with him, and he was planning to prepare it with some of Fosca's cheese and the last of the black pepper. He would definitely miss pepper when it was gone. Darkness was settling over the hillsides as he looked out the kitchen window. A bat swooped back and forth, and an owl gave the night's first cry. His whole life now felt like a constant letting go of things, a permanent state of grieving.

Some people probably did believe in dragons. Education had changed dramatically in the past twenty years. Everyone was in a uniform from the cradle to the grave. Like Michele, people were basically taught from age five to do the jobs they would do for the rest of their lives. There was no training for most in critical thinking or history or literature. If you were slotted to be a farmer, you were trained to grow and harvest crops and tend the soil, manage water and machinery. The Fascist Party controlled the licensing for all professions, including doctors and lawyers. This silo-ing of knowledge deepened divides. He could see it with Alessandro, Pap-pone, and Michele, three boys of roughly the same age who had grown up within a short walk of one another's houses. Michele was trained in agri-culture, Pappone in civil order, and Alessandro in literature. Their shared educational experiences were limited to primary school lessons about the glories of the Roman Empire, and the glories of Italy under Mussolini. "Education has always been an instrument of power," Eleanor had said, "nothing new there," when the dictator took a page from Stalin and began building a cult of personality around himself. But soon she was just as outraged as Lapo. "It's crazy," she said after a day trip to Rome where she saw the new sports stadium built for the ill-fated Olympic Games of 1940. Inspired by ancient Rome, with sixty marble statues surrounding the playing field, it also featured bas-reliefs of heroic soldiers, all of whom had Il Duce's memorable face, and an obelisk and fountain dedicated to the dictator. Plus he'd named the entire place for himself. "The Foro Mussolini?" she'd said. "What's next, sainthood?" The next month, Mussolini declared he was the reincarnation of Emperor Augustus.

Now it was up to Lapo to pull Mussolini's lies together in a narrative that would elevate him to a real-life Hercules and imply he would live forever.

At this thought, Lapo found it hard to choke down his wine. He had never written fairy tales, much less ghostwritten a mythical autobiography before. He was loath to borrow too heavily from the standards of the fantasy genre: Spenser's *Faerie Queene,* the Arthurian legends, and the popular Tolkien novel from 1937, *The Hobbit.* There were also the Greek and Roman myths, *The Epic of Gilgamesh, The Odyssey,* the Bible, the Ramayana, the Popol Vuh. Most Italians had never heard of the last two. He doubted anyone would notice if he wove together elements from them into some monstrous new whole. A trip to the underworld, maybe, or a plant that conferred immortality? He should add more demons. Demons were always good.

The important thing to keep in mind, Lapo told himself, was that Mussolini thought he was the hero. He thought he was restoring the glory of the Roman Empire. He thought he was saving Italy from exploitation by the rest of the world. Or did he? Did men like him even trouble themselves about "good" and "bad"? They saw things they wanted and they took them and called it self-defense and patriotism.

He decided that the next morning, he would go down to the henhouse and study the rooster.

Sally

On Thursday morning, I awoke with a start. I'd tossed and turned all night, worried and afraid to surrender to sleep, which would no doubt bring horrific nightmares. I'd heard planes going over but no air raid siren. The rumor was that Siena didn't have the money for a real siren, or for more badly needed shelters, or anti-aircraft measures. Last night's radio broadcast was full of the usual propaganda about Italian victories, but the gossip in the hotel was that Italy was struggling in North Africa, losing in East Africa, faltering in the Balkans. The country should never have entered the war. It wasn't rich enough or ready enough.

I wrote out a note for Allen and Terri and handed it to them at breakfast, telling them not to open it until I was out the door.

"What's going on?" asked Terri.

"Nothing to worry about," I said. I needed the Thirteen not to react when Anna took my place on the train with them that afternoon.

Once again, I thought of how little I actually knew about Anna—but it didn't matter, I decided. Whether she was a teacher, a mother, a factory worker, a librarian, or a petty criminal—she was a human being, and that was all that was important. She was someone who needed help, and I was someone able to help.

I pulled a cloche hat out of the steamer trunk and pinned on a veil and a voluminous chiffon scarf that hid my face as much as possible. I slid the armband over my coat sleeve, made sure my pass was in my pocket, and headed out into the streets of Siena. I made my way down Via Banchi di

Sopra to the piazza, feeling wild surges of nervous energy. It was important to make it seem as if this was just like any other day. I made myself walk slowly.

All the time I had been in Siena, no one but that one Fascist official had ever accosted me, despite the air raids and the fact that they were at war with America. But today, as I got close to the piazza, a man coming up the street in the other direction grabbed me. "What are you, English?" he demanded. "You bombed my city, you killed my family."

He went to hit me and I said, "American. I'm an American." I reached into my pocket and held up my passport, the golden eagle on the cover. His fist remained raised over me. A crowd had formed, but no one stepped forward to help. Finally, the man said, "I have cousins in Boston. You should stay out of this war. It's not right, Americans and Italians. It's not right." He put his arm down and walked away. I pushed through the crowd and hurried along the street.

✿

There wasn't time to do more than exchange clothes and documents and a hug. Anna held me tightly, looked deeply into my eyes. Clio said she would be back later. And then they were gone.

The apartment was silent.

I knew the rules: I couldn't move around much because no one was supposed to be in the apartment, given that Clio was out. She had rented it in her name, even though in reality she lived with family in another part of the city. I couldn't open or close windows or shutters or turn lights on and off in case nosy neighbors got suspicious. If I heard anyone coming, I had to disappear down the ladder and into the tunnel below. I padded around in bare feet. I tried to read *Eine kleine Prinzessin*. I waited, checking my wristwatch in the fading light.

I tried to be patient, but Clio didn't come back. Hours passed. Staying as silent as possible, I checked for food in the kitchen, and found a box of crackers and a small dry wedge of *pecorino* cheese. I ate half the box of crackers and the cheese. I watched the way the light filtering through the slats in the shutters crosshatched the room, and how those shadows shifted in the course of the day.

Clio still didn't arrive.

I went down into the tunnel with matches and lit one. I saw brick walls.

The tunnel was narrow—less than a yard, but tall; I could easily stand up. There was a narrow terra-cotta channel at my feet that carried a slow stream of water. I was afraid to go far—afraid of getting lost, of being stuck down there forever, like some Poe story. I kept lighting matches as I made my way uphill, or what felt like uphill, until I saw light. I came to a place where the tunnel dead-ended and turned upward. There was a grate overhead, about eight feet up. Sunlight came through. I could hear people moving around up there, the sounds of someone calling to a dog or a child. There would be no way for me to get up to the grate without a longer ladder than the one that went to the closet door. And it was likely the grate was latched. I turned around and started back.

I was partway back to the ladder when I stumbled and dropped the matches. They fell into the water. I was plunged into darkness. I fumbled for them quickly, but they wouldn't light. I stood there in total darkness, panicking, feeling the brick closing in around me. I dropped to my knees and began crawling in the water, terrified I wouldn't find the ladder. It felt like I went miles in the darkness, but finally I felt the feet of the ladder. I climbed up and reentered the apartment. *Never again,* I thought. *Not even to save my life.*

Still no one came. On the third day, having eaten the rest of the crackers, I decided to go out. I couldn't stay there forever and starve to death. The place stank because I couldn't flush the toilet. That would alert the neighbors eventually.

I decided to go out during the day, when the streets were busy. I put on Anna's coat and scarf and waited until there were no noises in the stairwell. I had no documents and no armband. I was a freckled, snub-nosed redhead in a city of raven-haired angular beauties. If anyone stopped me, I had no explanation for who I was or why I was there.

I held my breath and slipped down the stairs and out into the narrow alley.

I had never been to Clio's family's apartment, but I knew where it was, because, as the Bon Vivant, I was trained to observe. Clio always met me in the piazza, and we always said goodbye there after her outings with Anna, but I had discreetly followed her early in our friendship to see where she really lived. I made my way now to the address in the spot where Via degli Archi dead-ended into the narrow, covered walkway of Vicolo delle Scotte. There was a simple wooden door in a brick wall. People were passing by, children on the way to school, men in a hurry. I kept my face down and no one paid me any attention—just another girl on the street. I rang the bell. A woman about my age opened the door wearing a black skirt and a white blouse and a flowered apron. Her hair was tight and neat around her oval face. She frowned when she saw me.

I held out the notebook I'd copied Clio's stories into. "Is Signora Clio at home? This belongs to her."

The woman said sharply, "Go away," and slammed the door in my face.

That was strange. I stood there for a moment. I looked up at the windows, but could see nothing but plaid curtains. I dared to knock again. The door swung open, and a man in a black uniform stepped out. I was confronted with the Fascist's twisted gold braid, the shiny brass buttons, the flaming torch lapels.

"What do you want?" he demanded, eyes as black as his uniform. "Who are you?"

"Just a friend of the *signora*'s. Is she all right?"

The man also slammed the door in my face. People in the street had now stopped to listen and watch me, their eyes suspicious.

"You hear that accent? A foreigner," snarled one young man, moving closer. "What's she doing here?"

An old woman with curling, wild eyebrows stepped between us. She wore a black dress and black cardigan. "The old lady died last night," she said quickly to me. "Liked to feed the stray animals. I'm guessing you were one of them. Get along now. Be on your way."

I hurried back toward the apartment, panic rising into my mouth. But when I turned the corner into the alley, I saw Blackshirts. They were standing outside the apartment door, pounding on it. There was a woman in a gray shawl hanging out a window across the street, shutters thrown open, talking to them. She saw me and pointed and yelled, *"Eccola!"*

I ran. I was a child again, running through train yards, through cities, through unfriendly Midwestern towns. *No Okies. No hobos. No work.* I was running for my life, turning, dodging, scanning for an escape route in the terrifying labyrinth of Siena. I went through the market, doubled back, made myself slow down to appear normal, removed Anna's coat and discarded it. I'd be cold, but I wouldn't be dead. Finally, I darted into the cool darkness of a church, found it empty, and bolted under the altar behind overhanging drapery.

I hugged my knees like a child and sat as still as possible. Silence.

Clio was dead? Clio was dead. Yes, Clio was ninety-three, but she had seemed strong, immortal even. *Wrong decision wrong decision wrong decision.* A deep sorrow convulsed me and my mouth fell open in a sob, then closed again. I pulled myself upright. The feelings got walled over, encysted, the way the body closes over a piece of gravel embedded in skin.

I heard footsteps come and go, echoing through the stone church. Finally, after a long silence, I peered out at the cool candlelit gloom. I felt like a wild animal. Cornered. My heart pounded. All my senses were on high alert. I made myself stand up. *Steady. Steady. One foot in front of the other. Just another girl out for a walk. Stopped in to say a prayer.*

I strolled out of the church and toward the nearest of the medieval gates. It was just after lunchtime, when the city slowed to a sleepy crawl. Porta Camollia was ahead of me. I could see green hills through the gate. The guard was there, smoking and talking, the same one that Favagrossa had been annoyed with. He was stopping people randomly and checking their papers. None of it seemed urgent, and there was a fair amount of chatting. I noted that the guard stopped every beautiful woman who went through, while letting most of the men and older people through without question. I waited until a gorgeous young woman with long black ringlets and a tight-fitting wool coat sauntered toward him. He immediately stood up straighter and asked her for her documents, flirtatious and officious. While he teased her about her birth date, he ignored others who continued back and forth through the gate. I spotted a bike leaning against a wall near the gate, outside a bar. I prayed the bike's owner was deeply engrossed in conversation inside. I calmly put my hands on the bike, jumped onto it, sailed past the guard, who was still engrossed with the young woman, and pedaled through the gate. I kept pedaling, gasping for air, unaware until I was through that I'd been holding my breath. I coasted down the winding road to the valley below.

Sally

To avoid more checkpoints, I turned off the main road when I got to the valley floor below the city. I headed through a forested area. I was just pedaling blindly, trying to get away from Siena.

I turned down a narrow side lane. There was a stone wall on one side of the road and a steep drop-off on the other. I came around a curve and saw a house with blue shutters ahead, but then suddenly a car was coming right at me. Didn't the driver see me? I had time to register the car was small and white and moving fast. I veered, but the car grazed me, and my bike went off the edge of the road, down into a gully. I tumbled and smashed into a tree and felt a sharp pain in my arm. I didn't lose consciousness, but I could taste dead leaves. I heard a smack and the crunch of metal as the car hit the stone wall. I stood up—I was dirty and scratched, but I could walk. My arm ached but didn't seem to be broken. I felt something on my face and put my hand to my cheek. Blood. I could see that the white car was above me, stopped. A police car approached behind it, slowing down. An old woman in a black coat climbed out of the white car, brushing herself off. I watched from down in the leaves. Could I run? I needed to run, but there was nowhere to go.

"For God's sake, you were right in the middle of the road," the old woman yelled down at me as the other car stopped and the doors opened. There was something familiar about her.

"What's happened?" said the driver of the second car, a policeman in a black uniform. "Is everyone all right?"

"I'm fine," said the old woman. I finally recognized her—the woman with the wild eyebrows who had protected me outside Clio's house.

"This is why Il Duce wants women not to drive," said the man. "Signora Lucia, you don't have the nerves for it, not to mention the eyesight. Do you even have a driver's license? I'll need to see your documents."

"I've known you since you were a child, Ranuccio."

He huffed. "What about you?" he called down to me.

"*Tutto bene*," I said, pulling my scarf down farther over my hair.

"Sure? I can drive you to the hospital. I'm in a hurry, though. Urgent business."

I froze.

"Really, thank you," said Lucia. "I'm fine and I see she is, too. You'd better go take care of that."

"First I need to see her documents. Rules must be followed."

Fuck. Blood seeped through my fingers and my whole body ached.

"Come up here," ordered the man.

"Don't you recognize her?" said the woman.

"No."

"That's the shepherd's girl. Touched in the head. Doesn't speak much. Can't seem to learn to ride a bike, poor thing. Redhead. Mother was a Swiss whore. So stupid she's out without a coat on a day like this, *disgraziata*."

He frowned.

"You've gotten so big for your britches you don't know the country-people anymore," she said. "Well, I do."

"Fine, fine," said the man dismissively. "Hey, Heidi," he called down to me in a nasty tone. I played my role and stared blankly at him. "*Deficente*," he said. "There's no room in the new Italy for cretins."

"Absolutely," said the woman. "Couldn't agree more. I'll tell the shepherd to keep her home. Tie her up if he needs to. Have a good day and come see me for some *pappa al pomodoro* the next time you're hungry."

The cop said a courteous goodbye to the old woman and left.

She waddled over and reached a gnarled hand down the embankment and said to me, "Hurry. Come with me. Quickly."

"How did you find me?" I asked as I clambered up the bank. The whole thing had happened so fast. My arm and face were bleeding, but at least all my limbs worked.

"I followed you." This amazed me—I had seen nothing. She was good. "I'm sorry I had to hit you with the car," she said. "He was right behind me and I knew he would stop you. I've been looking for you all afternoon, ever since. None of us knew where Clio hid you, so we couldn't come to you. We had to just wait for you to appear."

"We?"

She shrugged. "Clio was not alone in opposing this insanity."

There was a network, I realized. I'd heard rumors of an organized resistance, but it was so dangerous and everyone in Italy seemed to watch each other so closely that I didn't think it really existed. "I didn't know where to go. Is Clio really dead?"

The woman nodded, her eyes full.

"Did Anna make it out of Italy?"

"I don't know."

We got the bike back up the embankment and looked it over. A little battered, but still working. "I'm glad you got a bike," she said. "That was smart. So all you need to do is head down this road. There's a safe house." She gave me verbal directions that she made me repeat back to her, and also gave me a set of three battered maps of the countryside around Siena that included farm roads and trails and the names of the farmhouses. To this she added a compass, a flashlight, and a wine bottle full of water. "You'd better take my shopping," she said, attaching two bags to the handlebars. "If anyone sees you, they'll think you've just gone to the market." She took the coat off her back and handed it to me. "You need this," she said.

"But what about you?"

"I'll be fine. There are people out there, good people, who will help you. I think you have good instincts, and you will know them when you find them. They're everywhere, even though it doesn't feel like it, and even though they may not know it themselves. Good luck."

✿

I wrapped myself in her too-big coat that smelled of cats and pedaled away down a path through the forest, following the directions she had given me. It was a strangely beautiful day, the sky deep azure, birds singing. I thought of how the women in prison had taught me to sing *"Volare,"* which means "to fly." The dirt track got narrower. Two crows twirled far above me. The fact that Clio and the old woman were part of a network made me wonder. Was Anna even Clio's granddaughter? Or just a stranger she was helping?

Riding the bike helped calm me, my legs steadily pumping the pedals. I was glad I was conditioned from riding and walking up and down Siena's hills. I turned down various bumpy dirt tracks, avoiding farmhouses, keeping my eyes down and trying to look inconspicuous, like I knew where I was going.

Finally, as the sun was dropping in the sky, I got to the address the woman had given me. The safe house was a remote farmstead, hidden in a small valley. I turned down the lane and rode through the lines of beech trees. I crested a hill, then dropped down again. The house was supposed to be right here in front of me. Instead there was a smoking ruin, with a message painted in black on the one remaining wall. IL DUCE HA SEMPRE RAGIONE. "Il Duce is always right."

Lapo

He sat on a small campstool in the center of Luisa and Roghi's yard observing the social dynamics of poultry. Several light-brown-and-gold hens pecked at insects in the dust and inspected the stone wall that surrounded the yard. They steadily gulped up ants, flies, spiders, and mosquitoes.

He remembered how alarmed Eleanor was when they'd first moved to Belsederino and they had no screens on the windows. "What about malaria?" she asked. She had screens installed on all their windows and those of the farmhouses. Mussolini, who to his credit recognized malaria as a major health crisis in Italy, worked with the Rockefeller Foundation on both medical prevention and treatment with quinine, as well as paying for the spraying and draining of swamps. Everyone at Belsederino received courses of quinine, and malaria cases plummeted. Now there was no money for the programs because of the war. Lapo watched as a mosquito landed on his arm. The insects and the disease were back, and people were dying of malaria again. Mussolini wanted to re-create the glory of the Roman Empire, and all he'd managed to do was repeat their mistakes.

Luisa was standing in the doorway with her arms crossed, looking amused.

"Would you like a little wine?" she called to Lapo.

"Always," he said.

The rooster was standing still, staring into the distance, as Luisa emerged and handed Lapo a small glass of white.

"What's he doing? Thinking?" Lapo asked.

"Yes. He's male, so he's thinking about sex or power."

"You have a dim view of my gender."

She didn't respond but kept her eyes on the rooster, who suddenly turned and attacked one of the hens, then immediately mounted another.

"Point taken," said Lapo. "So you don't think he spends much time thinking about foxes?"

She shook her head. "He worries about what he can control. Other chickens."

He wished he could sit there all day and stare at the chickens, but he had received a message from MinCulPop setting a deadline for his first draft. He wanted to write back in protest, "You can't rush art!"—but he knew it would be pointless. He had to just write, write, write.

So far, he had constructed a story of a boy discovering his secret destiny to reclaim Italian glory. In his version of Mussolini's life, the dictator was found as a baby on the slopes of Etna by a shepherd and his wife. They raised him in the fresh air of the mountains and the clear waters of the Mediterranean, where he could dive deeper and swim faster than any other child his age. Then his life was endangered by demons who knew his destiny, so he was moved in secrecy to Predappio and given to the Mussolini family to raise. Lapo had made Mussolini strong, brave, and loyal to the couple who raised him. Then he had introduced the idea of school, and students who picked on him, teachers who were unfairly harsh and didn't recognize his brilliance. That was when Mussolini's dragon had appeared, the personification of adolescent rage. Lapo made it so the youthful Mussolini had some control over the dragon and who it ate, but not total control. The dragon sometimes ate innocents, such as Mussolini's father, who happened to be standing in the wrong place at the wrong time and got torched when the dragon was blistering the skin of a young woman who was "immoral" and wore pants. The dragon was also supposed to represent the will of God, or something like that. He was making it intentionally muddy. He looked at a hen who had wandered over to his boot and was staring at it intently.

"I mean, how the hell did the beady-eyed, weak-chinned Germanic Windsors get people to think they were chosen by God to rule England?" he asked it.

The hen looked up at him as if it were about to defend the British monarchy, then wandered off.

Now he had to write the scenes of Mussolini becoming a man and as-suming his "rightful" destiny as leader of Italy. Mussolini as savior, Christ with a machine gun. It was agonizing to write this shit. Lapo studied the rooster, then made some notes in his notebook.

> *Confident, strutting, sudden unprovoked viciousness, then imme-diate calm. Keeps the flock in a state of unease. Attacks first and at random.*

He thought of Alessandro, and how he had taught him to manage his feelings as he grew up. Instead of saying "don't hit other children," he had told him stories of children who hit others and had no friends as a result. It wasn't a plan, it was just how his sense of fatherhood had evolved—he had seen from Alessandro's first days that a story carried more weight than a rule. Rules took away choices, but stories displayed the consequences of choices and helped you (in theory) make good ones.

Alessandro wasn't easy—he threw a rock through the schoolhouse window to hear the sound of glass breaking, he fell out of trees, he came home with notes from the teacher about talking back or scuffling. But all in all, he was an empathetic, honorable kid who showed no sign of cruelty. In Lapo and Eleanor's book, that was the definition of success. Also, thanks to the stories, he became addicted to reading, which was terrific, unless you needed him to fold laundry.

Alessandro learned not to crash his bike by crashing it. To avoid bees by getting stung. To be a strong swimmer by swimming in rap-ids that almost swallowed him. It made for seat-of-the-pants moments for Lapo and Eleanor, that was for sure. But Alessandro fully inhabited his body and mind—he was strong, confident without being cocky, and aware of his limits. Above all, he had an unselfish, unwavering sense of right and wrong. He was the total of all the things that had happened to him—his stories.

We are our stories, thought Lapo. People and nations.

Ettore growled and Lapo looked up. A figure was walking down the road toward them. Refugees from bombed cities like Poggibonsi occa-sionally passed by on their way to find family on the coast, but Belsederino was so far from everything that it was rare to have anyone appear.

The figure continued striding toward him, limping slightly. He reminded

Lapo of Alessandro, and he had the amusing thought that he had summoned his son by thinking about him. He could add that to the book, the idea that Mussolini could summon people with his thoughts. That was a good power to have.

As the man came closer, Lapo could see he was in uniform, though it was very dusty.

The figure saw him and raised his arm in greeting, and now Lapo could have no more doubts. It was Alessandro.

Sally

I pedaled away from the ruins of the safe house as fast as I could, then at a fork in the road, I crawled under the comforting branches of a huge oak tree and let myself feel fear, anger, sadness, anxiety, more anger, more fear, and a profound sense of abandonment that was all too familiar. Almost all the men I knew—my father; Patsy's husband, George; the men I'd met at parties—kept their emotions tightly laced as though expressing one would release an explosive Pandora's boxful. But I had figured out that my strength—like that of most women—came in a different form: I had to reach a catharsis in order to stop panicking, think straight, and make good decisions about what to do next. That's what men didn't understand about us—crying wasn't a sign of weakness, it was a source of strength. I thought of my mother back in Iowa, and I thought of Patsy. Like an incantation, I summoned both of my mothers to help me now, and they came to me with all their power.

I put my back against the tree to make a plan, no longer feeling alone. The solid expanse of bark was comforting. The tree had no doubt stood there for hundreds of years, a witness to so much—I tried to tap in to its wisdom. I had the maps of the area in my pocket. I pulled them out and scanned all the names, thinking about who I could turn to for help. I couldn't go back to Siena—they'd be looking for me, or for Anna, which was the same thing. I wouldn't endanger the old woman again. Who could I turn to? There were other people I'd met in Rome who came from this area. Alba's father, the old marchese who'd offered to hide me in his wine cellar. I hoped he really was an ally. He had talked admiringly about Carla Rossellini, enemy of the regime. Clio said she knew the marchese well. I knew his villa was somewhere near Siena. I tried to picture his wine label. God knows I'd downed enough of the stuff. An oak tree like the one I was leaning against, but even bigger. I peered at the map until I found the name of his estate, Cielocade. I calculated it would take me a couple of hours to get there on the bike, if I didn't encounter any patrols. I decided to ride cross-country rather than using main roads. I ate some of the dried figs and almonds in one of the bags the old woman had given me, but couldn't bring myself to gnaw on an onion or a beet. I got on the bike and started pedaling. I dared to cut through vineyards and pastures. A dog barked at me once, which scared me, but it stayed away. I passed many abandoned farmhouses. Clio had told me that Tuscany's villages were slowly leached of their inhabitants by poverty as Italy's centuries-long history of sharecropping came to an end. It was eerie, all these empty ancient buildings falling into ruin. As darkness landed on me like a stone, I got turned around and was afraid I was lost. It was impossible to navigate by the lights of the towns because of the air raid blackouts. But then the moon came out, and I could see the path in front of me. The danger was that I would unknowingly go too close to an inhabited house or even a town in the dark. I pedaled onward. I wouldn't say I was brave—what other choice did I have? When I was crossing a larger road, I heard a car coming, and I dove into the bushes and hid until it had passed, its headlights blacked out. My heart was pounding.

Just before midnight, I reached the cypress alley that led up to the villa. I thought of how many times I had attended parties at villas just like this. The alley would be lit by luminarias or torches. There would be uniformed waiters with trays of drinks ready to greet me. Now I was afraid I'd be met by guard dogs, Fascists, or armed family members. I wanted to curl into a ball and hide from the world, but I'd come this far, so I made myself smooth my hair and retie the scarf, apply some lipstick, and pedal up to the huge wooden front door and ring the bell. There was a long silence, then an upper window opened.

"*Chi c'è?*" asked a sharp female voice.

"I'm—I'm looking for the marchese."

"Sally?"

Now that was unexpected. I peered up through the darkness and tried to recognize the voice. "Alba?"

"Sally!" Alba called now. "I'm coming down."

The Alba who greeted me at the front door of the villa was almost unrecognizably plump. "Rubenesque" came to mind. Her cheeks were round, her dress about to burst its buttons. Her previously limp hair was lush and luxuriant about her round pink face. She looked startlingly beautiful and alive in a way she never had before.

"I'm so glad to see you! I'm here all alone. The beastly servants have run away and I don't have any news," said Alba. "What's happening? Have the Americans invaded?"

"No," I said, shifting smoothly into the lie I'd planned while biking along. "But I've become a war correspondent. Because, you know, I speak Italian and I know people."

"Like Virginia Cowles?"

I was grateful to the socialite turned war correspondent I'd never met. "Yes, exactly. That's how I'm allowed to still be in the country. I'm covering the war. Like Virginia." I was counting on the limited information available to Italians, and hoping incurious Alba might not realize there were not supposed to be any Americans left in Italy, even journalists. Virginia herself was apparently stuck in London, chafing to get permission to visit the front. It was a half-believable lie if you didn't think too hard about it or know the intricacies of diplomatic press exchanges.

"Write that the war is terrible," Alba said, inviting me into the villa's massive entrance hall. "It's boring. We got hit by a bomb. I think the plane must have been piloted by someone we know. All those handsome British boys, so reckless, with those unpleasant senses of humor. It would be so rude if one of them killed us."

"Quite rude. Very unsporting."

"Plus there's no food to eat."

I had to blink at this, given that Alba had gained at least fifty, maybe seventy-five pounds since I last saw her. We stood in the hallway of the villa, lit only by Alba's flashlight. I saw boxes of papers spilling out, and a thick layer of plaster dust over everything. A chair was overturned, and a vase had dead flowers in it. Golden walls had water stains that marred a ceiling fresco of dancing nymphs. It looked less like bomb damage and more like serious neglect. I thought about the many people who would usually be working here, answering the door, keeping the place clean and tidy, her table stocked with food and wine. Where were they?

"Your lipstick is a pretty color," said Alba, shining the flashlight in my face.

"Is your father here?"

"No, no one but me. I'm so lonely. Do you have ration cards?" Alba asked. "I don't have enough to eat. People think people in the country are better off, but we're not. The military requisitions everything. We're starving."

I raised the bags of onions, almonds, dried figs, and beets. "I brought some food. I just need a place to stay tonight. And, of course, tomorrow I want to interview you about your experience of the war." I took out one of my notebooks and waved it as proof, hoping she would believe me.

✡

I woke up curled into a child's bed in an upstairs bedroom in the villa, a painted troupe of monkeys and hippos dancing on the yellow wall. The sun was just coming over the undulating horizon that was dotted with a castle and some farms. It looked still and eternal, reassuring. Then a swarm of planes flew over, a high black buzz in the sky. I felt hot and edgy, as if nothing in the night was able to release yesterday's accumulated energy. I could hear someone walking below.

Alba said she was lonely and welcomed company, but I wondered how long I could stay there, out of sight. Alba trusted me because she saw me as one of "us," high society, her people. But how long would that last? I decided I must make myself useful, essential to Alba, as I had with Lila. It was hard to imagine the Alba I knew doing anything more effortful than lighting a cigarette.

"I'll make coffee," I said when I found Alba in the filthy kitchen. She was wearing a ratty pink-and-purple silk bathrobe that was too small for her. The morning light came in through a hole in the roof that was about the size of a volleyball. Bricks littered the floor, and dust was thick on every surface. I screwed a moka together, lit the stove, and waited for the water to hiss and burble.

"A stray bomb hit us a couple of weeks ago," said Alba. "I mean, what were they aiming for? The railway is miles from here. Were they drunk? This is all so stupid. When is America going to enter this war and end it? When they showed up in 1917, they were so *bravi*. Before you knew it, it was over. Back to normal, as if nothing ever happened."

I thought about the devastated landscapes I had seen in France, the entire generation of men lost. Not sure I agreed with her.

"This time it should all go even faster, no?" she said.

"I don't know."

"What are the Americans waiting for? An engraved invitation?"

I shrugged, eager to change the subject. I pointed up. "I can fix that hole in the roof for you. Tarp it at least. Do you have a toolbox?" I reached for a cabinet door.

"No, that's the pantry," said Alba quickly. The door swung open, revealing the pantry was empty.

"I'm sorry," I said. I knew that despite the vegetables I'd brought, having an extra mouth to feed with no ration coupons was not good. The moka overflowed and I poured the hot coffee into two little cups.

"There's no milk or sugar," Alba complained. "They've taken it all."

I nodded and sipped. The coffee was ghastly tasting, bitter, even worse than the fake coffee in the hotel in Siena.

"It's made from chestnuts," Alba said. "Chestnuts are the only thing the military hasn't requisitioned."

I thought of the wondrous coffee I'd had with Alba's father in Rome. Strange that he couldn't smuggle some up here to his daughter.

"If you kept bees, at least you'd have honey to sweeten it," I said. "I can show you how to build a hive and attract them." Ma kept bees back in Iowa. I always liked tending the hives.

"Silvio used to have vodka in his coffee every morning," Alba said. "He said it calmed him."

"He's not here with you?"

"I don't know where he is."

"He left you here alone?"

"He said it wasn't safe for him, that he was going to relatives in England." Now I saw why all those noble families intermarried: safe havens everywhere.

"But he didn't take you?"

"I hate England. All that rain. I feel like I'm rotting there. Like fruit on the ground."

I looked around, thinking about how quiet the place was, and asked, "Where are the children?"

"Hunting rabbits."

This was odd. I hadn't heard anything this morning. Alba's little boy was about three, and there was a girl, Lucretia, sixish. I began to study Alba more carefully. There were bits of straw in her hair. She smelled rank. Her pudgy hands shook a little.

"What can I do to help you today?" I asked.

"Go out and look for wild asparagus," Alba said. "It might just be coming up. And mallow. We can eat that for dinner. You'll have to go far though, up the hill and down the other side." She told me where to find patches of mallow, a mucilaginous weed, and wild asparagus. "Look for mushrooms, too," she said. "The edible ones, though, like this." She showed me a picture of funghi porcini in a dusty book. "I'll have to register you," she added. "If the militia comes by and finds I haven't registered you, we'll both be arrested."

"Oh, you don't have to," I said smoothly, flipping through the book, which contained pictures of all kinds of edible wild plants. "I have a press pass, so I can move around. Still, I'd love to avoid the authorities if we can. You know how annoying they can be. The bureaucracy. What a pain in the sweet patootie, right?"

"Then don't come back until dark," said Alba, seemingly relieved.

I took the book with me, and a cloth bag to put the wild foodstuffs in. I exited the villa, but I didn't go far. There were too many mysteries to solve before I could figure out whether to trust Alba or not. I found a thicket of raspberry bushes and hid there behind a stone wall. I watched as Alba left the villa and went into the chicken coop. After half an hour, she emerged. I stayed there, my legs cramping. Alba came out of the villa again a few hours later. Into the chicken coop, long pause, out again. Once she had gone back into the villa, I crept slowly into the chicken coop, finding only a small room encrusted with chicken poop, just like we had back in Iowa. Here two scraggly chickens pecked at the dirt. The henhouse was so small I couldn't stand up straight. I felt around in the dried poo until I found the false floor and lifted it, slipping down through a small hole into a hand-hewn cellar. I turned on my flashlight and discovered what my nose had already told me was three rows of massive prosciutto haunches, six wheels of *pecorino* cheese, baskets of dried fruit, jars of olive oil, and a huge supply of little dried sausages. There was enough there to feed fifty people for a month at least. The charitable explanation was that Alba was feeding people who didn't have enough ration coupons, maybe even escaped prisoners of war or one of the thousands of refugees, like Anna.

There were rumors of British pilots who'd crash-landed during bombing runs and were hidden in the countryside. The less charitable explanation was that Alba was feeding herself. But where were the children?

I returned to the villa at dusk with a basket filled with mallow, some stalks of wild asparagus, and mushrooms. I wanted to stay, but Alba was not to be trusted. I'd have to move on, which was terrifying.

"I'll interview you tonight for my article about life in wartime," I said. "And then I'll leave in the morning." I offered Alba the rest of my onions and beets, waiting to see if she would show signs of empathy or concern.

Instead her eyes were greedy. "Thanks," she said. She put most of the food away. We each ate a small plate of vegetables, and then had some dried fruit. My stomach was still gurgling after the meager meal. I watched Alba for flickers of remorse, but saw none. For her "interview," I asked Alba about her thoughts on the war.

"Well, I think Mussolini's a great leader," said Alba, chomping on the tough end of an asparagus stalk. "And I'm sure we'll win, but I really just want it to be over so we can go back to normal life. I miss parties, don't you?"

I thought about it. Did I miss parties and the whirl of high society? Not a bit. "Does your father come to Siena often?"

Alba's expression shifted, her eyes darting away. "No. I haven't seen him. He doesn't love me, you know, because I'm not a boy."

"Oh, Alba. I hope that's not true."

"It is true. He loves my son, my Livio, but not Lucretia."

"Where are the children?"

"They've gone to visit friends." Again she was vague, clearly hiding something.

"What do they think of the war? Do they understand it?"

"They don't know anything different. They think this is how life is. Do you think it will be over soon?"

"I don't know."

"No one knows anything. It's all very unsettling."

After dinner, Alba burrowed into the sofa with an old copy of *The Tatler* with Nancy Mitford on the cover. I took this to mean she wasn't interested in more conversation. It seemed important to stay on Alba's good side for as long as I was in this house. I grabbed a rag from the kitchen and started doing some dusting, waiting to see if Alba would stop me. She didn't.

A few minutes later, I'd made decent headway on the half-inch-thick dust in the salon when I heard voices outside. I instinctively slunk into the shadows.

"Don't worry. I have a gun," whispered Alba. She produced a hunting rifle that looked like it dated to the Napoleonic era.

The buzzer rang and the big knocker pounded. We peered out from the barred windows on either side of the door. There were four children standing there. The youngest looked to be about five, the oldest about eleven. They were skinny and their clothes hung on them. Alba kept the gun trained on them.

"We're from Genoa," the oldest called out. "Refugees. Our houses were bombed. They put us on a train to come here to live but no one met us at the other end."

It was like staring at my younger self.

"You must have been so frightened," I said. Alba gave me a kick and shushed me.

"You can't stay here," said Alba. "Go away." She went to close the shutters. I was horrified.

"Wait. Do you have anything to eat?" the boy asked.

"We have some onions," I said.

"Why did you say that?" whispered Alba. "They're little thieves."

"They're children."

Alba sighed, dug into the sack of onions, and threw them some through the bars of the window.

"Go to Colle," she said. "Up that road. There are people who will take you in there. But get off my property. Don't think about staying here tonight. I will shoot you."

I watched the hungry children disappear into the bushes, slinking off toward the next farm. Their houses had been bombed, their parents were dead or missing or had turned them loose because they couldn't feed them. Alba treated them like a pack of stray goats. I was pulled inevitably back into my own childhood exodus. I'd been turned away from houses this same way, and I remembered the shame and the hunger. I was furious with Alba.

"Why didn't you give them more food?" I demanded.

"I don't have anything for them."

"Come on. I saw you today. I know what's in the henhouse. Why didn't you give them at least a little something? You have enough."

Alba stared at me through narrowed eyes for a full five seconds, then picked up her gun and held it at her side. "I can't. If they know I have food, they'll kill me and eat it all."

"I'm not sure that's true. They might just appreciate your generosity. You could make them do a little work around here. You need help with this place. You would be saving their lives. They're children."

She shook her head. "They'll kill me and eat it all."

"Alba, not everyone is bad. I'm not going to kill you and eat it all."

"Not yet. You're not starving yet."

"It's more than that, I hope. I wouldn't ever kill you."

"You would if you had to."

"What's going on? What happened to you? Someone has done something terrible to you, haven't they? Do you want to tell me about it?"

Alba's eyes filled with tears. "I can't," she said. "I can't tell you. I'm going to bed now." She turned away, then said over her shoulder, "You're my friend. But don't try to steal my food." There was a plaintive note to Alba's voice as she went up the stairs to her room.

"And don't steal my lipstick," I joked, but I locked the door of the nursery that night, and shoved a chair in front of the door.

Alba was pleasant but wary in the morning, wishing me well with my war reporting. "Don't forget to tell them it's boring," Alba said. "I haven't had a new dress in ages."

I was a half mile down the road before I discovered my lipstick was gone. On the other hand, I thought, there was a distinct possibility that a hedgehog had saved me from being made into sausage.

Lapo

"Babbo!" Alessandro said, burying his face in his father's shoulder. Lapo could not contain his emotions. He wept, apologized, and wept again.

"*Che emozione!* I can't believe you're here," he said at last, leading Alessandro inside the castle. "Are you all right? You're limping. Let's go upstairs. Can you make it?"

On the way up, he apologized that Alessandro's room was occupied by a family of four. "You'll sleep in my bed," he said. "I'll use the couch in my writing room."

"You have guests?" Alessandro asked, puzzled.

"Let's hear your story first."

After his father had given him some water and a glass of wine, Alessandro sprawled on the sofa in the writing room with Ettore's head on his chest and told his father what had happened since he left home. Lapo could tell he was leaving things out, warping the story for his father, which was worrisome. He was glad to hear that Alessandro had two weeks' leave, though upset that they had already lost two days to travel. *He's here now, that's all that matters,* he told himself, but he still wanted his son to feel free to share his burdens with him.

"How bad is it?" asked Lapo.

Alessandro sighed and looked around. "Is it safe to talk?"

Lapo shrugged. He wasn't sure who was in the castle. "I don't know. Let's go for a walk."

"Ah, fuck it," said Alessandro. "I'm so tired. I've been walking all day. I'm going to tell you the story of a guy in my regiment, okay?"

Lapo smiled. "Yes. Tell me all about the soldier in your regiment. Maybe by talking through his problems, we can help find a solution to what ails him. So that he can further the glory of Italy as he should."

"You're good at this," said Alessandro. "Let's call him Schweik. Schweik is in trouble."

✡

It was as bad as Lapo had feared. Incompetent leadership, rampant corruption, and insufficient equipment, food, first aid. A mission of subjugation and mass murder. This was the story of war since the beginning of time, and it was still the story of war. He and Alessandro tried to decipher the big picture of what was happening, based on what each of them knew. Listening to American and British radio stations was illegal and could land you years in jail, but people still did it. It was clear Hitler expected Italy's help in holding the territory he had conquered and to keep order there while his army rolled farther across Europe and Africa. Rallies, radio broadcasts, and articles sowing fear, division, confusion, and conspiracy theories promoted the idea that only the benevolent authority of Berlin could bring order to the chaos in Europe. The Axis had occupied France, Poland, Czechoslovakia, Austria, Belgium, Denmark, Norway, the Netherlands, Yugoslavia, and Greece. Constant attacks on Britain from the air were meant to terrorize and exhaust the tiny island's inhabitants so they would demand peace at any cost.

"It all happened so fast, but I bet the Czechs are not falling for it," said Lapo. "It's such a young country. They remember what it's like to be part of an empire."

"Exactly." Alessandro said that every morning, there were anti-German slogans on buildings, and Nazi flags were defaced or pulled down. Homemade bombs were a regular occurrence. Garden gnomes were a humorous symbol of national pride and resistance. He explained that as the war had dragged on, shorthanded German commanders were putting pressure on Italian leadership to help keep order in Prague. "We're only supposed to guard the embassy and the ambassador when he moves around," said Alessandro. Now they were being asked to lend manpower to enforce curfews, staff roadblocks, and generally carry out the occupation.

"It's hard to imagine Italian soldiers in that role," Lapo said. "The Czechs are not our enemy."

Alessandro nodded. He told his father that many of the soldiers missed home, hated the cold, couldn't digest the food, and had nothing but sympathy for the people they were supposed to be terrorizing. "So the German generals ordered the Italian generals to start shooting those of us who are not ruthless enough. That happened the day before I was leaving."

Lapo struggled to make sense of what his son was saying.

"The morning I left, two soldiers in my battalion were shot by the commanding officer."

"Oh my God."

"It's insanity."

"Caporetto," said Lapo.

"What's that?"

"The last war. The Italians were refusing to go die in the mud, so at Caporetto, their own officers shot one in ten of them. They killed the ones with clean boots." Lapo was filled with panic for his son. "What are you— What is Schweik going to do?"

"He's thinking about killing himself."

"No! My God, no!"

"Come on, Babbo. Tell me why he shouldn't. He doesn't want to hurt innocent people. He's never going to make any headway with his commander. If he deserts, they'll find him and kill him. If he goes back and doesn't fight, they'll shoot him. All roads lead in one direction, the direction we're all going in anyway. By ending his own life, at least he's taking control of the situation."

Agony gripped Lapo's throat. He longed for Eleanor. He lowered his voice, hoping no spies were nearby. "But you're so young. Things could change on a dime. Mussolini—" He lowered his voice even more, keeping a hand over his mouth. "Mussolini is not invulnerable." He told Alessandro about meeting Il Duce and about the book.

Alessandro stared. "You're ghostwriting a book to make people worship Mussolini?"

"I have to."

"You have to?"

"I can get you transferred to a desk job. I can save Belsederino. These people who are living here, the prisoners from the city. I can't let them down."

Alessandro shook his head. "There's got to be a better way."

Lapo's heart sank. "I'm doing the best I can. What else can I do?"

Alessandro went to bed. Lapo sat up late into the night, smoking the last of his stash of little Tuscan cigars, trying to come to terms with the fact that he had lost his son's respect.

Sally

I rode my bike up a steep hill outside Colle di Val d'Elsa, hoping not to get shot, but also longing for relief from the pain of cycling uphill along a bumpy forest track. I hoped I didn't get a flat tire. The path was overgrown, and branches reached out to touch my shoulders as I huffed through them. They reminded me of Aida's orchids, the way they sent blind fingers into the air in search of nutrients. Aida's small room above the garage at Patsy's was filled with orchids, and she would let me stare at them and spritz water on them.

"Do you like working for Patsy and George?" I asked her one day when I was about thirteen.

"I like working better than not working, because I like eating better than not eating," she said. "This is a good job."

"You could be a movie star instead, like Lupe Vélez."

She laughed. "I don't think so."

"You're so smart and funny. You could do anything."

Aida sat me down and looked into my eyes. "Not in America. Most jobs aren't available for people like me."

"Then why don't you leave? Mexico is so beautiful."

"Beautiful and poor. Every place has its problems. But there's something I think you should think about. All work has dignity," she said. "Taking care of people is an important job. People may not see it that way, because they're idiots, but it is. What would happen if no one did Albert Einstein's laundry or cooked his food?"

"He'd have to do it himself?"

"A genius like him? That kind can't even tie their own shoes. Everyone plays a role in this life, and mine is to make sure that you and Patsy and George are clean and fed and the house looks nice so you can be your best at what *you* do. I'm proud of that."

"You call them stupid rich people who can't pick up their own underwear. I hear you, you know, when you mutter under your breath."

"Everyone's allowed to complain. Would I want my kids to do this job? No. I'd want them to go to school and be doctors who make very expensive house calls and fleece these people for every dollar they have. But this job is okay for me."

"When are you going to get married and have kids?"

Aida frowned. "Can't be a live-in and have kids. Folks don't like that. I don't want to give up my job."

"But wouldn't your husband take care of you if you did?"

Aida snorted. "I'd have to find one first. That's a risky proposition these days. Men can't even take care of themselves, much less their families. I'd like to have a little girl. But that's hard to do, to have just one."

"Why?"

"You'll learn the answer to that later."

Looking back, I realized what I had not seen then: Aida was profoundly lonely. She had been forced to choose between taking care of other families and having one of her own. It was cruel. I had just accepted things as the way they were, but that was not how they had to be. She deserved better.

Some of Aida's orchids were in terrariums, while others sat along windowsills. As a child, I was awestruck and alarmed by the tendrils they sent out. I worried they were going to encircle my neck and strangle me.

"They're aerial roots," she'd explained. "They're taking water and nutrients right from the air. Isn't that amazing—they live on air?"

Now I was wishing I could live on air. I'd spent the night after leaving Alba under a stone bridge. I ate the last of the food I hadn't given to Alba—a couple of very unsatisfying raw beets and a handful of almonds. I was hungry and had no place to go. Again. Several patrols drove over the bridge during the night, and I realized I was getting too close to Poggibonsi, a transportation hub that was crawling with military. I needed to head toward the least populous area of Tuscany. But first, I needed to eat. I'd done my best to memorize the edible plants in Alba's book. I wandered into the woods and found some mallow, and what looked like the first shoots of *ortichie,* which could only be eaten now, before it got horribly prickly. I chomped on the greens and swallowed, unsatisfied, dreaming of Alfredo's bowls of cheesy, creamy pasta.

I studied the map for names of places that sounded familiar. If I'd known when I was rubbing shoulders with the rich and famous in Rome that I'd soon be on the lam, I'd have made more of an effort to make genuine friends instead of polite acquaintances. I'd also have tried to remember where people lived and get a better sense of their willingness to betray their country by sheltering me.

There was one place-name I recognized. Villa Incantato. It conjured the smell of wine, sweat, perfume, and incense. The name meant "enchanted." I'd been to a massive party there that had gone down in infamy. The fete was so large that I'd never actually met the owner, but I knew he was a British lord famous for these scandalous parties. I had memories of topless people with furry satyr pants lounging in a grotto, holding martini glasses and snorting cocaine. The Bon Vivant had expressed shock and delight in his column, describing several acts of extramarital debauchery with droll precision.

That kind of over-the-top decadence was frowned on by Mussolini, which is why it stuck out in my memory. The whole time I was there, I was expecting a police raid that never came. I assumed the British lord was long gone, but maybe there was some food still stored there, or people sympathetic to foreigners. It was a very shaky reason for going, but it was all I had, and at least it gave me a destination. Not moving was making me jittery.

I rode my bike along deserted country paths. The weeds towered over my head, and I often had to get off my bike to fight my way through. Once, I am not kidding, I even came face-to-face with a wild boar, black and tusked. The *cinghiale* squealed at me, and I thought it would charge in retribution for all the times I had eaten its relatives in delicious stews and atop pastas. Fortunately, it reversed course and disappeared into the brush. That's how scary I looked.

I passed a couple of fields where people were tying up new tendrils of grapevines. They turned and stared as I rode past. I waved, but they didn't. People didn't trust strangers anymore, didn't give anyone the benefit of the doubt. And who could blame them, when the whole world was turning on each other, dogs fighting over bones.

I saw people farming with scythes, rakes, baskets on their heads. Horses pulled wagons; huge pairs of white oxen pulled plows. It was a quiet, clean landscape like we'd had in Iowa before things got bad. There were birds everywhere, and, now that spring was in full swing, insects galore. I felt like I was back home, among people who worked to eat and expected little more from life.

Finally, a huge pink villa appeared on the horizon. Incantato. It sat atop terraced gardens that were now overgrown. The lord must have left no later than June 1940, when England and Italy declared war on each other. I rode up the cypress-lined drive, then parked my bike next to the stone pillars that marked the entrance to the grounds. The pool in the formal gardens that I remembered as teeming with drunken, naked people was empty, leaving only a few leaves floating on a puddle slowly seeping into cracked cement. I remembered the masked ball that night. It was unseasonably hot and humid, and the people dressed as centaurs and gorgons began shedding their costumes and clothes. An "orgy," the Bon Vivant had called it with glee. Now the grotto was a thicket of vines. The topiary camel was a sort of cloud shape, the unicorn's horn softened into a halo. There was a sculpture garden I didn't remember of equally huge animal shapes in bronze and steel, cavorting giraffes and oversized, menacing lions. The lord must have added them just before war was declared.

The villa was chained shut, flaking blue paint on the huge front door, weeds popping up between the pea gravel. I walked around the building and down some stairs toward a cracked and weedy tennis court. I heard a buzzing sound. At first, I thought I must have disturbed a beehive, but then I looked up.

A swarm of planes was filling the sky over my head as if someone were pulling a black sheet over me. There were so many of them that I thought of when my teacher in Iowa told us about the passenger pigeons that used to blacken the skies overhead and blot out the sun for hours at a time. The planes were loud, and flying low—side by side, in formation. For a moment, I was frozen in awe—I had never seen such a thing before. The sound got louder and louder. I ran back up the stairs and flung myself under a statue of a hippopotamus. The planes began firing and bombing just as I rolled under the giant metal beast. I covered my ears as explosions boomed and bullets pecked at the dirt all around me. It was like the worst thunderstorm I had ever endured, with every raindrop replaced with a bullet, and every burst of thunder a bomb. Were these the Americans? British? "I'm on your side!" I wanted to shout.

I stayed in the fetal position, arms over my head, expecting to die at any moment. Then, when I thought I would lose my mind and run out into the rain of lead, it stopped. Like the end of a spring shower, the sun came out again. I listened and heard no more buzzing. I slowly rolled out from under the hippo. The ground was pockmarked with bullet holes. I could smell smoke, and looked behind me to see the villa was burning, great billows of black issuing from the broken tower. I walked to the top of the stairs and saw that where there was a tennis court before, there was now a large smoking hole in the ground. The metal fence was twisted and melted. *How silent it is,* I thought, then realized I was deaf.

I just about jumped out of my skin when I felt a hand on my shoulder. I flung myself around to face a sturdy young man in a white shirt and black trousers. Improbably, he was smiling at me. He held a bucket.

His lips mouthed something, and I pointed to my ears and shook my head. He nodded and held up one finger—wait, he was telling me. I obeyed, blinking, as he ran toward the smoking villa. The world without sound was so strange to me, all a pantomime, a silent film.

The shock started to wear off, and my hearing began to return. First, it was a faraway ringing, then it sounded like I was underwater. I was trembling, I realized. I sat down again. I felt like I was having a heart attack, and I began to cry. The shaking wouldn't stop, and I rolled back into the fetal position, willing my heart to slow. I catalogued what I could see. Green grass torn up, a dark green hedge. The gray stone of a walkway. I could smell smoke, and something more acrid. I could taste fear.

Finally, a pair of wooden clogs appeared in my field of vision. I sat up.

"Can you hear me now?" the man asked me. He was still smiling. I began to cry again at the sight of his smile.

"Yes," I said. "I'm sorry I didn't help you with the fire."

"It's okay," he said. "It's okay now. You were really caught in it. This time was bad. My mother and I were safe in our house and it was even bad there. Can you stand up?"

I climbed to my feet. I looked into his eyes. "I'm—"

"*Oi la,*" he said in surprise. "Wait. I remember you. You're the girl who paid me to tell you about the party that time."

I looked into his face, tears still streaming down my cheeks. "Yes," I said, wiping my face with my sleeve. "I remember you, too. I was just thinking about that party. You told me about the people riding horses into the ballroom."

"Lady Montague," he said, grinning. "Stark naked. What are you doing here?"

"Traveling around writing about life in wartime."

"Well, you got a good introduction to it, didn't you?" he said with a laugh. "Almost too good!" His laugh was so unexpected, so healthy, that it made me start crying again. And then I was laughing uncontrollably.

"I'm sorry," I said. "It's just the shock."

He reminded me his name was Giuliano, and I remembered he was Lord Desart's *fattore,* or farm manager. The family had gone to Switzerland. Giuliano was improbably friendly, with a heavy Tuscan accent.

"Come with me," he said, skirting the bombed-out tennis court and heading into the olive grove. He told me he'd avoided military service by farming the castle's fields and sending the wheat and sunflower seeds to the army. "Of course, I look after myself," he said, nodding to a few rabbits hanging limply from his belt.

"Could I pay you for one of those?" I asked.

"Pay?" He sniffed. "You'll be our guest."

Giuliano spent the short walk warning me that his house was humble, not like the villa, and a grand lady like me must understand the war was hard on them. I laughed and told him I was most definitely not a grand lady. His mother, Ilaria, in her sixties, was pruning an olive tree when we arrived at the neat stone farmhouse, standing on a rickety homemade ladder in her long black skirt and sweater, sleeves rolled up to reveal tanned arms. She climbed down as Giuliano explained I was a friend of the lord's, an American. I didn't correct him, since the lord wasn't around to do so either.

"Quite a day to be out and about," said Ilaria. "I bet you almost got more holes in you than a colander."

I nodded and took her hand in mine and thanked her for her kindness.

It was larger than I expected, the knuckles swollen with arthritis, and her grip was so strong my fingers ached as she smiled and nodded.

"Thank you," Ilaria said shyly. "It's nice to have a visitor."

We went into the dark kitchen of the farmhouse, and Ilaria skinned the rabbit in one movement, sliding it out of its pelt as easily as I rolled off a stocking. She opened a jar of tomatoes over my protests not to raid her larder, and soon a stew was simmering, the scent of rosemary in the air. Giuliano appeared freshly washed and shaved and poured me a glass of wine.

It was so strange—one minute I was hiding as death rained down in an apocalyptic hellscape, and the next I was having wine and laughing. I studied Giuliano's face as he told Ilaria about his attempts to stop the fire in the villa. "I was running here, I was running there," he said, his eyes crinkling with glee, "and wishing I had the old horse with me to pee on it." They roared with laughter at this.

Why were these people being kind to me? They didn't know me outside of one conversation, and I had but the most tenuous connection to their employer. They told me that Desart had left them behind without pay.

"What can you do?" said Ilaria. "Except make the best of it."

I wolfed down a huge bowl of rabbit stew and a large hunk of bread.

"I should probably be moving on for the night," I said. "You've been so kind."

"Stay, stay here," said Ilaria. "We'll make room for you. Stay as long as you like."

"I know you're supposed to register guests with the local officials," I said.

Giuliano rolled his eyes. "It's my house. I'll have who I like in it."

It felt wrong not to tell them. "I need to avoid the authorities. You could be in serious trouble if they find me here."

They both nodded, seemingly unworried.

"I can pay you," I said, but Ilaria refused. I took out Lila's diamond earrings and put them on the table. Ilaria laughed and gave them back.

"Such things have no value here," she said.

○

I loved staying with Giuliano and Ilaria. I woke up early every morning as they did, and helped Ilaria prune the olive trees. I helped Giuliano tie up the fronds of the vines. It made me feel connected to my family to be out in the fields again, with string in my hands, feeling the life inside each plant I handled.

Giuliano went to the village every couple of days to collect any mail and get the gossip. He told me that the planes—British—had apparently destroyed some Italian military installations. Lots of people and farm animals had been mown down in the rain of bombs, and people were terrified of another raid.

Weeks went by, and I began to relax, to feel that the war was far away, that I was safe there. But, of course, I wasn't.

✿

One afternoon, Giuliano came running up as I was sweeping the courtyard and told me to hide. As I rushed into the house, he said that rumors of a strange woman at his place had reached the mayor of the nearest town and three policemen were on the way there. Fortunately, a neighbor had tipped him off.

I climbed into the space Giuliano had created by building a false wall in one of the farmhouse bedrooms that could shift and then lock into place, not so different from Anna's hiding place in Siena. It was invisible from the room itself, though of course dogs might sniff me out. I heard the car pull up outside and began to calm my breathing, stilling my body and trying to slow my heart.

The hiding place was small and dark and I was sitting down, my face between my knees, buried in the fabric of my skirt. I listened as the booted footsteps of the officers came up the terra-cotta stairs. I realized with horror that I could smell the smoke of their cigarettes. I prayed I wouldn't sneeze.

To calm myself, I thought about Clio. "I think time is a fabric," she'd said. We were standing in front of the Fonte Gaia in Piazza del Campo, where we'd just eaten yet another giant bowl of gelato. Clio was telling me about the *eremo*, about how cool the mountain air was, how wild boar roamed the forest, and how as a child she had made chains of wildflowers and swum in the frigid stream.

"If time were a fabric, you could take it and embroider it, stitch points of it together," said Clio. "You and I are meeting here now, but we might also meet at another time, at different moments in our lives. I feel like that might be how it works." I stared at the marble folds of the fountain and wanted to reach out and touch them. I felt that if I could, I would make that stitch and bring myself at age eleven and Clio at the same age together to comfort each other and be friends.

"Maybe this is not the first time we've met," Clio said, completing her thought. "Maybe it's not the last."

Sally

From my hiding place, I heard the three officers remind Giuliano that the names of everyone in the house must be registered with the police in the required ledgers.

"It's just me and my mother," said Giuliano. "Same as always."

"I will shoot you right now!"

"Then who'll give you your black-market olive oil? And your rabbits?"

I heard a sharp *thwack* and then the sounds of the men leaving, their car backfiring as they drove off.

I waited until Giuliano knocked three times, then climbed out. His face was bruised, his lip cut, and his mouth bleeding.

"I'll go tonight," I said.

"Don't be afraid of those swine, overfed on their mother's *pappa al po-modoro* and confiscated *salumi*," fumed Ilaria as we went downstairs. "It's not safe for you to go. What if there's another bombing?"

"But you and your son aren't safe if I stay. They'll bribe the neighbors to watch the house and rat us out."

"Not enough money in the world for that," said Giuliano, washing his face at the kitchen sink. "We're close-knit around here."

"You'd be surprised."

Giuliano made the classic Italian "*pff*" of dismissal, then winced at the pain in his mouth. He dried his face and grabbed an onion and began chopping it.

"Listen. I couldn't live with myself if you were hurt or killed. You've been so kind to me, and for no reason."

"You're a friend of the lord," said Giuliano, tossing the knife in the air and catching it again with a grin. *He never lost his ability to play,* I thought. *What a marvelous quality.* For a moment, I thought I could fall in love with Giuliano and stay here forever, but I also realized that would probably seal his death warrant.

"I'm just someone who puts on fancy clothes and goes to parties."

"The lord has nothing to do with it," said Ilaria, stoking the fire in the kitchen hearth. "We're all just people. Of course we have to help each other."

I wished what was so obvious to her was that clear to everyone else.

Giuliano added, as he tossed another log on the fire, "You would do the same for us, my mother and I, if we were in trouble in America. Even if I were a stranger to you."

I hoped so.

Ilaria, practical as ever, had a possible solution. "You should go to my aunt, Fosca. She lives alone in a corner of a huge estate called Belsederino, far from everyone. Nothing but sheep and goats for company. You could help her, and she could help you." She handed Giuliano a carrot, which he expertly julienned.

"What about the *padrone*?" Giuliano asked his mother, his brows lowered in concern as he chopped.

"He's married to an American," said Ilaria. "If anyone is going to turn a blind eye, it's him."

I agreed to their plan. I would leave before dawn, with good directions, a letter from Ilaria to Fosca, and a knapsack full of food.

"You're one of us now," said Ilaria, as she blew out the candle that night. The embers of the fire glowed orange, the only light in the room.

✷

That night, I dreamed about Patsy, and my family back in Iowa. In the dream, I discovered them hiding in the dirt-floored basement of Ilaria's house. Patsy had been shot down over Japan and was wounded. My mother was holding Baby Margaret in her arms. The wooden beams over them were low, and at first, I thought they were hiding from an air raid, but then I began to worry that it was a grave, that they were all in a grave together. In the dream, they didn't speak, and kept shushing me to silence.

I awakened to no more certainty than I felt in my dream. Was Patsy okay? Were my parents and siblings alive or dead? Why did they disappear, like doves into the wind?

Maybe this was the fate I deserved, to wander alone in search of help in a hostile land.

Lapo

He prayed he'd convinced Alessandro not to kill himself. He was taking a break from writing to split wood for the refugee farmworkers' cook fires. He'd always loved the rhythmic action of centering the maul and then *whoosh*, the downward arc that neatly split the log.

He'd invoked Eleanor and the girls, and made Alessandro promise him, but what did that mean, really? He had in return promised Alessandro he would find a solution. *Whoosh*. The log fell into halves on either side of the stump, the grain of the wood bright and clean. At least his son seemed more optimistic when he'd left to return to Prague. Lapo often told himself when he failed at some menial task, like fixing a faucet, that it was okay because his real tools were words. But he couldn't find the right words to fix this problem. It was difficult to make someone see the importance of staying alive if they didn't already. He wondered if he and Eleanor had made a mistake not raising their children to be more religious. That was one upside of religion: ending your life was a sin, period. Lapo agreed with that—he could not see it any other way. So many things conspired to take life from us—diseases, accidents, violence, falling tree limbs—that it must be precious. *Whoosh. Whoosh. Whoosh.* More logs fell into neat halves. He was angry and frustrated at how calmly Alessandro could talk about ending it all. What had he, Lapo, done wrong? How could he fix it? *Whoosh.* For the millionth time, he wished Eleanor were there.

Enough wood for today. He decided to go up to see Fosca. He hadn't checked on her in a few days, and he could use some wisdom from his elders. She might need him, too. The sheep were lambing, and that was a stressful time for her. Ewes often had twins, triplets, or more, and sometimes died in labor. Lambs were attacked by foxes before they had even exited the birth canal, or died of cold or random diseases. They couldn't afford to lose any this year. Every life was precious.

Lapo saddled the young horse. This would be the animal's first longer ride. The horse danced a bit as Lapo got on, and he wondered if he was asking too much of him. But he settled when Lapo put him in a steady trot up the hill. Nothing like a hill to take the buck out of a young horse.

Lapo loved the rhythmic cadence of the horse's hoofs. He rose and sat in the saddle, and began to breathe deeply and really look around him. The landscape was quiet today. No planes sputtered overhead. One hawk circled, harassed by a couple of crows. He let the horse slow to a walk as they turned onto the dirt track to Fosca's. The path went through a patch of forest that had just leafed out, and Lapo kept his legs on the horse in case he spooked at wildlife. The sunlight was dappled and lovely, and the shade under the trees felt cool. He smelled the pleasant mulchy scent of leaves, heard the tinkling of the brook nearby. The breeze whiffled the leaves of the oaks and elms that sighed around him, and butterflies danced around the head of a salamander.

He found Fosca washing the cheese rinds. He was impressed as always with her strength. She had been born into a farm family in the 1860s and had seen so much change in her life. She remained largely unimpressed by it all.

Her face was like a dried apple. She'd lost her teeth, and her mouth caved inward. Still, her grin was bright and infectious, full of mischief.

"You look well, Fosca."

"Nearly dead," she said.

"I doubt that."

"Is the war over?"

"Not yet."

"Americans come?"

"Not yet."

"When are they coming?"

"I don't know."

"Are they coming?"

"I don't know. We're going to have to hang in there a bit longer."

"How are the city people doing?"

"Better than I thought they'd do. They're coping."

"Good. And the *signorino*?" This was her name for Alessandro.

"Headed back to Prague."

"So soon?"

He decided only to say "I'm sad about it." He admired her twenty new lambs, little white cloudlets frolicking in the field. Seeing them filled him with optimism.

"Cupcake had quintuplets," she told him, pointing to one tired-looking ewe. "They all survived, with a little help from some of the other mamas."

"What do you think of Mussolini?" he asked her on a whim.

Her eyes glittered at him. "Who?" Then she laughed, and he was left wondering how much it mattered to her who was in charge of Italy.

She gave him two new wheels of cheese to take to the refugees, and he gave her several bottles of wine in return. "I'd bring you a *damigiana,* but I can't fit it in the saddlebag," he said.

"You're a good man."

"I honestly don't know if that's true."

"You are."

She gave his horse a carrot.

"Don't waste those on him," he said.

"A carrot is never wasted on a horse. Buys you goodwill," she said. "You never know when you'll need it."

After days of tension, Lapo was so relaxed riding home through the beech forest that he almost fell off when the horse came to an abrupt halt and snorted.

"*Oi la,* Romeo," said Lapo, putting his heels into the horse's side. *Must be an animal,* he thought, likely a wild boar. Horses were terrified of boar.

The horse snorted again, then sniffed. Then he began to walk off the trail into the trees.

"What are you doing, you crazy beast?"

He snatched at the reins, but the horse made a beeline for one large tree, then stopped under it.

"What on earth? You're insane, Romeo, let's go. *Andiamo.*"

The horse looked up into the tree. Lapo looked up as well.

He saw a young woman sitting very still. The plain shock of it made him sit there for an embarrassing three or four seconds without saying anything. She had red curly hair and looked strangely like a Klimt painting, he thought, though he couldn't remember the name of it. Swirls of tree branches, and a beautiful woman in a robe. Then it came to him: *The Tree of Life.*

"*Ciao,*" he said. "It appears you have mesmerized my horse."

"It's the carrots," she said. "My sack is full of carrots." She opened her fabric sack and showed it to Lapo. A carrot fell out and the horse picked it up and ate it.

Lapo was amused, wary, but also a little confused. She was small, young, and had an accent.

"I thought you were a patrol," she said. "That's why I hid up here."

"I'm not, so why don't you come down?"

She climbed slowly out of the tree. She was indeed young, he saw—twenties. Short. Pretty. That red hair. Freckled face. Not Italian.

"Your accent," he said. "You're not from the group that Pappone brought. Who are—"

"I'm just bringing some vegetables to Fosca," she interrupted. "From her niece."

"What's your name? You're American. Or are you?"

"I'm from Rome."

He did not believe her. And she wasn't saying her name. Now he was worried. Who was she, and why was she lying to him? "Does Fosca know you're coming? She didn't tell me."

"It's a surprise."

"What's your name?" he demanded. "Tell me."

"Sara Crewe. You're the *padrone.* They told me about you. You're married to an American."

"Yes. Though she's gone away. Sara Crewe. I know that name. Do I know you? I feel like I know you." Her accent was good, but he still thought she was probably an American. Maybe half-American, raised in Italy, like his own children. She had an easy smile that made him relax a little. Still, he knew as the landowner he should ask the girl for her documents. If Pappone found someone unregistered on his property, he would be blamed. "I'll walk to Fosca's with you to keep you safe."

"I have a bike," she said, pulling it out of the underbrush. "I'll be fine."

He smiled at her. "Yes. Fosca will have to register you," he added. "I'll tell Pappone for her that you're there."

"I'm not going to stay. Just dropping off the carrots and going."

"Oh, that's good. Because Felice Pappone is not the person you want to catch you as unregistered."

"Why not?"

Lapo wondered if she was a spy, sent by Pappone. Maybe he was being tested. "He's brave and fierce, a real patriot. He lives down there in the valley. Well, his parents do. But he visits them, and this is part of his territory."

"I'm not going to stay, so you don't have to say anything."

"I should, though."

"But you won't?"

He sighed. She was afraid, clearly, and that brought out a protective side of him, which was probably foolish, given that his job was to protect his family, the farmers, and now the prisoners. *His* people. "I won't. But we don't want any trouble here."

She nodded.

"If I see you again, I will turn you in."

She nodded again and rode off on her bike.

"Addio," he said.

He kicked the horse into a trot and rode off.

Shit, he said over and over to himself as he rode back down the dirt road to the castle. *That's all I need. If Pappone finds her and her papers are not in order, he's going to think I hid her here. He's going to kill her, and he might kill me, too.*

It came to him. Sara Crewe. *A Little Princess.* His daughters' favorite book. She'd given a false name. With Alessandro already in danger, there was no room for error. He should tell Pappone now. Get out in front of this thing.

Sally

I realized with a sinking heart that I couldn't go to Fosca now. It wasn't safe. The *padrone* was not to be trusted. He said he'd turn me in. I knew it wasn't personal, but it still stung. There was a reason most ancient stories elevated kindness to strangers to a high moral good. Of course, there was also a reason that expelling, imprisoning, and killing strangers was the leitmotif of human history. The Giulianos and Ilarias of the world were rare.

I headed in the opposite direction, away from Fosca's and away from the estate of Belsederino. I'd steer toward Rome, where at least I knew more people. Yes, it was the center of Italian Fascism, but maybe it was better to hide in crowds than here in the countryside where everyone knew everyone and a stranger was immediately noticed.

I mapped a back route through the mountains outside Grosseto and then south through the hills above the sea. There was no way to completely avoid larger roads—the journey would be risky.

I left the woods near Fosca's, crossed back through the forested part of the Belsederino estate without seeing anyone, and headed south, skirting the paved country road while keeping it in sight so I could navigate by it. I'd planned to avoid the busy road and bridge that spanned the river valley just southwest of Belsederino and instead drop down toward the river and carry my bike across the shallows, but there seemed to be no one around. Still, better safe than arrested. As I scanned my possible route, I could smell the sulfurous waters below where Giuliano told me people had gone to soak their aching bones and soothe various afflictions since at least Etruscan times. The Romans, of course, were the big soakers—they created elaborate stone pools to catch the warm water for bathing. Now I saw only a few goats.

I looked down at the river below, and something struck me. The shape of the curve. A dogleg.

I flipped through the notebook where I had written down Clio's stories. I found the map she had made. I held up the drawing of the river. It was close, but rivers twist back on themselves all the time. I looked at the map again, then turned and looked behind me. There was the funny-shaped mountain, like an ice cream cone someone had taken a big slurp out of.

As I was pondering this, I caught movement out of the corner of my eye. There was a figure up on the bridge. I ducked down in case he saw me. It must be a sentry. Where had he come from? He must have been crouching down before, and I'd missed him. I watched as the sentry climbed up on the railing and stood there, peering out over the void, arms out. It took me a moment to register exactly what he was doing.

Before I really thought it through, I clambered back up the hillside and started running onto the bridge.

"Wait!" I said. "Hang on one second!"

He—a young man in uniform about my own age—was so startled at my appearance that he nearly lost his balance. He teetered for a second, then stood still on the railing. One strong gust of wind and he would sail off it.

I stopped when I was about ten yards away.

He was wearing Italian Army fatigues, and there was a backpack next to him. On the ground next to the backpack were a canteen and a pistol. If he did jump, I could claim them for myself.

"What do you want?" he said. "I'm busy here."

"Learning to fly? It's harder than it looks."

"I thought I was alone. Where did you come from?" he asked.

"Over there." I gave a vague wave to the west.

"Are you lost?"

"Yes. Looks like you are, too."

"No. Not lost."

"Are you sure about this?" I waved my hand over the empty expanse of air.

He sighed and said, "This is a stupid war and I don't want any part of it anymore. Never did."

"I think that's true of almost everyone involved with it. There are, I'd guess, six people who actually want this war, and they've dragged the rest of us into it."

"You're an American."

"How does everyone know that?"

"Your accent."

"I suppose I do have an American accent. I can't hear it."

"I'm half-American. Whatever that means."

"Means you have conflicting feelings about this conflict."

"Means I don't count as a 'real' Italian."

"Don't let documents define you."

He squinted at me. "Who are you? What are you doing out here?"

"I'm a socialite."

He gave a snort. "You're kidding, right?"

"I grew up to be an irresponsible party girl. Then all this happened. I gave my U.S. passport to someone who needed it more than me, and now I'm on the lam. Could use some help, actually."

He pointed back to where I'd come from. "Go to Belsederino. It's right over that hill. My father will help you."

"Oh. That guy? I . . . saw him just now. I left because I think he's going to turn me in. He sent me away."

At this, he frowned and climbed down off the railing.

"Seriously? What the hell is wrong with him these days? My mother is going to blow her stack. He's got slave labor working in the fields. And he's writing a goddamn autobiography of Mussolini!"

It was my turn to laugh, taken aback by his passionate anger. "Sorry, that is . . . bad."

"I think he's writing the book to save me, but still. He could have found a way out of it . . . some other way."

"So that's why you're a bird in training?"

He turned back to the railing. "I can't go back to the army."

"Well, before you do . . . *that,* can you at least help me? I mean, if your life is so worthless to you, then there's no reason *not* to help me. Right?"

"What do you want me to do?"

"Help me find a safe place to stay. Do you know this spot?" I showed him the map. He looked at it and frowned. "Please. I have no one. I mean, if they kill us both, at least you can claim dying was your plan all along."

He stared at me for a second, then nodded. "Yeah. Okay. Let's get off this bridge. We're way too visible—"

The words had barely left his mouth when a car barreled onto the bridge. There was nowhere for us to run. It screeched to a halt and a comically tall and skinny Blackshirt got out. Most Italians are pretty short, but this guy had to be six foot four at least. You could tell they didn't make uniforms in his size. The pants were well above his ankles, and the sleeves of his coat were three-quarter length.

"Documents," the patrol demanded.

The soldier produced his military ID and papers.

The patrol examined them and then practically spat in his face. "You were due back days ago. You're a deserter."

The patrol was way less comical when he took his pistol and with that long skinny arm hit the soldier as hard as he could across the face. The soldier dropped to the ground. Then the patrol stood over him, cocked the pistol, and took aim. "As a traitor to your country, you must die."

What the hell? What about military due process? I ran full speed at the scarecrow Blackshirt and pushed. Caught completely unaware, he fell over the railing screaming and plummeted a hundred feet down, disappearing with a splash into the water below us.

I watched as the man's body surfaced like a water bug, not moving, facedown. I was frozen in place for a full minute, staring.

The soldier was panting and heaving. "You killed him," he said. "Are you crazy?"

"That was the opposite of crazy. We've got to get out of here," I said. "We've got to find this place on the map." I grabbed his pack, slung it over my handlebars, and shoved the gun in my pocket. "Come on." I kicked him. He groaned. "Come on, buddy. Get up. Hurry." I pulled him to his feet. He was staggering and barely able to walk. "We'll leave a note in the car. Suicide." My mind was spinning as I turned my bike around. We'd have to work fast.

"Hurry up," I said again.

"It's no use. Now they'll have me for murder. They're always going to find me again." He lurched toward the railing. "You're safer without me. Go back to my father. He's a good man."

Before I could stop him, he climbed back up onto the railing.

Sally and Alessandro

I grabbed the back of the soldier's jacket with both hands and pulled with all my strength. For a second, I thought that not only was I too late, but his weight would pull me over the edge, too. Another bad decision, Daddy. We teetered. And tottered. Then he fell backward onto me. We lay there for a second, panting.

"This is war. He was going to kill you, so I killed him. It was the right thing to do. The only thing to do." It felt very clear to me. "Stop thinking and walk."

✿

We hid the bicycle and made our way in darkness across country, avoiding roads. Alessandro—that's what the soldier's name was—said he thought he knew the crossroads with the cypresses that Clio had drawn.

"There's no house there, though," he said.

We had a moon to guide us, but that was dangerous, too. Anytime we were out of the trees, we were visible. For safety, we moved in silence. In a clearing, Alessandro paused and looked down into the valley below. Because of the blackout rule, the castle where his father lived was totally dark, though he said he could see the faint outlines of the house where people he knew called Roghi and Luisa lived. The castle complex with its half-crumbled wall looked warm and inviting, even in the cold silvery moonlight.

"We can't go there," he whispered. "It's the first place they'll look."

"I think this hermitage will be safe," I said, holding the map. I trusted that Clio had given it to me for a reason, and left off place-names for a reason, too.

An owl began to hoot, and we slipped back into the woods. He led me deep into the forest. We emerged at a crossroads in the moonlight. I counted the cypresses. Four on one side, three on the other. We ducked back into the forest.

"It should be up there," I said, pointing into the darkness. We heard animal noises as the forest grew denser and denser. I tripped and fell, and Alessandro walked into a tree.

"I think someone played a cruel joke on you," he said.

But then, there it was. An abandoned stone building so covered in vines it was barely recognizable as a structure.

In the moonlight, I could make out pointed, arched doorways along the ground floor, and small irregularly spaced rectangular windows above that made it seem like there were secret floors inside.

"It really is an ancient *eremo*," Alessandro said in English, eyes wide in surprise. "I've lived only a few miles away my whole life and I had no idea this was here."

We crawled carefully through the vines into the half-ruined building, leaving the growth in place so no one would notice anything amiss. Part of the roof was open to the sky, and the vines had invaded the inside as well. There was crumbling stucco on some walls, whitewashed in some places and pale blue in others. Heavy beams crossed over our heads, with plenty of bird poo under our feet on piles of dusty bricks and leaves. On the far side of the house, Alessandro pried apart the vines until he found a door that led into a *cantina*, which was cut deep in the hillside. I felt cool air and the smell of mustiness waft over me.

"You go first," I said. "I hate spiders."

"Me, too."

We used our flashlights to find the spiderwebs and a branch to knock them down. The *cantina* was a short passageway into a large arched room made of stone. The ceiling was about twelve feet at its highest point. There were old wooden wine casks, lots of empty bottles of an uncertain vintage covered with dust, and a few demijohns still containing wine.

"We won't die of thirst," he said, picking up a bottle. "Though I think a lot of this might be past its optimal date. This one is dated 1837."

"Can you drink wine after a hundred years?"

"Not this kind of wine. This one looks a little newer."

"Let's try it."

We sat down on the dirt floor, which felt cool to the touch. I took off my pack and offered him some of the vegetables Ilaria had packed for me that morning, which seemed a long, long time ago. He used his pocketknife to open the bottle of wine and took a pull from it, then passed it to me.

"A little corked. Not as bad as I thought it might be," he said.

I drank, feeling the warmth of his mouth on the bottle's neck, then passed it back to him. Now that we were in what I hoped was a safe location, I wondered who this guy was, exactly. Good guy, bad guy, or something in between?

"We should use the light as little as possible, for safety," I said. "We need to get used to darkness." I clicked off the flashlight and we sat in the dark, breathing. My eyes kept trying to adjust, to make out Alessandro, or anything in the darkness, but there was nothing. I was putting a lot of trust in a total stranger, though I was still in possession of the pistol.

"So now we just wait out the rest of the war?" he asked.

"Raw carrots are going to get old fast."

"I don't do well in captivity."

"No one does. They'll be looking for you, but maybe you can at least go out a bit at night."

"I don't want to spend the last years of my life stuck in this room. That's worse than the army."

"Stop being so dramatic, Gary Cooper. And it's not worse than the army. The idea is that they won't be the last years of your life. Learn a little patience, my friend."

He laughed a little. "Yeah. Not my strong suit. I thrive on outrage and despair."

"Well, you could fight for the other side. There's a network of people. The woman who gave me this map, she was a part of it. And another woman I met."

"How do we make contact?"

His voice had lost its sad and angry edge. I could feel a new energy coming off him in the darkness. It spoke to something inside me.

"I don't know. We have to figure out who to trust." *We.*

"Not my father, apparently."

"If he's writing a book about Mussolini, does that mean he meets with him face-to-face?"

"I don't know. I would think so. I was too disgusted to ask."

"We could kill Mussolini."

I heard Alessandro shift. "I only met you two hours ago and already you killed someone and now you're proposing we assassinate the leader of Italy. You're one tough broad."

"Yeah. So you better not turn out to be a jerk." I took a swig of the wine. "I know I should feel bad about that guy. But I don't."

"You saved my life. But what do we do now?"

I laughed. "You wanted action. I was happy to spend the next few years hiding in this luxurious hermitage, drinking wine, sneaking out to harvest some truffles now and then, maybe taking up knitting or whittling a backgammon set. I'm just coming up with ways to pass the time."

He flashed the light on and for a strobing second, I caught him staring at me.

"You're very beautiful."

"I said 'ways to pass the time' and your brain went right to sex. Men are unbelievable."

"I didn't say anything about sex. You're making an assumption."

"So you weren't thinking about sex?"

"I gave you a compliment, that's all."

"On my appearance."

"Yes."

"Shallow." I was intentionally giving him a hard time. I didn't know why. It felt playful, which was fairly insane given the day we'd had.

"Didn't you say you were a socialite?"

"I didn't say I wasn't shallow, too."

"What if I am shallow? Like every other human alive."

I sighed in the darkness. "Don't you think judging each other on our appearances and who we're related to is the root of everything that's wrong with the world?"

I heard the slosh of the wine in the bottle as he took a swig. "I wish we were all blinded. Just universally, everyone on the planet, all at once," he said.

"I hope I'm not in a moving car when that happens."

"We would probably start discriminating against each other based on smell." I heard him take a long inhale.

I did the same. "Smells like old dirt in here."

"And wine."

"Speaking of which, stop hogging." I felt the air move as he shifted closer to me in the darkness and passed the bottle to me. It took me a second to find his arm and then the bottle. "I really can't see anything," I said.

"Flowers. I can smell flowers."

"I'm sure you're getting a little odor of sweat, too. I've ridden that bike pretty hard for quite a while now." I leaned toward where I could sense he was and took a big inhale. "Sweat. Yup. You're the only Italian who doesn't smoke. That's good."

"Anything else?"

I snuffled closer to him.

"Cotton. Laundry soap," I said. "That's in short supply." I reached out and my hand landed on his arm. He took the bottle from me, but I grabbed his sleeve and pulled it to my nose. "Gunpowder. Mud." I pushed his sleeve up and sniffed the skin of his arm, on the underside of his wrist, like a perfume saleswoman. I laid my nose against his warm skin. "Courage. Strength." I put my lips against his wrist and licked. "Salt. Now I'm kind of craving a pretzel." I dropped his hand. There was silence between us for several seconds. I heard the soft thump of his jacket hitting the dirt as he lay down.

"Fear. Can you smell that? It's all over me," he said.

"You'd have to be pretty stupid not to be afraid these days."

"This morning I wanted to die, but now I don't. But I'm not going back."

I could feel my heart beating in my neck.

"Are you afraid?" he asked.

"Yes. Not right at this moment. I actually feel safe here. I feel like maybe this place is okay." I wanted to say, "Please don't be a bad guy," but I didn't. Maybe I didn't need to.

"I won't let anything happen to you."

I exhaled. "Same here. Got your six."

I waited until I could hear his breathing. I lay down in the dirt. Then I must have fallen asleep.

I woke up to total darkness and panicked, flailing my arms around. A light flicked on and I could see part of a face. A friendly face. Whose was it?

"It's me. Alessandro. You're okay. Remember the *eremo*?"

"Better than I remember the Alamo." This joke of course meant nothing to Alessandro, so I was spared a groan. "Do I have any bugs on me?"

"Not that I can see." He reached out and brushed something off my cheek. "You're good."

He flicked the light off. I touched the place on my cheek where his fingers had brushed.

"Did you sleep?" I asked.

"Yeah. And I panicked when I woke up, too. The total-darkness thing is unsettling."

"What time is it?"

"Eight in the morning."

"Oh. We were out a long time."

"Yeah. You got a big day planned? Luncheon with the king and queen? Here, have an apple. A little shriveled, but still good."

I waved my hand around until I found it. It was strange to bite into something I couldn't see. The crunch of it was very satisfying, though, and the sweet tanginess filled my mouth, despite the mustiness that marked the beginnings of rot.

"Well. I thought I might spy on your father. Figure out if we can trust him. It would be nice to have someone who could drop off food for us somewhere, or different somewheres. I mean, I can go steal, but you know. . . ." I thought of Alba's hoarded food.

"I want to go outside with you."

"Let me get the lay of the land first."

"There's one thing you need to know," he said, suddenly serious. "Felice Pappone. He's the local militia leader. A real top-class jerk. His parents live on the estate. The house on the other side of these woods. His father is the gamekeeper."

"Your father mentioned him."

"Just know that he's armed and always looking for poachers on Belsederino, which means he's all over the woods. You want to steer clear of all the Pappones."

"Got it. Do you have any sense of a schedule Pappone Senior follows, or places where he usually patrols?"

"No. He changes it up so he can catch people red-handed. If he catches you, pretend to be one of the prisoners my dad is overseeing." He told me about how the Pappones hated his family. Having an American as the *padrona* of the estate was abhorrent to them, no matter how kind Eleanor was. And so Felice hated Alessandro, too, no matter how much Alessandro tried to be friends. He was mystified as a boy by this rejection, and his mother had done the painful work of trying to explain xenophobia.

I drank from my wine-turned-water bottle and wiped my mouth. "You must miss your mom. Dried fig?" Our fingers touched as I passed him the fruit. It was interesting that we didn't have to flail about to find each other's hand this time. I just reached out and his hand was there.

"So much. I'm terrified I'll never see her again."

The sweet scent of fig filled my nose. "Where is she?"

"Chicago. She didn't want to leave Italy, but my dad made her. My sisters are with her. I haven't seen her in so long. Even letters don't get through now. It's so terrible. Where are your parents?"

I explained and he listened in silence, then said, "I'm so sorry."

I was touched by the emotion in his voice. "Why did you and your dad stay in Italy?"

"I couldn't leave. Military age. They would have stopped me at the border. My dad stayed because I had to."

"So he's not a bad guy."

"I never thought so. But then he hit me with that 'I'm writing a book for Mussolini' news."

"That's what we're going to figure out. What that is all about."

"I wish I could come with you. Please be careful."

I reached out in the dark and put my hand on his chest. I could feel his heart beating under my palm. "I will."

I got up and walked toward the door, hands in front of me. I listened at the door to the *cantina,* then slowly pushed it open. Light burst in, making me blink.

I turned and could half see his face in the darkness, smiling at me.

Lapo

"Where is your son?"

Lapo was standing in the doorway of the castle. He channeled Ettore the Labrador and gave Pappone his blankest look. "By now back in Prague, I would imagine, unless the trains were delayed."

"He is not in Prague. He's a deserter."

"Impossible. He talked all about the mission. He was very excited about it. If he's not there yet, he's doing his best to get there. Is the militia keeping the train lines safe? Maybe he's been attacked." Turning the responsibility for Alessandro back on Pappone felt satisfying, but at the bottom of his stomach there was a churning feeling. Where was Alessandro? He issued a silent prayer that he had not done the terrible thing. *Please please please.*

"Your son disappears and a military patrol officer ends up at the bottom of a ravine. It's suspicious."

"He could have tried to stop someone who was attacking that officer and been abducted. Are you searching the area? This is very serious."

Pappone looked hard at him. Lapo held his gaze. He wanted to scream. But they had not found Alessandro's body, so he had to hope he was safe. "This is my son, Pappone. If he's in danger, he needs our help!"

"I know that."

"Andiamo! Let's find him!"

Pappone shifted. He preferred issuing commands to following them. "Of course we're looking. We have patrols out all over."

"I'll alert Mussolini's office that we have dangerous brigades of ruffians in the area who are attacking our noble Italian Army officers. I'm sure they'll want to help you control this zone."

"No need to do that. I have the situation fully in hand."

"Good. I'll expect a report from you at the end of the week."

He smiled to himself as soon as Pappone's car disappeared over the hill. Then his smile vanished. Where was Alessandro?

Sally and Alessandro

I stayed in the shadows of the woods, keeping my eyes and ears peeled for the scary game warden or his thug son. My terror was if the gamekeeper had a dog with him. But apart from a lot of squirrels, a stunning group of blue butterflies, and a very plump red fox, I didn't see anyone as I crept through the woods toward the castle.

When I had a good view of it, I climbed a tree and watched. It was a huge picturesque old wreck, a half-crumbled massive stone wall with crenellations, a slightly unstable-looking tower with small, irregularly spaced windows, and a farmhouse complex below. And I thought Patsy's house was a castle. It was hard to picture kids growing up here. Where did they go to school? Such a romantic but remote place. Did Alessandro have friends? I would bet he was very close with his sisters, and must miss them. He must also know a lot about nature, having lived immersed in it. I tried to envision what it would be like to grow up there in the countryside, surrounded by a large and loving family. It hurt too much and I thought about how much I hated Fascists instead.

I'd killed a man without hesitating. Did he have a wife, kids? Did he believe in what he was doing, or was he just following orders? I tried to tell myself he was a murderous psycho who disobeyed military procedure by not merely arresting us. But I realized I was believing in rules about honor, about valuing life and treating people nicely and fairly, about justice. Rules that didn't exist now. That idea was somehow more terrifying to me than anything.

✿

"He stares out the window a lot," I told Alessandro later. "The third window, near the top. For minutes on end."

We were sitting in the darkness. Alessandro had turned on his flashlight when I returned.

"Welcome home," he said with a grin.

I laughed. "I've been waiting my whole life to hear those words," I said.

He was eager to show off the improvements he'd made to our living space in the cellar. "Casual callers will be impressed with the comfort and beauty, and all on a shoestring budget," he said, imitating the American home décor magazines he said his mom loved to read. He'd created an "elegantly simple" eating area, with a couple of small crates to sit on and a makeshift table. There was a "highly luxurious" sleeping area, with smooth, soft dirt and our bedrolls, discreetly located on either side of a small table for the lamp. There was a "state-of-the-art" exercise area where one could do push-ups and sit-ups, run in place, and use stones as barbells. There was a "library" with one book. And there was a "discreet yet effective" latrine hole in the farthest corner of the *cantina*.

"I've never had a home before," I said. "I mean, not in a really long time. I appreciate the lack of gingham. Never liked that fabric. It clashes with my face."

We opened a bottle of Brunello to celebrate.

I realized I felt comfortable with him, even more than I had with Giuliano and Ilaria. It was strange. I wasn't used to feeling at ease around people.

"Dad looks out the window like that when he's writing," Alessandro said. "Or not writing."

"He also spent a couple of hours staring at chickens."

"Really? He doesn't usually do that. Luisa is the only one who cares for the chickens."

"There were a lot of people around, doing various chores."

"The political prisoners from Siena."

"And the Blackshirt came. I think it was the guy you said."

"Pappone?"

"Thrusts his chest out like a Ziegfeld girl?"

"That's him."

"He showed up around three and stayed for a few minutes."

"Hmm. Not good. He didn't seem to threaten my father or anything, did he?"

"No. He saluted him when he left."

Alessandro stared into his cup of wine for a second, then asked, "Are you sure no one saw you?"

"Sure."

"Pappone's looking for me."

"Finding both of us would be his lucky day." I took the bottle of wine and poured more into my tin cup. "Listen, do you think we should kill him if he does come here?"

"Geez. You're making me nervous, bloodthirsty American girl."

"But seriously. I mean, I think we need to talk these things out before they happen. That other thing took me by surprise."

"I guess we'd have to kill him." Alessandro frowned, and I studied the line of his jaw in the flat white light of the flashlight. "But I don't know that I could. I grew up with him."

It struck me that that was the key—familiarity might breed contempt, but it also breeds a sense of connection that makes you less likely to harm the person. Connection makes you see people as fellow humans.

I opened my pack. "I found the wild greens just where you said." I proudly showed him. "Can we eat these mushrooms?" I produced a couple of large fungi.

"No. Throw them in the latrine, please, so we don't accidentally consume them."

"Oh, well. I found some wild asparagus, too. And a nest of bird eggs." I showed him the tiny eggs I'd found. "We need something more substantial, though. I'm going to try to steal a wheel of cheese from Fosca. I'll leave her some money, so I guess it's not stealing. I don't think she'll tell anyone." I shivered. "It's warmer in here than out there."

"I wish we could make a fire. Cook something. Keep warm. It can get very cold at Belsederino."

"The temperature should be pretty steady in here, though, underground. God, this wine is good."

He drank from his cup. "Brunello is the nectar of the gods." He crunched on an asparagus stalk. "I want to go out."

"I know. Soon. First things first. Can we trust your father?"

✿

I was creeping along the edge of a pasture, staying in the trees, when a low-flying plane passed over me. I climbed under the bush, where I would be invisible, but I was unnerved. I stayed farther away from open areas the whole morning.

In the afternoon, I spied on Lapo as he worked with a young horse in the round pen, then watched as he rode him out of the pen and up the road out of sight.

"He's probably checking on Fosca," said Alessandro when I got back to the wine cellar. We were eating hunks of cheese from the wheel I'd stolen from Fosca's aging room, and grapes from the vineyard that were not as tasty as they looked. "He does that at least once a week."

"He's looking for you, I think. He looks worried."

Alessandro was silent.

"I think we should talk to him. I'm going to try."

Lapo and Sally

Lapo was riding the young horse along the trail that went up to the little lake. The trail cut through *macchia,* or brush, that was nearly impenetrable, unless you were a wild boar or porcupine. He had to admire the dense tangle of wild rosemary, broom, juniper, and erica, with the occasional cork oak rising above the fray. Lapo and Roghi had discovered abandoned fields and buildings under the ever-advancing *macchia,* and a big part of daily life at Belsederino was trying to keep the plants from reclaiming their territory.

In case anyone was spying on him, he was trying to appear like a slightly idiotic, inbred landowner just out for a ride, but in reality, he was checking on the hidden livestock, and also looking for any trace of Alessandro. He had to be here somewhere. Where else would he go?

The horse's ears went up and he stopped.

"Romeo? What do you see?"

The horse snorted.

A young woman stepped out of the bushes.

"Signor Lapo."

"I remember you. Go away. You'll get us all killed." A cuckoo sounded nearby. The birds were everywhere this spring, mocking him with their ridiculous, incessant calls. *Cuk-oo. Cuk-oo.*

"I need your help."

The horse insisted on sniffing her pockets. Lapo tried to use the height advantage he had to convey authority.

"I don't have a lot of help to give. You can't be here. I'm looking for my son. Have you seen him?"

"Is he missing?"

His face was hard. "He's been kidnapped by bandits." *Cuk-oo.*

"Bandits?"

"Rebels. Whatever you want to call them. The local militia is looking desperately for him. So am I." *Cuk-oo.*

"Oh. I'm sorry to hear that. I need some bandages. For a friend. As soon as we can, we'll move on."

So she was part of some resistance. He knew it. Dammit. That was the last thing he needed in his woods. "It's not Alessandro, is it?"

"No. Will you bring some bandages and anything you have to clean a wound?"

Oh God, he thought. Probably a downed British pilot or an escaped POW. Shit.

Sally and Lapo

The next day, I waited near the old washing tubs for Alessandro's father. I came hours early and hid so I could see anyone who came up the track before they saw me. My plan for escape was to run like hell down through the beech woods and into the *macchia*. I was pretty sure I could lose anyone in there except a dog.

I heard a horse coming, and soon Alessandro's father appeared. He dismounted, tied the horse to a tree, and sat near the washtubs, waiting, his back to me.

I watched him for a few minutes, then stepped out into the open.

As I did, I heard a twig break behind me. I turned and saw a black uniform in the shadows of the trees.

"Stop!" the man shouted. "Hands up!"

I bolted past Alessandro's father, who jumped to his feet, but my planned escape route was cut off. I ran the other way, into unfamiliar terrain, as fast as I could. I could hear the two men shouting, then footsteps behind me.

So Alessandro's father was a Fascist.

I was fast, and I tried to stay in the trees, but the forest was opening up, more sunlight coming through, not less. *Shit*. I could hear footsteps behind me. I accelerated, leaping rocks and bushes, my lungs burning, my heart pounding.

The path ahead of me widened again, and now I was afraid the guy could get a shot off if he stopped and took aim. *Pfft*. A bullet whizzed past me. I dodged, hoping he couldn't get a clear shot in the trees. *Pfft. Pfft*. Trees snatched the bullets on either side of me. Suddenly I was on the edge of a field—*shit*. There was a half-ruined barn ahead. Alessandro had made me take the gun with me. If I could get a wall between me and them, I could try to pick them off. The barn door was closed, but I saw a small, crumbled portion of the wall, about waist height, near the door. Was it big enough to squeeze through before they shot me? I ran straight to the barn, bullets whizzing around me, and dove through the hole.

Lapo

Lapo, huffing and sweating, ran up behind Pappone as he was aiming his weapon at the barn. Pappone fired several shots at the structure. There was no response. Pappone headed slowly toward the barn.

"I saw her go off that way," Lapo lied, pointing past the barn.

Pappone walked up to Lapo, threw an arm around his neck from behind, and put the gun to his temple. "Who is she?"

Lapo willed himself to stay calm. "I don't know. I stopped to water my horse. I've never seen her before."

"Why should I believe you?"

"Because it's the truth."

Lapo could smell Pappone's horrible breath, his foul, musky sweat. Pappone kept his arm around Lapo's neck and pushed him toward the barn, a human shield. "Drop the gun. Come out with your hands up," he called.

He pushed Lapo up against the hole near the door, then peered around him into the barn. Clearly he couldn't see anything, because he said, "If you move, I'll shoot you dead." He released his hold on Lapo's neck. Lapo stood still, hands up. Pappone tried to kick at the heavy wooden door. It didn't open, and he raised his gun to shoot the door open.

Lapo said, "A moment, please. Don't shoot me." He stepped forward and turned the doorknob. The door swung open, and the room was revealed to them. Light came in through the brickwork lattice along the top edge of the wall where it met the ceiling. It was completely empty except for a small scattering of straw on the terra-cotta floor. A bird cooed at them from a nest on a rafter, then flew out through the lattice. Pappone shot at it.

"A pigeon," said Lapo. "That's all. Just a pigeon." His mind was racing as he presented Pappone with a genial smile. How had she gotten out? There were no other doors and no windows. Where was the girl?

Sally and Lapo

I closed the trapdoor as fast as I could, feeling in the darkness for some kind of latch. I could faintly hear footsteps over my head, and I dared not move or breathe. I was worried that the trapdoor, having been opened recently, would appear different from the rest of the floor and reveal its secret, as it had for me when I ran in and found it slightly cracked open. But the footsteps receded, and I let myself breathe.

Where was I? I could smell a musty odor, but not like the wine cellar. And it was dry, not damp. When I'd opened the trapdoor, I'd seen only a wooden staircase, darkness hiding whatever was below. I was a little worried about turning on my flashlight now, in case a sea of snakes or rats peered back at me from around my ankles, but I finally counted to ten and pressed the button.

I inhaled in surprise and relief. Below me, I could make out a room filled with tall rectangular structures. Waving my arm at the sticky cobwebs, I made my way carefully down the stairs. They were creaky, and some of the boards looked questionable, but they held. I made it to the cool stone floor, which I imagined must be twenty feet underground. I was standing in an aisle of floor-to-ceiling wood shelving. *Must be some kind of root cellar or wine-aging room,* I thought. I shone my flashlight over the shelves. They held bundles of old documents tied with twine—really old, from the look of them. There were boxes, too, hand-lettered in careful ink. I centered the beam on one of the boxes. SALDI VINO E OLIO DAL 1712–1714. I scanned left and right, up and down. Most of the shelves contained heavy paper or leather binders bulging with documents. They were almost all tan, some with faded red stripes, and others with elaborate designs hand done in ink, scrolls and curlicues and crests. There were shelves of scrolls, and piles of wrinkled parchment tied with flat white cloth ribbons. The shelves were not numbered, and it looked like the documents had been transported here in haste—they were shoved, not placed, and the dates were not in order. There was a wooden box with a faded family crest of a pair of bears and the words FAMIGLIA CERVINI. I started walking, and realized there was more than just this room—six rooms, in fact, each filled to the ceiling with shelves of old documents. One room had brown paper bundles tied with white string that reminded me of panforte, and another had maps piled up on narrow tables. Everything I could see was wrinkled, tattered, water stained, rumpled, crumbling, and extremely fragile look- ing. The oldest date I could find in a quick walkabout was 1250, and the newest was 1861.

I heard faint footsteps, and a light tapping. Someone was coming. They hadn't given up. I took out the gun and hid behind a shelf, ready, willing my heart to slow down.

The trapdoor dropped open and fresh air cascaded over me.

"Hello?" a voice called in whispered English. "He's gone."

I said from behind the bookshelf, "Close the trapdoor and keep your hands up." I felt like I was in one of George's westerns, but the cavalry was not coming to save me.

The figure did as I said, plunging us into darkness as soon as the door was closed. I turned my flashlight on him. It was Lapo. "Come down slowly."

He did.

"Take your clothes off."

He raised his eyebrows but undid his belt and dropped his pants. Re- moved his tweed jacket, loden-green vest, and white collared shirt. He stood there in pink plaid boxer shorts, his hands up.

"Step away from the clothes."

"I don't have a gun," he said.

I took his clothes and began to check them.

"What is this place?" he said. "I had no idea this was here."

In his pocket, I found bandages and a bottle of iodine. I sighed with relief.

"You can get dressed again. It's a bunch of binders and ledgers," I said with distaste. "A bureaucrat's dream."

✿

"These are all the records of the estate," he said in amazement, after making a tour of the rooms. I hadn't told him yet about Alessandro. I wanted to hear more from him, find out where he stood. He could have alerted the Fascist officer and set a trap for me. "All the farm records—sales of farm products, property sales, wills and testaments, equipment inventories, menus for grand dinners, household expenses, sharecropping records. It's amazing. I thought all this was gone. That's what they told me when I bought it in 1919. 'It has been empty for sixty years,' they said, and that it was all gone."

"Looks like just a lot of numbers to me."

"But numbers that tell a story. A thousand stories. Look at this: '*Quadernetti delle Fattorie*' from 1632 to 1634. The estate bought a mule for six florins. A molly."

"Great. Why do you think they hid all this? Who would care?"

"My guess is to keep it safe during the war of unification. That's when the owner died, in 1861. He might have been the only one who knew this was here. After he died, the estate languished. His wife never came back. I think for a while the banks owned it, then maybe the state, for taxes. Anyway, when I bought the place, they told me there were no estate records at all, outside of what's in government archives. This is wonderful—it's the history I was looking for. Now I know exactly how the farm was run!"

I was less enthusiastic. "Why did you bring the Blackshirt?" I asked.

"I didn't. I don't know how to prove that to you. Where is the injured person?"

"There isn't one. It was a test."

"A test?"

"Of whether you're a good person or not."

"Oh." He shifted on his bootheels. "Well, I swear I didn't know Pappone was following me. To be honest, I'm sorry I didn't accidentally drown him when he was a child." He gingerly removed a book of accounts and opened it, his eyes greedily scouring the handwriting in the ink ledger. "I keep books just like these myself," he said.

"Man's eternal quest to keep track of things and thus control them."

He laughed. "True. But you're really in danger," he said, putting the book down. "Pappone is tenacious. He's going to take this personally. He'll be back with dogs to search the forest. You need to get out of here now."

I sighed. "Alessandro is here."

Sally and Alessandro

I was telling Alessandro about the archives. "Not a single mention of a human being. Just numbers. As if that's all that matters."

He was mad that I'd put myself in danger. I wondered if he was going to hug me after I told him about my escape, but he didn't. I realized I wanted him to. Dammit. The damn unfurling was happening. An attraction would only complicate things. But I wanted to touch him.

He smiled and dropped to do a set of push-ups. Was he showing off for me? Or just sticking to his plan to stay strong for whatever was ahead of us? This was all getting—

"My father bought the place. Don't confuse us with the Cervinis," he said. "My family isn't noble."

"'Noble.' A fancy name for those who exploit others and get rich. Who care about their kids but not other people's kids."

Alessandro lifted an eyebrow, then continued the push-ups. "Babbo used to tell us about the family that owned the place for hundreds of years and died out. The Cervinis are somehow related to the Spannocchis, like all Italian noble families are related. I did some research in the archives in Siena. Bankers that bought property all over Tuscany." Alessandro was panting now, squeezing the words out as his arms pumped up and down. He was definitely showing off. "They made a few catastrophic alliances along the way, but they always rose back up." Alessandro dropped to the ground and stretched like a swimming fish.

"Rich people tend to do that."

Alessandro rolled over and started on his sit-ups. "Tiburzio was the most famous of them. Military engineer. Died in Spain in the early sixteen hundreds."

"I'm impressed by your detailed knowledge."

"History major, remember? Tiburzio built fortresses. Lots and lots of fortresses, in Cádiz, Santander, Zaragoza, Jaca, San Sebastian, Havana."

"Cuba?"

"Cartagena, in Colombia, too."

"War and subjugation—always a good way to make money."

"You a communist?" He finished his exercises and sat back and drank some water, panting.

I leaned against the rough stone wall of the *cantina*. The cool felt good against my body. "I'm not anything. I hate politics. It's all men trying to help their own. Women don't matter. Only sheaves of wheat and florins matter. But look at it this way. Everyone on earth is descended in the same way, right? We all had two parents, four grandparents, et cetera."

"Yes. Barring incest."

"Barring incest. Thank you. Some people have detailed histories of their ancestors because they were rich and literate, like these people. Other families don't know their history because they were poor and illiterate."

Alessandro nodded.

"But that doesn't mean they didn't exist. I guess that's what bothers me. It's like anyone whose history isn't written down doesn't exist."

"Is that why you write everything down? I see you, with your notebooks."

I shifted. "A bad habit. This isn't about me. I'm talking about everyone who didn't build a castle or name a mountain after himself." I looked at my own hands for a moment. Sometimes when I was sad, I would tell myself they were my ma's hands, stuck onto the ends of my arms. I would pretend my mother was caressing my forehead or rubbing my back. "The rich hold the pen of history, and all that."

"I want to drink to that, but I'm afraid you'll get out a guillotine."

I leaned forward and gave him a playful swat on the arm, feeling the muscle beneath as I did. Cue more unfurling. "The rich and powerful think they have immortality, but one fire, one flood, one infertile generation erases it all," I said. "Nature is a great cure for hubris." I could feel the heat radiating off his warm body in the cool cellar. He leaped up and grabbed an iron bar that extended across the arched ceiling of the *cantina* and began to do pull-ups. His shirt rode up and I could see the skin of his lower abdomen above his pants. I felt my face flush hot, and turned away.

I covered my unease with words. "Rich people use writing—banks and wills and real estate records—to pass on their wealth, and their children get richer. Poor children start over every single generation."

I heard his feet drop to the dirt floor. I turned and he was standing there, shirt off, looking at me. His body was beautiful—strong, smooth, alive. He came close. I could feel his breath.

I swallowed to ease the dryness in my throat. I sat down at our table, and he pulled on a shirt and sat opposite me. I said, "We're obviously in a very charged situation. Isolated from the rest of the world and facing death at any moment."

"You faced it today." He put his hands over mine for a second, and then released them. "You're beautiful. And so brave. You're amazing."

I thought about Patsy's rules but found I couldn't remember them. I had a sense Patsy would like Alessandro, that she would approve.

He lowered his voice. "Let's face it, appearance matters because deep down, we're animals."

I could still feel the lingering warmth of his hands on my skin. I found my voice. "But is this a good idea?" I could hear Patsy in my head screaming, "Yes!"

He got up and grabbed a bottle of wine and opened it. He said, "Of course not." He poured each of us a cup, and set the cups down on the table. I tried to pretend I was not disappointed.

We each took a sip. And then promptly spat, stuck our tongues out, and made faces.

"Uccch. Corked," said Alessandro.

"Icchhh," I said, wiping my mouth with my sleeve. "Hang on, I'll get another one." I walked the thirty feet back to the far end of the *cantina*. I lingered there for a second. I was about to complicate things. But if I were about to die, I wanted to have loved someone like Alessandro first. There was no time to lose. I grabbed a bottle of Brunello and headed back to the front of the *cantina*. My heart was beating faster, already anticipating the feel of his hands on my body.

Except Alessandro was gone.

Sally

I stared at the place where Alessandro had been standing. I blinked a few times and shone my flashlight around. The door was open. There was no sign of a struggle. I'd heard nothing, but then again, I was far away behind heavy walls.

I turned off my lamp and crept forward to look and listen outside the *cantina* door. The crumbling old *eremo* was silent. I crept out, letting my eyes adjust to the darkness. I realized I was holding my knife—I didn't remember pulling it out of its sheath at my hip. I looked for the gun, but it was gone. Dammit.

I moved silently through the *eremo* and exited from the side of the building, not the front. I stepped carefully over the vines and used my hands to guide me when I couldn't see. I felt like a cat, wondering if I was the stalker or the stalkee. I was about to move around the front of the building when I heard a voice.

"Where are you taking me?" It was Alessandro.

I froze. Could I overcome whoever or whatever had him? Or was I going to get caught, too, in which case I would be no help whatsoever? I heard footsteps. I crept through the dense trees parallel to the footsteps. It seemed to be one person who had him. They were moving in darkness. I guessed that the person must have a gun on Alessandro, and was behind him, because I could hear no struggle.

"You know me," said Alessandro. "Please, Signor Pappone. You know who I am. Your son and I grew up together. You're like a second father to me."

The game warden.

"You're a traitor. A deserter."

"You don't know what I've seen. The way the Nazis are killing civilians. It's not right. I stood up for Italian dignity and values."

"By running away?" The old man snorted. "You're a coward."

"We're losing this war. We all know that. At what point is it more noble and patriotic to admit that, to put our children's future above our pride?"

"The radio says we're winning."

I was forming a plan. I could make a noise, distract the man. I could glide up behind him and stab him, or jump on top of him. Anything to give Alessandro a chance to get the gun.

The two men passed into a shaft of moonlight along the dirt track and I saw Alessandro first—his hands were tied behind him. That was bad—it would be hard for him to get the gun. The older man was medium height, holding a rifle, walking behind Alessandro as I had imagined.

"The Germans are cruel," said Alessandro. "It's dishonorable how they behave. Confining people in ghettoes and camps. Putting women and children in cattle cars. They're killing them. It's a wholesale slaughter of innocent people."

"It's a war," said the man, lighting a cigarette. "That's what war is."

"Why are we in it? Can you answer me that?"

"Because we're fighting an enemy who threatens our survival."

"Who is that enemy? The Czechs? The Poles? The British? How are they threatening Italy?"

"The Americans. It's all the fault of the Americans."

"You know Americans. My mother. Do you feel threatened by her? Do you remember our American friends who came to visit? How much they loved our culture?"

"Things have changed."

"Mussolini has told you to hate them. That's the only thing that's changed. He's demonized them, made false accusations, lied about them. Every dictator needs a scapegoat, and he chose the British and French and Americans. He's just making us afraid so he can stay in power."

I got ready to jump. I would tackle the old man, fight for the gun. Give Alessandro a chance to run. Then the smoke from the gamekeeper's cigarette hit my nose.

Sneeze.

The old man started firing in my direction. I ran, hiding behind tree trunks, as bullets whizzed past me, then dove under a bush in a hollow in the earth.

The bullets stopped, and the footsteps receded.

I waited until they were gone, then raced forward after them, as silently as possible, running in the sandy soil down the track. I would burst onto them, I hoped, and go for a tackle.

I got to where the path met one of the rutted winding dirt roads that cut through the forest. Moonlight illuminated the road, which was empty. It was only then, as I stood there on the edge of the forest, that I realized I was bleeding.

Lapo and Sally

Lapo stared at the panicked young woman, trying to quell his own panic. "Maybe we can trade," she said. "Give me up for him."

He sighed. "They'll just keep both of you." She'd snuck into the castle to get him, bleeding and upset. She was so quiet that Ettore had not even stirred as she slipped into the room. He rushed her out before any of the other castle inhabitants were awakened. He sent her to the basement of the barn where all the Cervini family archives were stored. Of course, there were now pigs, lambs, and chickens there, too, hidden away from the authorities. It wasn't a perfect hiding place for her, but it was easy for Lapo to access and seemingly unknown to the Pappone family. He brought her bread, and some of their precious prosciutto, and arugula from the castle garden. He had already moved some hay into the barn so he had a reason to be there, in case Pappone happened by. The hay also muffled the happy squeals of the pigs when they heard him coming with scraps for them.

Pappone came to Lapo and told him that Alessandro had been arrested. He didn't tell him how it had come about, only that his son was "safe" and in jail in Siena. He was denied any visitors, but Pappone promised Lapo he would make sure he was well treated. Lapo had expressed shock, disappointment, and gratitude, though inside he was seething with one emotion: rage.

He spent the day in despair and anger and more despair, and he had little emotion left to muster now as he washed and rebandaged Sally's bicep where the bullet had grazed it.

"I'm fine," she said. "We've got to rescue him."

Ciano was now out of Mussolini's good graces, relieved of his post as foreign minister, so that was a dead end. "I'll go to Mussolini himself. It's the only way."

"Do you think that will work? That he'll intervene?"

"I don't know. Things are not going well for him."

"What are you going to say?"

Lapo stood there, mute and agonized, then sank down on a bale of hay, his face in his hands. "I don't know." He petted the Labrador, who was shedding tufts of white fur.

"How is the book coming? Does he like it?"

He looked at her. "So you know about that?"

"Alessandro told me."

He exhaled. "I haven't sent the draft yet. It's long overdue. I'm to deliver it in person."

She brightened. "That's perfect. You can ask him then."

"What if he hates the writing?"

"Will he? Does it make him look good?"

Lapo shrugged.

"Show it to me. It needs to be brilliant. It needs to move him to tears, make him incredibly grateful to you."

✡

The next time he went to see her, Lapo brought her the small stack of paper.

"This is it? Sixty pages? Isn't it supposed to be a whole book?" she said. The pigs were snuffling in the straw behind her, and the odor of their manure caught in his throat, strangling him.

"I don't know how to write this. It's supposed to make people believe he's a gift from God, a magical leader for the centuries, a living divinity. It's supposed to enthrone him forever. Make him impregnable to all challenges." He was convulsed with despair.

"A fortress of ideas to protect him. Lies."

He nodded and sank down onto a wooden trunk. The pigs grunted and squealed. "What is a fortress in an age where the enemy is truth?"

She sat down on a bale of straw. "That is a bit of a task, isn't it?"

"Alessandro . . ." he said. "It's all my fault."

"Don't. You'll paralyze yourself. Go, and let me read."

✿

He returned later that day. He had to be careful, not draw attention to the fact that he was visiting the barn, but at the same time he couldn't stop himself. He had to know what she thought. No one else had seen the pages.

She was holding a pen, which was disconcerting. Where had she even found a pen? They were back in their previous spots, he on the trunk, she on the straw bale.

"First of all, shouldn't it be an 'I' story if it's Mussolini telling it?" she asked.

"I guess, but it's also supposed to be a story about him and how amazing he is."

"I have some ideas," she said.

Sally and Lapo

Table of Contents

"Maybe we should flip chapters one and seven," I said. "Flying cobras is kind of a Ziegfeld showstopper."

Lapo shook his head in exhaustion and despair. I had grown fond of him as we'd worked on the manuscript together over the past few weeks. I could see he was a kind man who was in an impossible position. "The whole thing is way too over the top. He'll shoot me on sight," he said. We had no news of Alessandro except that he was still in prison in Siena. Felice Pappone had just been named as the new podesta of Siena, which put him in charge of the city and the Fascist militia in the area. I knew Lapo had reached out to him to ask for clemency for Alessandro.

"What did Pappone say?" I asked. "Did you hear back?"

A shadow passed over Lapo's face. "He said no. Mussolini is our only hope."

"I saw the man speak in Piazza Venezia. Nothing is too over the top for him. I happen to know he has different women brought to him every afternoon."

Lapo considered this. "He does have a pet lion," he said.

"See? I think this can be even crazier." I had channeled every movie Patsy had ever made, with their outrageous plots and clichéd characters. I felt I had a handle on the kind of story Mussolini wanted to shove down Italian throats.

"In chapter three, I think he should behead the little girl because he knows she's a demon. Then he should climb out the window and drop to the ground and get in the plane and fly it to the island where he . . . wrestles a giant lizard. No, a mummy. It's Egypt, and it's a mummy."

Lapo had brought the manual typewriter with him. He rolled a new sheet of paper into it and began typing.

✡

Several days later, I put down the last page onto the now larger pile of paper.

"Perfect," I said. "You almost made me believe this guy really is a god among men."

"That's it then. Thank you. I'll leave in the morning."

Lapo

Dear Eleanor,

I'm about to do something that may turn out to be the end of me. If it is, and if somehow someday you find this letter, I hope you will forgive me. I do not see any other options, and time is running out. I wish you were here, but I'm glad you're not. This is a terrible place to be. As beautiful as ever, which somehow makes it worse. The roses are blooming. The grapes are plumping up. There are nests of swallows in the tower. What is it that Milton wrote? "The mind is its own place, and can make a heaven of hell and a hell of heaven," or something like that. I don't have the text to look at, so forgive me if I am misquoting. Belsederino is heaven, but it has become a hell for me. Like a character from Dante, I cannot find my way out of this. I cannot see what the right thing to do is. I wish I could be the happy warrior, heading off with the knowledge that I am pursuing a just war, but I do not know. It is the historian who decides what was a just war. The person holding the pen, who looks back in judgment on decisions made in agony.

Alessandro

Alessandro put his hands on the red brick walls of his cell, feeling for a hold. He used his mountaineering skills to scale up to the tiny barred window. He stared through the bars at Siena. He could see the Duomo, San Domenico, and the tip of the Torre del Mangia. This view was intentional on the part of the builders of the Fortezza Medicea. It had not been constructed as a prison. When it was built by Cosimo I de' Medici, Siena itself was the prison, full of unruly subjects, and the *fortezza* was built to keep the occupying Florentine forces safe from them. It was a watchtower and a garrison. He dropped to the floor of his cell.

If he spread his arms, he could touch all four walls. Prisons had not really changed much in two thousand years. Well, there was some comfort in that, he thought. So many people before him had suffered the same fate for standing up for the truth. Famous people, certainly, like Galileo and Giordano Bruno, but thousands, if not millions, of faceless others.

His body hurt where the Blackshirts had beaten him while they called him a traitor, a deserter, a foreigner, a coward. His mind had drifted to other places, other times, other souls. Toad, his ideas about kindness. His faith that there were enough people out there who cared, and that someday things would be different. He was probably dying in an infectious disease laboratory now.

Sally. He wanted not to care about where she was, what danger she was putting herself in. It was so much easier not to care, to be one of those people who walled off their feelings for others, or maybe never had them in the first place. Life without empathy. With a scar where your heart once was. What a strange kind of peace that would be.

He could remove his belt, which they had not taken from him, and hang himself. He would be free. His captors' desire to cause him pain would be thwarted, so in one sense, he would win. But, he realized, he couldn't do that. He couldn't leave his father. He couldn't bear for his mother to hear that news. His sisters, their sweet, awful, funny faces, contorted in confusion at the idea that their brother would leave them forever. He couldn't leave her. Sally. Her face, her eyes, her hand on his. The goodness that radiated from her. For a moment, he was filled with resentment at her and his family. How dare these people put these chains on him, these chains of love? But were they chains? Or were they the roots of a tree?

He was tired, but here they were, the Blackshirts again, opening the doors of his cell. Forcing him to his feet, dragging him down a dark hall-way lit by torches toward . . . what was this? Some kind of medieval iron torture device? What the hell? They were laughing, all of them, jostling, laughing, pushing him onto it. Laughing. Pain shot through him.

His body was the prison, he realized. His body was the torture device. So he left his body behind and sailed away like a butterfly, through the brick walls, high above the ramparts of the fortress.

Rome

July 25, 1943

Lapo

He navigated through the outskirts of Rome toward Villa Torlonia. At first glance, Rome did not seem like a city at war. After all, so much of it had always been half-ruined. Toppled columns and roofless towers were nothing new. But now the past was actively encroaching on Mussolini's futuristic vision for Italy. There were vegetable gardens everywhere—to help feed a hungry populace, but they made the city seem more medieval than modern. Not a tractor, but a pair of giant white oxen plowed the Via dell'Impero in front of the "wedding cake" monument, the seat of government, and neat rows of tomatoes sat at the foot of Castel Sant'Angelo. Bicycles, scooters, and dinging trams mixed it up with horses and carriages clopping along the narrow cobblestone streets and across wide piazzas. Dark-eyed men with slick hair and white V-neck shirts and wide trousers, ladies in straw hats, bricklayers in workman's caps, older women in large white collared dresses, skinny-legged little boys in shorts and sandals, and older men in suits without ties gathered around legal and illegal vendors selling everything—oysters, antique candlesticks, baskets, fruit, goats, and naughty postcards. Sidewalk cafés were full of people reading newspapers, arguing, and smoking. Girls in summer dresses swished past. A peddler pushed a cart of rags, singing. It all seemed peaceful enough, but on second glance, the signs of war were clear: painted white arrows pointed the way—AL RICOVERO—to air raid shelters, and smoke from the devastating bombing of a few days earlier hovered over the city. Refugees limped past, bandaged, wide-eyed, and trembling. Soldiers on leave lingered in doorways. Women in black shawls kept children close on their way to Mass, glancing up in fear, awaiting the buzz of planes. Massive Fascist posters trumpeted Italian strength and virtue, while the whispered words on everyone's lips were "When will this end?"

He turned the car and headed down the Via XX Settembre. The traffic slowed to a stop in front of a greengrocer standing guard over a small pile of rather sad-looking oranges. Lapo rolled down the window and rested his elbow on it. In the countryside, people like them were still eating fairly well, because they could grow and hide food, but here in the city, people were stuck with ration cards or the black market. Despite the bustle, Romans were hungry. A huge poster of Il Duce glowered down from a building nearby.

Siena

July 25, 1943

Sally

As soon as Lapo left, I disguised myself as best I could in a black scarf, plain cardigan, and skirt. I hoped I looked like just another Italian girl and not a red-haired American. I was worried that Lapo's book might not please Mussolini enough to convince him to release a deserter. If Lapo even got in to see him. Mussolini was a little bit preoccupied. He was losing the war. The Allies were already in Sicily. They were bombing Rome. We needed a backup plan. I was not going to let Alessandro be shot by a firing squad.

I thought of Clio, and the risks she had taken to help others. She could have sat out the war knitting by the fireside, and no one would have blamed her, but she quietly and bravely did the right thing, with pluck and good humor, to her last day. The least I could do was honor her by doing the same.

I found the bicycle Alessandro and I had hidden near the bridge. For several hours, I rode down country roads under blue skies, until Siena appeared in the distance, black clouds behind it. It was strange to be out in the world again. Using Lapo's typewriter, I had created a crude forgery of identification papers for myself, but I prayed I would not have to put them to the test of scrutiny. As I got closer to the city, I passed ox carts, horse carts, people on bicycles and on foot. I made eye contact with no one. I pedaled up to the city walls and glided through Porta Romana into Siena. I had hoped fatigue from the long bike ride would calm me, but it was hard not to quiver in terror. I leaned my bike against a brick wall and slipped into a bar just inside the gate. It was crowded with people who seemed to have just come from a wedding. They were laughing and talking and I felt like I stood out horribly. I kept my eyes down and made my way to a brown wood-and-glass call box at the back, avoiding curious stares. "Office of the Carabinieri," I told the operator.

Rome

July 25, 1943

Lapo

Gaetano Polverelli, the minister of popular culture, took Lapo on a stroll around the grounds. Apparently, he was early. They made small talk about mutual acquaintances. Lapo noted an air raid shelter amid the classical statuary in the garden. "There's a third-century Jewish catacomb over there," said the minister offhandedly. "And a Swiss hut, a Moorish grotto, and a round theater. Is it not spectacular?"

Lapo found it all a bit too playful in that forced way that becomes crassly poignant. But he said, "Magnificent."

The day was hot, and cicadas buzzed. As they walked, Lapo could feel his shirt sticking to his back under his suit jacket. There was an eerie still-ness to the afternoon, like that moment when all the students go silent as the teacher walks into the room. A layer of clouds was lightly obscuring the sun, and he heard the sound of glass breaking as if from a great distance across a lake. Polverelli took out a pale blue handkerchief and wiped his brow as they passed two carabinieri standing sentry at the front door to the villa.

He led Lapo through the white columned entrance and down a long marble hallway and said, "Wait here, please."

Lapo decided that the Villa Torlonia smelled of lemons, leather, and cat urine on old rugs. The villa echoed with the sounds of bootheels on mar-ble, a grinding of an engine, the whine of an abandoned dog. And fear. *The money is running out,* Lapo thought. Just like Ciano predicted.

The minutes ticked on as he waited.

Siena

July 25, 1943

Sally

I had to keep pumping *gettoni* into the phone to keep from being cut off. A small boy peered through the folding glass doors at me, fogging the glass with his breath. I smiled and kept talking. Finally, I made the arrangements.

✿

I tried not to hurry through the narrow streets of the city. If I asked for directions, my accent would give me away, so I wandered through Siena's labyrinth until I wound my way to a huge palazzo right in Piazza del Campo. There I found an officer of the carabinieri striding back and forth.

"Favagrossa," I called. He turned, the plumes on his majestic hat waving.

"Sally Brady! My favorite enemy!" he burst out, then restrained himself as people turned to look. He leaned over me and whispered theatrically, "Imagine my surprise when I got your call. How intriguing! I can't wait to hear how you evaded our border controls and why you decided to stay in Italy. Is it because you are in love with me? Or is it this soldier you have decided we should release? It's all so romantic."

"Is he free?" I asked. "Alessandro? You gave me your word of honor."

He bowed. "He has been released. But the podesta demanded to see you before I take you away."

I nodded, relief flooding my body. Alessandro was free.

He waved to the Blackshirt guarding the entry to the palazzo, and we went through a huge arched doorway into an inner courtyard. The brick walls were imposing, with small windows looking down on us. We climbed a stairway and entered a long corridor with giant oil paintings of officers on horseback holding swords aloft.

"May I freshen up first?" I was eager to paint on a new face.

Favagrossa led me down the corridor. He stopped in front of a door and nodded.

The bathroom was surprisingly utilitarian—plain white water closet with a pull-chain toilet and your basic sink with slightly rusty stains on the white marble where the water ran. I could imagine Favagrossa complaining, "What is the point of having power if you have a lousy bathroom?"

I tucked in a loose curl and freshened my lipstick, pinched my cheeks. I stared at my reflection. I met my own gaze, surprised at the apparent confidence of the person I saw staring back at me.

"What do you think?" I asked Favagrossa when I emerged.

He gave me a big grin. "I am madly in love with you, Sally Brady."

I laughed and Favagrossa walked me back past the sword-waving generals. I watched his cape swish as he walked, the bounce of the feather on his hat, and the shine of his black boots. This was part of their power, the sexy and menacing style. I told myself to focus and observe. Spy. I noted piles of newspapers in one room we passed, and stacks of gas masks. Maps. The whole place was less busy than I'd imagined. This was the HQ of a city at war. Where was the energy?

"It's very quiet," I said to Favagrossa.

He nodded, uncharacteristically silent.

"How is your father?"

He stopped and looked around, although we were alone in the hallway. "He's very angry," he whispered. "The war is going badly." He led me to a doorway. "The podesta will see you now," he said, and opened the door.

Two people sat at a square table in the center of a room covered in tapestries and full of globes. A man in riding attire I recognized as Felice Pappone. I realized that he was not only the jerk who'd shot at me in the woods at Belsederino but also the jerk who'd ordered me to remove my pants in Siena. Super. I was further shocked to recognize the woman Podesta Pappone had his arm draped possessively around.

"Those are my earrings," said Lila.

Rome

July 25, 1943

Lapo

The minutes ticked on, and Lapo felt he would lose his mind. He wanted to overturn the chairs, smash the vases, stab the sofas, bite the damn lion. Instead, he sat quietly, obsessively tracing with his fingertip the fleur-de-lis pattern in the jacquard fabric on his chair. He was a failure as a husband, as a father, as a son, as a writer, as a landowner, as a person. He couldn't think of any way in his life he had not failed. His self-loathing was complete. *My greatest success is in failing,* he thought. *I am a perfect failure. I deserve the Nobel Prize for Failure.* What would the prize be? A gilded turd?

And yet, he was not done with this life. He would keep trying to get it right, keep trying to reunite his family, keep the people he loved safe. He would even keep writing. Every day, he would try to make Eleanor and his children proud and make the world a better place, knowing he would never succeed.

He jumped up as the door finally opened. It was Patrizia, Mussolini's assistant.

"Il Duce is pleased with your manuscript," she said.

"He is? Can I speak with him? Just for a minute?"

"He'll see you tomorrow."

"Tomorrow? It's just for a minute. I've come all the way from Siena."

"We've booked a room for you at the Minerva," she said. "Il Duce will see you tomorrow at nine." Patrizia escorted Lapo back to the front entrance of the villa.

Siena

July 25, 1943

Sally

"Wait outside," ordered Pappone to Favagrossa. I saw Favagrossa flinch as he stepped out and shut the door behind him.

"It's lovely to see you again," I said as politely as I could while trying to compose myself. Lila? With Pappone? "I thought you were in America."

Lila looked away and lit a cigarette. She looked older, I thought. Her makeup was heavy, her eyebrows drawn with pencil. Her hair was different. She had lost the natural sweetness she'd had—it was painted on now. And spritzed—I could smell her cloying sugary perfume from where I was standing.

"You escaped me in the forest like a red deer," said Pappone. "And yet here you are."

"And how did you two meet?" I pressed.

Pappone tightened his arm around Lila. "Alba Farnese introduced us. You remember Alba? The daughter of the Marchese della Gherardesca? Oh yes, but of course you do. You saw her only a few months ago. She told us all about your visit. She thought you were probably an enemy of the regime."

"Better than a lot of other things I could be," I said, glancing at Lila. I had always seen her as an adventuress, a young woman willing to play the beautiful wife to an older rich man she didn't love so that she could travel, meet interesting people, and experience as much as she could of life. But now I saw something else. Someone who had nothing but her beauty to protect her from the world, a beauty that was fading.

"We have released your *boyfriend*," Pappone interrupted, using the English word. "But he will not soon repeat his crimes, I think. He's always been weak, that one. Even as a child." His black uniform was tight and spotless, like a snakeskin.

I swallowed my anger. "Then I will keep my end of the bargain," I said. "Which enemy alien camp are you sending me to? Not that it matters, because the Allies will soon be here to free me."

Pappone's pig eyes glittered.

"Lila, wait for me upstairs. I have business to attend to."

"I guess this is goodbye," I said to her.

Lila stared hard at me and then said, "Keep the earrings. I have lots of others." She left, slamming the door behind her.

Pappone nodded at me to follow him. I assumed there would be some arrest paperwork to do, transport papers. He led me into an adjacent room with tall ceilings and paneled walls full of stuffed animal heads looking down at a large desk. Stags, boar, lions, rhinos, oryx, elephants. It was like the hunting lodges I'd visited in Scotland during my Bon Vivant days, but somehow tackier, if dead animal heads could be any tackier.

"Someone's quite the avid sportsman," I said.

He walked toward the desk, then whirled and grabbed at my breasts and pawed at my skirt, hiking it up and pushing against me. "You make me hard," he said, pulling at my garters.

"This wasn't part of the deal." I pushed him away and darted around the desk.

He sneered at me, panting a little. "I could send soldiers right now to recapture Alessandro." He reached for the phone.

"You would be breaking your word."

He snorted. "You don't matter."

The truth of his words hit me like a punch. He was right. I wasn't human in his eyes. My pain, my fear sparked no empathy in him because I was not of his tribe. He came around the desk and lunged for me again.

I sidestepped him, keeping a stuffed wildebeest between us. I struggled to find my words, to use them to stop him. "How romantic you are. With your girlfriend right upstairs," I said as lightly as possible. "She's a tigress," I said. "With sharp claws. Be careful."

"I'm a busy man. We'll have to make this quick." He picked up the phone. "Get me the *fortezza*."

"Why are you doing this? You know Alessandro. You were children together. He's a good man."

"A good man," he scoffed, then said into the phone, "Hello? That prisoner you just released? Is he still in sight?" He paused and looked at me, holding the phone in the air. "Pick him up again, would you?" To me he said, "He's always thought he was better than me." Deep-seated anger and resentment burned in Pappone's eyes. He didn't want to fuck me, he wanted to humiliate Alessandro the way he had felt humiliated by his very goodness. He wanted to fuck *him*. He wouldn't leave him alone until he succeeded.

I stepped around the wildebeest and put my hands up. "Please," I said. "Okay. Fine."

He barked into the phone, "Hold him until I tell you to release him." He hung up. He stepped around the desk and pushed me against the paneled wall. I let out an involuntary gasp. I wanted to smack him, put a knee into his balls. Out of the corner of my eye, I saw a gilded dagger on the desk. I could grab it, plunge it into him. I realized I was fully capable of that—I had the strength, and I was as ready in real life to kill this asshole as I'd been when Alessandro and I talked about it in the cave. I would have no regrets. But I couldn't do anything, or Alessandro would die for certain, and probably Lapo as well. Definitely me. Pappone put a hand over my mouth and shoved hard against me as he fumbled with his pants. I closed my eyes, trying to will myself away, away to somewhere else. To Belsederino. Then I heard a click.

"Take your hands off her."

Pappone turned and I could see Favagrossa standing there.

"Ha," said Pappone. "You want a turn when I'm done?"

I held my breath. I looked at Favagrossa. His hands were shaking. He was afraid. I could see he had acted on impulse, rushed in to save me, and was now trying to think this through. Pappone turned back to me, grabbed a handful of my hair, and pushed against me again. "Have it your way. Watch."

"Leave her alone, sir. Please," Favagrossa pleaded. "She's not like the others."

Pappone smirked and began to undo his pants. "They're all the same from the waist down."

I kept my eyes on Favagrossa. I saw his hand move as he stepped forward and then *bam*. He smashed his pistol into the back of Pappone's skull. The podesta of all Siena and its environs dropped to the floor.

Sally

"*O Dio!*" said Favagrossa. He kneeled over Pappone and put a hand on his throat. "He's still breathing," he said to me. "Thank God. I have to call a doctor." Then he added, "He's going to kill me. That was so stupid."

"You're a good man. Honorable."

"I couldn't stand it. I just . . . And now look. Stupid stupid stupid. *Porca miseria!*"

I kneeled next to Favagrossa, put a hand on his arm. I looked around and all the animal heads looked back at me. "Who can hear us right now?"

"No one. They've all gone to bed."

"Okay. So let's think this through. He had too much to drink. He fell. He hit his head."

Favagrossa nodded. "But when he wakes up . . . he'll remember. He will have me shot."

I looked at him and said, enunciating very carefully, "Call your father. Tell him what happened."

Favagrossa's eyes widened and the feathers on his cap bobbed. "My father? He'll kill me, too. *O Dio! My father!*"

I shook my head. "Your father will not shoot you. He'll protect you."

"You don't know him."

"I know men. He'll be mad at first, then he'll see this as an opportunity. Pappone is a terrible person, right? Everyone agrees?"

Favagrossa blinked, unable to comprehend what I was saying.

"Trust me. He will talk to Pappone and tell him to keep his mouth shut if he knows what's good for him." I moved to Pappone's feet. "Let's get him comfortable in case anyone comes in," I said. With some difficulty, we hefted Pappone up and onto the sofa, where he appeared to be resting.

Favagrossa's pupils were huge and he was pale. I tried to speak very calmly, even though I was just as full of fear and panic. "Lock the door. Go tell the others that the podesta is not to be disturbed. Call your father. But please, have Alessandro released."

"What about you? If I let you go and Pappone finds you, he will kill you for sure."

Rome

July 25, 1943

Lapo

Though he wasn't hungry, Lapo couldn't sit in his hotel room alone, so he went down to dinner at nine in the hotel restaurant. The hotel was surprisingly busy, given the war, the food shortages, the blackout, and the curfew. But, he noted, the rich and powerful always found a way to break the rules. The maître d' gave him a quiet table away from some noisy German officers and whispered that MinCulPop had arranged carte blanche for him.

He didn't order anything, but waiters brought a slow procession of prosecco, and pasta with lobster, and a huge *fiorentina* steak. The sommelier brought him Belsederino wine. "In your honor," he said. "Our finest wine."

He sat there without appetite in front of the obscenely delicious meal that seemed to go on forever, consumed by his failure to protect those he loved most. Even these obsessive interior monologues were a failure, an indulgence. *Too much thinking,* he thought.

The waiter had just taken away the uneaten food and brought him a huge crème brûlée when the maître d' banged on a glass and called loudly for silence. All talking ceased. The maître d' walked over to a large radio over the bar. Of course. It was eleven, when the Italian state programming came on, and everyone had to listen.

The radio crackled as a woman's voice said, "*Benito Mussolini's Italian Adventure,* written by Il Duce himself and dedicated to his good friend and ardent Fascist—"

Lapo put his head in his hands and groaned lightly as the announcer said his name. She began reading the first lines of the book. He kept his hands over his ears.

"Deep in the bowels of Etna, a true Italian soul was forged by fire. . . ." The narrator recounted the story of Mussolini's beginnings, and the magic they portended. People around Lapo went back to eating while pretending to listen to the radio respectfully. Lapo saw a woman nearby roll her eyes.

Then, in the middle of a sentence about how Mussolini could repel bullets, talk to birds, and control the weather, the narrator stopped. She said abruptly, "And now the news?"

Military music came on, but it wasn't the usual "Giovinezza." The diners began to murmur. The officers frowned.

Lapo finally realized what he was hearing. "Fratelli d'Italia," the old national anthem of Italy, which the Fascists had banned. People stood up.

"What's going on?" said one Blackshirt angrily. "This is illegal!" He and the German officers left the room. The civilian diners stayed put, listening. Lapo sat quietly, feeling the blood leave his head.

A male announcer came on, loud and clear. "We have some breaking news from Villa Torlonia. As of tonight, Benito Mussolini is no longer the head of the Italian Armed Forces or the government. He is under arrest in a secret location." There were gasps. One woman screamed in shock. The announcer went on, nearly shouting, "The acting head of the armed forces has issued a statement saying that he knows Italy, 'through the valor of her troops and the determination of her civilian population, will find, in the respect of old institutions, the way of recovery.'"

"Fratelli d'Italia," unheard for two decades, resumed at top volume. It boomed through the hotel and all the streets, alleys, parks, and piazzas of Rome.

As soon as the song began again, everyone in the hotel who wasn't in a black uniform, and a surprising number who were, leaped to their feet screaming with joy. Lapo saw people's faces open up like flowers. They were kissing, hugging, and shedding buckets of tears. A mother pulled her little son so close Lapo thought she was going to crush him.

Mussolini was gone! He wanted to shout for joy, but—

Oh God, he realized. Alessandro was an army officer in the hands of a Fascist militia at the moment the armed forces had turned on the Fascists. And if anyone in the army had heard the broadcast and knew Alessandro's father was the "ardent supporter" of the dictator the armed forces just arrested? *Shit,* he thought. *I've managed to endanger my son in every possible way.*

A priest pulled Mussolini's picture off the wall of the hotel lobby and smashed it.

✡

It seemed to Lapo that all of Rome piled out into the street at once. The piazzas were filling with people as he tried to make it to the car. He watched a little boy on his father's shoulders take a hammer and smash a Fascist eagle insignia on a building. Then the boy threw the hammer through a window. People ripped Fascist insignia off hats, and he saw two men strip off their black uniforms and light them on fire themselves before the crowd could do it for them. *"Viva la libertà!"* was the cry of the night. No Germans were visible.

From windows six stories up, portraits of Mussolini were sailing into the street below and smashing on the cobblestones. People were dancing, laughing, screaming, drinking long-hidden bottles of wine. The Trevi Fountain was full of people splashing and hooting.

It was pandemonium, but not everyone was happy. A woman sat on her front stoop, sobbing. Frightened eyes looked out from behind shutters while angry people pounded on their doors.

"Is the war over? But is the war over?" was what everyone he passed kept asking.

Siena

July 26, 1943

Lapo

The road from Rome to Siena was strangely silent, the roadblocks gone. Lapo drove straight to the *fortezza* in Siena. He found a crowd had gathered, demanding the release of all the political prisoners. He pushed his way to the locked iron grate, where a nervous guard who kept a gun trained on him told him Alessandro was not there.

He drove like hell straight back to Belsederino. The landscape was quiet, wary after the chaos of Rome the night before.

The political prisoners were gathered in the courtyard of the castle when Lapo's car pulled in, his heart in his mouth. "We need to talk to you," said the theater director, a tall man in a frayed tweed cap.

"Is Alessandro here?" he shouted to Roghi as he leaped from the car. Roghi shook his head.

"*Padrone! Signore!*" came voices from the crowd surrounding him as he waded through them to the castle's front door. He caught glimpses of worried faces, shovels, pitchforks.

"There was a note for you." Roghi handed him a piece of paper. Sally's handwriting.

Lapo scanned it, blinked, then turned to address the crowd, which had now coalesced in front of the tower. He saw fear in their eyes. Women clutched their children close. They fell silent, except for a bleating goat.

"You have probably heard that Mussolini has been arrested," Lapo said. "The rumors are true. I saw no Blackshirts on duty in Siena or on the roads."

"What does it mean?" a young woman asked.

"I think it means you can go home."

The crowd murmured in confusion. "Is it safe?" an older woman called out.

Lapo shrugged. "I fear we're in a civil war," he said. "The Blackshirts have disappeared today, but they won't give up that easily. And the Germans . . . I don't know what tomorrow will bring."

"He's a friend of the Fascists," said one young man angrily, pointing at Lapo.

"Yes," said another. "He needs to be punished."

"Blackshirt! Fascist!" some voices at the back of the crowd called out.

"Fiorentino di merda!"

Lapo felt a collective wave of energy come off the crowd, years of pent-up injustice and anger unleashed, primitive rage. He backed into the doorway as the crowd pressed forward toward him.

"Son of a bitch!" snarled a man with a red face.

Lapo felt hands around his throat.

"Enough! *Basta!*" shouted Luisa, appearing at Lapo's side.

She shoved the man aside and pushed her way into the middle of the crowd of angry people. Fearless. "This man took you in. He showed you kindness. He saved your lives."

"He kept us prisoner. He's a rich asshole Florentine!" someone called out.

"Signor Lapo gave you his own room so you and your children could sleep indoors," Luisa said to him.

"Why do you let him own you?" called another man with an axe.

"He doesn't own me. He owns the land we're all standing on." Luisa's eyes blazed with anger.

"Florentines don't own Sienese land. Siena for the Sienese!" shouted a woman with a scythe.

"Listen," Luisa said. "We can't exist without laws. When you were sent here, you had your property unjustly seized by the Fascists. Don't you want it back?"

Some of the older people nodded.

"If you think Lapo is a Fascist collaborator, which I don't, then you can sue him when the war is over. What we want is a return to justice, not the end of it. Go home. Go back to Siena. Reclaim your homes. If you want to stay here and continue growing food so we can all survive, you're welcome to, but you'll need to pull your weight."

"Will the Florentine pull his weight?"

Luisa looked Lapo up and down. "Cosimo de' Medici here will pull his weight," she said.

Campo Di Concentramento No. 12

Vincigliata, near Florence
1943

Sally

I expected barbed wire and mud. Instead, Favagrossa took me by train (late, slow) to a huge castle, larger and more forbidding than Belsederino, complete with crenellated battlements and a guard tower.

"This is a prisoner of war camp?"

"It was restored by a crazy Englishman in the eighteen hundreds," said Favagrossa. "Thanks to him, there is no chance of escape." I looked at the forty-foot-high stone walls and had to agree.

"There are some very important people here," he said as we walked across the drawbridge. "And the camp superintendent needs a secretary who can speak English and Italian and who can type."

Of course, I thought. Secretaries were a prime commodity during a war. Generals gave orders. Secretaries, personal assistants, and aides-de-camp had to turn those words into food, ammunition, airplanes, shoe-laces, mules. Bureaucracy at its finest. At the prisoner of war camps, it would no doubt be the same.

"Vincigliata is not just any camp for prisoners of war. It is where the captured enemy generals and higher-ups are kept," Favagrossa said with his usual flourish. "The VIPs of the POWs."

I had to laugh. In war, just as in regular life, rank and privilege mattered. "Three Michelin stars, I hope."

"Nothing but the best for Sally Brady."

✡

We went past the sentry at the gate and Favagrossa handed me over to the camp supervisor, a man called Sardella. Neither Sardella nor his junior officers or his guards spoke English or French, which were the only two languages the prisoners spoke. In addition, there was correspondence to censor, Red Cross contacts to deal with, and other matters needing attention.

"You will help him," Favagrossa said to me. "And you will treat her well," he said to Sardella.

✡

I worked in a small, cold office in the tower, just inside the main gate. I had a little wooden desk and a typewriter and a cot. There was a lighter square on the wall where I guessed a portrait of Mussolini had hung. In Sardella's office, there was a telephone and a radio. There was a tiny bathroom that, except during working hours when I shared it with Sardella, I had all to myself, which seemed like the height of luxury.

The prisoners were allowed to write one twenty-six-line postcard per day that would go from us to the censors, then to the Red Cross, then to the addressee. Sardella was very strict about the twenty-six lines—if they tried to add anything more, he tore up the postcards. Parcels arrived for the prisoners and had to be opened and logged in the omnipresent ledgers the Italians loved so much. Some of the parcels came from friends and families of the prisoners, while others came from the Red Cross itself. I logged board games, musical instruments, mosquito nets, socks, Ping-Pong paddles, cans of butter, soup, Spam, tuna, buttons, thread, brownies, notebooks, chocolate, soap, seeds, and coffee.

"In some camps, guards steal things," said Sardella. "Because these are things we do not have in Italy. But here, we run a very tight ship. If it comes to a prisoner, it goes to a prisoner."

That is, unless he wanted it for himself. I saw him leave with aftershave, foie gras, cocoa powder, coffee, and a pair of size nine black patent leather dancing shoes.

I was not supposed to have any contact with the prisoners—only guards were allowed into the main housing and recreation areas—but after a couple of weeks, I was called into Sardella's office. It was a hot day in August and heat radiated off the stones of the castle.

"Come with me," he said. A guard escorted us through a rock passageway that gave me an unpleasant reminder of the prison in Rome. We came to a door with a metal grate. A handsome man in a patched but neat uniform stood on the other side of the grate.

"Hello there," he said in a British accent. "Aren't you a sight for sore eyes! I hear you're a Yank."

Sardella grabbed my arm. "You say only what I tell you to say," he said in Italian. "Tell him to say what he wants and nothing else."

I shook off Sardella's arm and said in English in a falsely grim tone, "I have to use the longest possible words in the fastest and most confusing way so he won't know what I'm saying, but I'm going to try to help you in any way I can. Make sure you look frustrated and ticked off at me for being so uncooperative. What can I do?"

The British officer swallowed a smile and did indeed manufacture some disappointment. "Can you get near a radio and if you can get any news possible and try to get us civilian clothes and hide them somewhere and any money you can and ask him if we can have a ladder for picking the olives in the garden?"

"He'd like a ladder for picking the olives," I said to Sardella. "They say it's a shame to let fine Tuscan olives go to waste."

"They're not going to use it to try to escape?" He flicked a dust mote off his sleeve.

"You're not planning to escape?" I said.

The British officer narrowed his eyes. "How do I know you're not some Italian Mata Hari here to trick us into revealing our secrets?" he said. "What is your name?"

"Sally Brady," said a figure from behind him I didn't recognize. The man limped toward the grate using a crutch. I saw one of his legs was missing, and his uniform had faded bloodstains on it.

"Roddy," I said.

✡

In brief conversations where I was supposed to be translating Sardella's orders, I learned Roddy had been traveling in a plane that was shot down over Puglia. He was an aide-de-camp to a general who had also survived the crash, and they had been taken to a camp at Sulmona, which was apparently awful, and then here, which was boring but tolerable. He was thin and looked sick, but still managed a smile and a flirt. He told me some of his compatriots had apparently escaped in the spring by tunneling out, so Sardella had taken all their shovels away.

"You'd beat me down the ski slope now, and probably at arm wrestling, too," he said, then added, "I didn't treat you right, Sally."

"My motives weren't as pure as the snow that day, either."

"I realize it's too late, but please allow me to try to apologize. I was an ass, and I'm sorry if I caused you any harm."

"Don't think that means you don't owe me a dance," I said.

"I'm afraid my dancing days are over."

"Only if you decide they are."

He reached out and squeezed my arm. "You really are a most extraordinary girl."

Sardella frowned and stepped between us. "I don't think you are talking about dysentery medicine," he said.

✧

The days passed more quickly than I would have imagined, because I kept myself busy. Whenever I could, I passed on news I overheard from the guards' radio, encoding it on the spot so that Sardella didn't figure out what I was saying. The trick was to avoid words that sounded the same in English and Italian, like city/*citta*, capital/*capitale*, and troops/*truppe*. This made for some crazy games of verbal charades.

"Tell the prisoners their bread rations are being cut," Sardella said to me.

"The people on our side are just on the other side of the large place where the Christians and the lions went toe to toe," I said, trying to convey that the Allies were south of Rome.

"'Toe to toe'?" said Sardella. "What is 'toe to toe'?"

"A kind of bread product," I said. "Like a cracker."

I could send letters myself via the Red Cross, so I wrote to Aida, telling her where I was and that I was okay. I had learned that letters sometimes took up to five months to reach their destination, so I didn't expect to receive any mail for a while, but I received a letter only a few weeks after arriving, in early September.

I didn't recognize the handwriting. It was neat and square, and post-marked "San Diego."

> Dear Sis,
> You probably don't even remember me, but this is Victor, your long-lost brother.

My heart began to race. Victor! He would be twenty-two now. That was hard to imagine.

> A woman in Los Angeles tracked me down and told me you got cap-tured. She told me to come rescue you, which I'm pretty sure is a tall order given that I'm in the navy and I think we're headed to the Pa-cific, but I'm going to do my best. I sure hope they're treating you okay there. They're shipping us out tomorrow and I don't know where I will end up or if I will ever see you or home again. If you get out, will you go home? They're having a hard time and I hated to leave them. Ma died a few years back. Sorry to have to tell you that. Gee, I wish I could see you and we could catch up. I sure do want to hear all about your life.
>
> Love from your little brother,
> Victor

I sat back and stared out the small grated window in my office. I could see trees, and birds, and blue skies. A village on a hilltop in the distance. Never had the castle felt truly like a prison before—I was aware of what others were suffering in the war, and how good I had it—but now I wanted nothing more than to fly through the window and get away. Home! There was an address at the bottom. Ames, Iowa. Only a few miles from where I'd started. It was hard to absorb the news about my mother's death. I re-alized I had always expected that, someday, I would see her again, that we would sit together and talk and laugh and I would tell her about all the things that had happened to me since I got on that train. I put my head down on my desk and let the tears come.

✿

I was prohibited from listening to the radio myself, but Roddy suggested I take some cigarettes from one of the prisoner packages and bribe the guards for news. I chose a guard from Milan, to start with.

"Paolo," I said quietly one day as he stood outside my door, ostensibly guarding it.

"*Sì, signorina?*" His smile was kind.

"Do you have a light?" He lit a match for me. "Would you like one?" I said. "Chesterfields." I knew the Italians coveted British cigarettes. They were only allowed to smoke the Italian state brand.

"That's very kind of you," he said, accepting one and lighting it.

I was about to ask him for news when he offered, "I don't think you'll be here much longer."

I raised an eyebrow.

He told me that Mussolini had been arrested on the same day I was, and that Italy was in a strange state of limbo and confusion. "The Fascists are not giving up so easily," he said. "Many soldiers are deserting." The guards themselves were nervous, worried about the prisoners falling into the hands of the Germans, which apparently Badoglio, the new head of Italy and a military officer, had given strict orders was not to happen.

"Italians, we never like being on the side of the Germans," Paolo said.

The next time Sardella asked me to translate, I passed this on to Roddy, and the next day, his general requested a meeting with Sardella.

The general was a blond man in his fifties, I guessed. Erect military bearing, but lively eyes and a clipped accent. His brown uniform, cap with its red stripe, jodhpurs, and brown boots were immaculate. Sardella, in his gray-green Italian Army uniform, jodhpurs, and black boots, looked like a color-adjusted version of the same person.

"The writing is on the wall, my good man," said the general to me. I translated for Sardella. "Release us now and I will make sure you are treated well by our side."

Sardella did not scoff at this as I expected. "I will take this under consideration," he said meekly.

✤

The seventh of September was sunny and warm. From my window, I could see nothing. I knocked on my door and called for Paolo, but got no answer. I sat there anxiously all day, but no one came to bring me food or news. The waiting was agony, worse than my empty stomach.

That night, I awoke when Favagrossa burst into my room. I hardly recognized him out of uniform, in workman's trousers and cap and a tattered black jacket. "Sally Brady!" he whispered, grabbing my arm and pulling me out of bed. "Pack your things. We don't have much time."

"I don't have any things," I said. "Where are we going?"

"I can't tell you."

I followed him outside and found a car waiting. "What about the others, the prisoners?"

He shrugged. "I cannot protect them from the Germans. There are too many Germans. My God, they're everywhere."

"Then let the prisoners go." The Germans would be eager to get their hands on Roddy and the other Allied officers. I had managed to help them get some civilian clothes and money they had hidden in the castle. But Roddy had only one leg. If they did escape, how would they make it to Allied lines, which were hundreds of mountainous miles away? "Let everyone go," I said. "You'll get favorable treatment when the Allies arrive."

"I hope so," he said. "That's why I'm helping you. You're my calling card. You will tell them I'm not a bad man. I helped you, right? I've been good to you, Sally Brady."

"You did jail me twice."

"For your own safety."

"I don't want to go. Let me help the others. I can translate for them, help them find the partisans."

He drew his gun and pointed it at me. "Get in the trunk," he said. "You don't understand. It's chaos. I will shoot you."

He forced me into the trunk and shut it. It was not a large car. I was curled up like a dog. It was dark, cold, and smelled like gas fumes. I was jolted for hours as he drove like a madman. Finally, the car came to a stop. I was shivering and bruised. I blinked as he opened the trunk and helped me out.

"I'm sorry," he said. "It had to be done."

"You'll help the Englishmen?" I said. "Otherwise, I won't say nice things about you."

He nodded. "I give you my word." In the predawn light, I saw only a field surrounded by trees. We waited and I heard a buzzing get louder and then a small plane landed. It bounced to a stop and Favagrossa led me over to it. It looked rickety and I saw patches on the wings. I was terrified. The skies were full of bombers, and the ground full of anti-aircraft guns.

"I think I'd rather take my chances here," I said. "Please. I need to get back to Alessandro. Please," I said.

He stared at me. "I'm sorry. He's dead."

He shoved me into the back of the plane and handcuffed me to one of the doors.

"Goodbye," he said. I hardly heard him. "It is very important that you tell them that I saved you. I did it. Don't forget," he said.

All I could see was the back of the pilot's head as we took off into clouds. We lurched and bounced in the air. I was sick the entire flight, retching quietly, crying, convulsed with grief and nausea. We landed once to refuel, and then took off again.

Finally, we dropped sharply down and landed in a field and bumped to a stop. I could see little else than rocky cliffs and a vast blue ocean in the distance. It reminded me of the day I had met Patsy and she'd shown me the Pacific.

It was only when the door of the plane opened that I realized the pilot was a woman. She had dark eyes under a leather helmet, her goggles pushed up. She said nothing as she took off my handcuffs.

"Where are we?" I asked her.

She pointed toward the sea. "Head in that direction and you will find Lisbon," she said. "Go to the American embassy. You're going home."

"Who are you? Are you Carla Rossellini?"

She winked at me and got back in the plane. I watched as it taxied and lifted off again into the blue sky.

Siena

September 8, 1943

Lapo

It was just like any other day on the farm in the lead-up to harvest time. They worked all day in the vineyard tying up vines and thinning the grapes. When Mussolini was arrested on the night Lapo went to Rome, he and most Italians had hoped Italy would withdraw from the war. Unfortunately, Hitler was not going to give up Italy so easily. He had spent August moving huge numbers of troops across the border from Austria and down into the Italian boot. Lapo saw endless convoys on the main roads and rail lines, and suddenly every town had a German unit "protecting" it. And these troops needed to be fed, so they raided Italian farms like his for anything they could find.

Groups of partisans were also coalescing, and armed men and women would emerge from the forest now and then and demand food. Lapo always gave what he could, despite the fact that he would be shot if the Germans found out. He kept hoping for a miracle, that Alessandro would reappear one day. The thought that his son's body might be lying somewhere unburied ate at Lapo. No news was somehow better, somehow worse than finding Alessandro's name on one of the endless lists of the dead.

Mostly Lapo just kept putting one foot in front of the other. Life on the farm continued in its ancient rhythms, despite everything. Olives were ripening to a deep purple. Wheat turned golden. Grapes swelled. Lambs frolicked, unaware and uncaring of what Rome, Tokyo, Berlin, Moscow, London, or Washington thought of them.

That morning, Lapo came back from Siena and told Roghi and Luisa it felt like the kettle was about to boil. When the Germans began firing at the Italians, it would get very ugly, very fast. Swarms of Allied bombers were passing regularly over the farm. German Army trucks stirred up dust on the roads.

That evening, he joined Roghi and Luisa for dinner. They ate tiny amounts of *pici* with a thin *cacio e pepe* and declared themselves full, a shared lie. No one left the table, but they didn't speak either, just sat there in the darkness. They were drinking wine, as if it were a party, but there was a strangeness in the air.

Instead of going to bed as they always did after dinner, they moved silently into the sitting room of the castle. Dilapidated sofas were covered with threadbare sheets. Ettore had claimed one whole sofa for himself. Luisa squeezed in next to him, put the dog's head on her lap.

Lapo clicked on the radio, which was broadcasting Rossini's opera *The Barber of Seville*. *"Calumny is a little breeze,"* sang the tenor. *"Slowly, slowly, under the breath it goes hissing, skittering, leaping and sliding, through the ears and into the heads of people, stunning and inflating them. . . ."*

The comic opera of mistaken identities and true love felt somehow apt for the moment, less absurd than reality. *"May love and faith eternally be seen to reign in us"* went the closing aria. Crickets trilled along.

Lapo felt his eyelids getting heavy when he was startled by the trumpets of "Fratelli d'Italia." An announcer introduced the head of the Italian Armed Forces. His basso voice made the radio rattle. "The Italian government, recognizing the impossibility of continuing the unequal struggle against an overwhelming enemy force, in order to avoid further and graver disasters for the nation, sought an armistice from General Eisenhower, commander in chief of the Anglo-American Allied forces."

He gasped.

Luisa jumped up. Roghi jolted awake. "What just happened?" he asked as Luisa began to bounce around the room.

"Italy just changed sides," Lapo said, as if unable to process the idea. Luisa was hooting with glee, laughing and crying at the same time. *"Grazie a Dio!"* Roghi shouted with joy, an emotion Lapo had not seen in him for years. Luisa and Roghi began to spin and dance.

Still, Lapo sat unmoving on the sofa. "But how do the Allies think that is going to work?" he asked them, his face a mask of confusion. "Nazi soldiers are garrisoned in a villa not twenty minutes down the road from us." The

Germans had used prison labor to construct a huge line of trenches, bunkers, machine-gun nests, and barbed wire all the way across Italy to stop the Allied advance.

The others stopped dancing, the reality setting in.

They were an occupied country, and Belsederino was now on the front lines.

Ames, Iowa

1944

Sally

I thought of Alfredo, the restaurant owner in Rome, as I made dinner. I found some cream in the refrigerator, and though margarine would have to substitute for butter, and cheddar for parmesan, it would be a fun treat for us. I rolled out the pasta and cut it into thin strips that were as close to fettucine as I could get.

I had been home for a week. "Home" was an interesting term for it. I had never seen the one-story white house on the outskirts of Ames before, but I found objects in it that evoked memories for me. An old bedstead that Victor and I had slept on as children; a faded photo of my mother, her dark eyes peering at me across time. The house was very small, and I shared a room with my sister Margaret, now fourteen years old, while my father occupied the other bedroom. Victor was away in the navy, my sister Mary had gotten married and moved back East, and my brother Michael had died of polio as a child. Only Dad and Margaret were left now.

There was running water and a bathroom, which was a step up from the house I'd left at age eleven, a house my parents had lost to the bank not long after they put me on that train. This house had neighbors close on either side that I could hear talking and yelling and sometimes even snoring, and an empty lot behind it that turned into mud when it rained.

My father and Margaret stared at me in shock when I knocked on their door after a thirteen-year absence. I held a small cardboard suitcase that contained the scant few items I had purchased with money Aida wired me from Los Angeles. She was still working for George, who was married to a singing cowgirl. "I will pay u back," I said in my telegram.

"*De nada,*" she'd replied. "Go find your family."

America was not the place I remembered from when Patsy and I left in 1935. The war had changed everything. I saw posters for metal drives, rubber drives, and war bonds. All the young men were gone, off in Europe and the Pacific, except for the wounded. Women carried lunch buckets and went to work in factories. Everyone was busy, focused on victory. Rationing was strict—food items, but also typewriters, fuel oil, shoes, bicycles. For two days, I sat upright on a wooden bench in a second-class compartment from New York to Chicago, passing women in kerchiefs tearing out old rail lines and dismantling unused bridges so the steel could be recycled for the war effort. Nothing was trash anymore—as the posters said, AN OLD SHOVEL CAN MAKE FOUR GRENADES!

In Chicago, I changed for the line to Iowa. I was stiff and dusty when I got off the train in Ames and walked to the address from Victor's letter. Cars drove slower than I remembered—to conserve rubber and gas, no one was supposed to drive more than thirty-five miles an hour.

I stood in front of a small white wooden house in a row of identical houses. The paint was chipping and the front steps were crooked. Curious children stared at me from down the dusty road. I had left Iowa in 1931 with no photos of my family, and I wondered if I would even recognize my father. For so many years, Patsy had been my family, and I loved her for that, loved our wild life together, but now I needed to be someone else.

I took a deep breath and knocked on the front door.

As soon as the door opened and I saw his face, I knew it was him. A thousand memories hit me like a fire hose all at once, and I was thrown off-balance by their weight.

"It's me, Daddy," I said, staring at this older version of the father I remembered. His expression was suspicious as he opened the door, like he thought I was a stranger who was going to ask for help or money. His red hair had turned mostly gray, and he was a couple days unshaven, but maybe using your razor less was part of the war effort, too. At last, his face twisted into surprise, and he put his hands on either side of my face. "It's you," he said. "You're all grown-up."

I would never have recognized "baby" Margaret, taller than I and thin in brown pigtails and a white dress. She hung back, shy, until I folded her into my arms in the narrow hallway.

"Victor wrote to me," I said. "I'm here to help."

"Victor's in the navy," my father said, as if I had insulted my brother. "Serving his country." He turned to Margaret. "Get your sister settled. Then you two get supper ready." That was it. It was as if I had never left, just walked back through the door and resumed my same eleven-year-old life—cooking, cleaning, and not making noise. It was as if he didn't think I'd existed at all when I was away. He seemed utterly uninterested in anything except Victor, checking the mailbox every day for letters and scanning the newspaper for news of his ship. I remembered my father from childhood as laughing, often making fun of my mother, teasing her about her English, but this man didn't seem to enjoy talking at all, as if it cost him money to speak.

"No need to talk about that," he said when I asked him at supper about my mother.

The next morning, Margaret waited until Daddy left the house for his job at an ordnance plant, then she did her best to fill in the gaps for me. My mother had coughed up blood one day, and the doctor diagnosed tuberculosis. She was supposed to go to a sanatorium for six months of rest. "The doctor told her she had to stay in bed," Margaret said, "but she didn't. She continued to stay here and take care of us and Daddy. I was eight when she died."

I shook my head. I hated to think of my mother getting sicker and sicker from something she might have been cured of.

"When did you move to this house?"

She shrugged. "I don't know. I don't remember living anywhere else."

I found it so frustrating that they were living only a few miles from where I had looked for them. "Did anyone ever talk about me?" I asked. "Did they try to find me?"

She looked away as she ironed a shirt of my father's. "Victor used to tell me about you," she said. "But he told me not to talk about you in front of Ma and Dad."

Tears sprang to my eyes, and I walked outside to take the rest of the laundry off the clothesline.

✧

I had intended to stop being Sally Brady when I stepped back into my life here, but I found Patsy and Aida and even Elsa were always whispering in my ear that the woman who worked at the pharmacy had the sense of humor of a turnip, and that it was a good idea to fox-trot while walking to the mailbox. And my ghosts—my mother, Clio, Alessandro—they were with me, too, asking me to laugh, to savor the feel of the sun on my skin for them, to hold tightly to what they had lost.

Margaret had made supper every night since I arrived, usually a boiled potato and a tiny bit of chicken or canned tuna. "Let me cook," I'd told her this morning. I had used more of our ration points at the market than I probably should have, but I felt like we all needed a lift. Honestly, we had laughed more at the prison camp than my father and Margaret did here. I spread out the noodles to dry and set a nice table in the kitchen, thinking about how my mother had handled these same plates and silverware, how she had spent most of her life washing them every day.

Daddy arrived home promptly at five fifteen, and I told him I had a surprise for him.

"A letter from Victor?" he asked.

"A special dinner." I called Margaret, and had them sit down at the table.

"Ta-da," I said as I set heaping bowls of perfectly al dente fettucine in front of them, glistening with cream and cheese. "It's a recipe from a famous restaurant in Rome," I announced proudly. "I used to eat there all the time."

My father frowned. "You made *foreign* food?" He squinted, his mouth forming a snarl. "Foreign food, with my ration points?"

"It's fettucine Alfredo," I said. "People came from all over the world to eat it. Royalty. Movie stars. It's delicious."

Margaret flinched before he even moved. He picked up the bowl and seemed to think about throwing it. Then he dumped it into the trash and left the room.

✿

I lay in bed with memories flooding in like water that rose and rose until I began to choke and drown. These were bits and pieces of scenes from my life that hadn't made sense to me when I was a child. I'd thought they were just fragments of bad dreams, but now they came together into a narrative that made terrible, real-life sense. Ma only cooked her special food when Daddy was away. She warned us not to tell him she'd made tortillas, Chile Colorado, or flaky *coyotas*. She grew her chile plants behind the barn where he wouldn't see them, disguised among spinach and beans. "Speak English," he said to her whenever he caught her saying anything in Spanish to us.

"Margaret," I whispered to my sister in the dark. "Have you ever had a tamale?"

"What's a tamale?" she asked.

Siena

1944

Lapo

Dearest Eleanor,

I think of you and the girls constantly and pray you are safe. We are out in the fields every day, planting, weeding, harvesting. We try to hide what we can from the passing armies. Both sides are just as bad about taking what they need. Italy is in a state of chaos. Even if you have ration cards, the store shelves are empty.

Mussolini tried to revive Italian nationalism, thinking our sense of self lay in monuments and empire. I think it lies in empathy, curiosity, creativity, a sense of humor, and a desire to see everyone lead a good life. "Also," I know you will say with a smile, "pasta and wine." You and I are neither politicians nor historians, but we know what we love about Italy, and no change of government will change that.

Things will get worse before they get better. But I believe they will get better.

There's a hawk circling outside my window, hunting for snakes in the vineyard. I want to call him over and ask him to carry this to you. I must go now and help dig the potatoes.

Ames, Iowa

1944

Sally

My father expected the house to be tidy. I guessed I hadn't realized as a child how obsessive he was about cleanliness, but now it made sense why my mother was always cleaning. He would explode in a rage if there was a teaspoon in the sink or dust on the radio. His socks had to be clean and darned, his shirts pressed the way he liked them. Every day, Margaret came home from school and cleaned the house top to bottom and got supper ready for him. She ironed his sheets, washed everyone's clothes, and tended our victory garden. On weekends, she washed windows. I did my best not to leave muddy footprints in the hall or fingerprints on the light switches, but I felt too big, too messy, too *much*.

Before enlisting in the navy, Victor had worked in town at a meat market. His salary was sorely missing from the weekly budget, and I could see Margaret had not had a new dress or pair of shoes in a long time. She was a faded sort of girl, already old at fourteen. I saw a lot of my mother in her: the shape of her face, the curve of her arm, but also the sense of resignation, and duty.

The morning after the fettucine incident, I went to the Employment Office and told them I wanted a job. I knew about the ordnance plant and a local military training facility, and that Iowa farmers were producing record crops to feed the busy nation. I figured there were probably plenty of ways I could help.

"What skills do you have?" the woman at the desk asked me. "Carpentry? Metalwork?"

I liked this woman right away, and wanted her to like me, too. I shook my head.

"That's okay, honey. We can all be useful in some way. Can you drive? Type?"

"Yes, I can type. And I speak some Spanish. And Italian. I'm fluent in Italian."

Her eyes widened. "You are?"

I nodded.

She stood and went through a glass door in the back. I saw her lean over and whisper to a bald man in round glasses who turned in his swivel chair to peer at me. He turned back and nodded. The woman came back through the glass door.

"You're in luck and so are we. Turns out they need a secretary at the camp in Clarinda."

"The camp?"

"For prisoners of war? No one knows what to do with the Italians, since they went and switched sides. Apparently it's a madhouse over there."

Siena

1945

Lapo

One night not long after the Allies breached the Trasimene Line and took Siena, Lapo was sitting outside the castle doorway on the stone bench. He was removing his boots in the semidarkness and feeling an ache in every muscle. A figure appeared under the linden tree. He held his breath, but it was not Alessandro, it was Felice Pappone. Not dead, of course. Some people just don't die that easily. He was trembling, trying to blend in to the bark. "You've got to hide me," he said. "They've come to my father's house looking for me. They'll kill me."

Lapo stared at him. It might feel good to take his anger out on Pappone. If Lapo shouted now, Roghi would come running. The last of the former political prisoners from Siena, the ones who couldn't yet return home because their houses were destroyed, the ones who had joined the partisans, would be right behind them. They would not spare Pappone. Maybe he didn't deserve sparing. Who was Lapo to decide? Without his black uniform, Pappone was a slob. He was not strong or smart or kind. He was a bully dethroned. Lapo wanted to push him down and shit on him.

"*Padrone,* please," said Pappone, putting his hands together in prayer. "For the love of our two families. For my father's loyal service as your gamekeeper. Remember the hunts? The way we would dance? Feasting on wild boar and pheasant until the sun came up?"

Lapo well remembered the joys of the prewar days, the *sagre,* the dances, the folk songs. It was people like Pappone who had drained those joys from the land.

"Go to the barn," he said at last, sick of the man's whimpering. "I will bring you some food." And he did. Pappone whined about the injustice of it all. He was only following orders. He loved Italy. He had not killed the people from Siena, he had brought them here to save them. He *had* saved them. Lapo half listened to him, unwilling to let the younger man get under his skin. When the war ended and the trials began, he would produce him and let others decide his fate. In the meantime, he gave him books. Novels by Italians, novels in translation.

"Learn something," Lapo said, throwing the books down on the dirt floor.

"These are fake stories."

"Try to find something of yourself in someone else. Feel what it's like to *be* someone else. Try."

Ames, Iowa

1947

Sally

Finally, the war ended. Soldiers and sailors and flyers came back, and suddenly it was unpatriotic for women to work. We were taking jobs from men who needed them.

Victor was one of the ones who did not come home. He died on an island in the Pacific. I cried for someone I knew only as a child, my adored younger brother, my ten-year-old partner in crime. My sister cried for the older brother she loved, her protector. My father did not cry, but sank further into himself, his eyes dimmed, his heart broken.

The prison camp closed, and I found a job as a secretary for a local real estate agent. It wasn't exciting work, and the wages were low, but I was grateful to have it. My boss was kind and funny and loved finding people their dream houses. Sometimes I filled in for him on showings. "This is the kitchen," I'd trill to a wide-eyed young couple, "complete with all the modern conveniences to keep life running smoothly. And this will be Junior's room, unless Janey nabs it first because it has the better closet, and over there you can put the Ping-Pong table, and—"

"Wow," said one of the young brides. "It's like you can picture my home better than I can."

I was amazed by all the *things* Americans had. So many things that they needed more things to take care of their things, like fur storage and rug cleaning and auto repair, not to mention garages and walk-in closets. As a reminder that it was not the same elsewhere, there were ads in every newspaper for companies that shipped premade food and clothing parcels to Europe: 1 LB. TIN OLEO, 12 OZ. TIN CHEESE, 1 LB. HARD CANDY. It was a generous impulse to help countries destroyed by the war, but it was hard to imagine Italians embracing the American love of all things powdered, dehydrated, canned, plastic wrapped, and freeze-dried. I couldn't say this to anyone, but to me, American food no longer looked, smelled, or tasted like food at all. I laughed to imagine what Giuliano and Ilaria would think of instant soup. Remembering all the wonderful meals I'd had in Italy made me miss the taste of fresh basil and pungent rosemary, the smell of fresh bread. I missed meals that were a chance to linger, laugh, and tell stories instead of refuel and return to work. I felt like I was the only American left unthrilled by Reddi-Wip, French's instant mashed potatoes, and Minute Maid Frozen Concentrated Orange Juice.

✹

"You're so dependable," said my boss with a smile when I dropped a pile of contracts on his desk. "So steady." The word hit me like a punch. Instead of walking home that night, I wandered into a cornfield and traipsed up and down the rows in search of something.

"Let's throw a party!" I said to Margaret when I got back to the house.

I invited my boss and his wife, the neighbors. I strung lights in the backyard. I made paper hats for us to wear.

"What's the occasion?" they all asked as we stood around holding glasses of beer.

"Life," I said.

"To family," said my boss. His pregnant wife blushed.

We toasted, and even my father danced a little when I put a record on. I taught Margaret how to waltz, fox-trot, and tango.

"You're good," my boss's wife said when the record stopped and we all fell, breathless, into folding chairs. "Where'd you learn to dance like that?"

"I used to attend parties for a living, if you can believe it," I said. "I lived in Rome."

"See?" my boss chimed in. "I told you, Sally had quite the Italian adventure."

I waited for someone to show some curiosity about all the years I had been away from Iowa, the things I had seen, the people I had met. Instead, conversation moved on to the weather, the new Jimmy Stewart movie, and which one of the neighbors now had a television. I stared into my beer, unsettled. The men returning from the war didn't talk about what they had experienced overseas, and people didn't ask. I didn't much want to talk about what I had seen, either, but it stung to have all those years summed up and dismissed, as if I had spent two weeks on a beach flirting with a lifeguard. And yet, I had not seen the horrors that others had, so maybe the label fit.

"Life is different there," I said out loud, interrupting their conversation about baseball.

"Different how?" Margaret asked.

I looked around at our little grassy backyard, the lit-up windows of the neighbors' houses, moon coming up over the flat black horizon of the field behind us.

"Just different," I said.

Then the ordnance plant closed, and my father bounced from job to job. Whisky was available again, and he began to drink away his paychecks, so that there was very little left for us to live on. I hid what money I could, using it to pay the rent on our small house and buy things for Margaret to make her smile. She was seventeen. I knew there was a boy who liked her.

"Do you like him?" I asked her in the dark one night. I expected a teenage girl's response, some giggling at least.

"I don't know," she said in a serious voice. "Maybe." She rolled over and faced me. "But if I marry him, then I'll have to take care of him *and* Daddy. And our children."

"I'll be here," I said.

I heard her sigh. "You miss those places you talk about," she said. "I think you're going to leave again."

I stared at the ceiling. "What I miss is gone forever," I said at last. "There's nothing to go back to."

✡

One morning, I was on my hands and knees in the bathroom, scrubbing the tiles. If cleanliness was next to godliness, I was ready to join Team Satan. And what was worse, it felt like all of America was on Dad's side. Magazines and billboards were crowded with women in full-skirted dresses and heels excitedly mopping and dusting their immaculate homes. Women helped win the war so we could live like Sisyphus?

Dad was in an especially foul mood today, thanks to one of his regular hangovers. At breakfast, he had once again poured whisky in his coffee. "Hair of the dog," he'd said. It was becoming a daily habit. At least he was sitting quietly downstairs now, listening to a ball game on the radio. I could hear the announcer calling the outs.

I heard a buzzing noise in the sky above our small house. I looked out the little bathroom window. A small red plane made one pass above the field behind us. A crop duster off course? I stood up and wiped my hands on my apron and went downstairs.

"What is that noise?" called my father. "Bases are loaded and I can't hear a thing with all that racket!"

Margaret was busy with her needle and thread, her legs curled under her on the armchair my mother used to sit in and sew. She reminded me so much of Ma. I left them and went out the back, the screen door slamming behind me.

The field behind our row of houses, the dividing line between city and farmland, stretched flat and golden. The farmer had recently cut it to stubble. I shielded my eyes with my hand and stared up at the red speck in the vast blue sky. I was surprised as the plane came back toward us, dropping lower and lower, until it bounced to a stop on the stubble. A figure got out. It was a small person, as if a child had been given the magical power to pilot his toy plane. I walked toward the plane, my heart beginning to soar and leap. The pilot removed a leather cap, letting a wave of black hair loose. I began to run toward the plane. My legs pumped as I jumped the rows of stubble, my lungs filling with air.

"Patsy!" I shouted, waving my arms. "Patsy!" I grabbed her and hugged her tight. She felt strong and alive. "I've missed you so much!"

"Hey, kiddo," she said.

"What are you doing here?"

"It's a damn Jap!" my father shouted from the backyard. "A Jap!"

"The war is over, Daddy," I called. "And she's as American as you are!"

"You killed my son," he shouted. "I'm getting a gun."

"He's drunk," I said to Patsy, "and he doesn't have a gun." I called to the slim figure beside my father. "Margaret! Come meet someone!"

"I'm calling the police!" said my father as he staggered up the steps and went back inside the house.

Margaret came shyly forward like a deer, towering over Patsy.

"This is . . . my other mother," I said to Margaret. "Patsy Chen."

Margaret reached out and Patsy shook her hand. "You can fly this?" Margaret asked.

"Any girl can. I have a letter for you," said Patsy to me. "From Italy. It came to Aida, but it's for you. We opened it."

"Of course you did," I said with a laugh, but I grabbed it eagerly. I had thought of Lapo often over the years. I wanted to write to him, say how sorry I was, how I had tried to save his son, but I couldn't find the right words.

I stared at the envelope, but it wasn't from Belsederino. It looked official, on heavy paper with stamps and seals.

"You've inherited a house," said Patsy. "In Italy."

"A house?"

"Someone named Clio left it to you. She died a while ago, but you know—"

"There was a war on."

"Exactly. I looked on the map. It's near Siena. Out in the countryside." Patsy grinned at me. "I miss Italian parties," she said. "And there's an airfield not far from there."

The *eremo*. Clio had left me the *eremo*. Dear, wonderful, brave Clio. My own house. A place no one could take away from me. A home. The gesture, the sheer generosity of it, brought tears to my eyes.

"That's amazing," I said.

My sister's face contorted, and she turned away.

"Margaret," I said, putting a hand on her shoulder.

"You're leaving," she said. "I knew it."

"I'm not leaving. I won't ever leave you again." Waves of guilt washed over me. I would sell the property in Italy. Buy us all a house here. Try to keep the money away from Daddy.

"I have a knife," called my father as he came out of the screen door. He fell on the lowest step and got up again, came toward us slowly, tacking back and forth like a small boat in a high wind.

"You'd better go," I said to Patsy. "I don't think he'd really hurt you, but still. I'll write."

"Get in the plane," said Patsy.

I shook my head. "I can't. I can't leave them again."

"I know what you've said in your letters to Aida." I had shared with Aida, who would understand better than anyone, what I had figured out about my mother's marriage, her life.

"I'm going to kill you, you Jap bastard," called my father again. He tripped on the stubble and went down. I was afraid he might have stabbed himself with the knife, but then he was up again and staggering toward us.

"They're my family," I said to Patsy.

"So am I. Get in the fucking plane," she said.

I looked into Patsy's face, her black eyes glittering under her cap of black hair, and I loved her with an intensity that made me dizzy.

"Margaret," I said. "Get in the plane."

Her eyes widened in shock. "What? I can't."

"Get in the plane. Get out of here. Have a real life doing things you choose to do. Not taking care of someone who doesn't really love you." I could hear my father huffing and puffing. He was about fifty yards away. "He treated Ma like a slave, like a human mop. He erased her culture. And then he let her die. The best way you can honor her memory is to go away."

"He's our father," she said. "We can't just abandon him."

"That's what he did to me," I said. "Putting me on that train wasn't about me saving the family, or saving me, it was about having one less mouth to feed. They didn't leave me a forwarding address because they didn't want me anymore." I corrected myself. "*He* didn't want me anymore. The *girl*," I said. "He sent the *girl* away and didn't care what happened to her. I'm not human to him, and neither are you. Not really, fully human."

My father was ten yards away. Patsy got into the cockpit and started the engine.

"What about you?" Margaret shouted to me over the buzz.

"Oh, I'm coming too," I said. "But not without you."

Margaret turned and looked back at our father, the kitchen knife flashing in his upraised hand, his face contorted with prejudice and rage and drink.

Then the two of us ran to the red plane, opened the back door, and threw ourselves inside.

VII

Housewarming

Siena

1947

Sally

Margaret and I crossed the Atlantic on the Italian ocean liner *Saturnia*. The ship had been through the war, too. We were both a little battered, but Margaret was fresh and bright and alive in a way I had not seen before. We had the cheapest cabin—no porthole, and next to the engines, but she didn't care. It was a grand adventure. On the upper decks, there were parties every night. Elegant women in gowns and furs danced to live music. Or so I heard. We weren't invited.

When we docked at the port, I could see that Genoa was still in the process of being rebuilt. The debris had all been bulldozed, but the devastation was still very evident. Whole sections of the city were leveled. There were cranes everywhere, and new apartment buildings popping up out of the rubble. We took the train from Genoa to Siena. It was hot and slow, and we were packed in like anchovies, but I loved every minute of it. I was teaching Margaret Italian. There was a lot of talk on the trains about the battle for the future of Italy, the Communists versus the Catholics. But mostly about the shapely ladies of the Miss Italia pageant. *"Bellissima,"* I taught Margaret.

We checked into the Hotel Excelsior in Siena. I asked for room 602. "It's nice to be able to look out the windows this time," I said to Margaret. If the manager remembered me, he had the good grace not to mention it. When we unpacked, I pulled out the small yellow envelope I had always kept with me, ever since Aida gave it to me all those years ago.

"What's in that thing?" Margaret asked. "You always have it with you."

"Yes, I do. Funny. It's just a packet of seeds," I said.

"Seeds? Why don't you ever plant them?"

"I guess I was waiting for the right place." I dredged up the name Aida had told me when she helped me identify, after much trial and error, the exact spice I remembered from my mother's cooking. The taste of my mother's home back in Hermosillo, and the taste of my home back in Iowa. "They're chiltepin chile pepper seeds," I told Margaret. "It's a wild plant from the place that Ma came from. Someone who loved me gave them to me so I could make Ma's special dishes and know I was home."

It was strange to be back in Siena. The city had mostly been spared in the war, except for the train station. I met with the lawyers about the *eremo*. I signed papers, and it was mine, though I hadn't been there since the night Alessandro was arrested.

"Are we going to see it?" Margaret asked.

"We could sell it," I said. "Buy an apartment somewhere." It felt wrong to think about rejecting Clio's gift, but I wasn't sure I really belonged there at the *eremo*. For me, it was a place that was full of ghosts.

"Don't you want to see it first?"

Instead, I showed her Siena. We tromped up and down hills to museums and climbed towers to see views and revived ourselves with salty sliced *finocchiona*, *pici* dripping with melted *pecorino*, and crispy, tangy *rucola* salads. "I've never tasted a tomato like this before," said Margaret in amazement. "I've never tasted anything like any of this before." Afterward, we sat in the piazza and devoured bowls of gelato as I had with Clio. I read between the lines of what the waiters told me, just as in my days as the Bon Vivant. The society pages in the newspapers were not quite so prominent or expansive, which felt appropriate. I had the sense that people wanted to forget the past and look to the future, to a vigorous new Italy that was free and prosperous.

✡

We had been in Siena for five days. I showed her the alley with the apartment where Anna hid, and ran my hand over the bench that Clio sat on.

"You were so brave," Margaret said, but I could see it all felt long ago to her, already just another part of history. She was more interested in the dresses in the shop windows, in the boys who ogled her. *As it should be*, I thought.

I didn't show her the prison where Alessandro had died.

Maybe Rome. We could settle in Rome.

Then I saw Favagrossa. He was coming around a corner in Piazza Tolomei, resplendent as ever in his carabinieri uniform, the plume on his hat waving. He saw me and stopped. He squinted to make sure his eyes were not lying. I gave a little wave, and he spread his arms and came running, his cape flying behind him. "Sally Brady!" he boomed, then gave me a salute. "Welcome back to Italia!"

"This is my sister Margaret," I said.

He bowed with exquisite courtesy. "I have wanted to thank you for very long," he said. "It is because of you that I am not—" He mimed slitting his own throat. "These have been difficult years," he said.

I felt uncomfortable. "Well, you're welcome, I guess. I really didn't do anything."

"But there is somewhere I need to take you," he said. "I really must insist. I am off duty at five. Meet me here."

"We really can't," I said. I had had enough of Favagrossa for one lifetime. "We're leaving Siena this afternoon."

"Then I'm afraid I must place you under arrest."

Margaret's eyes widened.

"You wouldn't dare," I said.

He pointed to a black car with a red light on top. "Get in the car, *per favore*."

✿

"Where are we going?" Margaret whispered to me. Favagrossa drove like a madman along the curving country roads, and we slid from side to side in the back seat of the Alfa sedan. "I'm scared."

"He's crazy," I said. "But I don't think he'll hurt us."

I stared out the window and didn't ask Favagrossa any questions on the drive, not that he would have heard me over the siren.

✿

The tiny Alfa crested the hill at what felt like ninety miles an hour and went briefly airborne. Margaret gave a little scream, which seemed to please Favagrossa, and then we landed again with a thud. I saw Belsederino spread out below us.

Favagrossa skidded into the courtyard in a cloud of dust and turned off the siren.

"*Arrivati,*" he said.

I got out and looked up at the tall gray tower set against the deep blue sky. The tufts of caper plants sticking out of the walls like hair out of an old man's ears. Luisa and Roghi's stone farmhouse with the red tile roof and the jasmine climbing the walls. Surrounding the buildings, neat green rows of grapes, and bushy rows of silvery olive trees. And sunflowers—there was a huge brand-new field of yellow sunflowers, their gaze turned to greet me.

I stared up at the castle and turned slowly so I took in the whole façade, stones peeking through flaking stucco, reddish water stains where iron fixtures attached the peeling green shutters, ivy climbing up and tearing at the stonework. I kept turning, looking at the low granary building, the large pots of struggling lemons, the battered door to the underground cellar where the olive oil was stored, the curved arch of the fermentation room for the wine, the cellars underneath the hayloft, the stables. I remembered how in the right light, the place could seem romantic, magical, mysterious, and welcoming. In the wrong light, it was a testament to futility, nature constantly reclaiming what was rightfully hers. It was cold, forbidding, even dangerous.

The front door of the castle opened and Lapo emerged, confused at first at the sight of the police car and the unexpected guests. He was grayer, I saw, but otherwise just the same, twinkling soulful eyes behind round glasses.

"*Caspita!*" he said when he recognized me. "Sally!"

I felt a bit embarrassed to be intruding this way, but, ever the gentleman, he shook my hand and kissed my cheeks, and I introduced him to Margaret.

"Is this a castle?" asked Margaret in amazement, looking around her.

"We have running water now," said Lapo proudly. "Well, most days. The boiler is giving me some problems. Mice. Fiamma and Allegra are at Smith College. And Belsederino has two tractors now," he added. "Fords! But I hear you're the new owner of the *eremo.* The surveyor told me. This is wonderful news. We're neighbors! You must stay here while you renovate. We will help you."

A tall, slim woman in canvas trousers with auburn hair piled up on her head came out of the door to the tower. She was in her fifties, I guessed, and very beautiful, even in work clothes.

"This is Sally," Lapo told her. "And her sister Margaret."

Her face broke into a smile and she grabbed me and hugged me. It startled me, and I gasped and fought back tears. "You didn't tell us you were coming," she said.

"This is Eleanor," said Lapo. "My wife."

"Lapo, show Margaret and Tenente Favagrossa the puppies," Eleanor said to him.

"Puppies?" Margaret cooed.

"I love puppies," said Favagrossa with his goofy grin.

Eleanor took my hand. "Come with me," she said. Her grip was strong.

She led me around the back to the walled garden. "Go," she said, and gave me a little push. I walked under the arch and into the garden. The willow had grown tall. The purple irises were blooming. It looked cool and peaceful. I saw a figure there. He had his back to me. I knew it was him. This was why Favagrossa needed to bring me here. Alessandro was alive. Alive. He was sitting on the grass with two small children. Twins, I guessed. Boys. One of them was climbing on him, and the other was taking his shoe off. They looked just like him.

I'm happy for you, I thought. My face felt funny, half-frozen in relief, joy, mortification. A young woman was sitting on the bench under the linden tree reading. She was pregnant.

My sensible black pumps were sunk deep into the grass. I started to back away, unwilling to disturb them, but the young woman looked up from her book.

"Buongiorno?" she said.

Alessandro turned, blinked at me. He tried to stand up, but he had a child attached to his leg. "Sally!" he said. "I can't believe it! It's you."

"Oh," said the pregnant woman. "The famous Sally." She didn't stand up. I couldn't read her expression.

"Hi," I said. "I'm sorry to just show up like this, but I'm so happy to see you."

He managed to free himself from one of the children, but the other held fast to his leg as he limped over. The child looked up at me like a koala, eyes wide, cheek pressed to Alessandro's ankle.

"She has red hair," said the child, gazing up at me. "Like a witch."

Alessandro stared at me, apparently just as amazed to see me as I was to see him, then kissed my cheeks politely. "How are you?" he said at last. "Let's have a glass of wine."

Looking at him took my breath away. His face, the curves of it, the way the light glinted off his dark eyes, the black curls falling over his forehead. The scars.

"I'm going to take that as a yes," he said. "Come with me."

☼

"Your family is beautiful." We were sitting at the kitchen table. There seemed to be no room to eat. There were piles of paper and books everywhere. Brown eggs, placed in random spots. *Vogue, The New Yorker,* and Italian farming magazines. A pot of parsley. A fireplace poker, and a rubber ball. Alessandro pushed things aside to make room for the mismatched heavy green wineglasses, slid a cat off a chair for me, and we sat down. I could see Margaret through the French doors, playing with yellow puppies outside.

"It's so strange to see you," he said. "It's like no time has passed at all."

I nodded, but didn't trust my voice to speak.

He retreated, unsure. "You're married?" he asked.

"Your kids look just like you," I said.

He frowned and said, "Oh," and smiled. "Those are Michele's kids. That's his wife, Elena."

"Michele's children?"

"I'm not married," he said.

"Oh. I—I thought you were dead." I stumbled over the words.

He gave a little laugh. "I almost was, many times. I joined the Resistance. So did Favagrossa."

The realization hit me. "You sent him to get me out."

He nodded. "I'm sorry for the lie, but I knew you wouldn't leave. We did get the British officers safely out, though it was a little trickier than expected."

I nodded. There was so much I wanted to ask him, but I felt tongue-tied.

"You saved my life," he said. "I've wanted to thank you for a long time, but I didn't know how to find you. And now here you are."

I couldn't speak.

"It's hot in here. Let's go outside," he said.

☼

Lapo watched Favagrossa playing with the puppies. Living side by side with those who had once been ardent Fascists was not easy. Yet Italians managed to collectively put the past behind them, even when they failed individually. They had awakened from a twenty-year-long dream that had begun with the hope of unity and pride and ended in a nightmare of blood, division, and shame. Lapo wondered how people would look back on this fevered pair of decades, how his generation could explain that it came on them so gradually, the proverbial frog in the pot. But no, that was a lie—they had known. He had known.

His daughters had ripped the poster of Mussolini off their wall and burned it with the same savagery with which they had worshipped it. They merely shifted allegiances to other gods: movie stars and singers and soccer teams. He knew they would love their children with that same primal fire, their spouses, too, God help them. Was it better to see subtlety, motivations, nuances, understand your enemy's position, question your own, be constantly open to changing your mind, reversing course, making the million small adjustments that a thoughtful, bloodless life demanded, or was it better to live inflamed, passionately, even if it meant your god was strung up by his heels from a lamppost alongside his mistress, their expressions unrepentant even in death? Of one thing he was certain. They must never forget what a seductive tyrant had done to them, what he had turned them into. They must not turn away from the story, not inscribe it on clay tablets and then bury them. They must tell the story, over and over. They must never let it happen again.

Alessandro and I took our glasses of wine and walked back out through the French doors into the cool of the garden. The willow tree swayed slightly in the breeze, and the purple irises joined the dance. A book lay open on the bench.

We stood side by side looking out at the hills. I knew the *eremo* was up there. Waiting for me. Ready to come back to life. I was, too. I wanted to celebrate birthdays and holidays there, and have guests for the weekend, and have Patsy fly in, and convince Aida to get over her fear of the ocean and come. I wanted to grow chiltepin chile peppers in my garden and make my mother's salsa for Margaret. I wanted to throw parties.

"Welcome home," said Alessandro.

Author's Note

This is not based on one person's story; it's a mosaic of true bits and pieces from many people's stories held together with a lot of fictional glue. Most characters are of my own creation; some are blurred versions of real people and should not be taken as historical fact. I've changed the dates of events—for example, the bombing of the train station in Siena—to suit this narrative. At first, I was deeply uncomfortable fictionalizing such a massively important and painful period in world history. So many people have written firsthand or carefully researched accounts of what actually happened during World War II. I decided that in creating this story, Sally and Lapo's story, I would paint with less accurate strokes, abstracting the details in order to create what I hope is a watercolor version of events rather than a photograph, an interpretation that puts emotional truth above factual truth, and invites the reader to find resonances of their own, resonances that unfortunately feel stronger with each day that passes.

In researching the novel, I visited battlefields and villages still in ruins from World War II bombings eighty years ago, talked to survivors of the war, and of course also read extensively, including memoirs and diaries of women who experienced the war firsthand. What struck me was how many of them faced terror and tragedy with not just the proverbial stiff upper lip, but with surprising good humor. They acknowledge their grief and then, as Hermione Ranfurly says in her memoir *To War with Whitaker,* "You put on your gayest frock, paint your face . . . and determine to be cheerful." This attitude has in some ways disappeared from our world, branded as inappropriate or inauthentic. I found it intriguing. Maybe it will help us face what is to come in our own lifetimes.

Some real people, places, and events referenced or echoed here that you may want to know more about include Elsa Maxwell's raucous parties, Bomarzo, Margherita Sarfatti, Virginia Cowles, the Bottini of Siena, the Corsini Archive, Teddy Getty Gaston (who was interned in Siena and has a fabulous chapter in her memoir *Alone Together* about her time in the women's prison in Rome), Anna May Wong, Delfino Cinelli, Iris Origo, Galeazzo Ciano, Hermione Ranfurly (whose husband Dan was a POW at Vincigliata), and Richard Massock (whose account in *Italy from Within* of being interned with his fellow journalists and Mrs. Getty at the Hotel Excelsior is delightfully matter-of-fact).

✿

It took a World War II–size army of readers, friends, and professionals to bring this novel to life. *Mille grazie* to the real Sally Brady and the wonderment of writers at the Stone House and Moshup, including PK Simonds, Anna Kovel, James Lansill, Tracy McArdle Brady, and Kate Risse; wildly generous readers and listeners Charlotte Sommer, John and Jennifer Brancato, Keri and Paul Hardwick, Eileen Daspin, Lisa Bannon, Kathleen McCleary, Sheridan King, Maya Ricci, Lynette Cortez, Mark Ganem, Loren Segan, and Martin Velasco Ramos; early blurbers Glynis Costin, Julia Johnson, Jessica Barksdale Inclán, Cesare Casella, Diane Leslie, Andromeda Romano-Lax, Peter Gumbel, Conan O'Brien, Virginia Hume, and Chris Pavone. Nancy Cunningham introduced me to Gioconda Cinelli McMillan, who introduced me to the work of her grandfather. In Italy: stalwart and knowledgeable tour guide Danila Bracaglia; Helene Cadario and the much-missed Ranieri Polese; Maureen Kline and Gianna Esclapon; Elisa, Sarah, and Giugi Sesti, and their wonderful friend Fosca. My amazingly supportive students and colleagues at COS, especially Jamie Moore. A special shout-out to the members of Five Writers: Amir Bibawy, Susan Matsumoto, Zach Liebhaber, and Maureen Loftis. Stacy Brand: you make me look good, and make my pony look even better.

And, as always, this book would not be in your hands without the brilliant and wonderful Elisabeth Dyssegaard and the incredible team at St. Martin's, including eagle-eyed Susannah Noel, Jamilah Lewis-Horton, Dori

Weintraub, Danielle Fiorella, Meryl Sussman Levavi, Diane Dilluvio, Ginny Perrin, Laura Dragonette, and Lizz Blaise.

Finally, to the steadfast and buoyant Claudia Cross at Folio Literary Management: Can we buy that castle now?